RETURN TO EARTH

A Science Fiction Anthology

KEN PELHAM   TRACIE ROBERTS   BRIA BURTON

VERONICA H. HART   JOHN HOPE   ELLE ANDREWS PATT

C. L. ROMAN   CHARLES A. CORNELL   KRISTIN DURFEE

BARD CONSTANTINE

BLUE BEECH
PRESS

Front and back cover design by Charles A Cornell

Cover images licensed from Shutterstock.com

Return To Earth/ A Science Fiction Anthology

First Edition (PRINT) First Edition (Ebook) NOV 2025

BLUE BEECH
PRESS

ISBN-13 (Ebk): 978-1-960974-15-0

ISBN-13 (PB): 978-1-960974-16-7

All rights reserved, including the right to reproduce or distribute this book or portions thereof in any form whatsoever. For information, contact The Alvarium Experiment or Blue Beech Press.

Contents

About the Alvarium Experiment

The Alvarium Experiment is a consortium of writers working "independently together" to create short stories based on a central premise. The name comes from the Latin *alvarium* meaning beehive, a colony working towards a common goal for the benefit of all involved.

The stories that form the anthology *Return To Earth* represent the second creative collection published by this collective Hive Mind of award winning and bestselling authors. Stories from the Alvarium Experiment's first collection, *The Prometheus Saga* collectively won seven literary awards including five prestigious Royal Palm Literary Awards from the Florida Writers Association.

To follow The Alvarium Experiment's current and future projects online, please join the conversation at these websites:

Website: AlvariumExperiment.wixsite.com/ReturnToEarth
Blog: AlvariumExperiment.wixsite.com/ReturnToEarth/blog
Facebook Page: Facebook.com/TheAlvariumExperiment

About Return to Earth

Return To Earth is the second project of the Alvarium Experiment, a consortium of accomplished and award-winning authors. In this anthology, each author was given a central premise that mankind's first contact with extra-terrestrials might be with humans returning to Earth. The authors were allowed the freedom to independently interpret this premise and were unaware of the contents of each others' stories before the stories were individually published. The stories do not need to be read in any particular order as any story can become an entry point for the reader.

The *Return To Earth* stories and authors are:

"Under the Whelming Tide" by Ken Pelham. The Aethir, space-born descendants of the mythical planet Earth, are returning home at last to fulfill their destiny. But not all believe the great homecoming will be the heaven they have been promised.

Visit Ken at www.kenpelham.com.

"Coming Home" by John Hope. Finally achieving his dream of being an astronaut on the Jupiter missions, Jasper's mind is else-where, on the recent loss of his stepfather, Bud. But Jasper's space mission is interrupted when he is sucked into a wormhole that transports him to a different time, 30 years in the past. And now, doctors don't believe where he's from. Fortunately, his loving nurse at his side comforts him and a love builds. That is, until he realizes that his nurse's son is Jasper as a young boy.

Visit John at www.johnhopewriting.com.

"Project Bright Star" by Kristin Durfee. A once thought failed secret mission to colonize a distant planet, named 0X3B1, is discovered to have been successful when descendants of that mission return to Earth fifty-one years after their grandparents left, much to the surprise, and fear, of the world.

Visit Kristin at www.kristindurfee.com.

"Someday Loyal" by Elle Andrews Patt. Alien invaders are lobbing fireballs at Peoria, but Grandmama is holding tea. When the military arrives in search of Mrs. Suniol, Alice is drawn into the mystery of Lake Snow, a missing husband, and securing the key to an entire civilization's survival.

Visit Elle at www.elleandrewspatt.com.

"AOB" by Bria Burton. Aona, an Alien-Operated Bot (AOB), suffers a malfunction that could jeopardize her mission on Earth and could lead to the extinction of an entire species from another planet.

Visit Bria at www.briaburton.com.

"Social Experiment" by Tracie Roberts. For the past two years Dr. Olivia Tate had led a satisfying life with her alien spouse, Kya Dumont. As a scientist and cancer survivor, Liv is on a mission to discover a cure for the deadly disease. But something equally deadly has put Kya's people, the Oo'mahn, in danger of extinction. With an order to evacuate Earth, Kya struggles between helping her people and remaining with the woman she loves, especially now that Liv has also fallen ill. Now Kya's ship is approaching and the couple must not only find a cure for Liv and the Oo'mahn, but also devise a plan to remain together despite the objection of the aliens.

Visit Tracie at www.tracieroberts.com.

"Children of the Stars" by Charles A. Cornell. In modern day Japan, an American medical researcher discovers the deadly secret behind an eighty-year-old woman's ageless appearance and incredible fertility, and her connection to the bizarre disappearance of the freighter the Ourang Medan in 1948.

Visit Charles at www.charlesacornell.com.

"Gaia Returning" by C.L. Roman. Pirates steal things. It's what they do... When Captain Irina Demyanov's first mate disobeys orders and steals the crown jewels of a vengeful alien race, she knows she's out of options. Desperate to escape, Irina takes her chances on a dangerous vortex leap and lands near an unnamed, yet strangely familiar planet. The gamble may have paid off, but between hostile inhabitants and inevitable discovery by their pursuers, the pirates' chances of survival appear slim. Can the human remnant find refuge, or will their enemies put a permanent end to the human race?

Google on C.L. Roman for links to her work.

"The Paradoxical Man" by Bard Constantine. Albert Rosen is one of five explorers who vanished on a deep-sea expedition into the Bermuda Triangle. He returns to earth centuries later, transported across space and time through a mysterious wormhole. However, Earth is not the home he remembers. Humankind has been evacuated, and the survivors lie in hibernation aboard the Locus, an orbiting space station. Rosen is forced to match wits with Deis, an artificial intelligence determined to keep humanity in stasis until he is convinced they are fit to return.

Visit Bard at www.bardwritesbooks.com.

"Recovery" by Veronica Helen Hart. When a virus threatens the lives of everyone on board a transfer station for intergalactic travel, it's up to Dr. Candace Bertram to retrieve the only known vaccine from Earth. The risky, untested method of transport could mean catastrophic mission failure, and grave danger for Dr. Bertram.

Visit Veronica at www.veronicahhart.com.

For additional info about the stories and authors, visit the website: www.alvariumexperiment.wixsite.com/returntoearth

Facebook Fan Page: The Alvarium Experiment

Introduction to Return to Earth

Looking at these stars suddenly dwarfed my own troubles and all the gravities of terrestrial life. I thought of their unfathomable distance, and the slow inevitable drift of their movements out of the unknown past into the unknown future.
—H.G. Wells, *The Time Machine*

Earth's story is littered with fantastic tales of alien contact with Earth, both past and future. Some of these tales bring light and hope, while others make us shiver with horror. But what happens when the foreign visitors look remarkably like us? How will the world react when instead of extraterrestrials, it's humans who Return to Earth?

~The Authors of Return To Earth

RETURN TO EARTH

Under the Whelming Tide

Ken Pelham

Heaven and Earth. What they mean is really just a matter of perspective. ~KP

Whilst thee the shores, and sounding Seas
    Wash far away, where ere thy bones are hurld,
    Whether beyond the stormy Hebrides,
    Where thou perhaps under the whelming tide
    Visit'st the bottom of the monstrous world…
—John Milton, "Lycidas" (1638)

Excitement grew like a living thing within the ship as it hurtled through the endless void of space. The Aethir living within the vast ship, thousands of them, for thousands of generations, knew it only as Great Vessel. And a vessel is just that, a container, a ship, something serving only to carry them.

It was carrying them home.

Giddy with anticipation, the Aethir greeted each other with unabashed hugs and smiles and laughter and claps on the back. After sixteen times sixteen times eight generations, the Aethir were returning home, to the Heaven promised by the Masters, to the planet of their origin.

They had now entered its solar system.

The Aethir pressed to the great triangles of windows, awestruck. There, sunward, a tiny blue speck hung in the blackness of the void. They were so close now they could actually *see* Heaven.

They were returning to Earth.

ALONE WITH HER husband in the Library of History, Daneeth studied the shimmering images Tonven had selected and listened to him with growing despair. She shook her head; she loved Tonven but this heresy would get her and her unborn killed.

She glanced about to make sure they were alone, and placed her hand on his. "Tonven," she whispered. "Please. We can't think of these things."

"We have brains."

"You know what I mean. This…" She waved her hand at the flickering images of the Aethir in the air before them. "This hardly seems the time to undermine our salvation."

"There's no other time. In another sixteen sleeps we will arrive at Earth."

"At Heaven, you mean."

"Yes, Heaven. Heaven on Earth."

"Don't you think it's a little late to question Heaven?"

"I'd have questioned it a thousand sleeps ago if I'd been ready but I've just been piecing it together, bit by bit." He paused, and his eyes avoided hers for a moment. "I lacked courage. I feared my own conclusions. They seemed so… bizarre, and I couldn't be sure."

"But now you are?"

Another pause, longer. "One can never be absolutely sure of anything."

"How sure are you?"

"Enough to be afraid." He gestured toward the images. "Look close, Daneeth. What do you see?"

"Us."

Tonven nodded. "Us. As we are now. Don't you wonder about

us as we once were? How the first of the Aethir were?" He paused. "How different they were from us?"

Daneeth watched the images. The Aethir filled the images by the sixteens, by sixteens of sixteens, all so beautiful and slender, so full of grace. She placed a hand on her swollen belly, then both hands, and felt the miraculous small movement of their child within her. Soon the child, a tiny girl, would be born, another of their beautiful kind. "Of course they were different," she said. "All things change."

"That's the problem." He motioned with his finger, and the visions of Aethir shimmered. "Look back across generations, Daneeth."

The tall, beautiful Aethir began to change with the reversal. Generations flitted past in the span of mere heartbeats.

The Aethir changed. Their long slender fingers shortened, by half. Their arms, legs, torso, necks, all shortened too, and grew thicker. Impossibly shorter, impossibly thicker, brutish in their new dimensions. Shrinking as the time of tens of thousands of sleeps receded. Shrinking to a mere half of the height of the Aethir, and growing in girth by more than double. Their skin, so tan in color, a caricature of the purest white of the Aethir, and so vulgarly bulging with muscle.

The images stopped regressing.

"That's us. That... *creature* is us. That is what the first Aethir looked like."

"It's... well, ugly to be sure. But everyone knows these pictures, and how we changed over ages."

"But what caused this change?"

Daneeth blinked and shrugged. "Who knows? But things always change for the better."

Tonven shook his head. "Even the Masters never claimed that."

"But it's obvious, isn't it? Look how beautiful we have become, how graceful. These first Aethir were clumsy and hideous."

"I'll grant you that. But that's how they appear to us. We would be equally hideous to them."

Daneeth giggled. "Tonven, please be serious."

He paused, looked from her to the ancient Aethir images. "I am. And I've done something about it."

Daneeth felt her face flush suddenly hot. "What do you mean?"

The portal shimmered and rippled like disturbed water, and eight scowling Guardians strode in. They divided into two fours and formed a half-circle around Tonven, each of them awkwardly fingering a field controller. The portal shimmered once more and Monitor Ghed strode in.

Daneeth stepped closer. "Stop it, you men! Tonven means nothing and is a hopeless thinker!"

"Ah," Ghed said. "The heretic awaits us. Most accommodating of you, young Tonven."

"Frankly, Ghed, I'm disappointed in your slowness getting here. I thought Great Vessel's finest would be a bit quicker to catch their quarry."

Ghed nodded to his Guardians. "Maybe your wit will keep you company in solitary. Very well. We'll fetch you after eight sleeps time. That should afford you ample opportunity to reconsider your crimes against us, against all humanity."

Tonven shook his head. "Eight sleeps are too much. We haven't time. I demand we speak right away."

"Do not rush things, Tonven. You must be represented and your counsel must be appointed. She needs time to prepare a case."

"She? So you've already selected someone."

"Vena will represent you."

Vena. Daneeth felt the blood again flow hot into her face. She imagined her face would be a vivid pink by now.

Vena!

EIGHT SLEEPS. That was decreed. But Daneeth paced, fretted, tossed, turned, and felt her baby move. She wept for her family's future. Eight sleeps, yes, but not once among them did she sleep soundly and long.

They had removed Tonven from her and placed him in a cell, with no contact.

Vena called upon Daneeth after the seventh sleep. Daneeth greeted her with a piercing glare, and blocked her at the entrance to her apartment.

Vena hesitated. "Will you please let me come in, Daneeth? We must talk. If you love Tonven, we must talk."

"One sleep until Tonven is tried for heresy, and *now* you decide to do something about it?"

"Please? Let me in so we can talk."

Daneeth hesitated, but stepped aside and nodded her in.

"You despise me," Vena said.

Daneeth offered no argument.

"Well, there is nothing to be done about that. But I am Tonven's appointed counsel, and there is nothing to be done about that either. So I must do my best for him."

"What do you want?"

"I am his counsel and they have yet to let me speak to him."

Daneeth felt a twinge in her stomach. The baby? No. Fear. "But that would be criminal."

"They decide what is criminal. Remember that time-worn catch-all, the First Law of the Aethir: society before individual. It's the truth, but it can be subverted to justify anything."

"I'll go to them right now!"

"No you won't. Ghed, as Monitor, sets the pretrial rules and he doesn't intend to lose this case."

Dizziness passed through Daneeth, a moment of a tilting world closing upon her, a slow-drawing cloak of shadowy specks. She sat upon her bed and recollected herself. "If the outcome is already written why are you his counsel?"

"The outcome is not written. Not yet, and not if I can help it. Listen. There are at least a couple of magistrates that are sympathetic. If I can sway a couple more…"

"Why are you doing this?"

"I have been ordered to do so."

"Don't hide behind that. You can defend Tonven in appearance or you can defend him in fact. Which will it be?"

"I will represent anyone I'm assigned to the best of my ability."

"I did not take Tonven from you, Vena."

"Whether you did or did not is irrelevant."

"And yet it colors your every thought."

"I assure you, the past remains in the past."

"It *never* does." Daneeth rested her hand on her swollen belly. "We have a future, Tonven and I. At least, we did. He never wanted one with you."

"I am not so sure of that. Nevertheless, duty compels me in this."

"Tonven will refuse your counsel."

Vena shrugged. "The assignment cannot be changed."

"You may go now."

"Don't you want to discuss the case?"

"Not with you."

"Then you are a bigger fool than I imagined. You may not realize how serious a charge of heresy is; there hasn't even been such a charge brought in my lifetime." Vena sighed, looked at her in silence. "I will tell you this," she said at last. "Be prepared to testify. The Council of Magistrates will leave no matters aside. With child or without, they may question you, and in Tonven's defense so will I if I must."

DANEETH ARRIVED at the Hall of the Aethir at the appointed moment, summoned by the eighth chime after the eighth sleep. The portal shimmered as she approached, enveloped her, and she passed through it and into the vast bright chamber.

Thousands of shallow, gigantic bowls lined the upward curving walls. The ancient seats of the Masters, all empty and unused, just as they had been since the last of the Masters died ages ago. In the concave floor of the room sat or stood a handful of the Aethir. To one side stood Tonven, Vena whispering to him. He appeared not to hear, or listen, and turned to smile at Daneeth. He took a step toward her, but three guards stepped to block his way, hands raised. Monitor Ghed scowled and shook his head.

The chimes struck eight times more and the High Council of

Eight, the magistrates of law and governance of all the Aethir, entered, dressed in gossamer robes of white. The light within the Hall brightened with their approach.

"Ah, the enlightenment," Tonven said. He bowed grandly.

Vena frowned and shook her head at him.

Daneeth felt a stab of dismay at Tonven's effrontery. He gave her a smile and a wink, drawing a rebuking glance from Ghed.

The Eight ignored them all and took their seats behind a semicircle dais. Ghed nodded and the Guardians pulled Tonven—with only token resistance—into the center of the half-circle of the Eight, Vena at his side.

Monitor Ghed stepped forward, a grave look on his face. "Illustrious Magistrates of the High Council, as you are aware, on the eve of our greatest achievement, our destiny, we are threatened with heresy of the worst order. We are threatened with the very proposal that we must not achieve it at all. That is the charge; I leave it to you to act upon, and I remain your humble servant." He executed a respectful bow and stepped back, his eyes downcast.

"Well put, Mister Monitor," Tonven said.

High Magistrate Soola looked from Ghed to Tonven. "You understand the charges, Tonven?"

"More or less."

"You do not wish to recant, or to plead insanity?"

"I do not."

She regarded him for a moment. "This is your opportunity to do so. We do not—*I* do not—particularly wish this affair to go any further."

"If I did so, you wouldn't hear what you need to hear."

The High Magistrate sighed. "Very well. Monitor Ghed?"

Ghed coughed delicately into his slender fingers and looked in turn at each member of the High Council for what Daneeth guessed was meant to be dramatic effect. "You know the charges, my Magistrates," Ghed said. "This man of the Aethir, this Tonven, has spread great untruths, solely for the purpose of sedition and fear-mongering. He has stated that—"

"Enough," Soola said with a dismissive wave. "The man can

speak for himself without you to filter it. Tonven, tell us what you will."

"Thank you, High Magistrate." Tonven stole a glance to Daneeth. "I have considered this problem for thousands of sleeps now. I won't bore you because time is short. Am I correct in saying we arrive at Earth after just eight more sleeps?"

Vox, known to fancy himself the only true technocrat among the Magistrates, cleared his throat. "More or less, eight and three-eighths."

"Unless we abandon this plan," Tonven said, "we will not live to see nine."

"Nonsense," snorted Vox.

"Nonsense," repeated Ghed, emboldened.

Soola glared at Ghed. "Perhaps. Perhaps not." She returned her attention to Tonven. "Continue."

"I've long had doubts about who we are, what we are. Why we are. So some thousand sleeps ago, I began to attack these doubts and research our histories."

"Already I take offense, young man. Everyone knows our origin story and our history. These have never been hidden."

"I do not mean to imply that the truth has been intentionally hidden from us, or even lost. The records are glorious and detailed." Tonven turned and faced the man slouching at the end of the semi-circle. "Magistrate Deriss, you are the greatest historian among the Aethir. Tell us of it, and I'll tell you what we're missing."

Deriss straightened and beamed. "Why, I will be happy—"

"Do keep it short, Deriss," Soola said. "No one here wants to die of starvation."

Deriss's face sank. "Well. There's so much…"

"Then I'll prompt you, Magistrate Deriss," Tonven said. "Who are we and where are we from?"

"You know that already."

"Pretend I don't. I want everyone to see the picture anew."

"Well. I shall attempt an abbreviated version. In the beginning, the Masters came to Earth and—"

"From where?"

"They were always here."

"Here? What is here?"

"Here. Within Great Vessel. They were always here."

"I doubt it. They came from somewhere else. Not from here. From one of the billions of worlds in the galaxy."

"And so the heretic speaks," Monitor Ghed mumbled.

"They were ship-bound," Deriss said. "They claimed so themselves."

"Yes, they *were* ship-bound, probably for thousands of generations, just as we have been," Tonven said. "But they came first from one of the myriad worlds."

"They never claimed that."

"After so long in space, they probably no longer cared."

"But we care. We want to return to Earth, the Heaven. Why would the Masters be so different in their desires?"

"They *were* different. So completely different from the Aethir we can't begin to fathom their thoughts, their psychologies. And they felt no need to explain because it would have been pointless. Suppose for a moment that they did care where they were originally from. Why then did they never return, if they were so similar in thought to us humans?"

Deriss fidgeted. Daneeth thought he wanted to shrug, but that would be a sign of doubt. Unsafe doubt.

"I'll tell you why," Tonven continued. "Because they couldn't return. Like us, they had been too long, too many generations, in space."

"How can one be too long in space?" Soola asked. "It's a natural home."

"Remember your teachings, Magistrate. You know how the first Aethir looked."

Soola regarded him for a moment, and traced a small circle in the air with her finger. An image flickered into existence. A First Aethir, a woman, short and stout. Another gesture, another image, this one a man. More gestures, and dozens of unique individuals, men and women, boys and girls, stood about, moving, accomplishing odd tasks.

"Now us, please," Tonven said. "And at true scale to these first Aethir."

The images shimmered, so like the images Daneeth and Tonven had viewed just a few sleeps ago. The first Aethir, short and impossibly stout. The modern Aethir, graceful, ethereal wisps, towering by more than double over the first Aethir.

"Ah," Tonven said. "Modern human and ancient human. Aethir all, and yet so vastly different."

"Not so different," Deriss said, leaning forward. "Same features, same eyes, same noses, same mouths. Five fingers on each hand, five toes on each foot."

Tonven nodded and raised a hand, fingers extended. "Five. Five plus five makes ten. Another example of how different the psychology of the Masters was from that of the Aethir. Did you ever wonder why all our maths, all our figures, are expressed on the number eight?"

"Eight-form is the simplest, most logical, form of mathematics," Deriss said.

"To the Masters it was. They possessed two digits on each of their four appendages, and eight stalks upon which they carried themselves, each stalk also with two digits. Naturally, they expressed figures in eights. If we had developed our own culture, we would have expressed in groups of ten."

"Then why don't we?"

"Because we were handed eight-form math and told to use no other."

Deriss settled back and studied his hands as if for the first time.

"Remember the teachings," Tonven said. "We changed drastically from the first Aethir. I suspect that the Masters also changed drastically from the first Masters to live aboard Great Vessel."

"Perhaps," Vox said. "The histories are vague on that point. However, you conveniently forget that the Masters themselves taught that all species, on all worlds, change slowly over time."

"That's my point. The Masters changed. We changed. We aren't like those first Aethir, and neither will we be like the Aethir that still dwell on Earth, if any do."

"But if we change over generations, and all species change over generations, then the Aethir of Earth will have also changed. They will be just like us!"

"I don't think so."

"Well, young man?" Soola asked. "Why on Great Vessel should different populations of the same species evolve differently? It makes no sense."

"Great Vessel is not Earth, and not remotely like Earth. Of course we would turn out differently."

"But apart from being enclosed, Great Vessel *is* like Earth," Soola insisted. "The air we breathe is the same as it has always been, since the first Aethir were taken in. Chemical records prove this. If the atmosphere in Great Vessel differed from Earth's, that very first generation would have perished."

"Granted, the air is probably the same, or nearly so. Something within the tolerances for human survival at the least. But the similarities end there. We enjoy all comforts and have never wanted for anything in all our ship-board existences. The humans of Earth had to evolve and adapt to the rigors of that world. Therefore, their shape and form were appropriate to survival in that world."

Vox gave a little chuckle. "Perhaps the air was slightly different. Without question, the interior of Great Vessel is unlike the exterior of any world. So? Give me a reason to believe any differential changes could occur."

"I suspect an inherent laziness in our Masters holds the clue."

Daneeth's heart seemed to skip a beat.

"Heresy piled upon heresy," Ghed said. "You do not defend yourself well."

Vena seemed jarred to action. She placed her hand on Tonven's arm. "My client expresses his beliefs as best he can under duress," she stammered. "He does not mean to impugn the integrity of the Masters."

"I'm not impugning them," Tonven said, pushing Vena's hand away. "I'm pointing out the reality of the extreme comfort of their existences. They perhaps took to Great Vessel to escape a dying world. This ship is a marvel and a testament to the great powers and brilliance of the Masters. It was a perfect home for them, but it rendered them ship-bound and space-bound for the remainder of their time as a species. Why do you suppose, after many generations in space, they decided to take in the Aethir amongst them?"

"Out of kindness and love," Vena said, smiling. "It is written."

"Out of boredom, more likely," Tonven said. "They were sick of each other and needed pets, just as we Aethir need the little robotic pets we keep to amuse ourselves."

Deriss waved a dismissive hand. "But upon the passing of the last living Master, some six generations of Aethir ago, Great Vessel was programmed to return us to Earth. Does that sound like the workings of a pet owner?"

"I imagine owners of live pets frequently set them free. Maybe from a sense of guilt."

Daneeth thought that Soola's pale skin turned a slight bit paler. Ghed positively reddened.

"This speculation is irrelevant to the charges before us," Vena said, still smiling.

"Hardly," Vox said.

"Hardly," Tonven agreed. "It fits my theory. If the Masters abandoned their home world by necessity and couldn't return, they must have created Great Vessel's atmosphere to be identical to that of their home planet. Then, after eons, they sought and found an intelligent pet—us—that could readily live in Great Vessel. There-fore, their home planet's atmosphere was also similar to Earth's. But if we have changed dramatically from the first Aethir, something else was dramatically different about Earth."

"I'll indulge you," Soola said. "What was this great difference? Sunshine? Water? Food? We have these things in endless supply, and the Masters taught us that our home, Earth, was abundant in such things. A Heaven bathed in sunshine and comprised mostly of water, the stuff of life. The stuff dreams are made of. What would compel humans on Earth to change so much since we have been gone?"

"They didn't change. Only us."

"Pray tell, why?"

"Our environment is different. Recall, I said that the Masters grew lazy. Banished forever to lives ship-board, comfort grew to be their aim. They made themselves comfortable by making themselves lighter."

"How?" Tovi spoke for the first time. A quiet woman, but with a reputation for fairness and a passion for understanding the science of things. "Did they eat less?"

Tonven shook his head. "I don't know. The Masters knew more of the cosmos and its laws than we could ever suspect. But I've got an idea. Picture for a moment the entire galaxy. The Masters taught that it's an incomprehensibly vast spiral of stars. The greatest mass of stars is at the center. The others revolve about this center."

"True," Tovi said. "Go on."

"Now each of the stars has its own disk of revolving debris. Planets, gas, comets. Many planets have moons revolving about them. What I propose is that each mass attracts each other mass. I don't know what this attraction is, but I call it pull. The greater the mass, the greater the pull. The pull of the Masters' home planet must have been similar to the pull of the Earth. Our own philosophers recognize that some materials of the same size are heavier than others. Even gases. Some gases are lighter than others."

"Nonsense!" Vox slapped the table. "Great Vessel is a vast, hollow sphere, and would take an adult Aethir four sleeps to walk from one point around to return back to the same point. Vast, yes, yet it's the tiniest of fractions of that of even small planets. Earth is said to be many times the size of Great Vessel. If, as you say, our atmosphere must be similar to Earth's, then logic demands that it must also be of similar size." He sat back, a look of angry triumph burning in his eyes.

"Our atmosphere is managed by Great Vessel itself to remain at original pressure."

No one spoke for a moment. Tonven had thrown common knowledge at them.

"I admit, this troubled me greatly," Tonven continued. "Great Vessel is a hollow sphere. The mass of it must be a tiny fraction of that of Earth. Therefore, the pull must be a tiny fraction also. Somehow, in their quest for comfort, the Masters manipulated the pull within Great Vessel. They lessened it so that they weighed far less and could move about with the least exertion."

"And so with magic they reduced their weights. By how much?"

"This is unknowable, but I imagine it to have been between an eighth and a sixteenth of the original pull. This then enabled them to reduce consumption of food and water."

"And this made us change as well?"

"Think of it. Generation after generation were free of the bonds of pull, no longer bound to produce short, thick, muscled bodies with heavy bones to support the great weight of the first Aethir. Imagine, Vox, how your body must look and feel if you weighed sixteen times more than you do!"

"If all is as you claim," Vox said, "why then did the Masters not teach it to us?"

"We were pets. Nothing more. Why do you think, of all the vast wealth of knowledge they possessed, they taught us only the fewest scraps of it? Because educated pets might challenge them."

Silence hung in the Hall of the Aethir. At last, Soola spoke. "Imagine the struggle of those early humans! The torture such existences must have been!"

Daneeth shot her a glance. Was she being swayed by Tonven?

"No, Magistrate Soola, they were adapted to it. Built for it. We are not." He paused. "And that is why we will die if we return to Earth."

Vena stepped forth, her face drawn. "Tonven. Is this true? This is what you would risk your life for?"

"I believe it to be true. I lay awake at sleep-time hoping with all my heart that I am wrong, a misguided heretic, or just a fool that worries over everything. Never have I wanted so much to be wrong." He paused, gestured toward the myriad images of modern and ancient Aethir. "But the images don't lie. They tell a story, and this is the only explanation for these images that makes any sense."

Soola let out a long sigh. All eyes turned to her. "Have you anything more to say, Tonven?"

"I could go on, but I've summed up my thoughts for you."

"And still you do not recant this fairy tale?" Vox said.

Daneeth moved closer. "What will be his fate if he does not?"

Monitor Ghed glared at her. "Quiet, girl. *You* are not to question the Magistrate."

Vena placed a hand on Daneeth's forearm and squeezed. "A conviction, by majority vote, carries expulsion into the void."

Daneeth felt her world, her love, being stripped away. "Cast out into space? That is instant death!"

Soola said, "It is harsh in the extreme, but it's a law held sacred since the last of the Masters passed away. Discipline has kept the Aethir from passing as well."

"It's barbaric!"

"It's the law."

Daneeth trembled. "Tonven, please, my love, recant. I can't raise our child by myself."

Tonven shook his head. "Unless we abandon the notion of this supposed Heaven, you won't have to." He looked at Vena. "Represent me now as I wish."

"Magistrate," Vena said, her voice breaking, "Tonven restates his position. And I add my voice to his; I am convinced by his logic. You may prosecute me as well. If he has just a chance of being right, you must change course and study this issue until it's resolved with certainty. Anything less than delay is tantamount to a crime against humanity."

"We may well indeed add you to the casting-out, Vena," Ghed said.

"That's enough, Ghed," Soola said. "Tonven's musings border on paranoid mental illness, but Vena has a point."

Hurix, the most ancient of the Magistrates, cleared his throat and pointed a shaky finger at Tonven. "I for one have made my decision. I see no reason to beat a dead Master any longer."

"Hurix, vulgarity has no place—"

"Spare me, woman, and call a vote."

Soola tapped her long fingers nervously. "Very well. You all know the charges of heresy and maliciousness, and the defendant is clearly in control of his faculties and competent to have been placed on trial. Vena, is there any closing statement you'd like to make?"

Vena trembled. "I…we wish to state once more that Tonven is a loyal Aethir and believes what he is saying. And now so do I. In the least, I urge the Magistrates to delay Heaven. Heaven can wait."

Ghed muttered something inaudible.

Daneeth trembled. "Vena, that is no defense! My husband stands to lose his life!" She turned to Soola, and wiped a tear from her cheek. "Tonven has not been himself. Clearly he has great passion and beliefs. That's why I fell in love with him! But passion leads to conviction and stubbornness. Tonven does not say these things out of malice, but out of love for his people. You cannot find a lie in that. No one has ever caught him in a lie because he says the things he believes, right or wrong. Please, I beg of you. Let him live. In a few more sleeps all will be forgotten as we enter Heaven. Joy will reign over the Aethir. Do not make my beloved perish for his thoughts. Lock him away, muzzle him until the blessed moment arrives; by then all will be right with the world. Please. Please!"

"Crime and the law do not make adjustments based upon circumstance, dear child," Vox said. "Call the damned vote."

Soola looked at Tonven. "Your last chance."

He grimaced and shook his head. "High Magistrate, I cannot recant the truth."

Soola nodded. "We now vote. A simple majority will determine guilt. As High Magistrate, I vote first as prescribed by law. I find the defendant not guilty."

Vox slapped the table. "What? You cannot be serious."

Soola ignored him. "Hurix, your vote?"

"Guilty."

"Deriss?"

Magistrate Deriss looked down at his hands. "Not guilty."

"Vox?"

"Guilty!"

"Serena?"

"Not guilty. This whole trial is a corruption of our ideals."

Daneeth's heart surged. Three to two for acquittal so far! She looked at Tonven. He kept his eyes on the floor, and trembled slightly.

"Tess?"

"Guilty."

"Zissen?"

"Guilty."

Four to three in favor of conviction.

Only Tovi remained. Daneeth held out hope. The most reasonable person in Great Vessel held her husband's life in her hands.

"Before the final vote," Soola said, "I must point out that a tie vote constitutes an acquittal. Guilt requires a majority. Tovi, your vote?"

Tovi closed her eyes. "This is the most difficult vote I have ever cast. I've heard compelling arguments from Tonven today. They ring true. Yet at the end of it all, guilt or innocence in our system is not always a function of truth, nor whether we should wait, nor whether guilt or innocence will even matter when we reach our destiny after eight more sleeps. Rather, it is a function of whether a violation of admittedly antiquated laws has occurred. And in that regard, Tonven is guilty."

Vox and Hurix simultaneously shouted approval. "Then it is done!"

Blood drained from Daneeth's face. Her vision darkened, her beloved condemned to die, her world dying with him. Faintly, distantly, she heard Tonven imploring Vena to catch and steady her.

Vena took Daneeth's arm and eased her into her seat.

Soola said, "It's settled then. The court has delivered a verdict of guilt."

"And justice must be immediate," Hurix said.

"Into the void with the heretic," Vox said. "And not soon enough."

Soola said, "Settle down, old men. The law says that, in a verdict of guilt, if the High Magistrate sides with the dissenting opinion of innocence, he or she may replace the prescribed sentence with an alternate. I have decided to invoke that law. Tonven will not be consecrated to the void. I hereby sentence him to probation, without penalty or restriction, until the end of his days, or until the Aethir return home."

A rush of relief and joy swept into Daneeth, and she caught her breath. *Tonven would live and be free.*

"No!" Vox screamed. "This is an outrage. I won't stand for it!"

"Magistrate Vox," Soola said, "might I point out that you now come dangerously close to sedition yourself? Shall I open a new trial here and now to determine if indeed you do?"

Vox opened his mouth, thought better of it, and sank back into his seat.

"And our arrival on Earth?" Tonven asked, his voice flat and devoid of hope despite his reprieve.

As if in answer, a slight change in the floor of Great Vessel could be felt.

"That will not change," Soola. "We have begun the braking. Descent into Heaven has commenced."

EXCITEMENT RIPPLED THROUGHOUT GREAT VESSEL. The moment of destiny had arrived, the moment of prophecy and promise. The ship had braked for eight straight sleeps.

The populace had hung on every announcement from the Magistrates. Great Vessel had passed the outer planets of Earth's planetary system. Each milestone revealed itself just as the Masters had promised. They flew past the outer gas giants, one with shining rings of ice; past the largest with its vivid bands of color and red spot like a benign observant eye; past a small planet of red; past the brilliant glowing whiteness that was Earth's lone moon.

And there before them grew the third planet from the star, blue, green, brown, and white, the indescribably beautiful planet Earth. Daneeth watched it, mesmerized by the beauty and mystery. It took her breath away, this shimmering planet of life and bounty and sweetness.

Great Vessel approached, slowing ever more, and dipped into the upper atmosphere, and descended.

The entire population, many sixteens of sixteens of men and

women and children of the Aethir gathered in the vast hold of Great Vessel. The mighty ship, after nurturing thousands of generations in space, would gently kiss the fertile ground of Old Earth, and the people would at last be home.

Daneeth had gathered with all the others, giddy with the infectious euphoria. Her fears, stoked by Tonven's own fears, had evaporated. She felt their baby kick and squirm, and she caressed her bulging belly. Her sweet baby girl would be the first born of the first generation of the returned Aethir.

She looked at Tonven standing beside her. His eyes were drawn and gray from lack of sleep. She smiled, took his hand, and squeezed it gently. He forced a smile in return.

Next to him stood Soola, beaming, her grin infectious. "We believe we are landing in a region of advancement," she said. "Great societies abound there, and great numbers of people. I'm glad you could be with us, Tonven."

Almost imperceptibly, a slight bump and shudder were felt in the floor of the ship. A chorus of cheers rang out all about them.

They had landed on Earth.

"See, Tonven?" Daneeth said. "We are here and all is well. All is perfect."

Tonven gave a slight nod.

Through the great rows of triangled windows, Daneeth saw the dust of landing drift and clear. She gasped.

As far as the eye could see, magic and beauty surrounded them. She had seen the archival images of Earth and knew what to expect, yet it still had defied her imagination, outstripping her expectations many time over. Plants, much like those grown in Great Vessel, but in limitless variety and size and numbers, abounded. The ground stretched away, rippled and uneven and beautiful, and in the distance towering heights of ground—mountains—reached into the brilliant blue and white sky. To her right in the distance, a great plain of blue—a sea—shimmered and stretched to the horizon, dappled with golden light from the sun.

And people—*humans*—gathered by many sixteens on the hills and watched and pointed. Some appeared riding on the backs of great four-legged beasts. Many fell to their knees and bowed. Many more turned and fled. None came closer.

Tonven said something, inaudible below the buzz and cheer of the thrilled Aethir. Daneeth asked him what he had said.

"Look at them," he said. "They haven't changed."

Soola squinted into the distance, and a look of horror flooded into her face.

A hiss of air. A seam, like a broad malignant grin, appeared in the hull of Great Vessel as the vast bay door slowly opened.

The simulated gravity of Great Vessel vanished in an instant.

Screams pealed all about.

Daneeth felt the weight, the horrific pull, of the home planet throughout her entire body, as if each tissue, each fiber, each cell of her being were bearing down. Agony seared her. Her lungs felt sodden and gorged, her head shot through with pain, and she struggled to hold it upright.

She heard a snap, and then another, as first her left leg and then her right, buckled and broke under her sudden weight, too thin, too frail to support her. The splintered femur of her right leg broke through her flesh with a splatter of blood. She stumbled and collapsed to her knees.

Soola lay nearby, writhing in agony. All about, the Aethir collapsed in great heaps, their screams filling the air.

Tonven collapsed last, and slowly, as if he'd known what was to be. Tears filled his reddening eyes, and he whispered, "I failed you, Daneeth."

She felt the child within her, their child, sink through her abdomen, its great sudden weight pressing down, her thinly boned pelvis cracking under the strain, her body unable to resist the great demanding pressure.

The destiny of the Aethir fulfilled, Daneeth closed her eyes and prayed for a quick end to the crushing pull of home.

Author's Notes—Ken Pelham

AMONG EVOLUTIONARY BIOLOGISTS, study and debate continue about the rate of evolutionary change. Charles Darwin envisioned slow, gradual change. In 1972, Stephen Jay Gould and Niles Eldredge offered a modification to gradualism with their "punctuated equilibrium" thesis of evolutionary change, arguing that significant change in a species occurs at a relatively rapid rate when that species is subjected to environmental change. During periods of little environmental change, species change at a much slower rate. Bear in mind, "rapid" and "slower" are relative terms here; it would still take many generations for the emergence of a new species of human, which is what the Aethir represent.

This story tears a population of ancient modern humans—the Aethir—from Earth, drops them into a spacecraft, and sends them hurtling off on a never-ending voyage through interstellar space in an environment much different than that to which they had evolved.

Another notion I explore in this story is that of a space-faring population with incredible technology at their disposal, yet remaining pretty much children as far as their understanding of what they possess. We always expect extraterrestrial visitors to have giant 1950s B-movie brains, and to be able to break down the complexities of the Universe into complex mathematical formulae. But why? What if they were taken from their homes as a pre-literate and prehistoric group and kept at that level? Perhaps after the Masters passed away, the Aethir began to finally grow and study in the fields of math and science. So I placed them at perhaps a medieval level of science. A brilliant young Renaissance man like Tonven, slowly piecing together a working knowledge of the Universe, is seen as both genius and heretic, a Galileo of his culture.

Thanks for reading, and I hope you enjoyed the story.

~KP

Coming Home

John Hope

I never felt so far from home. The Belle 46's command module console blinked dozens of tiny lights. My mind reeled through the standard checklist of items in which the Academy had trained me. Power subsystem. Environmental subsystem. Oxygen levels. Temperature. Communications. Alarms. All normal.

Focusing on this dry grocery list of items was better than thinking about what I'd left behind, the ache that tapped at the child inside me. My gaze wandered from the controls to the round portal that provided a window to the outside. Somehow, the stark black and white of stars and space felt comforting, like staring unfocused at waves crashing on a beach.

Earth, home, and the memory of Bud, my stepdad, floated a galaxy away, so it seemed. In truth, I was only about 385 million miles away from Earth, drawing close to the Victoria substation orbiting around Jupiter. The timing of Bud's passing before liftoff didn't give me a chance to feel the loss. Now, the hectic launch and subsequent hibernation had ended. Like leaping into a freezing lake, only now had I a chance to surface and breathe. The capsule's ventilation system provided little comfort.

The Belle's console beeped, waiting for me to confirm my checklist.

I wiped my eyes, scanned the remaining monitors, and typed in my code. The console chirped and glowed green. This mission should have felt like everything I had worked so hard to achieve. It had been my dream to astronaut the Jupiter missions, taking up-close measurements of the stormy red spot and the violent storms underneath. But now, at the zenith of my career, I couldn't shake my thoughts of home.

I closed my eyes and felt Bud's warm, heavy hand on my shoulder. His powerful presence always anchored my restlessness.

When I was thirteen, I sat bruised in the dirt, one eye swollen shut and the other fixed on the gang of boys laughing and running from me, bragging about how they successfully kicked my ass. The slow crunch of gravel from behind tensed my spine. I knew it was Bud. The embarrassment of my defeat made my battered body feel worse. He knelt next to me, his hand on my shoulder. He said nothing except my name. "Charles." I knew he was waiting for me to explain.

I looked down the road. The boys had already disappeared around the corner. "They..." Tears choked me. "...they called me an orphan." I peered up at him through my teary eyes.

His dark mustache speckled with gray twitched. His deep brown eyes, matching mine, stared steady and straight. "You're never alone with me."

I swiped an arm across my snotty nose and sucked in. Focused on him, I asked, "Bud?"

His face brightened.

"Can I call you Dad?"

He smiled. The wrinkled creases on the sides of his eyes pointed toward the gathering tears. "Of course." He spoke in a strange whisper. He smiled as if he knew I'd pose the question. Yet, the joy in his face revealed how he felt about the request.

I twisted and wrapped my arms around his broad shoulders. His squeeze made it hard to breathe, but with him it seemed I didn't need to.

A few years before that day, the last day of fourth grade, I ran down the sidewalk, happy to be free of school. Opening my front door, I called, "Mom!" But my feet screeched against the hardwood floor when I saw a house full of adults.

They wore dark suits and looked serious.

Sweat dripped down the side of my face and I breathed in the cool, stale air. "Where's Mom?" My eyes zipped from one stranger's face to the next.

They stared down at me like I interrupted their meeting.

I shivered, feeling extremely out of place in my own house.

The bodies parted and Bud approached me. His face appeared damp like he'd been crying.

I knew it was bad even before he spoke.

"Charles," his voice cracked. He coughed, then placed a hand on my shoulder. "Your mom…"

I shook my head. He didn't have to finish. I dashed past him, through the crowd of adults, down the hall, and to her bedroom.

It was empty. She'd been camped out in her bedroom for months.

"Mom!" I scream and spun. "Where's Mom? Where's my mom?"

The dark bodies around me said nothing. They stared, dark and looming.

Bud approached me again.

"No," I shook my head. "No. No. She's not dead. Where is she? Where'd they take my mom?"

Bud folded his giant body around me.

My knees buckled.

Mom's cancer had finally gotten her. When I said goodbye to her this morning, she seemed weak and frail as she had been the past several months. I had no idea that was going to be the last time I'd see her.

I pulled away from Bud and looked up. "Mom…"

"I know," his deep voice grumbled.

I shook my head. "I… didn't know she'd die today. Not today."

"I know."

Tears rained down my face. "Why didn't she tell me?" I shook. "I talked with her this morning. Why didn't she tell me she'd die?"

He shook his head and hugged me again.

The Belle's alarms ripped me from my memories.

I blinked away the blurriness and tapped through a series of menus on the console. Repeated 313 alarms appeared. I tapped for more details.

"UGP alarm?" I mouthed.

Throughout my years of training for this mission, I'd never encountered this particular alarm. I yanked out a reference manual from the shelf next to me and flipped through the pages.

"313...313..."

I flipped, stopped on a page, and my fingers scanned the text that read, '313. UGP alarm. Unmapped Gravitational Pull. Sensors have detected a nearby unidentifiable gravitational spike. Forces may exceed booster's threshold for maintaining intended path.'

I pressed some buttons and the craft's trajectory monitor came to life. A three-dimensional map appeared over a silvery plate, a blue icon of the ship against a mostly black field with a series of dots showing a relative path of the ship. I pressed another button. I checked the thrusters. They were at normal power. I increased to full power. The engines whirled and the ship lurched as the thrusters responded to my command.

The 3-D display showed the craft returning to its flight plan, but only for a couple of dots. The ship shuttered then resumed its deviation. It was moving toward a dark area that appeared to be unknown to the computers.

I tapped through a series of menus. The academy's regimen trained me to remain relaxed, focused and rational.

"Stay focused. Stay focused," I chanted.

I typed in commands to search star charts for possible celestial bodies that might be causing the gravitational pull. The console beeped and the computer searched the database. The screen displayed a rotating hourglass icon, spinning. The image slowly blurred.

I looked to the 3-D display. The ship had deviated so far from the flight plan, I could no longer see the intended course. Out the portal, an area of stars had disappeared. In its place, black. The void grew quickly, swallowing up the tiny dots of stars.

"A black hole?" I theorized.

I checked the monitors. The ship approached the darkness fast. But its proximity to the vessel was far too close to be a black hole. I recalled from the academy, the gravity from a black hole light years away could easily crush a ship this size. Whatever this was, it had a strong gravitational pull, but it couldn't be a black hole.

"Maybe it's…"

The ship lurched and I rapped my head against the console.

Everything shook, the console, the monitors, the tiny lights, and the portal. Books and manuals rattled against each other and toppled off the shelves. The walls creaked and moaned as if the ship was getting crushed by giant hands.

I peered out the portal. Complete blackness. The stars were gone.

Alarms continued to wail.

I attacked the controls, trying to do something. Nothing responded.

The shaking grew so fierce, the illuminated buttons on the console became streaks of light.

Cabin air pressure spiked, increasing.

I grabbed the sides of my head.

Screeching.

Buzzing.

Crying.

Shaking.

Then, silence.

Black.

I WOKE SURROUNDED in complete white.

My voice cracked, "Am I dead?"

Objects took shape within the whiteness. One of which was a

gentle, smiling face. A girl. She was gorgeous. Dark eyes. Long wavy hair. Something strikingly familiar.

She spoke with a smooth, calming voice. "Welcome back to the living."

"What? Where?" I tried to sit up. My head spun. I felt nauseous.

"No." She placed a hand on my chest. "Rest."

I lay back and turned my head. White tiled ceiling and floors. A large, open window exposed a green, leafy tree, birds chirping on a nearby branch. Beyond the tree, I heard sounds of vehicles rumbling and the occasional shout of children playing. To the other side, an open door lead out to a hallway. A nurse in a sky blue uniform pushed a woman in a wheelchair.

I coughed and touched my chin. My head was bandaged. "I'm..." my voice sounded weak. "I'm in a hospital?"

"Yes."

"On Earth?"

"Of course, silly."

It occurred to me the girl was likely a nurse, though her uniform appeared far more pleasant, flowery and calming. "You..."

"Yes?" she asked with a smile.

"You're beautiful." I felt my face redden. I couldn't believe I said it out loud.

She smirked. "That's the meds talking." She stood.

"Do..." I coughed.

She stood next to me, waiting.

"Do I know you?" I looked at her badge. 'Louise'.

Another flash of her perfect teeth. "Well, I've been taking care of you the past couple months, Mr. John Doe."

"My name's Charles."

"Fantastic." She picked up a clipboard and jotted.

"Wait. Did you say months? What's today's date?"

"June 16."

I rubbed my head. Then I saw him in my mind. Bud. He died April 29th, a date forever etched inside me. I'd been standing in the ready room. A half dozen engineers and specialists in puffy white jumpers surrounding me, working me into my astronaut suit and gear. The liquid cooling and ventilation garment. The EMU electrical harness. The urine collection device. The lower and upper torso assemblies. The display and control module. Everything needed for an emergency spacewalk should the slingshot around Earth encounter a critical failure. Lieutenant Merlin, a lean nerdy but muscular friend of mine, delivered the news. I was so lost in my piece by piece assemblage, the news hit me like being told a trivial weather report. I thought at first he'd showed up to make fun of me.

"What?" I said, at hearing the news.

Not smiling, he nodded. "11:30 this morning."

"You… sure?" My mind was slow to fully interpret his words.

Merlin touched his nose, coughed, and nodded again. "He… uh." He swallowed. "He had stipulated no resuscitation or life support."

"I know. I know." I stood frozen.

The specialists surrounding me stopped their work. They paused and watched, as if waiting for me to give them the go-ahead.

I looked to the floor and uttered, "Bud…"

"He said…um…" Merlin began. "The nurses attending him said that his last words were about you."

"Me?"

"He asked if you were on your way, and then said no matter what, you should go."

I frowned. "He said that?"

He nodded.

I knew Merlin well enough that I knew I could trust him. I turned to the surrounding men. Swallowing, I nodded.

They resumed their duties.

Now, in my strange hospital room, I wiped my eyes and I wondered for a moment if Bud had died in a room like this. His illness came so swift and the last days of my mission prep so intense, I hadn't had the opportunity to see him.

But the more I looked, the odder this room appeared. The bed rails. The nightstand topped with fake flowers. The rotary telephone underneath. Wait. A rotary phone?

I looked to her. "What kind of hospital is this?"

"Huh?"

"I'm not at the Academy, am I?"

She sat at the end of my bed. "Academy?" She spoke like I'd slipped into another language. She touched the side of my face with the back of her hand. "You really had a spill, didn't you?"

"But—"

"Just rest." She stood. "You've been through a lot. I'll let your doctor know you're awake." She stepped out.

***

Days passed. My frustration grew. Every time I brought up the Jupiter missions, the Belle 46, and the unknown gravitational field I'd encountered, they regarded me like a nutcase. Particularly the doctors, all of whom spoke to me like a child.

Louise was the only one who'd even listen. She'd sit next to me in bed. I'd explain. She'd smile and touch my cheek. Her touch was warm and comforting. I felt something in it, a calmness that deflated my anger towards this white-walled prison.

Three men in uniform marched into my hospital room.

Louise stepped aside but didn't leave.

Their sudden presence brought an air of discomfort. I inched up in bed, my pillow to my back pressing against the wall.

The oldest-looking man, his chest decorated in a multi-colored tiny ribbons, stepped forward, his arms locked behind his back. His heals clicked when he stopped, his chest puffed out like he was trying to overpower me with the assortment of ribbons. The pins lining his shoulder indicated general, three stars. He snuffed his huge nose and smiled slightly. "So, you're Mr. Charles Zinsser."

"Yes, sir."

"You've been the talk at the Pentagon." He looked to Louise. "Ma'am."

Louise took the hint and stepped toward the door. She tossed a wary glance over her shoulder before disappearing.

The general held out a hand to the side. One of his cronies slapped a folder into the general's palm. He flipped the folder open, thumbed through the few papers inside, and smirked. He lifted out an enlarged photograph and held it out to me.

My eyes lit up.

The Belle 46, or what was left of it, sat spread out on a concrete floor, each busted piece labeled with a yellow tag sitting on the ground next to it.

The general hit me with, "Where'd you get the fuel for this craft?"

"Fuel?" I touched my chin. "It's just standard rocket fuel, I guess. I... I just piloted the Belle."

He lowered the photo. "The labs found traces. Seems your standard rocket fuel was purer than anything the good U.S. of A. has ever produced. So I ask again..." He folded his broad, hairy arms. "Where'd you get the fuel for this craft, Mr. Charles Zinsser?" He said my name with a hint of disbelief, as if doubting it was my actual name.

His cronies gave me comparable glares.

"Like I said," I started. "I don't know. I just piloted the Belle."

"That's another thing." He held out a hand. His aide gave him another folder. Opening it, he thumbed through the papers. "We have no craft on record named the Belle 46. Though interestingly, Intelligence found a political community called the Belarusian Assembly of Forty-Six Communistic Oblasts, or the Bela-46, created to put the kibosh on anti-communism movements in Eastern Europe."

"Communism? Are you kidding?"

"Oh, no. All this talk about the disillusionment of Communism has a strong push back from those who aren't so crazy about relinquishing their power."

My head spun, not fully grasping everything the general was dishing out.

He flipped a page and continued, "And even more interesting, one of their forty-six-member committee has just gone missing. So, Mr. Charles Zinsser, perhaps you can be a little more open with us." He pulled out a pen from his shirt pocket and clicked it against his chest. "Let's start with your real name."

"My real...?" My head spun. "Look. I have no idea what you're talking about or what this Bela-46 thing is, whatever it is. I'm just a pilot. An astronaut."

The general leaned in.

I smelled his sharp aftershave. The gray stubble jutting out his nostrils shimmied.

He said, "We'll see."

He snapped his heels against the tile, spun and shot out of the room. His cronies followed close behind.

Seconds later, Louise slipped in, as if she'd posed just outside the room, waiting for her moment to return.

I dug my hands onto my face, feeling the stress. When my eyes cleared, I turned to her. "I'm not crazy."

"I know."

"I just wish they'd listen."

She sat and placed a hand on my leg. The touch jolted my senses, warm and comforting. "Tell me again about the Academy." Her wide eyes stared like a child ready to be read a bedtime story.

I shook my head. "You're just humoring me, aren't you?"

Her head tilted ever so slightly to the side. She answered in a tone I'd never heard from her before. "No, Charles." She stared for a long moment.

I saw in her face there was something bubbling underneath.

"I have a confession. I've been spending way too long with you over the past months. In fact, Ms. Kiski, the head nurse, has been on my case to keep up with my rounds." Her eyes glassed. She gave them a quick swipe. "But... I don't know. There's something about you. The second I first saw you. It was... I had to take care of you."

"Funny." I held her hand in both of mine. "The first time I saw you I felt I'd met you before, too."

Even with a crooked smile, she was beautiful. "I guess this is one of those classic nurse-patient stories." She shook her head and wiped her eyes.

"Why are you upset about it?"

Her chest rose and fell with a deep breath. "Two weeks before they wheeled you in, I lost my husband." She stopped, as if waiting for the words to sink in.

I gave her hand a soft squeeze.

She looked down. "I don't know. I guess you came along at just the right time." She looked up. "I needed a man, and there you were."

I petted her hand with my thumb. "You know, right before I left on the Jupiter mission, I lost someone close as well."

"Really?"

I nodded. "My dad. It's not like losing a husband, but we were close. He was actually my stepdad. But... he was all I had." The days of frustration had distracted me from thinking of him until now. The weight of his loss pressed on me. My breathing rattled. I tried to swallow the feeling.

She leaned in and kissed my forehead.

When she pulled back, my eyes were wide open, staring at her.

She touched her bottom lip. "I'm sorry."

"What? No. Don't be."

She turned away. "I don't know why I did that."

"I needed it."

She gazed at me and smiled.

"Thanks." I squeezed her hand again. "Sometimes the most unexpected things gravitate people together. But I'm glad they do. Especially when two bodies are alone in this universe."

She shrugged. "Actually, I'm not completely alone."

"What do you mean?"

Another nurse entered the room. The day shift had ended. She carried a two-year-old little boy dressed in a Pink Panther shirt and matching cap. Behind her walked a little girl, maybe four, holding a plastic doll. "Louise. Nursery's shut down early today. And I gotta head out."

Louise stood and took the boy from her friend. "Hey, big boy."

The boy wrapped his chubby arms around Louise's neck.

The other nurse waved. "See you bright and early tomorrow." She grabbed the little girl's hand and headed out. "C'mon."

Louise stepped to the bed and sat, resting the boy on her lap.

I started to say, "And who's...," but one look at the boy's face and I knew exactly who he was. A second later, everything made sense. The unknown gravitational force the Belle had encountered. Louise's familiarity. Our connection. Everything.

The boy's big brown eyes blinked. He looked at me with a silent uncertainty that I knew all too well.

Louise smiled and wiped a speck of dried food from the boy's face. "Meet my son—Charles." She patted the boy's back. "You two have the same name."

He looked up at his mom.

I reached out and touched the boy's hand.

He looked at me.

I felt a jolt of bizarre recognition. "Hello," I said softly. "You can call me… Bud."

Author's Notes—JOHN HOPE

THANK you for reading COMING HOME, part of the Return to Earth, Alvarium Experiment series. I find it exciting to share my love of storytelling with you that will, I hope, make you feel and make you think.

If you've enjoyed the story, I have a favor to ask. User reviews on Amazon.com are fantastic resources for fellow readers to gain a basic assessment of a book or story. I'd be eternally grateful if you can take a few minutes to login Amazon and let others know your thoughts and feelings about COMING HOME.

And if you didn't like the story, well… keep it to yourself.

~JH

Project Bright Star

Kristin Durfee

"Man has gone out to explore other worlds and other civilizations without having explored his own labyrinth of dark passages and secret chambers, and without finding what lies behind doorways that he himself has sealed."
— Stanislaw Lem, *Solaris*

I

The sound of Lizbeth Stevens' shoes clicked on the linoleum floor of the Johnson Space Center in time with the second hand on her watch. She was late as she walked down the long corridor to her office and passed the plaques that lined the windowless hall. Some of the names would have been familiar to her, like those of the *Challenger* astronauts. One small bronze sign bore the name of strangers. Not only had she never heard of these ten men and women, but no one else living remembered them, either.

The top of the plaque simply read:

Project Bright Star
July 4, 1969

Command Pilot Robert Williams
Pilot Frank Joseph
Science & Recovery Commander Harold Combs
Flight Engineer Raymond Carter
Recovery Specialist Charles "Chuck" Thomas
Monitor Vikki Barnes
Flight Engineer Mary Decker
Recovery Specialist Mildred "Millie" Parker
Flight Engineer Ruth Evans
Monitor Shirley Miller

If she had paused, just once in the times she'd passed through this space, and read the sign she may have wondered what this mission was. How was there some sort of launch twelve days before the *Apollo 11* mission? But as it were, the sign was allowed to tarnish over the years until the patina caused it to blend further into the background.

On this night, like each night of the previous seven years, Lizbeth kept her eyes straight ahead as she walked to the second to last door on the right. The building was quiet. She was the only one who worked on this floor at such a late hour. Her job was to give support to any Americans on board the International Space Station. It had been two weeks since her sole charge had returned home. She was late to a job that didn't require her to even be there. The irony was not lost on her.

When she got settled at her desk she turned her comm system on—more out of habit than anything else—and listened to the transmission between the Russians and their lone man. Two hours into her shift, she'd almost finished the current New York Times bestseller when her focus was redirected to the radio. She had a working knowledge of the Russian language, a mixture of *Rosetta Stone* and hours listening to chatter. The cosmonaut reported picking up a large object on his radar. She jumped into the conversation and asked if it was a comet, but the Russian didn't think so.

Lizbeth looked through her charts and records. No orbiting devices were scheduled to be in view during the next four years.

There were also no telescopic reports of asteroids. She got on the radio and relayed this information. There was a pause on the other end.

"Something is coming," the Russian said in a thick English accent.

Lizbeth picked up the phone and punched in a three-digit code. The recipient picked up on the second ring despite the late hour.

She didn't wait for the director to speak first. "I think you need to come in."

"You think?" His voice was rough with sleep.

"You need to get here as soon as you can."

II

GLADYS JOSEPH TURNED to stare at the large instrument panel. She was alone in the cabin. Her six other companions were in the sleeping quarters. *Four other companions*, she reminded herself. It had been a year since they'd lost Helen and Virginia, but somehow Gladys still forgot that they were no longer with them and that their bodies floated somewhere off in space. She had to remind herself of this fact almost daily. It never seemed to sink in.

John probably took it harder than the rest of them. Helen was, after-all, his sister. After his parents, brother, and another sister died early on in the sickness, he probably thought he'd escape with one family member. It wasn't meant to be.

They'd all suffered unimaginable losses. Their parents and grandparents were all dead. Gladys was the only one to have a living blood relation in her sister, Margery, though she still mourned the losses of her other sister and two brothers. Raymond had not only lost his family, including two sisters and a brother, but his betrothed Virginia didn't even last long enough to see what OX looked like from high up in space. Thomas was an only child, so Gladys thought he would be the least affected, but he'd barely stopped crying since they'd left.

It got on everyone's nerves.

She checked the countdown clock as it ticked on the wall behind her. 2221 Days 12 Hours 03 Minutes. Their journey would take them the better part of seven years. She wasn't sure how accurate the clock was, but John swore the elders had shown him how to correctly set the homing beacon and that the ship should do the rest. All they would have to do was sit back and wait to return to their new home on a planet called Earth.

III

LIZBETH CHEWED on what little was left of her right thumbnail. Her boss and about half a dozen higher-ups she'd never seen before were crammed into her office. She wondered why they didn't move to a larger conference room or the main command center. Not being able to take it anymore, she tried to sneak out of the room, the heat of claustrophobia making her sweat. Her boss chose this exact moment to call her forward.

"Ms. Stevens, can you relay a message to the Russians? Our translator is still thirty minutes out."

She took a deep breath to remove the shakiness from her voice. "Of course, sir." She awkwardly turned and pushed through the room and was handed her comm system by a man with countless medals which adorned his left lapel.

"We need some more info. Speed, course projections, origin assumptions," the man said as casually as if he were making a grocery list.

In what she assumed was woefully inadequate Russian, Lizbeth asked the questions. After the few seconds radio delay, the cosmonaut answered her in a slow and calm voice.

The sweat on her face and under her arms turned cold.

"He said it appears to be on a direct course with Earth, estimates it to arrive in one month, give or take a day, and—" He had to be mistaken. She asked him the last question again.

"*Da, kosmicheskiy korabl*," the voice repeated.

She turned slowly to the group. Twelve pairs of eyes fixed on her. "A ship," she whispered.

"What was that?" someone called from the back.

"It's a spaceship." Her voice carried this time, her words a bomb that detonated the room.

IV

GLADYS TURNED three knobs in quick succession. She'd gotten quite adept at the workings of the ship after years of practice. She glanced up at the clock for the millionth time that day. 31 Days 06 Hours 37 Minutes.

The hatch behind her opened and Thomas walked in. She saw his eyes were red-rimmed, but thankfully dry. For now at least. If anything the last few years had made his homesickness worse, while the rest of the crew seemed almost to forget they'd ever had a life that wasn't on the ship.

Their ancestors had arrived at 0X3B1, or "OX" as they called it, in the year 1972 after seven years of traveling. Gladys was too young to fully understand the stories they told her about Earth, about the secret project they worked on, about their arrival to colonize a foreign planet, but she had gleaned quite a bit of information from the documents on the ship during her years of travel.

A man named Harry Truman created a group called the National Space Exploration Center. They had a team of scientists use alien technology that had crash-landed on Earth in 1947 to launch a craft into the sky looking for a planet that would eventually become her home. A man named Lyndon B. Johnson that, to the best of Gladys' understanding, ruled their former world, sent her ancestors into space on their celebration day: July 4, 1965. They'd talked constantly to those back at Earth, but her grandmother told her the story of how a terrible storm broke their communication device four years after they left. They never heard from anyone again.

According to John, the ship was on a course for somewhere

called Roswell, New Mexico. It had a homing device that would return it to the place it left from. Gladys hoped that this Roswell would look like—or at least how she remembered—home.

"I can take over if you want to get some sleep," Thomas said. His voice pulled her out of her daydream.

"I'll do a quick check of the greenhouse then turn in." She unbuckled her seatbelt and patted Thomas lightly on the shoulder as she left the room.

The small space dubbed "the greenhouse" barely lived up to its name anymore. There was such little food left it made her stomach clench in fear. If their travel projections were off even by a few days, it could spell their demise.

They were on near-starvation portions, each having lost about ten-percent of their weight over the last few weeks. Gladys wasn't sure what this Earth place had in store for them, but she hoped some kind of food would be involved. She examined each of the plants and checked their humidity levels. Everything looked good.

She passed through their small rec room on her way to the sleeping quarters. When her grandparents had made this trip there were double the occupants. It was a wonder they didn't kill each other.

There was a small collection of books which Gladys knew by heart. They also brought with them a tattered flag. It had thirteen red and white stripes on it and a blue rectangle with fifty carefully affixed stars. It was a gift from Earth's leader and had a prominent place in their community on OX. There was much discussion on what items they would bring with them. The ship would only hold so much, but the flag came without question or protest. It was strange that it was such a huge part of their home when it really originated millions of miles away.

She quietly opened the sleeping chamber and crawled into her bunk, her stomach growled loudly as she closed her eyes.

V

"MADAM PRESIDENT?"

"I asked not to be disturbed."

Her aide shifted from foot to foot. "I know, ma'am."

She sighed and sat up in bed. "Fine, what is it?"

"NASA. They said it's an emergency."

Twenty minutes later, President Rebecca Adams sat in the War Room surrounded by top military and government officials. The space filled with a strained silence. She couldn't fault them that. Being summoned to the White House at zero three-thirty rarely meant something good was happening. She had debated this already with the head of NASA, to settle whether this should come from her or him. He was en route to DC but wouldn't arrive for three hours. She would go ahead and tell them what she knew.

There was no use in delaying or sugarcoating it. She dove right in. "At twenty-three hundred forty-five, Central time, a Houston NASA employee overheard a radio transmission between the remaining Russian cosmonaut on the International Space Station and Russian mission control in Korolyov. An object was noted approximately twenty-one million miles from Earth."

Several seats squeaked as their occupants shifted.

"What kind of object?" General Fuller asked.

"A spaceship of some sort."

The squeaking stopped.

Secretary of Defense Jeffery Loman leaned forward. "A spaceship, Madam President? From where?"

"That information is still being gathered, Jeff. We don't want to raise any alarm bells until absolutely necessary, so some of our information gathering has been slow. Communication between us, Russia, and the Space Station is also on a delay."

"How long is twenty-one million miles in travel time?" Secretary of the Interior Jules asked.

"About thirty days." Her words landed flatly in the room.

After a long pause Jules asked, "And where is it headed?"

"Earth." An intake of breath was heard in the room. "At this point we know little. We don't know what or who may be on this craft or what they may want." She paused, still struggling with this next decision. She wondered if her ancestors, who included two past presidents, would agree with her plan of action. "This information is not to leave this room. You tell no one. Your husband can keep secrets? I don't care. Your one-hundred year-old grandmother is deaf? If you even whisper it to her, you will be executed for treason." She looked around the room and paused at each person until they nodded in agreement.

Adams' lead strategist, a woman ten years her senior named Robins, shifted in her chair before she addressed her boss. "What about the American people, ma'am?

"When we have more information, I will tell them, but there is no need to risk panic when we don't even know what this thing is or what threat there may or may not be."

"It's not right," Robins said. "This is information they need to know."

"They need to know what I *tell* them."

Robins shook her head. "You know that is crap." The mood of the room stiffened. Whether the rest of the occupants agreed with the strategist or not, no one was going to voice their support. She was on her own. "If you keep this from the American people..."

"I tell them—"

"If you *keep* this from them." Robins stood with such force, it made her chair fly back into the wall behind her. "This will be your legacy. It won't matter the millions of good things you have done. Your elimination of the deficit, your jobs and approval ratings, it will all be for nothing."

"That is enough!" Adams said. Robins opened her mouth, but shut it right away and retrieved her chair. "This decision is final. I am more serious about this than any single matter during the eight years that I have been your commander. If you tell a single soul, not only will I know right away, but I will personally push the button that will kill you on the spot."

The president left before any of them had a chance to call bullshit on her threat.

VI

21 DAYS 04 HOURS 07 Minutes.

Gladys was pretty sure she was about to lose her mind in anticipation. She'd read and re-read every textbook about her ancestors' home. Now she just wanted to see it for herself.

"I just wish," Thomas said with tears in his eyes, "that our families could have been here to see this."

"Well, they're not," Margery snapped.

The deaths started in 2004, but they didn't know it's cause right away. Robert died first. He was seventy-four and succumbed after a short illness. Shirley died soon after, but being seventy-one, it was just assumed that the elders had reached the point in age where it was time to move on to whatever was next after this life. When Theodore, Richard, and Frank—the latter two only five and previously vibrant and healthy—died in quick succession, they got worried.

No amount of herbs or rubs seemed to help. The sickness started with a cough. It then spread quickly to the chest and caused the person's lungs to fill with fluid. After a few days or a week, death would follow. It wasn't until Gladys was much older, thousands of miles from home, that she realized that her parents and siblings had died from the liquid slowly drowning them. She tried not to think about it.

She remembered little from the time before. At eighteen, Gladys was the youngest of the group. Thomas and her sister Margery were both nineteen, Raymond twenty, and John twenty-two. They were about the same age their parents had been when they had each of them.

"What do you think it will be like?" Raymond whispered to Gladys.

"The books talk about the future a little bit."

Margery rolled her eyes and went to join John in the controller cabin. Gladys knew her sister hated it when she talked about history and the books. It was a wonder that she agreed to come with them at all.

"What do they say?" Raymond asked. Gladys was pretty sure he knew, but she liked to talk about it and he liked to hear her speak.

She grabbed one of the volumes from the shelf, sat next to him, and opened it to her favorite page, a full color two-page spread. She still remembered the first time she'd seen it.

Her father had her on his lap; she was five. It was two years before he got sick. He flipped through the book and read to her. The pictures were in black and white and she'd squirmed with boredom. Then he turned the page and a sudden burst of color appeared.

It was filled with the most beautiful images she'd ever seen. Cars with bubbled roofs flew through the sky. Boxy robots walked four-legged creatures called dogs. The dogs were her favorite. All Gladys wanted in the whole universe when she was young was a dog. She wondered if they still existed. She wanted a dozen of them

"What do you think they'll say when they see us?" Raymond asked.

"I'm sure they'll be glad we came back safely. Our grandparents must be in books just like this one," she said and patted the page lovingly with her open hand.

VII

LIZBETH WAS PRETTY sure she was going to throw up.

She followed several steps behind her boss, who turned around and motioned for her to walk faster.

It was surreal to walk through the halls toward the Oval Office. She'd been surprised to see how accurately represented the place was on TV shows and movies, to the point that she expected Martin Sheen or Michael Douglas to walk around the corner and spout some clever line.

The past ten days had gone by in a blur. There were secret meetings, trips back and forth between Houston and DC, but this was the first time she was asked to join. The president wanted to thank the person who made the initial contact with the Russians and who continued to be their point person for communication. Lizbeth wasn't the most qualified translator—luckily she had a team now to assist her—but she was the one the cosmonaut wanted to talk to.

Lizbeth was one of ten people in NASA and possibly twenty people in the world who knew about the ship. Today's meeting with the president was supposed to be about how to tell the American people. Lizbeth wondered if other world leaders would weigh in as well. The Russians knew, of course, but they had promised the same level of secrecy that the Americans did. As soon as it got out, though, it would be sure to go viral in an instant.

Would panic ensue? Would people believe that this was the end of the world? Lizbeth had been twenty during Y2K and she remembered how crazy people went over the threat that computers would blow up the world. She dreaded to think how they would react with the knowledge that some possibly alien beings were on a crash course for Earth.

She was lost in thought as the white doors opened and the oval room presented itself. The carpet was plush and blue and a large rectangular desk sat at the top of the circle. Couches flanked it while the presidential seal separated the striped upholstery.

"Director Morgan." President Adams came from behind the desk and moved to shake his hand.

The president was much taller in person than Lizbeth expected. The woman almost came up to the same height as the director. She released his hand and turned to face Lizbeth, who momentarily forgot how to breathe.

"And you must be Ms. Stevens," she said.

"Yes, Madam President." Lizbeth had practiced this line the whole flight over, afraid for some reason that she'd mess it up and call her the wrong thing. The president shook her hand before she motioned for them to take a seat on the plush couches. She asked one of her aides to bring in the others, though who that encompassed, Lizbeth didn't know. She felt terribly out of place.

"Now," the president started. "I understand that we have entered a twenty-day window for arrival?"

"Yes, ma'am," the director said. "It's an estimate, but we're pretty sure they are going to maintain the same near-constant speed they have been. If that's the case, that'll put them in Earth's atmosphere somewhere around the beginning of July."

"Fitting," she said. "Do we know yet where the craft may be projected to land?"

The director stayed silent. It took Lizbeth a moment to realize he waited her to answer the question. "No, ma'am. Right now projections appear that it's Earth, but it's still far enough out that they may change course, possibly even avoid us altogether."

"Do you think that's going to happen?"

"Honestly?" Lizbeth paused. "No. I don't see any reason why they would be on a straight course for us only to veer off at the last second. I think they are coming to Earth, we just don't know where yet."

"Thank you for your honesty." The president turned to face Director Morgan again. "And when will we know an exact location?"

"Our projections are being updated every fifteen minutes, so we're hoping that they will pinpoint something soon. We're also working with the Space Station on getting positions and better views of the craft, but that's still a few weeks out, two, three at the most. When we have a better idea of what's coming in, we may have a better idea of where they are coming in."

"So what am I supposed to tell the American people? I'm set to address them at twenty-hundred hours. We have six hours to come up with something to tell them. Something we are comfortable with and the other nations are comfortable with."

A soft knock at the door was followed by three men who wore dark navy suits and blue ties. For a moment Lizbeth wondered if they were in some sort of uniform before she realized there were slight color and cut variations on them.

"Director, Ms. Stevens, I would like you to meet the secretaries of defense, communications, and the interior, Loman, Rodriguez, and Jules."

They stood and shook hands before they sat once again.

"I brought you all together," she continued, "to figure this whole mess out. I need something to go to the people with that will inform them without scaring them."

"They are scared of everything," the secretary of security said to the laughter of the other two.

"Yes, yes they are, but this may actually *be* something to be scared of. I'm scared, aren't you?" The three lowered their eyes momentarily as she spoke. Lizbeth found it interesting that the showing of vulnerability was used as a weapon against them. She'd have to remember that.

"Can we claim the mission as our own?" Secretary Rodriguez asked. "Tell the people that it was a manned, or even unmanned, mission that we knew about but was top secret."

"And if they end up being human-hating bomb-toting aliens?" the president asked sarcastically.

"We're screwed either way," Secretary Loman said. "No one will remember we lied to them when they're fighting for their lives." He was completely serious. Lizbeth's blood turned cold and she itched to escape this place. How could they talk so casually about people's lives?

President Adams glared at him. "That's enough, Jeff. Jesus, you think this is a joke? "

"No joke. We tell 'em a little lie, we earn a little wiggle room. Let 'em eat cake."

"Maybe Jeff's right," Secretary Jules said.

The president slapped the wooden arm-rest on her chair. "Enough!"

A hard, strained silence fell upon the Oval Office.

Lizbeth raised her hand. She wasn't sure what the protocol for speaking was. She saw the director shoot her a look out of the corner of his eye, but she needed to say something. "How about the truth?" The room broke out in muffled laughter.

"The truth?" the president asked.

"Most of the truth. Let the people know that there's an object heading to Earth. We're not sure what it is yet, but we're working on it, and in the meantime, you're putting together a crew of the best and brightest to intercept it."

"Are we?" Secretary Jules asked.

"No," Lizbeth said. "Well, not really."

"So much for the truth," he said.

"We're working on how to achieve communication, but that way people will know what's happening, but also that we're working on protecting them. I know it's what I'd want to hear." Her words hung in the air.

"Interesting," President Adams said. She turned to Rodriguez. "Get with the staff writers and come back with a rough draft. Within the hour."

He glanced at his watch and gave an exasperated sigh.

"Is there a problem?"

He shook his head and left the room, his lips pressed so tightly together, they formed a straight line.

The president stood which caused the rest of them to scramble to their feet. "I want to thank you both for coming." She reached out her hand and shook the director's and Lizbeth's. "We have some work to do before the press conference, but the two of you are free to get a tour if you would like. We're having a follow-up meeting at seventeen hundred hours. There will be two seats reserved for you."

The director nodded as a woman appeared from a door behind them. She introduced herself and said that she would be taking them through the residence to see the White House from behind-the-scenes. Lizbeth looked over her shoulder as they exited the room. President Adams gesticulated with her hands in quick movements as she talked to the two remaining secretaries as the door closed.

VIII

SEVEN DAYS HAD PASSED since the president and other world leaders addressed their people. Life continued. People still went to work. The stock market, closed for fear of a crash, had reopened the previous day. Farmers harvested their crops and teachers spoke to rooms of bored children.

But there was an underlying fear in the world that threatened to consume it at any second.

It was all anyone talked about on TV. Even stations that weren't supposed to be twenty-four-hour news became so. In countries around the world, commentators brought on a bevy of experts ranging from former NASA scientists to psychics, the latter claiming that they could speak with the "aliens" on board. Reactions were mixed regarding whether the impending invaders were friendly or not.

Lizbeth tried to avoid television in general. No one had any answers. Those plastered on the screen had as good a guess as any of those in the inner circle of knowledge. The team was scheduled to return to Houston from DC in a week's time before they headed to the anticipated destination.

The projections showed the spacecraft touching down in New Mexico, though the exact location wasn't known. It was hoped that more specifics would be revealed in the coming days.

There was no radio communication to the ship. Whether because they had none or because they ignored their signals, her team didn't know. She wanted to believe, deep down to the core of her being, that the occupants meant them no harm. She'd seen one too many Fourth of July blockbusters to know how this could end for Earth. Part of her wanted to run and hide, but part of her couldn't possibly dream of looking away. So she sat in a hotel room close to the White House and waited, along with everyone else, for what the craft would bring them.

IX

02 DAYS 04 HOURS 47 Minutes.

Gladys sat and stared at the clock. It was about all the activity they could manage these last few days. They had eaten their last ration of food the previous morning. Now all they could do was wait.

They'd passed the moon a few hours before. Each of them

pressed their faces against the two small windows at the side of the ship. It was massive and looked like it was made of ice. Gladys was surprised that there didn't seem to be people living on it. The books she read talked about the space race. With the success of their grandparents' mission, she had assumed that the moon would be occupied by now. It seemed like the goal of all those racing toward it.

"Maybe they live on the other side?" Thomas wondered as they flew by it.

"Maybe," Gladys said quietly.

The Earth came into greater focus with each passing minute. She couldn't help herself. She knew she should conserve her energy, but she had to check on it, as if it could disappear from view. It was the most beautiful thing she had ever seen. Even better than the color pictures in the book. There was so much blue it made her dry throat ache worse from thirst. While they still had some water left, it was rationed almost to the level of pointlessness.

Swirls of white clouds covered large swaths of the planet. She wondered if they would be able to fly through them or if the storms would jostle them off course. John assured her that they would land right where they were supposed to.

Gladys was in awe of his abilities with the ship. As the oldest, he'd obviously gotten the most information about how it worked, but his troubleshooting skills had to have far exceeded what he'd been taught.

When the adults started to get sick, there was renewed fervor to get the ship back in working order. It had never been abandoned by her elders, but they seemed to tinker with it more than anything else. She remembered being very small and her grandfather Frank showing her around the inside of it. He spoke of their journey and how he and the nine others had come to this strange planet and made a life for themselves.

The alien space craft gave them the information to build their ship and the technology which allowed them to convert the elements in the air of OX to oxygen. A huge sphere made out of some material Gladys wasn't allowed to touch enclosed her whole life when she was young. Now she was in an even smaller bubble. She couldn't wait to get to a planet where she didn't have to be afraid to step outside her house. Where she could go anywhere she wanted and take big gulps of air.

In less than three days their new future would begin. Terror and excitement mixed into a new feeling. It churned together and boiled within her.

A crash behind her made her jump. Margery had come through the sleeping quarters and slammed the door. If hunger had made the rest of them docile and quiet, it threw her sister into a new level of fury. They avoided her as much as possible in six-hundred square feet, which is to say, not at all.

"I swear, if they don't have food waiting for us when we get off this terrible thing," she said.

"What?" Raymond asked. He was the only one still on speaking terms with her, the rest didn't bother to engage her in heated conversations anymore. "You'll fall over in weakness and hope they take pity on you?"

"Speak for yourself." She huffed.

"Two days," Gladys whispered. "Two days and our whole lives change."

"Any more than that," Margery said, "and our lives will be over."

Gladys stood and walked to the window. She stared as the blue orb grew closer and freedom moved toward her inch by inch.

X

THERE WAS a single camera on a tripod at the edge of the asphalt runway. No one manned it. It stood sentinel against the desert skyline. Its operator had grabbed something to eat in the barracks. His future task gave him little worry. Two seats down from him, Lizbeth pushed her food around, unable to take even the smallest of bites.

Her whole world, actually, *the* whole world was about an hour from changing forever. The space craft had entered their air space, the projections from six days ago spot on. For whatever reason, the ship was headed straight to Roswell. Most of the Army base had evacuated. Only critical personnel remained. Somehow Lizbeth was on that short list.

The president liked her and Lizbeth's boss in a move to try to gain favor, kept Lizbeth close by. She didn't mind the power play. She was glad to have a front row seat to either the start or end of the world. Plus, she figured this was probably the safest place to be. Or, at the very least, if this was the beginning of the end for the human race, she wanted to be one of the first to go.

In any form of apocalypse, when people joked and made plans for what they would do first, Lizbeth always knew her answer was nothing. She would gladly go in the first wave of whatever it was. She didn't want to be around when friends and family died, or worse, having to kill them herself. Her weapon of choice was surrender.

President Adams entered the room and everyone quickly stood. She announced that the escorts of the shuttle gave their ETA at forty-two minutes. Lizbeth's stomach formed another knot. Someone asked if the occupants were visible.

"No," the president said, disappointment filled her voice. "The windows have some sort of heat or sun guard on them. We cannot see in."

This really was the unknown, Lizbeth thought.

The team moved outside. The base had two large runways through the middle of it. It felt surreal to Lizbeth to stand in this place. She would have bet anyone that she'd never step foot here and she never gambled. She'd been interested in all the Area 51 stuff just like every other American probably was at some point in their life. To actually be here was both over and underwhelming at the same time.

The place didn't look impressive to Lizbeth, on par with bases she'd visited before. A large, three-story building stood at the edge of the complex, and she assumed a lab was inside due to the number of people in lab coats who exited while they'd evacuated the grounds.

A large hangar stood to the right of the runway. A team in hazmat suits manned plastic quarantine bays which awaited the strangers' arrival.

There was some outrage that the president hadn't allowed more people to view this historic event, including those from other countries. It was going to be aired on television and the internet, but on a delay. If this turned out to be something bad, they wanted to buy themselves enough time to figure out what to do. An incorrect location for landing was given an hour ago, some place close to the Canadian border.

Roswell already had an extensive no-fly zone, so it wasn't difficult to keep planes and helicopters away. They had taken every precaution they could think of. Now all they could do was wait.

At three minutes to seven, as the sun began to make its descent behind the mountains, a rumble could be heard in the distance. A black speck appeared. As it flew forward, Lizbeth counted six more objects—jet fighters—that surrounded it. This was it.

Its form came into better view the closer it got. The body of the craft was white, and while it had a similar appearance to the modern space shuttle she was used to, there were slight variations. Instead of a single pair of wings, this ship had three. The tail also split in two, giving it the appearance of a winged whale. Gigantic sets of wheels littered its underbelly in an amount that seemed unnecessary for its excessiveness. It flew straight for the blackened strip and bounced hard twice and skidded before it came to a halt halfway down the runway. The escort planes did one more fly over before they landed on the strip one over. No one paid them any attention.

The tail had a flag on it—an *American* flag—Project Bright Star was written in faded script.

The doors of the hatch opened and a Tyvek-clad technician wheeled a set of stairs toward it. Lizbeth took several steps forward before Director Morgan put a hand on her arm.

"Just wait," he said. She held her breath.

A woman walked through the door on the side of the ship and took one shaky step forward before she collapsed against the railing of the stairs. Someone else in a Tyvek suit rushed up to meet her which caused her to recoil in fear. Lizbeth broke away from her boss. There was a pull in her that she couldn't ignore. Danger or not, she had to get closer. Those around her must have felt the same way because they moved forward with her.

Lizbeth was mere feet away from the steps now. She let out a gasp as she saw the woman's face. A girl, really. Teenager? Her mild whirled. Who was this person? Behind the stranger more faces appeared. A boy. Another boy. A girl. And a third boy. They slowly crawled down the steps with the help of another suited figure. When she reached the bottom the girl in front turned to look at them.

"Hi," she said, and lifted a perfectly normal looking hand in greeting.

Lizbeth felt her legs buckle as the world blackened around her and she hit the ground.

XI

GLADYS'S EYES burned under the bright lights. She'd asked several times for them to be dimmed, turned off, anything, but her pleas were ignored.

It was almost funny. First, she was in a huge bubble. Then a smaller one in the space ship. Now she could reach her hands out and graze both of the plastic sides of this tiny one when she stood in the center of it. This certainly wasn't the homecoming any of them had expected.

She hadn't seen the others since they'd gone through decontamination. They'd stripped them of their clothes, their last remnants of home, and sprayed them with foul smelling water. She was so thirsty she opened her mouth to drink some of it, but it burned her throat. She was desperate for a drink.

They gave them all new outfits of blinding white and told them to enter different areas of the place they were in. She turned and locked eyes with John, her own fear reflected in his. He stood up tall and nodded to her, wordlessly telling her it would be all right. Her heart pounded in her chest, but she nodded back and moved to where they told her to.

A few minutes later a person about her mother's age flanked by two older gentleman sat on the other side of the plastic from her.

"My name is Lizbeth," the woman said. One of the men held out a small rectangular object with a small light in the corner. Gladys wondered what it could possibly be.

"Water, please," Gladys croaked. They still had given them nothing to eat or drink. Lizbeth looked at the two men. One nodded and walked away, returning moments later with a tall glass of clear liquid. There was a small drawer and he placed the glass in it and slid it toward her. Gladys took it with both hands and drank deeply, some of the cool water spilled down the front of her. It tasted strange, but she finished the whole glass anyway.

"More," she said.

Lizbeth shook her head. "Not yet. We don't want you getting sick. When is the last time you had food or water?"

Gladys's stomach growled. Now that she'd had some of her thirst quenched, food was all she could think about. "Four days for food, one day for water. Please, food, anything. Please." The same man left again, but didn't return right away.

"I need to ask you some questions," Lizbeth said slowly. "Do you understand what I am saying?"

"Yes. Why wouldn't I?"

"So you speak English fluently?"

Gladys didn't understand the question. "What else would I speak?"

Lizbeth looked at the man who held the rectangular object before she turned back to Gladys. "Of course. Why don't you tell me about yourself? Who you are, where you come from, why you are here?"

"My name is Gladys Joseph. My parents were Sue and Vick Joseph. Their parents were Frank Joseph and Vikki Barnes and

Raymond Carter and Ruth Evans." She paused to allow that truth to sink in to them. There was no flicker of recognition.

Lizbeth leaned forward."Who?"

Gladys's heart sank. "My grandparents. From Project Bright Star."

"Project Bright Star?"

"You don't know about Project Bright Star? The mission to OX? Or..." She leaned forward. She desperately wished for this woman to understand. "0X3B1?"

"No," Lizbeth said slowly.

Panic coursed through her. "No? But how? How is that possible?" Gladys looked back and forth between the two. The third man returned with something small in his hand that he pushed through the door. She was no longer hungry.

XII

LIZBETH'S EYES felt sharp with dryness. The notebook she clutched was filled with pages of notes. Her muscles ached and buzzed at the same time.

When she entered the room she saw the president was already seated at a table toward the front of the space. The director sat to her left along with other officials she recognized from the White House. The director met eyes with her and nodded. She took an open chair near him and settled her various papers down.

She noticed a stack of books in heavy plastic wrapping which sat by the president. Were they from the ship? Lizbeth wished she could hit pause on this moment so she could be everywhere at once. She wanted to look inside the ship, speak to all the passengers and scientists, and have time to digest what she'd learned before the rest of the world had to be let into the information. As the president cleared her throat, the fantasy floated away with her words.

"I have a team at the State Department looking through old records trying to determine the exact origin of this project." The president gestured to the wrapped books. "These were found on the ship and they contain some lineage records and history books from the 1960s. They are going to be taken to the on-site lab here momentarily for testing, but they appear to be authentic to that time frame. Now." She looked around the room. "What have you all found out? Let's start with the first person off the ship." She looked down at her list. "Gladys."

The room was quiet. It took Lizbeth a moment to realize everyone looked at her as they waited for her to speak. She shuffled a few papers. "Yes, Gladys. Her full name, according to her, is Gladys Joseph. She says she and her crew left a planet called 0X3B1 seven years ago after some kind of sickness wiped out most of their population."

"Do we know if they are sick? If this sickness can be spread here?" the president interrupted. For the first time fear flickered over her features.

"We don't know, Madam President," one of the men in a Tyvek suit said. "We're still running labs and blood work on them, but as of right now we are working under level three contamination protocols with capabilities of upgrading to level four if that is warranted. They will stay in their separate air-filtered enclosures and anyone making direct contact will need to wear PPE gear."

"Has this same story of community loss been echoed by the other occupants?" she asked. There were nods of agreement.

"I interviewed John Williams, the oldest of the group. He remembered life on"—the man looked down at his paper—"on what they call 'OX'. He was part of the group that helped rebuild the craft to allow them to escape and come to Earth.

"And they were under the assumption that we would know who they were?" the president asked.

"Gladys seemed surprised that we didn't have a welcoming parade set up," Lizbeth said. "They don't understand why we aren't excited to see them, why we don't know them."

"I don't understand that myself, frankly," the president said.

XIII

EXHAUSTION HAD SETTLED IN, but Gladys knew her day was far from over. She wished she'd slept better the night before instead of staving off sleep to look out the port windows. All she'd wanted to do was get out of the ship. Now she longed for the simplicity and safety of its tight quarters.

The team that interviewed her had left, but Gladys didn't know how long ago. She'd eaten whatever it was they brought her. It was square and didn't really taste like anything, but she felt it expand in her stomach and it helped with her hunger pains. She still longed for more water though.

Someone who wore the same suit as the people who met them off the ship came into view in front of her. The person gestured for her to come to the front of the bubble. He spoke, but his voice was muffled from the many layers of plastic between them. He unzipped the lining of the bubble and held his arm out and motioned her to step out and follow him.

She looked left and right as she walked out, but didn't see her four companions.

"Where are we going?" she asked. The man turned and mouthed something to her, but she wasn't able to make it out.

He handed her a mask right before they went through a large white door, and gestured for her to put it over her face. It made her feel claustrophobic even though they were now outside in the open air.

He brought her across shiny black Earth. Gladys was afraid to walk on it. It looked like liquid and she was sure they would fall straight into some abyss, but the man stepped on it fine so she followed.

She searched the horizon for their ship, but it was nowhere in sight. Her chest tightened. What if she never saw it again?

They didn't seem to walk very far, but Gladys huffed and tried to catch her breath through the re-circulated air of the mask as they moved toward a large, white structure. She looked up at the now blackened sky. It was illuminated with stars. She wondered where OX was in this sea of lights.

The man made a noise and she looked back down. He held the

building's door open for her. She hesitated for only a moment to catch one last glimpse of the night sky before she walked through.

She followed him down a long hallway. It felt strange being out of the ship, like everything was a little too big. When they came in for their landing, the world below looked expansive and huge. The thought of it overwhelmed her.

He took her through another set of doors where her friends sat on shiny silver chairs, each of them in white outfits. She rushed forward, ripped the mask off her face, and threw herself into the outstretched arms of John.

"Oh my gosh," she said into his neck. "I didn't know if I'd ever see you guys again." He shushed into her hair and rubbed her back. It felt so good to see them she had to fight back tears. She hadn't realized how scared she was until that moment.

She hugged the rest of the group and sat with them. The man who brought her closed the door. Gladys turned and realized they were in a large room with glass walls. It felt both open and closed at the same time.

"So what do you think?" she asked the group.

"We couldn't stay where we were," Margery said. "But I'm not sure if coming here was the best plan."

"Did any of your people know who we were?" Thomas asked. They shook their heads. Gladys's stomach twisted.

"What are they going to do with us?" Raymond asked.

"They can't keep us here, like in prison. I mean, our families back here must be worried about us," Thomas said. "At least they must remember who our grandparents are, right?" He looked at the group, but no one nodded.

"Do they not know who we are?" Gladys asked, her voice tight and small with fear.

John stood up straighter. "They have no idea who we are. They don't believe us, but there is no explanation for our arrival that makes sense, other than what we tell them."

"When will we get to leave?" Thomas asked.

"I don't think they are going to let us," John said.

XIV

MADAM PRESIDENT," Secretary Loman said.

She waved a hand at him. "I need a minute."

"We don't have a minute."

"Make one," she said sharply. Gosh, she longed for a cigarette and a shot of Jack. Too bad she'd given up both nine years ago. Poor timing, she decided.

"Madam President," Secretary Rodriquez said quietly. She looked up at him, aware of the two sets of eyes on her. "I don't think I understand what you are saying. How could this have been a secret for so long?"

"The truth was buried," she said.

She looked down at the papers in front of her. Classified documents, blue prints, flight manifestos, all unearthed for the first time in a generation. She was angry she hadn't been made aware of this and wondered how she would tell the American public.

Could she just go on TV and simply admit that the US Government had lied all this time about what happened in the desert in Roswell sixty-eight years prior? That a team spent the better part of two decades in the 1950s and '60s building a secret spacecraft only to have thought it failed? There were notes that some sort of communication loss happened in 1969 when the ship passed by Saturn. It was assumed the ship and the entire crew was lost. But somehow the ship had continued on. How could she tell the public that the descendants of the mission had just walked into their midst and possibly held not only untold information about life on other planets, but also a deadly virus that could wipe out the residents on this one?

It was an impossible question.

"How much longer until Kohl takes office?" she asked. The men laughed politely. It was only a half-joke.

"We need to know how to proceed," Loman said again.

"I think we need to tell the American people," the president said.

"Is this how you want to be remembered?"

Rodriguez shifted from foot to foot and lowered his eyes from hers. "I have an idea," he said. "I think you need to address the people. We will have a press conference. You will explain about the mission, about it all. We will not open it up for questions so we can contain it."

"And how is this supposed to help me?" she asked.

"You can claim that the space agency held secrets. It's the only way to save face and your legacy. Say that you were a victim of lies passed down to you from your predecessors. You will go down in history as the president who finally delivered the truth. It will be your last great act."

"And the director?" she asked. The idea was impossible, but what alternative did she had? She'd worked for eight years. Fought for twenty before that to even get to this place. Should she let this be what she was remembered for?

"A panel will be held and Director Morgan will be publicly fired. It will be career-ending for him of course, but you can make sure he is taken care of. Put together a handsome severance package, tax-free, and give it to him a few months after his dismissal. He may go down as the scapegoat, but he'll be a rich one at least."

"And the occupants?" Loman asked.

"Are the scientists still outside?" she asked. Rodriquez poked his head out of the room and called down the hall. Moments later three people in white lab coats entered. She posed their question to them.

"Medically, they are in remarkable health," one of the women said. "Malnourished and dehydrated, sure, but over-all it's incredible how good they look after surviving seven years in space. They are suffering few of the effects normally seen in long-term space travel. I've never seen anything like it. Whatever gravity technology they have on that ship we need to reverse engineer."

"But?"

"But..." She pulled in an audible breath. "Something killed the rest of their colony. DNA and antibody mapping is happening now, but we won't get results for twenty-four hours. But our technology has its limitations. If it was an alien virus, we may never know what it was."

"So how do we proceed?" Loman asked the doctors.

"It may not be safe for them to be in public, at least not now. Just like we can get sick from them, they could also get sick from us. They are unvaccinated. They've never been exposed to germs from Earth. Frankly, there have been some exposures already to the outside world. We may want to limit that."

The president jumped on the woman's words. "So what you are saying, is that it is in *their* best interest to be held."

The doctor hesitated so another jumped in. "For the time being, yes. Until we can figure out what they may or may not have been exposed to and start an anti-viral and vaccination rotation, I think it's best for everyone."

"We're going to keep them in a cage?" Rodriguez asked, incredulously.

"Sometimes cages are just as much for keeping things out as they are for keeping them in," the president said.

XV

LIZBETH CUT through the reporters as she passed through the gates at the base. They had thinned in the last year, but still represented a decent sized group. She wondered if they'd ever leave and be content with just the regular press releases NASA put out about the "OX Five" as they had been dubbed.

Pandemonium ensued after the Director's announcement of Project Bright Star, who the OX Five were, and the secrets of the last sixty or so years regarding the use of alien technology. He said that there had been no further alien contact outside of the 1947 crash in Roswell, but people didn't believe. They'd lied to us before so spectacularly, they reasoned, why not again?

Her boss had been promptly and publicly fired after the announcement. Lizbeth was glad. To have kept such a secret, even as all of this had unfolded, was unforgivable.

She had been transferred and kept on to stay with the OX Five, which was fine with her. She never ended up taking that plane ride back to Houston. Instead, she paid a few friends to pack up her things and ship them to New Mexico. They had visited once along with her parents. They'd hoped to get some face time with the "human aliens", as some called them, but Lizbeth was unable. There were twelve people with clearance to be in contact with them and she wasn't going to jeopardize her opportunity because her mom nagged her about it.

She wasn't sure how much longer they would be able to keep the group in containment. It was clear that they weren't sick. They had been immunized and checked and rechecked for antibodies. There was no medical reason to keep them out of the population, but there was a still a fear to do so.

Once the names of the five were published along with the lineage documents from the ship, people came out of the wood-works and claimed to be related to them. One man in his early fifties said he was the long lost son of one of the original astronauts, Vikki Barnes. His birth records didn't support this, but he swore that she was his mother. He wanted to see his nieces, but it was impossible, at least right now.

There were three lawsuits going through the lower courts at the moment. They weren't going anywhere, but they were an annoyance to the team all the same. Two were from claimed family members, though they had no records to back this up. The third was from a group of alien trackers who were suing the government for slander. They claimed that the years of ridicule they suffered from their peers over their conspiracy theories were the fault of the United States for not setting the record straight.

Lizbeth found it an unappealing aspect of human nature to try to capitalize on this information, whether they had a right to it or not. She wondered how much longer their project was going to be allowed to continue under the increased pressure from the public. They wanted to see the group, and not just from stock photos that NASA released to the press. They wanted access. Wanted to be able to see and touch these people, kids really. Human rights groups claimed that they violated about a hundred treaties against imprisonment.

Were they?

Lizbeth struggled with how the group was kept. At first she trusted that it was for their own good. But as time wore on, she also longed for them to be incorporated back into society. She felt badly for the group; they had lived in a series of bubbles their whole lives.

She was enthralled to hear all about OX. Gladys, Thomas, and Margery didn't remember it very well, but Raymond and John were able to speak endlessly about it.

For their part, the five were flabbergasted to hear about the world. Their books on the future had been so wrong, yet the truth was even stranger than they could have ever imagined.

Lizbeth brought in movies and books to fill their time. They laughed over Star Wars and cried over Charlotte's Web. Gladys constantly asked for a dog and was delighted when one of the scientists brought his Golden Retriever in. She buried her head in its soft neck and sobbed. It was agreed upon that no more dogs would visit.

Margery kept mostly to herself. She only interacted with the researchers when it suited her, which was rarely. John was protective of the rest of the group. Lizbeth had learned that any new tests or activities had to be passed through him first. While he really didn't have any veto power, giving him the appearance that he did made all the difference in his cooperation. The rest of the group went along with what he said, Margery included.

Lately he'd questioned their captivity with increased fervor and Lizbeth found it difficult to give answers that satisfied him. She'd gotten off the phone with President Kohl that morning and he'd given her permission to allow short trips outside for the group. They were limited to the grounds directly behind their current building, but it was a start.

No protective equipment would be needed for the group or the handlers, a big step in their introduction into the world. The space was chosen specifically because it was outside the scope of the reporter's high-powered lenses so they could be left in relative peace.

"I have big news today," Lizbeth announced when she entered the third floor. Thomas watched the TV while Raymond and Gladys looked over a picture book Lizbeth had brought them last week about the natural wonders of the world. They'd been trans-fixed ever since.

John jumped up to attention. "What?"

"We're going outside!"

The other four sprang to their feet and talked at once and over each other. Even Margery's attitude was brightened. Lizbeth helped them pick out clothes. It was much colder outside than in their temperature regulated floor.

She escorted them through the halls trailed by a team of doctors. She paused for a moment before she opened the door. Cold air rushed toward her. She took a deep breath and stepped into the crisp afternoon.

XVI

THE BURST of air hit Gladys with such force, she found it difficult to breathe. She tried to take a big gulp in, but it burned even more and caused her to cough. She staggered for a step and felt John's hand encircle her upper arm.

"I'm okay," she said.

The five of them filed outside and stayed pressed into one another. The sun was bright and Gladys had to shield her eyes. She took several steps and looked around her. Directly in front of them was a giant expanse of land that looked similar to OX. She tried to look past the fencing and focus on the horizon. For a moment, if she squinted hard, she could pretend to be back home and not in this foreign place.

Earth was nothing like she thought it would be. It didn't help that their welcome was far from what she'd expected. And the follow-up wasn't much better.

After the initial onslaught, she'd had exactly twelve people in her life. Lizbeth was nice and she liked a couple of the doctors, but mainly the NASA team was cold toward them. Every day a rotating crew checked their vitals and wrote notes on clipboards. Once a week they took their blood and made them do various other tests. A few times they even hooked them up to sensors and made them run on treadmills.

The whole thing exhausted her. She wondered if they could escape and go back to OX. Heck, at this point she'd even take just circling the universe in their ship until they ran out of food and slowly went to sleep.

She longed for the safety and simplicity and strange freedom the craft held. She walked forward and laced her fingers in the fence and pressed her face as close as it would go. John moved up beside her.

"Kind of looks like home," he said.

"Do you think we'll ever get back there?"

"I hope so."

He placed his hand on top of hers and pushed his face forward like hers while they looked out on their past and future, together.

Author's Notes—Kristin Durfee

WHEN I WAS FIRST APPROACHED to participate in this anthology, I jumped at the chance. To be able to stand beside the other excellent authors in "the hive" was a true honor. Then I realized I had to actually write something.

It started with the project's premise: humans returning to Earth. I sat down with my trusty notebook and decided to jot down a few ideas first before deciding on one. *Project Bright Star* entered my mind and wouldn't let go. I started writing complicated family trees for made-up people and did research on the solar system, the history of space travel, and how long it would take for the average space ship to travel to different planets.

I by no means consider myself an expert in these areas, but where I could, I tried to make this story based on fact and reality. Any oversights on my part are unintentional and can be considered the "fiction" part of science fiction. Nice how we writers can play with reality in this way to suit our needs.

While there are a great many resources in the universe that is the internet, I found the Planetary Science Institute (www.psi.edu) and Astronomy Café (www.astronomycafe.net) great places to start if you are interested in learning more about our solar system and what lies beyond it.

~KAD

Someday Loyal

Elle Andrews Patt

I'm a mess of a person but I'm loyal and I'll love you with everything I have.
—logicaldreamer.tumblr.com

A lice brought the tea out onto the porch. "I do believe the world is ending," she said.

"And why is that?" Grandmama asked, scooting forward in her wicker rocker to snag the nearest blueberry puff as Alice set the tray down on the porch table.

"The holo's gone dead. And there's a least a dozen fireballs falling through the sky."

"Really," Grandmama said. She set her puff down and licked her fingers. "Let's see."

Alice helped her stand and then followed her down the front stairs on tippy-toe, peering up the whole way because she didn't want to get hit in the head by falling things. Her skin crawled as she stopped on the bottom step, ready to take cover as fast as possible.

Grandmama stood all the way out in the front yard, her head tilted back, hands on her hips, and studied the arch of blue overhead. Puffy clouds floated lower than the streaking fireballs, which seemed high up and far away to Alice.

Mrs. Suniol came out of her front door with a pink overnight bag and her lime green purse with the zebra stripes. She closed the door and made a show of locking it up although everyone in the neighborhood knew she didn't really lock it, just in case her husband, Loyal, ever came home from the grocery store run he made years and years ago.

"Mattie," Grandmama called.

Mrs. Suniol turned, looking all around like she didn't know it was Grandmama hailing her although they had been arms-length friends for sixty-some years. "G," Mattie called back. Grandmama's name was Granada, but everyone called her 'G'. "Isn't it just awful? The world is ending."

"And why is that?" Grandmama asked.

"The spaceships, didn't you know?"

Grandmama shook her head. "Alice," she said over her shoulder. "Do go fetch the bourbon, would you?"

Alice, glad to be sent back indoors, said, "Yes, ma'am." She scurried across the porch and let the screen door slap-slam behind her. The holo remained blank. Static hissed from the speakers. She went to the furtherest corner cabinet in the kitchen, where Grandmama stored all her various liquors: cherry cordial and peach sherry, two kinds of vodka, a dusty bottle of tequila, butterscotch rum, bitters, bourbon and an ancient pint of Jack Daniel's whiskey. Not a single bottle had ever been opened except the bourbon. Grandmama bought a new bottle of Ansell's every two weeks.

Hand shaking, Alice took the bourbon and then two small water glasses. The static from the holo's speakers and the hum of the refrigerator cut off. When Alice looked for the time on the microwave, it wasn't there. Lordy, the world really was ending.

Out on the porch, Grandmama had coaxed Mrs. Suniol across the street and into the yard. "Now, Mattie, we just need to wait and see. Where is it you think you're going?"

"Teddy's cabin. It's on Lake Snow."

Grandmama glanced over at Alice, disbelief written all over her and then gave Mattie a big fish-eye . "Mattie! We spent every child-hood summer together at Teddy's cabin. You think I don't remember?"

"You couldn't remember me when you went off to that tootin' foolutin' women's college overseas. How do I know if you remember Teddy's?"

Alice closed her mouth, set the glasses down, and tucked herself into the swing to watch from afar. She had no idea Grandmama and Mrs. Suniol had been girls together, and she'd never heard the name Teddy. She did know of Lake Snow on account of David Wilkins' broken neck way back in tenth grade, but she'd never been there.

"Matilda," Grandmama demanded. "Get over here on this porch right now. You ran off with Loyal and nobody knew where to reach you for near on three years."

Mattie's mouth quirked up at the corner even though her gaze stayed on the sunburned brown lawn. Finally, she looked up at Grandmama through her eyelashes. "I'll give you that," she offered. "But that was over a year after you left."

Grandmama nodded. "I'll give you that."

Mrs. Suniol finished walking across the crunchy grass and climbed the stairs behind Grandmama. Grandmama gestured her to the chair Alice had vacated when she left to assemble tea.

"Hello, Alice," Mrs. Suniol said as she settled herself and placed her bag and purse at her feet, as if it were just any normal early summer afternoon in Runyonville. "How are you, dear?"

She didn't appear any more concerned than Grandmama. "I think the world might be ending?" Alice said.

"Well, as G says, let's wait and see, dear, wait and see. Maybe you all can join me at Teddy's after tea."

Grandmama nodded and poured the tea. "Where were you, anyway, Mattie?"

Blowing on her tea, eyes on the bourbon, Mattie said, "Why, in my living room, G, where the holo TV is, for heaven's sake."

"Not just now," Grandmama said, clucking her tongue on the roof of her mouth in that reproving sound she made when Alice left her dinner plate on the counter instead of loading it into the sonic. "With Loyal, while I was at school."

"Hiking. In Japan.

"Hmmm," Grandmama said. She set her tea aside and poured the bourbon.

"Thank you," Mrs. Suniol chirped, taking her glass.

A strange, distant hissing sound echoed across the sky and Alice saw that the fireballs were falling closer to them now. "Grandmama, maybe we should leave," she suggested, using the calm voice Grandmama insisted upon whenever Alice felt most hysterical.

"And go where, Alice?"

"To Teddy's cabin," Mrs. Suniol said.

"Why, Mattie? The sky's on fire," she pointed out. They all watched the fireballs fall for a few seconds.

A blue Mini-V came zigzagging down the street, bumping the curb all along the right hand side. The driver was crying and using her right hand to swat at the Labs hanging over the backseat, their tails smacking three crying children strapped in their seats and helpless against them. As they veered past, both dogs slid into the baggage-loaded front passenger seat. The woman gave up, faced front, and apparently stood on the accelerator. The hybrid coughed out a puff of blue smoke and zipped away towards Fremont and the highway.

Richard, the old neighbor who lived kitty-corner to them, came out onto his front-stoop. He peered down the street at the trail of smoke, glanced at the sky, raised a hand in greeting to Alice, Grandmama, and Mrs. Suniol, who raised her glass in return, and then shuffled back inside.

Now that Alice thought to listen, she could hear horns honking, and sirens and voices from the next street over. A car alarm blared from somewhere two or three streets over. Another car came by and then a third, both loaded with stuff and kids and pets. The hissing rose and fell like far away surf.

Grandmama had a thoughtful look on her face. Mrs. Suniol drank the rest her bourbon before she placed the glass back down and once more took up her tea. Grandmama leaned forward and poured her bourbon directly into her tea.

They sipped.

Suddenly cold despite the heat of the August day, Alice lifted her feet from the porch floor and wrapped her arms around her knees. "Are we going or not?"

"Yes," Mrs. Suniol said, as Grandmama said, "No."

They raised their ancient, hopelessly plucked brows at each other. Alice sighed. A sheet of lightning flashed across the sky to the west and she ducked further into herself. Grandmama rocked back in her chair. "I do believe that's the Epley building downtown."

Peeking out over the twin humps of her bony knees, Alice followed their gazes. Just visible through the porch columns and across the last of Mr. Snyder's summer flowers, flames jumped from the Epley's dome on the distant skyline of Peoria and licked at the drifting clouds and smoke above.

"Why should we go to Teddy's cabin?" Grandmama asked again.

Mrs. Suniol pulled her attention from the Epley dome and studied the assortment of Girl Scout cookies Alice had laid out back before the world had started ending. "Loyal said if there should ever be an emergency, like a civil emergency, a disaster of some sort on a wide scale, he would meet me at Teddy's cabin." She picked up a Peanut Butter Patty and nibbled the edges while Grandmama stared at her.

"My Mattie," Grandmama said after a long moment of consideration. "Do you believe that? Really believe it, with all your heart?"

Mrs. Suniol swallowed her mouthful, sipped her tea, and then declared herself. "Yes."

"Alice, go pack a bag, dear. All I shall need is my toothbrush and my pair of lacy purple underwear, if you will, please."

"Yes, ma'am," Alice whispered and scuttled into the house.

She went to her room first, because she wanted more than underwear just in case the world took a while to end. Her suitcase, when she finally managed to tug it out from under the bed, seemed too big to manage if they had to walk. When she'd left her dorm to live with Grandmama, it had seemed too small to hold her life. Rolling it along was easy on the city sidewalks, and there'd been men who slung it easily onto the monorail to Runyonville and off again, but she remembered wrestling it up the porch steps. She'd never get it up and into the trunk of Mrs. Suniol's old GuntherMobile.

Sighing, Alice groped around in the dark under the bed and found the Adidas duffle bag she'd left behind last summer. She half-heartedly slapped the dust off while she thought about what to take. Her pink tee shirt from Blackberry Fun Park, a couple of polos and her favorite denim shorts, which she was already wearing. Her black shorts, socks, all her underwear and her extra bra. A sleep shirt. She stuck in a notebook she liked to draw in and the romance she was reading and her toothbrush. The photo disc her Mom had given her, but when she checked the charge on it, it was dead. She packed it anyway. Maybe Teddy's cabin would have power.

In her Grandmama's room, she stuffed in a couple of blouses, a tan pair of slacks she knew her Grandmama favored, and three pair of lacy underwear, including the purple pair. Besides the requested toothbrush, Alice took a full tube of Colgate and all three jars of Grandmama's moisturizer from her bathroom drawer.

Slinging the duffle's shoulder strap over her head, she settled the bag sideways across her back. Through the open closet door, Alice spied the gleaming tips of Grandmama's extensive collection of dress shoes. She looked down at her grubby but sturdy tennis shoes. Grandmama was wearing her tea slippers. Alice grunted and dug out the waterproof suede hiking boots she'd only seen Grandmama wear once, to some summer camp function when Alice had been ten or so. They were in perfect condition.

In the living room, she re-adjusted, smoothed her hair and sweat from her temples, took a deep breath, and walked calmly out onto the porch. Grandmama put down her glass, once again filled with bourbon, and nodded at the boots in Alice's hand. "Excellent idea, Alice, thank you."

Mrs. Suniol snorted. She was wearing white sandals.

"You do have more appropriate footwear, Mattie?"

"I do. But I'll wear these, thank you."

"Suit yourself," Grandmama said mildly. She gestured for the boots and Alice brought them to her. When they were properly laced, Grandmama said, "Alice, dear, leave that bag and fetch the cookie jar."

"What cookie jar?"

Grandmama looked at her cross-eyed. "*The* jar, of course, Alice."

Alice had no idea what Grandmama meant. The only cookie jar they'd ever had was a bear with outstretched arms.

"On the top shelf in the pantry. In the back."

Mystified, Alice lowered the duffle bag to the white plastic porch boards. "But—"

"The cookie jar, Alice," Grandmama said.

Alice trotted back through to the kitchen. She opened the pantry door and reached as high and far back as she could. Her fingers brushed a cool and smooth surface. Fumbling along the shelf, she scrabbled along the smoothness, turning the object to inch it forward to the front of the shelf. Finally, she could grasp it. She drew it down.

It was a mason jar, filled with real metal coins and precious stones of all sizes and colors. Alice remembered to breathe when her lungs began to ache, but the air squeaked into her tight chest. The cookie jar, which Grandmama had called the cookie jar when Alice was little, so that if she talked about it, the coin jar would remain safe. It went with a bedtime story her Grandmama used to tell her. About how the fairy Godmother was saving the coins from the end of the rainbow, and sometimes jagged pieces of the rainbow itself, for someday. Someday.

Today was someday.

Alice's vision wavered and burned. Her tears fell hot on her cheek.

"Alice," Grandmama called from the porch.

Alice swiped at her tears and snuffled. Stooping, she snatched at a pile of mini-thermal lunch bags from a lower shelf, wrestled one away from its brothers, and zipped the jar into it. "Coming," she shouted back. She stumbled over the kitchen threshold, which made her cry harder.

Wiping her face, she wasn't even aware of the four young men at the foot of the steps who held her Grandmama's rapt attention until the weighted silence on the porch registered. Embarrassed, she sucked in a breath, stood taller, and quit her crying.

"Are you quite done now, Alice," her Grandmama asked without looking at her.

"Yes, Grandmama,"Alice replied meekly.

The men were soldiers, maybe Marines, Alice thought, but she was hazy on who wore what uniforms except from pictures on the holo. Sailors wore white, and the Army wore green, except when they wore camouflage. Marines never seemed to be dressed all the same. And everybody wore camouflage at war, right? But something in their bearing, maybe, whispered Marine to her.

"You were saying," Mrs. Suniol said, her voice sharp, all giddiness from the bourbon slapped right off her by the seriousness on the men's faces.

"Yes, ma'am," said the one standing with his toes against the edge of the bottom step. "Are you, after all, Matilda Suniol?"

Mrs. Suniol drew herself up, but without standing, and gave him the imperious Queen look she used at Halloween when the teenagers came to her door in shoddy, last minute costumes. "I am."

"Do you have ID, ma'am?"

Mrs. Suniol stared at him a moment longer and then deflated. She motioned at the purse lying against her overnight and Alice eased over to give it to her. Mrs. Suniol dug around in the deepest pocket for a moment, her tongue creeping out the corner of her lips and came up with a pink zebra print wallet. She flipped it open and held it out to the man.

He trotted up the steps, and examined it carefully. Alice saw that his hands were clean, with buffed nails, but the skin looked rough and lived in. His boots were shiny, but worn. He threw a glance at her, noticing her looking at him. His eyes were clear blue and not hard, exactly, but the soft edge of youth she saw in the boys at college was gone. Alice shook her head. What was she thinking?

The man gave Mrs. Suniol back her wallet. His men in the yard relaxed. One turned and walked back toward the hard top jeeps parked at the curb. The other two followed their leader onto the porch. Alice stepped back to make room for them.

"Ms. Suniol, we have received an important communique from the, um...invaders."

Grandmama looked startled. Mrs. Suniol frowned.

"The aliens?" he tried.

"So, there really are aliens?" Alice asked.

He nodded. "Sort of. They're a lot like us, apparently. They claim they 'planted a flag' here," he said, making air quotes, "thousands of years ago and we're them, or they're us or some non-sense like that. They aren't really invading."

"But," Grandmama said, waving a hand at the fireballs still streaking the skies. The entire skyline was aflame now. Smoke roiled into the heavens like writhing black snakes all tangled together.

"I know," he said, dragging the word out. Alice stifled a giggle. She was certain he'd have rolled his eyes if he hadn't been working.

"Whatever do they want?" Grandmama said. She sat back, looking for all the world like she might be sending Alice for more teacups for the men.

"They want you," he answered. "Well, Ms. Suniol, anyway."

"Why?" Mrs. Suniol cried, her voice trembling.

"We don't know, ma'am, but we're under orders to bring you to Central Command."

The soldier beside Alice shifted his hand to the butt of his gun. Alice gasped. He dropped his hand, looking sheepish.

Grandmama, ever practical, asked, "And where is Central Command?"

"Iowa."

"Iowa?"

"Yes, Ma'am."

"She's not going without us," Grandmama declared.

"That's fine, ma'am, we're authorized to do whatever it takes to get her there."

"Alice, are you ready?"

Alice surveyed the duffle at her feet, felt the weight of the coin jar on her shoulder, scanned the beloved street she might never see again through a fresh blur of tears and nodded. Grandmama held out her hand and the head soldier graciously helped her to her feet.

AT THE SMALL airfield near the mall where Alice once worked at a pretzel kiosk, a wide black helicopter sat hunkered on the weedy asphalt like a massive Japanese beetle. The two soldiers driving the jeeps remained behind as the leader and his second handed Grandmama and Mrs. Suniol up through the rear doors to a waiting fellow. The rotors began a slow twirl as the leader turned to Alice, his hand palm up in invitation. She mounted the pipe step before leaning over. He canted forward so she could talk into his ear. "Are you Marines?"

"Yes, ma'am."

"What's your name?"

"Sam."

"How old are you, Sam?"

"Twenty-four, ma'am."

Just two years older than she, but seeming so much more mature than she felt. "Thank you, Sam," she said and started forward again, but he still had her hand and tugged her back.

"Your name, ma'am?"

"Alice."

"Thank you, ma'am," he said and let her go ahead of him. The fellow handed her black ear protectors as Sam's second climbed in behind her and Sam slid the door shut and took his seat. The three Marines sat with their backs to the pilots, facing Alice, Mrs. Suniol and Grandmama. Sam's knees bumped against Alice's as the beast roared and lifted tail first from the ground before leveling off. The acceleration pushed Alice back against her seat.

Sam pointed to his left and Alice turned her head. Runyonville lay in gridlock chaos below. Cars lined Valley Road in both directions, all of them trying to get to the interstate, which was suffering its own obstruction. Emergency lights flashed from a dozen different points. The roads branching out into Baxter County were in better shape, but still heavily traveled. Several minutes into the flight, the helicopter banked to the left. Smoke obscured the view momentarily and then devastated Peoria lay out the side window, the now fully engulfed Epley dome dead ahead.

Sam's mouth opened in a bona fide gape. Lifting a hand to his right headphone as he stared out at the flaming skyline, his lips moved rapidly as he spoke into the mic in front of his mouth. Alice looked again, trying to see what had alarmed him. Three airliners were visible, in an obvious holding pattern far above them. Distant fireballs continued to fall. She guessed there were more she couldn't see.

The helicopter turned a bit, now on a heading that would sweep them closer to downtown. Sam's lips moved. The copter dropped several hundred feet. People crowded every sidewalk. Some were walking, but most stood still, watching the flames...and the buildings completely visible through them. At least fifteen skyscrapers at the city's core were ablaze in light. Police cars and fire trucks cordoned off large portions of the affected blocks, but there were still people out on the streets. Standing still. Watching.

The pilot kept them well to the northwest as she circled downtown. Black smoke washed over them every few minutes. Parts of the Epley dome blackened, scorched by the flickering light, and then the darkness retreated, the dome rose as if building itself back into its proud arch, then burned before it darkened once again with smoke and soot and ash and began to collapse.

It was a hologram. A repeating loop of flickering light. Fake. No flames. No smoke. People stood still, the tiny ovals of their upturned faces clearly visible as they watched the spectacle. Grandmama's hand, which Alice hadn't even noticed, squeezed her thigh and she turned to face her. Grandmama's eyes brimmed with tears, just one spilling over as she blinked, a big grin lighting her face.

Beyond her, Mrs. Suniol's relief made her look like a young woman once more, her hazel eyes bright with wonder. Alice rejoiced to see that the two old friends held hands as they met her gaze before all three turned back to the amazing holographic view.

A bright flash startled Alice. Straining against her safety harness, she cowered back into Grandmama's side, who lifted her arm to protect Alice's head. An incoming fireball collided with the helicopter and exploded into a shower of sparks. The copter dipped to the right and then swung up again hard to the left, lifting fast. Grandmama's hold on her tightened, her fingers digging in. Alice forced her eyes open to see what Sam was doing.

The middle Marine, Sam's second, blocked her view as he had his arms outstretched to encompass all three of them as they huddled together. Peeking over his shoulder, Alice watched Sam hold onto a bar above the window, half-standing to see out. His jaw worked as he yelled into his mic. Glancing the other way, she could see the Marine that helped them aboard doing the same on the other side, though his jaw was clenched tight.

Transparent flames flickered past the windows and then the windshield filled with them, thin black smoke swirling. There was no heat. No sharp odor. In fact, now that she thought of it, she hadn't smelt any smoke all day, even though the neighborhood reeked of it last year when the wind off a forest fire two hundred miles away blew smoke their way. She pulled away from her Grandmama. The Marine watched her with sharp eyes as he straightened to allow her to sit upright again.

Grandmama and Mrs. Suniol continued to clutch each other, but now also seemed to be taking stock of the situation. The very fake situation, although they were now on a definite downward trajectory. She wished she could hear what they were saying. The Marine's lips moved and Sam twisted around to glance at her. He nodded at her, the corner of his lip twitching up, and she smiled back.

Fifteen minutes later, the copter bounced down into the tall fescue of an unmowed pasture surrounded by an endless sea of mature pines. The pilot shut the rotors down. The Marines made no move to get out. Alice took her ear protectors off when Sam removed his headset and the others followed suit. Both the pilots removed their helmets, unstrapped, and scrambled back to join them.

"Captain Ingram," one of them said. "This is ATO Jones." Both of them were in their thirties, dark-eyed dark haired women wearing competence and confidence like second skins. "We were ordered down. We're to make our way to the nearest town, make contact, and await transport."

"You can't just call them?" Alice asked.

"Wireless is blocked," the Captain said.

"They can do that?" Grandmama said.

"But," Mrs. Suniol said. "It's all satellite these days."

The captain nodded and cut her eyes toward the holographic flames and smoke still playing on the surface of the copter.

"How are they doing that?" Sam asked.

She shrugged. "Think we're good to bail, Jones?"

"Let's find out." Jones shouldered past Sam's second and grabbed the handle of the door. "On one, Kreager," she said and Sam grabbed the handle of the door on his side of the copter. "Three, two, one."

They wrenched the doors open and jumped out through the fire. Alice saw Sam land on the long grass and roll. She whipped her head around to see Jones regaining her feet. Sam yelled "Clear!" with Jones echoing him.

The captain stepped out first and the other two Marines followed before reaching up to help Grandmama and Mrs. Suniol out. Alice dropped Mrs. Suniol's pink overnight out and then slung her duffel over her back and the lunch bag holding the cookie jar across her chest before she joined them. The hologram crackled against her skin like static electricity as she passed through it.

ATO Jones stood halfway in and halfway out of the holographic flames. "Wow. This isn't touch tech, though you can feel it. Not sound waves. This is just crazy. How are they directing and maintaining these?"

Alice knew from the stiffness of her shoulders and the expression on her face that Grandmama was about to become intimidating. "Why is the military helping maintain this illusion of attack, Captain Ingram?"

"Because it's no illusion, ma'am," Captain Ingram said in a firm tone, giving Grandmama her complete attention. Alice was impressed that the captain had such a fine sense of self-preservation. "We are not in control of the electric grid. Our most important defense mechanisms have been neutralized."

"Not destroyed?"

"Rendered inoperable."

Grandmama softened her stance. "Thank you for your honesty. Now why not continue to fly despite this"—she waved a hand at the helicopter—"showmanship."

"We were ordered down, ma'am."

Grandmama gave her a long, measuring look and then turned to Mrs. Suniol. "Mattie, you really should have changed your shoes."

Mrs. Suniol rolled her eyes. "We should go to Lake Snow like we planned. Loyal won't wait forever."

"How long have you waited for him, Mattie?"

"Forty-three years, twenty-two weeks, five days and fourteen hours, but who's counting?"

Sam's thick eyebrows shot up and Alice didn't miss the glance he shared with Captain Ingram. "We were ordered to locate and transport you to, um, a location in Iowa, Ms. Suniol, as soon as possible. Afterward, I'll ask arrangements be made to transport you—" he looked a little wild-eyed as his gaze darted to Grandmama and Alice and back to Mrs. Suniol's feet—"anywhere you'd like to go."

"If he's there, he'll wait for you," Grandmama declared.

Mrs. Suniol sniffed. "He's there."

"Nearest town is west, Captain," ATO Jones said.

ALICE HAD BLISTERS. She had no idea how Mrs. Suniol had walked through the field, down the macadam a ways, and then three miles up and down a hilly gravel road shortcut, upon which they'd been joined by locals who had abandoned their cars along the way and were turning back towards home. The Marines were the pied pipers of Orange by the time they passed the town welcome sign.

Made-up of a single intersection and maybe ten streets branching from it, Orange boasted all of twelve hundred some residents. Half had managed to make it out of town to other locations, Alice guessed. Some had remained behind. At least a hundred and twenty trudged back in beside them, all of them talking at once.

The mayor, barber, and town veterinarian were standing on the railroad bridge over the main road when they came around the last curve. Several of the kids ran ahead, shouting out hellos. After a short conference between Sam, the captain, and the mayor, bar-b-que dinner was offered and accepted. There was plenty due to the power failure. The mayor made a short speech announcing that the town was not in eminent danger, though the forest outside of town was laced in holographic fire.

Two elderly women hustled Grandmama and Mrs. Suniol into their nearby home for clean-up, tea, and a lie-down. Alice and the Marines were escorted to the plasti-tek front porch of the general mercantile, pointed to the restroom, given bottles of water, and offered rockers. Sam followed a tall man into the back to what was promised to be a short-wave radio in working condition. After a few minutes, Alice toed her tennis shoes off, folded her legs to tuck her feet under herself, and closed her eyes. The distant hissing rose and fell. Rose and fell.

A gentle hand on her shoulder wakened her. "Hey, Alice, transport'll be here in five minutes," Sam stage-whispered. Two little girls sat at her feet, giggling into their hands. She looked up at Sam.

"You, um..." He rubbed his thumb across his own cheek.

Heat flooded her face as she kicked upright, swiping the back of her hand across her mouth. "Did I sleep through dinner?"

"No, ma'am. Your grandmother is wrapping the first burgers off the grill to take with us."

Alice shoved her feet back in her tennis shoes and stood. Sam ducked and grabbed her duffle and the lunch bag holding the coin jar. She took the lunch bag from him as they went down the steps.

Minutes later, she found herself waving good-bye to the solemn people of Orange from the identical twin of the helicopter they had abandoned.

．　．　．

ALICE DIDN'T KNOW what she expected, but this was not it. They landed at a tiny airfield much like the one at home, only in Iowa, which was not as green as she always imagined. The ripply brown landscape shining under the brilliant red rays of the setting sun and fake fireballs did not compute. Where was all the corn?

Heat rose off the pavement in waves as the open-backed truck they rode in trundled past copters and small jets and Cessnas. Three bi-planes sat at the edge of the field. "Are those, like, actual crop-dusters?"

Sam shrugged. Grandmama and Mrs. Suniol didn't hear her, focused as they were on the building they were headed towards. It was just a plain sheet metal warehouse with all the roll-up doors across its front wide open. Eight people stood out front, five of them men with military bearing. Mrs. Suniol's expression fluctuated between anxious and excited. Sweat beaded on her upper lip.

They crunched to a stop. Alice's thighs left a slick mark on the vinyl seat as she stood. Sam and the other Marines formed a line as they hit the ground. It felt oddly formal after all the hiking and front-porch sitting of the late afternoon. The greeting committee did not step forward. A woman with her hair arranged in a tightly braided bun detached herself.

"I'm Commander Lisette Boros," she said, sweeping an arm towards the cavernous interior of the warehouse. "This way, please."

Swamp coolers pushed the hot air around. Maps, papers, and laptop computers covered the surface of a long conference table at which at least a dozen techs in sweat-stained shirts worked. More stood talking to one another in front of three whiteboards covered in numbers and symbols. Alice had taken college math through calculus, and even a physics course, but several of the symbols were utterly unfamiliar in a way that seemed wrong somehow. She craned her neck trying to decide why as she followed Grandmama into a blessedly air-conditioned room.

"Please meet Thrunk Sink," Commander Boros said, indicating a short, dark man with piercing blue eyes. "And Kevin."

Kevin bowed. He looked like any other white, fair-haired mid-westerner. "Ladies," he said.

Unimpressed, Grandmama lifted her brows. "Are you going to share the alien communique with us or must we continue on in the dark?"

Kevin laughed even as Thrunk Sink frowned. "End of the line, Ms..." He raised his brows.

"You may call me G," Grandmama said archly.

"G," Kevin said. "We are the aliens in question."

Alice's heart thumped and dropped into her belly. She glanced behind herself, suddenly aware she'd left Sam on the tarmac without even a thought. Commander Boros shot her a questioning glance and Alice straightened her shoulders. "I believe this calls for tea," she said in the firmest tone she could muster.

Mrs. Suniol smiled as Grandmama nodded. "Just so, dear Alice. I agree."

Commander Boros only looked at them like she'd never heard the word 'tea' before.

"Please," Kevin said to Commander Boros, although his appraising gaze remained on Alice.

The Commander nodded at someone hovering near the doorway.

MRS. SUNIOL SET her teacup back into its saucer. "I'm sorry, gentlemen, that you've come all this way and gone to so much trouble—"

"Caused so much trouble," Grandmama said.

"Yes," Mrs. Suniol agreed. "Can you believe this, G? That aliens are just more men?"

Kevin snorted.

Thrunk Sink clasped his folded hands tighter together and spoke quickly in a language Alice didn't understand. Kevin translated.

"This is a matter of grave importance to Councilman Sink's planet, Mrs. Suniol. The native peoples are dying."

Mrs. Suniol picked up one of the images of a man named Rand May. "This does look like my Loyal. My Loyal, you understand, many years ago. This is not what he would look like now."

"Time moves differently depending on where you are in the universe," Kevin said.

"And how fast you're moving," Alice interjected.

"Correct," Kevin continued. "May left only a few days ago from the perspective of Councilman Sink."

"The truth remains that Loyal, if he is still alive," Grandmama said, "would be closing in on eighty years old."

"Seventy-five," Mrs. Suniol corrected.

"The average lifespan on Earth for a male is currently ninety-one," Commander Boros said.

Kevin nodded. Thrunk Sink nodded. Mrs. Suniol said, "Of course he's alive. There's an invasion going on. He's going to meet me at Teddy's cabin."

"Mattie!" Grandmama exclaimed throwing her arms up in the air. "He went for butter and sour cream forty-three years ago and never came home."

Clutching her bag in both hands, Mrs. Suniol lifted her chin. "I would know, G, if he was dead. And he said, if ever—"

"We know, Mattie. Teddy's cabin."

Thrunk Sink leaned forward, his clipped words passionate as he watched Mrs. Suniol while he talked.

Kevin listened to him intently and then rubbed the back of his neck and sighed. "Where, may I ask, is this Teddy's cabin?"

LAKE SNOW WAS everything Alice expected. Fireballs continued to light up the dark night sky. Their flame sparkled across the ripples on the lake's vast dark surface. Fireflies blinked in the air above it. Cicadas and crickets and frogs dimmed the ever-present hiss that still filled her ears. Ringed in dark green firs and brilliant, multi-branched white flowering shrubs that towered overhead, it not only looked magical, it smelled magical as well. Fresh and bright somehow.

She breathed in a deeper breath than she'd ever taken in her life before—the air rushed into her and right down to her toes, making her muscles thrum and skin tingle.

She knew it was Sam come to join her without turning around.

"No one's here," he said in a low rumble. He lifted his hand as he took in the view. "God, I've never seen anything so beautiful."

She held her hand out and he took it. His hot, calloused skin against hers felt like a promise.

"Ms. Suniol is crying," he said.

"She truly believed Loyal would be here."

"Councilman Sink and Kevin are searching the cabin, hoping Rand May left something here for them."

"Is this really happening?" Alice asked.

"Do you mean are there really aliens and other planets and a whole intergalactic community we never knew about until today?"

"Yes."

"Yes. I don't know much," Sam said, focused on the dark shadows of the lake. "But we were briefed by Kevin before we came to pick up Ms. Suniol. Her name? Suniol? In Councilman Sink's language, it's a term that refers to the royal guard of his native country. It's one of the reasons they suspected she might know of Rand May, in combination with the English name of Loyal."

"Loyal Guard. How did they find her, though?"

"A public records search turned up the marriage certificate."

"In just days?"

"Years. Here on earth. A major I overheard said they've been searching for May's trail for years here."

Unable to respond, to untangle time in the way they'd talked about it, Alice committed the light on Lake Snow to memory and then she and Sam walked back to Teddy's old cabin, which looked just like every lakeside cabin in every movie she'd ever seen. While Captain Ingram and ATO Jones remained with the helicopter in the dirt parking lot of a bait shop about a mile from the lake, Sam's crew was back up to five Marines, who were ranged around the ragged edge of a security perimeter. His second's deep, "Sir," as they passed the lightless hollow under a large spreading oak startled her, but Sam's rumbling chuckle as she lurched into him did interesting, pleasurable, things to her insides.

Grandmama and Mrs. Suniol sat like girls out on the top porch step, reminding Alice of the little trusting girls in Orange. They looked at Alice and Sam's hands in the low light of a portable lantern and Alice realized she'd forgotten. Sam didn't seem inclined to let go, so she held on. Grandmama smiled.

Kevin let the cabin's screen door slap closed as he came outside. "Nothing."

"Maybe you could tell us what you're looking for," Grandmama sensibly suggested.

Folding his sturdy farm-boy frame, he dropped down onto the wooden step next to her. "A stone," he said. He held his thumb and index finger an inch and a half apart. "Yay big. Rough. Clear except for a dark red center."

Alice's belly went topsy-turvy as she met Grandmama's startled gaze.

Kevin continued to talk to his own feet. "Rand, I mean, Loyal, he's—he was—a royal guard. He took the stone off-planet during an uprising. To keep it from falling into the hands of the rebels. But then—"

"He got lost." Mrs. Suniol said. "He told me that when I met him. That he was lost. But I found him. Finders—"

"Keepers," a voice said from the darkness.

Mrs. Suniol lifted her hands to cover her mouth, her eyes already wet.

A man stepped out from around the front corner of the cabin. Grandmama and Kevin stood up. Even as she caught the movement of one of the other Marines closing in, Sam angled himself in front of Alice, lifting his hand in a 'hold' motion. As sweet as that struck her, she couldn't see. She shoved him back over. Just to see what she already knew.

Loyal Suniol looked no older than the photos in Mrs. Suniol's front hallway or on the table at the Iowa airfield. Roman-nosed and firm-jawed, wide shouldered, young. Less than thirty. He drifted past them all and took Mrs. Suniol's hands in his. "My love."

"Oh, Loyal," she sighed. "I was so afraid for you."

And Alice saw the truth then, that Mrs.Suniol had known all along that she would not see him again. That she knew she would not grow old with him.

"Did you not move on?" Loyal said. "In all these years?"

"I've had companionship," she said.

Grandmama raised her brows.

"Richard has been very kind to me. I've had a good life."

Grandmama tilted her head with a considering look. Alice turned the name over before it came to her. Richard was their kitty-corner neighbor, the one who had come out and waved at them only that morning. Alice watched him potter around his yard watering and weeding nearly everyday. Her hand rose to cover her mouth, to contain the delight that burst in her at the thought of him and Mrs. Suniol together.

"Richard is a good man," Grandmama agreed and Loyal smiled, transforming him from merely attractive to gorgeous.

Alice did squeak then. Grandmama grinned at her. Sam shook his head and squeezed her hand once. She squeezed back as she glanced up to see him smiling down at her. Amusement looked good on him.

"G," Loyal said and leaned over to kiss her cheek. "I didn't think that someday would take so long to get here."

Someday. Alice grabbed the strap of the lunchbox, her thoughts spinning so fast she couldn't get her vocal cords moving before Thrunk Sink cleared his throat and threw open the door to join them.

Loyal kissed each of Mrs. Suniol's hands and then her lips, a chaste, soft kiss. Letting go of her, he stepped away from her and straightened, coming to attention in a way that Alice guessed must be human nature, if even space invaders did it.

Kevin leaned right from his seat on the steps and the councilman stepped between him and Grandmama to come down the steps and stand on the sparse grass facing Loyal, who bowed his head. Thrunk Sink returned the gesture, looking every bit an officer now. Sweeping an arm out to encompass the lake and the night and the fireballs, Loyal spoke in the language Alice didn't know.

"When it became apparent the palace would be overrun," Kevin translated, "his superior tasked him with safeguarding the—" He tilted his head, his lips moving as he considered what word he needed. "Through stone. And sent him off-planet. He came here, to a feral world, to hide. He hid the stone when he discovered rebels had followed him to Earth and then led them on a wild-goose chase to protect the woman he loves." Alice shifted, opening her mouth, but Kevin patted the air to hush her as he listened. "He was...else-where. Off-planet, but not far. His attention was drawn to the unmistakable message of both royal victory and distress being broadcast across your skies and cities. When he saw the signal, when he knew his planet was safe, he turned on the rebels."

"Turned on them?" Alice wondered if that meant—

"Killed them," Kevin said.

Sam shifted beside her, tension spilling off him onto her, his fingers tight enough on hers to bruise. "The holographic fireballs, taking the power grid offline, that was the signal? People probably died."

Alice nodded, thinking of the crying children in the smoking station wagon, their dogs falling into the front seat, their mother giving up.

Councilman Sink spoke, his face earnest.

"No one died," Kevin said.

"But—"

Kevin gave him a slow smile and a trust me look. "Sam, no one died from our actions. And now no one will die on Loyal's planet, either. That's all you need to know."

Grandmama laid a hand on Kevin's thick forearm and he immediately covered it with his. "What do you mean by through stone?"

"It channels the natural energy that rises from the mantle of Loyal's planet through a purifier that allows his people to continue living there," he said.

"And how long have they lived there?" Alice asked.

"Countless millennia," Loyal said. "No one remembers who discovered its power. The existence of the stone and its purifier has been lost and found several times, but it has never been removed for long. The people suffer from its absence."

"What did you mean, Loyal," Mrs. Suniol suddenly said. She sniffed and dabbed at her eyes, careful, as always, not to smear her mascara. "That you didn't know someday would take so long to get here?"

Loyal looked to Councilman Sink. The councilman nodded. Only then did Loyal return to Mrs. Suniol's side.

"I saw G the day I left. The rebels were near, but hadn't found me yet. I needed to go before they knew of you, lead them away. I told her I'd found a stone here, at Teddy's, that I needed a hiding place for it, someplace you would never look, as a special gift for someday. But I didn't know that you had told her about me. Somehow she knew I was leaving." He glanced over at Grand-mama, his quick glance filled with regret and the cost he paid for doing so. Alice hurt for him. For Mrs. Suniol. For the years she and Grandmama barely spoke despite seeing each other everyday.

"She brought butter and sour cream over later," Mrs. Suniol blurted.

Grandmama's strangled half-sob drew everyone's focus. "The potatoes were cold."

It bubbled up before she could stop it. Alice barked out a sudden laugh at the image of them hunched together over cold potatoes and steak. And then they were all laughing, save Councilman Sink, who frowned at them all. When they sobered, Mrs. Suniol said, "I was mad at her for not stopping you."

"I understood, Mattie," Grandmama said. "And even more when I found my own husband."

Councilman Sink said something short, in a prompting tone.

"She said she had the perfect hiding spot for it," Loyal contin-ued. "That she would keep it safe. Until someday."

Alice was already lifting the strap of the lunch bag over her head. She held it out to Grandmama.

"No, my dear Alice, please," Grandmama said with a go ahead gesture.

Aware of all eyes on her, Alice tugged her hand free from Sam's and ripped the velcro open, the sound harsh in the moist, summer dark.

"You have it here?" Loyal breathed. "How did you know?"

"Mattie believed in you," Grandmama said.

Reaching in, Alice grasped the cookie jar. Sam took the bag from her and she stooped as she unscrewed the top. She tapped the contents out onto the second step, between Grandmama's boots and Mrs. Suniol's white sandals. Buffalo Head nickels, Kennedy half-dollars, gold Pandas, Walking Liberties, Sacagawea dollars, Smithson dimes, copper Codes, crystal amethysts, raw rubies, uncut emeralds and garnets and tourmaline, white granite, tiger's eyes, blue stone, opal, spinel, moonstone. She used to know them all.

Crouching down, Loyal ran a finger through the pile, clearing them away in spirals until the stone, his stone, lay exposed.

Kevin hummed, a little nervous sound, and then spoke. "He's a casberacyk. A worker of the stone, for lack of a better term. Very rare among his people."

Alice remembered the unusual heat of it when she was little, something she didn't question back then. She'd thought it only a clear spinel with an odd red core. He stroked it before plucking it up and raising it to the moonlight. It fractured the light, sending bright sparkles into the night. Raising his other hand, Loyal placed the brilliant stone on his open palm.

"Close your eyes," he whispered.

Alice didn't.

Grey smoke rose from his hand, along with the stench of burning flesh and Loyal's slight whine as the glowing stone threw a clear, hard light onto them, the scraggly yard, the under branches of the nearest water oak. Sam took hold of the back of her shirt. The stone's red center burst, a miniature sun that mirrored the fireballs until it filled her vision and still she couldn't look away. Whole worlds appeared in the swirl of stars streaming through the light, galaxies of them.

Loyal closed his fist around the stone.

Alice blinked hard.

Lake Snow lay placid under the quarter moon. Silent. Very, very dark without the holographic fireballs and distant flames. The kitchen light winked on inside and then others all around the lake came on like steady fireflies guiding their families home. The crickets and cicadas and frogs found their voices.

Alice stared at Loyal's handsome face, absorbing his youth, his determination, his loyalty to his people. It was all true. All of this was real. "So they know you have it? What now?" she said, breaking the trance they'd fallen under.

Loyal opened his brilliant blue eyes, a trait he shared with Councilman Sink. "Now we go and you carry on."

Hand still clenched in her shirt, Sam pulled Alice into his side and tucked her under his arm. "But we know now. That you're out there."

"We've known for decades," Grandmama piped up.

Kevin stood and brushed his jeans off. "A thousand years from now, no one will remember."

"Oh, Loyal," Mrs. Suniol cried out, lifting her arms. He shifted over to hug her, the through stone still held tight in his fist. "I'll never forget you."

"I'll see you again, Mattie. In the meantime."

"In the meantime, my love."

"MY MATTIE," Grandmama declared. "You are lovely. That pink overnight is hideous, though."

"It used to be red."

"And you used to be young."

Mrs. Suniol huffed and sipped her Ansell tea. "Young is a state of the heart, G. Richard thinks I'm still a teen at heart. Alice, what do you think?"

"I think Richard is very glad you're making an honest man of him, Mrs. Suniol." Mrs. Suniol's radiant smile reminded Alice of Loyal's. She folded the lacy nightie she and Grandmama had bought for Mrs. Suniol's honeymoon into the overnight and zipped it back up. "He's a good man," she said, echoing her Grandmama's words that fateful night a month ago.

If they all teared up for a moment, it was no one's business but their own.

"Hey, Alice," Sam called from the living room. "How old is this Jack Daniels?"

Grandmama smiled, her eyes glistening. "He's a good man, too, Alice, you know that, right?"

Alice tweaked Mrs. Suniol's veil. "Are you going to tell him that you bought that bottle the day I was born to open the day I graduate from college?"

"Are you going to tell him you just applied to the master's program in astrophysics?"

"Hey, Sam, I'm going to study the stars for a couple more years before I finally graduate," Alice yelled.

"That Jack is for when she graduates," Grandmama shouted.

"I joined the space program," Sam yelled back.

"A match made by Loyal," Mrs. Suniol murmured. "You better crack the Jack now, G. Time waits for no one."

Grandmama flourished the tweezers in her hand. "You're right, Matilda. Sam, dear, bring the Jack! We're going to need more tea, Alice."

"Yes, Grandmama."

Author's Notes—Elle Andrews Patt

SOMEDAY LOYAL IS the first published story set in my 'Annunaki' universe. Kevin also appears in my unpublished novel in progress. I hope to produce other small story tags as prequels/sequels in this universe as time goes by.

Research for this story was interesting. Spinel rocks come in a range of colors including clear, and red/pink spinel is more common, though spinels in general have a limited availability. I combined the two. Holograms are indeed progressing to the 'touch' stage. I based the helicopter on the Huey/Venom. Illinois does indeed have large pine forests!

http://www.gemselect.com/gem-info/spinel/spinel-info.php

https://www.newscientist.com/article/dn26640-haptic-holograms-let-you-touch-the-void-in-vr/

http://www.military.com/equipment/uh-1y-venom

~EAP

AOB

Bria Burton

When a healthy marriage struggles, check for faulty wiring.
—Bria Burton

1 - A Malfunction

At the marriage counselor's office, I noticed a problem. My left eye twitched several times. A minor inconvenience. Minutes later the twitching resumed, only it wouldn't stop.

"Maybe you could benefit from time apart," said Marisa, the counselor.

I closed my left eye, but that didn't abate the involuntary movement. To my right, my husband sat with his legs apart, arms draped across his knees, head down. Erick's sandy brown hair covered his eyes.

I glanced out the window to my left, hand cupping my chin to appear pensive. Her question deserved consideration. But how long could I look away? Sooner or later, one of them would draw attention to my twitching eye. Our session wouldn't end for thirty more minutes.

Relax. Your siradons should be moving in to repair the area.

No one else could hear the Guide, who spoke in my thoughts. She helped me navigate this human existence that I was tasked to live. Without her, I would've broken The First Rule—*don't get caught* —long ago.

They're not moving in. Something's wrong, I informed her. I scanned my systems. The left eye flagged as an error, yet my siradons didn't assess and repair as they should.

My good eye relayed the scenery outside the window with perfect clarity. Beneath a cloudless sky, the grass and trees surrounded a lake with a fountain in the middle. When I lifted my twitching left eyelid, everything darkened and blurred.

You may have to leave, said the Guide. *It could cause further friction between you and Erick.*

Not ideal, but I'd do whatever was necessary.

My sometimes robotic reaction to things irritated Erick. Two months ago, I had veered off the Guide's suggested responses, to my detriment. We descended into a period of constant conflict. My decision to ignore the Guide nearly cost me everything. I learned from my mistakes. From then on, I followed her prompting unquestioningly.

The Second Rule—*sustaining your marriage is the most important task* —had an exception. *Nothing will jeopardize The First Rule, not even The Second.* Both rules were embedded in the fibers of my neural network. In this moment, avoiding suspicion was greater than the need to preserve the marriage.

"If you think it's best." My response to Marisa's suggestion broke the long silence.

"Time apart?" Erick shifted. "Really?"

My siradons needed more time. He needed a reassuring glance from me, but the Guide suggested that I resist. *Give them another minute.*

"Marisa's probably right."

"Will you look at me, please?" he begged.

When we first started dating, Erick showered me with flowers, cards, and anything else he thought I'd like. He worked as a manager at a shipping company, so he worked overtime to buy my heart-shaped pendant studded with diamonds for our one-year anniversary last month. His fear of displeasing others meant the idea of separating frightened him. I didn't have time to discuss it. The twitching continued. I needed to leave.

You're going to Yvonne's for the night to think it over, said the Guide. *Cry.*

I covered my eyes and spilled real tears. "This is too hard!" I rose, striding across the room.

"Aona? Where are you going?" Erick asked.

I kept one hand over my left eye, weeping. I turned back. "I'll be at Yvonne's. I just need time to think. I'll call you tomorrow."

"You don't have to leave," said Marisa.

I opened the door and walked out.

2 - The Guide

IN MY REAR VIEW MIRROR, Erick ran outside with one hand on his forehead. He lifted the other, dropping it to his side. As I drove away, he disappeared from my sight.

For the first time, I'd risked the marriage for the sake of not getting caught. I hoped to resolve the problem quickly and avoid future recurrences.

Just get here, said the Guide. *And don't worry. He still loves you.*

It wasn't in my programming to "worry."

Twenty minutes later, I parked in the driveway of a two-story brick house. Although Erick and I had a lovely home, the single-story ranch style had a small yard. Yvonne's manicured front lawn stretched across two lots with a lavish garden out back.

Yvonne opened the front door and waved. "Hi, Aona! Come in."

I waved back, approaching her with my left eye still shut and quivering.

We were the same height and build, but otherwise not very similar-looking. She had blue eyes and peach tones in her skin. A platinum blond bob cupped her round face. Her lips were full and pouty. My long, wavy hair matched the color of coffee beans. My face was square-shaped, my eyes green, my lips thin.

We were the only two AOBs on the planet.

I entered, hanging my purse on the coat rack before following her into the recently updated kitchen. She'd paid for the granite countertop installation, but sanded and painted the cabinets herself. At the island, she poured iced tea. "How is everything?"

"Erick and I are struggling, but we'll work through it."

The Guide kept Yvonne and me informed about each other. We played our parts, even without an audience. The odds of someone monitoring were slim, but the Guide took no chances.

"Let's talk downstairs," said Yvonne.

We took our tea into the basement where several chairs and couches faced a giant flat screen mounted to the wall. Yvonne sat in a recliner near the stairs sipping her tea. I set my cup on the coffee table and went straight for the closet.

Inside, I shut the door and stood in darkness. My good eye switched to night vision. Yvonne's winter coats hung to my left. I pressed my thumb on a spot against the back wall. A panel opened. I stepped through.

As light penetrated the darkness, my vision returned to normal mode. The room on the other side matched the size of the basement living room. There was a mini-kitchen. A bed pressed up against the far wall. Books piled on the nightstand. The bathroom door was ajar.

The Guide sat behind several computer screens at a long desk. Behind her, countless devices, cords, and wires were piled on shelving against the wall. A refrigeration unit housed important samples.

She was a Rogarian from a planet called Pewt and could almost pass for human, but her eyes gave her away. The bright pink irises moved fluidly, as if filled with mercury. Contacts couldn't block the brightness of her true eye color. When she spent time outside in Yvonne's garden, she wore sunglasses. But she never interacted with humans and never told us her name. She preferred that we think of her the way humans would—as an alien.

Yvonne and I were modeled after the Guide's slender build, but we didn't resemble her. The Guide's pixie cut was caramel brown. She had an oval face with dark eyebrows and good symmetry.

Yvonne and I had the same First Rule but a different Second Rule.

Sustain the Guide at all costs, even if it means jeopardizing The First Rule.

In essence, Yvonne dealt with the Guide as I dealt with Erick. Yvonne took care of her and provided companionship. The Guide left Pewt sixteen years ago and had no contact with them. Although she never expressed it to me, she might've been lonely. Maybe not with Yvonne and me in her head. She would often silence Yvonne's thoughts, but took few breaks from mine.

"Hi." She looked up and spread her lips into a perfect smile. Her pink eyes flashed and danced. "Good to see you."

"You, too." The rhetoric came easily to me now, even if I couldn't claim any real feelings.

"Have a seat."

I obeyed and opened my left eye. The room went fuzzy.

She swiveled around in her chair, facing me. With my good eye, I caught the panicked grimace spreading across her features. "What is *that?*" As she leaned in, her face blurred. "Look." She held up a hand mirror.

More astounding than the twitching was the metallic sheen of my left eye. It reflected right back at the mirror. The green in my iris was gone.

"What happened?" she asked.

"I'm not sure." I stared ahead, not moving while she raised a magnifying glass.

"Why haven't your siradons fixed it?" she asked.

We didn't have to speak aloud, but she must've enjoyed verbalizing when so much silent communication passed between us. For the hundredth time, I scanned my systems. No viable answers turned up. "I don't know."

She sighed, frowning. "I have to do an injection. I don't know what else to try."

I held still as she brought the point of a syringe filled with siradons toward my left eye. "Yvonne's hand is steadier than mine, but I'm not wasting a moment." She pressed the needle into my cornea and through the pupil.

The expected level of pain for a human meant that I should cringe and cry out. However, I held my position unmoving. In reality, I felt nothing.

She inhaled slowly, pushing the needle farther in through the lens. The tip sank into the vitreous humor. Her steady hand began the slightest of tremors. With her thumb, she delivered the injection. The pressure was brief as my eye filled with siradons.

The Guide brought a limited supply of the super-microbes—for lack of a better Earth counterpart—from her planet. Siradons were the building blocks for AOBs. Rogarians discovered them two centuries ago, causing an exponential surge in technology.

"What's happening?" she asked.

My own siradons flooded the area. The twitching slowed. "It's working."

She drew out the needle, lowering the empty syringe into the case. Her strange look indicated confusion. "How does it feel?"

The twitching slowed to a complete stop. My eyesight normalized. "I can see. No more spasms." My system scan acknowledged the eye repair, removing the error flag.

"But..." She held the mirror up again.

The metallic sheen, the mirror effect, and the lack of green in my iris remained.

"This isn't good." Her words understated the situation. She spun around. "Oh, no."

To the left of her computer, a security monitor showed images on a six-split screen. The top left corner was Yvonne's front porch and yard. A familiar car had pulled up and parked. Erick got out and shuffled toward the door.

The Guide spun back around. "What do I do?" she asked, staring at my damaged eye. Terror marked hers. The pink swirled.

Seconds passed. She did nothing except gape at me with a mixture of fear, calculation, and resignation. In that time, Yvonne opened the front door—most likely on the Guide's silent orders.

Here, wear these. I suspected fear made her go silent. She handed me a pair of sunglasses and gave me instructions.

I rose and walked to the wall. I pressed my thumb against the panel and went through the closet.

Yvonne is leading him around the side of the house to the back yard. Hurry.

I ran upstairs.

She's taking her time opening the gate.

I took a left and went out the back door. A trellis covered the large wooden deck where an iron rod table and chairs sat off to the right. To the left, I slipped into a mahogany-stained deck chair.

Yvonne and Erick approached from the side yard.

"Erick." I rushed down the porch steps into his embrace. "I'm sorry I ran off."

He hugged me with trembling arms, calming enough to speak. With his fingers, he wiped at the redness beneath his eyes. "It's okay. It's my fault. I shouldn't have accused you of being cruel when that wasn't your intention. It's taken me this long to figure out that I'm causing the problems, not you."

Progress. I smiled at him. As soon as the Guide fixed my eye, we could move on to Stage Two.

"I don't want time apart. Do you?"

Considering my eye problem, maybe. But the Guide was silent. "Marisa suggested it."

"True." He stroked my hair, moving it behind my ear. His hand knocked off my sunglasses.

In the two seconds it took me to bend and pick them up, planting them back on my nose, a flash of confusion marred Erick's face. Unfortunately, he was like most humans. He possessed a desire for answers.

"What's wrong with your eye?"

The Guide screamed, *STALL HIM! STALL HIM!*

"Nothing. I'm so glad you came to see me." I reached to hug him, but he took my glasses off.

With my finger, I sent a high voltage current through his body. Enough to knock him unconscious.

THE THREE OF us carried him inside, down the stairs, and into the Guide's secret room. I assumed the Guide would order a lethal high voltage current, but she didn't. She wanted to try something else.

The truth.

She implanted a device behind his ear. Resuscitation took longer than anticipated. The Guide wanted to inject him with siradons to keep him from dying. I objected. Too many unknowns to introduce siradons into a human. His heartbeat restarted and he breathed.

I understood her desire not to terminate a good man. If I told Erick the truth, I'd be breaking the First Rule, but she was not subject to the rules and had the final say about the mission.

He coughed and sat up, jittery. "What happened?"

"Sit on the bed. You were shocked with high voltage," I said.

"What?" I helped him up off the floor to a seated position on the bed. He stared at me. "What's wrong with your eye?"

Yvonne stood with her back to the closet panel. The Guide leaned against her desk with a pair of sunglasses on.

Erick's gaze darted around the room. "Where are we? Who's this?" He pointed to the Guide.

She removed her sunglasses and lifted her chin. "My name is Aven-eleth-alk-thalia. You can call me Aven."

I finally knew her name.

"Are those contacts?" He gawked, mesmerized by her eyes.

"No. They're not."

3 - The Truth

AFTER AVEN EXPLAINED her origins and mine, Erick let go of my hand. "What is going on? This can't be true." He sat up on the bed, his look of confusion transforming into a mask of terror.

"Everything Aven said is true. Yvonne and I are Alien-Operated

Bots. AOB for short." I raised my pointer finger. "I'm the one who zapped you."

His chin dropped, resting on his chest as he digested the facts. The woman he married wasn't human. Neither was her best friend. The stranger with pink eyes was an alien. It was a lot to take. I suspected that somewhere deep inside of him an eruption brewed, nearing the right temperature to explode.

Instead, the fear on his face shifted again, hardening. He turned to me. "But you've been to the doctor. You're telling me they didn't notice?"

Aven continued half-sitting, half-leaning against the desk with her hands gripping the edge of it. She crossed her black boots at the ankles. Her pink eyes followed Erick's every movement. "Siradons are undetectable by human technology. We used them to create Aona from skeleton to skin and everything in between, including her electrical system which allows us to communicate telepathically. And they sustain her."

"You expect me to believe all this? Where's your proof? Your eyes could be something from a tattoo parlor."

"I can prove it."

After a moment of silence, Erick shot to his feet. "How'd you do that? Wait, stop. Talk to me with your mouth and tell me how this is possible." He was transitioning back to fear, back to the possibility this was real. That explosion might not be far off.

"I implanted a device behind your right ear. I have one, too. I can hear your thoughts and you can hear me when I want you to."

Erick's eyes widened as he touched the spot on his head. "I feel something." He paused, mouth gaping.

I waited, glancing at Yvonne who likely shared my thoughts. *Here it comes.*

"Just stop!" He paced, hands cupping his skull. "Don't talk." The eruption seemed to focus inward. He circled the small space in front of the bed, cringing as if in physical pain, as if ready to cry again. But he wasn't making sounds. He gritted his bared teeth. His face reddened. He dropped to his knees, fists and head meeting the floor. "Why?!"

Prepare for a low-voltage shock, said Aven.

He wouldn't lash out. This was as violent as I'd ever seen him. But I didn't contradict her.

He rose to his feet. For a moment, he stood panting at the wall, palms face up. "*My* wife. A robot." He turned his red face toward me, his gaze aimed over my head. Slowly, he lowered his chin.

"Are you sure you want that?" asked Aven.

He glared silently at me, expressing his wishes in his mind.

"Okay. Aona, please stand," said Aven.

I rose in front of him. He stared at my damaged left eye.

She came over with another siradon-filled syringe. *He wants a demonstration that will make him lose all doubt.*

Understandable, I replied.

"This would cause any human excruciating pain," Aven explained. She pressed the needle tip into my eye, repeating the process from before. *A second dose might clear up the problem for all we know.* She injected the siradons.

Erick covered his mouth, his face going from red to green. "Oh...no, please..." He rushed to the bathroom and threw up.

4 - Plan B

THE SECOND INJECTION didn't help.

When Erick returned, plopping onto the bed, he held up a white towel. "I surrender. Take our planet. I don't care."

He dropped into the familiar posture of our counseling sessions. Legs apart, arms draped across his knees, head down, hair in his eyes.

"Erick, I'm very sorry." I sat in a chair beside the bed. "Nothing will ever make up for what I am. But I never wanted to hurt you."

"Really?" I couldn't see the tears, but I could hear them in his voice.

"I'll live here from now on. You won't have to see me anymore."

"Permanent separation. Fine with me." He didn't look up.

"Erick?" Aven still hadn't moved from her position leaning back against the desk. "I want to explain everything."

Even Stage Two? Unwise, but I waited for the outcome.

"It's very important that all I've said and everything I'm about to say remains a secret between us. No one can know about me, Yvonne, or Aona." She spoke gently, displaying deep pity for Erick. Maybe that's why she felt the need to confess. She had nothing else to give him. No other way to comfort him. More likely it would anger him further.

"Your secret is safe," he whispered. "It's not like anyone would believe me, and I wouldn't want to get zapped again. Or worse." He was taking this hard. But who could blame him?

Aven said, "We don't have to do this now. If you'd like to go home and come back later, I promise to tell you everything."

"It's just..." He threw down the towel. "I can't believe this is happening."

"I know," she said.

He raised his chin, looking at my damaged eye. "What do you expect from me? How am I supposed to reconcile that our marriage is a lie? Worse than a lie. I don't know what to call it." He shook his head. "Counseling. What a joke."

"You're right," I said. "It was a lie. Aven often told me things to say. The goal was to make you happy, but that doesn't make up for the pain I've caused. When she tells you everything, I hope it will help."

More silence. He straightened up, sighing. "I don't want to wait. Just tell me." He folded his arms as if bracing for the impact of whatever words she would throw at him.

I knew Aven would be gentle. "A plague wiped out all of the men on my planet. The virus is not one found on Earth."

"What about your techno seer things?"

"Siradons. Not a cure, although we found one later. Too late." She dropped her gaze for a moment, quickly raising it to meet Erick's again. "Without a living male, the siradons can only replicate females. And those are bots, not Rogarians."

"How long does your species live?"

"About two hundred Earth years. In less than that time, we will be gone. I'm here to prevent that."

"How old are you?"

"Thirty-five. Same age as you."

Erick's inquisitiveness was a positive sign. Moments of skepticism surfaced in his eyes, but this was interesting to him, like his science fiction novels come to life. Aven's intuition had been correct. Knowing the whole truth might help him more than anything else could.

"I studied Earth," Aven continued. "It's the only planet with a species compatible with mine. Sixteen years ago, we arrived in a cloaked ship. In Stage One, Aona and Yvonne blended into society. Yvonne's online business makes the money we need to live on, and she protects me from the outside world. Aona's purpose was to find a mate. I needed someone who would marry her." She lowered her chin, her cheeks reddening. "Someone who wanted children."

Erick raised one eyebrow.

"After counseling, she was going to see if you were ready for a baby."

"But..." He glanced at me. "She's not human."

"My eggs are frozen," Aven said. "Once I implant an embryo, Aona can carry and deliver without complication. That was Stage Two."

We waited for his reaction. The bigger, potentially more hurtful reveal was yet to come.

Erick's brow lowered. Creases marked his forehead. He might not like what was coming next, but his half-open, unspeaking lips suggested that he still wanted to know.

Let me tell him, I suggested. *You'll be maintaining your relationship so long as you're in his mind.*

Aven agreed.

"Erick," I said, drawing his attention. "A few weeks into our marriage, while you slept, I injected you with a tranquilizer to extract—"

"Don't." Erick clenched his jaw, blinking at me. "I don't want to hear it."

Aven said, "I'm very sorry."

"It wasn't enough that I had a fake marriage. You took something you had no right—" His hands shook. Not a good sign. He was angry again.

Aven's lip trembled. "I didn't want to," she whispered. "But I had to."

"Sure. You *had* to con me into marrying a robot. You *had* to steal from me, from my *body* without asking. All because the men on your planet are dead," he said, and then exclaimed with sudden hysteria, "Or this is the most elaborate hoax anyone has ever played on a sucker like me!"

A tear escaped from the corner of Aven's eye and slid down her cheek. I rarely saw her cry.

"It's no joke, Erick," I said.

He glared at my left eye. "I know."

"I won't do it." She wiped her face with the back of her hand. "If you say no, I won't make any embryos."

Yvonne and I exchanged a glance. *Aven, what are you doing?*

Tears streamed freely down her cheeks. She was ready to abandon the mission over...nothing.

"How can I believe you?" Erick's hands stilled. "Aona's not coming home. I won't know if she gets pregnant."

"I give you my word. My oath. It's not something Rogarians take lightly."

An idea formed, something I hadn't considered before. *Aven, are you in love with Erick?*

She stiffened and shot me a panicked glare. *No!*

Unlike me, she had feelings. She'd been in my head throughout our courtship, guiding me through it and into the marriage. Plus she kept me from killing him. She risked the success of the entire mission by confiding in him. Her race did not condone violence or taking things by force, but this situation called for extreme measures. Yet she not only revealed secrets Erick was never meant to know, but was also prepared to abandon her mission. His whim could dictate whether or not we started over from scratch. Which meant sixteen years wasted and, in the worst case scenario, extinction for her entire species.

At the very least, her feelings toward Erick equaled affection. More likely, it was love.

Aven's voice tightened, changing to unemotional professionalism. "I'll destroy the container." She picked up a tissue and wiped her eyes.

"People here lie all the time." He squinted, lips pursed to the side. I'd seen that look before. Her tears tugged on his compassionate heart, making him feel bad. "What bothers me is that you took without asking. Now that you're asking..." He exhaled, "Fine. Do what you have to do. It's a little creepy to think about my seed going to a galaxy far, far away, but hey, I won't have to pay child support. Go ahead and repopulate your planet." He stood. "If that's all, I'd like to leave now."

"Thank you." She strode up to him, extending her hand. Erick mirrored Aven's formality. They shook on it. She turned on her heel and walked to the panel. Yvonne and I followed them into the closet and up the stairs.

"What if it's a girl?" he asked.

"Statistically, we'll have a boy before running out of embryos," Aven answered.

In the foyer, he stood at the front door. "How many babies do you think you can handle?" he asked, one eyebrow climbing his forehead. The more information he received, the more he seemed to accept what had happened. It wouldn't be instant for him. He would need time.

"Yvonne and Aona are very helpful," she said.

"The boy would only be half Rogarian."

"We're willing to settle for that."

"I see." He faced me, opened his mouth, but closed it again. "Aona, I don't know if there are words to say. Except goodbye."

"Goodbye, Erick."

His mouth tightened into a line. "A clean break is best here. But I guess you'll be around, Aven." He tapped above his ear. "Don't expect a filter just because you invaded my privacy." He reached for the door handle, but paused. "One last thing. What was Plan A? This is Plan B, right? What if Aona and I had a baby without me knowing any of this?"

Aven's throat moved when she gulped. I guess she hadn't planned on telling him *everything*. She took a deep breath, speaking slowly. "As you know, Aona planned to use a midwife and give birth at home whenever she got pregnant. Yvonne found someone who could help us replace the baby with an unwanted infant."

His face puckered like he'd swallowed a lemon drop candy. That couldn't be good. "Clever. If you're willing to pay for that, why not put a sperm bank sign out front? Much simpler. Removes the taking without asking aspect, and you'd end up with plenty of boys."

I knew when Erick was using sarcasm. From her expression, Aven recognized it, too.

He opened the door.

"Erick, please understand. I'm very sorry for all of it. But I'm desperate. My people are desperate."

He stopped on the front porch, swinging around. "Not desperate enough to cut to the chase and find some guy who'd just give you what you wanted. Men sell that stuff all the time. Why mess with me and ruin my entire life?" He stormed down the steps, not waiting for an answer.

I knew what Aven would've told him. That type of man wouldn't meet Rogarian standards as a mate like he did.

She loved him.

5 - The Garden

I WAS surprised when Erick knocked on the door the next day. Yvonne led him into the kitchen where I sat beside Aven as she sipped her coffee.

"Can we take a walk?" He addressed Aven calmly, but didn't acknowledge me.

Aven agreed, a bright smile lighting up her face.

In the garden, Yvonne and I scanned the rows of vegetables,

corn, flowers, and plants for threats to Aven's security. I wore a patch over my left eye. As we flanked them, I overheard their conversation.

With a head tilt, he gestured toward Yvonne and me. "I'm not ready to talk about what you're doing with those two."

Aven had already begun the fertilization process. We would tell her when we became pregnant.

"It's going to take some time to get over losing the wife I thought I had. Thank you for what you said last night. It helped to 'talk' about it." He made air quotes.

Aven clasped her hands behind her back, nodding. "You're welcome. Thank you for forgiving me."

After he left last night, they must've continued the discussion through the implant. Whatever Aven had said obviously impacted him.

"I'm not one to hold a grudge. But you already knew that." He grinned. "You know more about me than I'll ever know about you."

Considering how he had stormed away, the fact that he smiled and acted friendly toward Aven meant he'd made major strides already.

In the past, Erick and I had stayed up all night talking. He loved discovering things about me, mostly Aven's inventions. In general, he was a social person. In groups, he met new people and found out what he could about them because he was genuinely interested. He had many friends, but never one like her. I could imagine him getting lost in all the questions he wanted to ask. If I had to guess, neither of them slept.

They ambled past the tomato plants. "I'm not as angry as I thought I would be. It's more like I don't know how to grieve when she's right there." He brushed his fingers over the green leaves.

"You may find some comfort in talking to her. Maybe you could become friends."

Erick stopped, facing her with incredulity. "Is she your *friend?*"

"She and Yvonne are the only friends I have here."

Erick had been in her life, too, albeit from a distance. But I didn't think she would admit any of her feelings for him, no matter how minor.

As he gazed into her eyes, he relaxed his grimace. "Do all Rogarians look like you?"

"The eyes? Yes. Women's are pink like mine. Men's are—" Both her smile and her eyes dimmed. "Were green." She turned away, strolling ahead.

Erick caught up. "All the men died. You must've lost family. Friends."

She squinted, lowering her Aviator sunglasses from her head onto her nose. "Everyone did."

"Was there someone you loved?"

In front of the rose bushes, Aven stopped, staring at the yellow buds.

"Sorry." Erick shoved his hands into his pockets. "That's probably really painful to think about."

I didn't know anything about the men in her life. *Were you married?* I asked silently.

Yes. We had three sons.

I echoed Erick's sentiments. *I'm so sorry.*

"It's hard," she said aloud. "I got through the stages. Even acceptance doesn't wash away all the sadness. But it's one of the reasons I volunteered to come here. My experience with ROB technology landed me the job." She turned her face toward him. "Rogarian-Operated Bots. Here, for mission purposes, we refer to them as Alien-Operated."

Erick and I made eye contact before he shifted his gaze back to Aven. "Am I the first human you've met face to face?"

"Yes."

"You're in Aona and Yvonne's heads. You tell them what to say?"

"Many of their responses are mine, but not all."

"You studied humans. Was it specific people or general species?"

"General. Specific once we arrived, oriented ourselves, and established this place."

"Did you study me?"

Aven nodded.

Erick's head bobbed along with her. "So...why me?"

Aven's hands fidgeted. "Rogarians have high standards for behavior. We didn't want just anyone. You were an ideal choice." She cleared her throat.

Yvonne walked inside. She came back out and set a pitcher and drinking glasses on the porch table.

"Would you like tea?" Aven asked.

They stepped up onto the deck. Erick pulled out a chair for Aven before sitting beside her. They sipped iced tea. From the opposite end of the porch, I sat in the deck chair and observed.

"I appreciate that you told me the truth," he said, "and asked before doing anything. After you got what you wanted, you could've had Aona leave me, or even kill me. Make it look like an accident. Continued on with your plan."

"That's not the Rogarian way."

They were quiet for a few minutes.

"So it's like I'm talking to you when I talk to Aona. You're leading her."

"She and Yvonne don't need me in order to function, but they wouldn't pass for human as easily without some guidance. In fact, they refer to me as the Guide."

"Why only you with two AOBs?"

"The sensitive nature of the mission. We don't want war. We don't want interaction as a general rule. We simply want to save our species from dying. Because yours tends toward violence, we hoped to avoid any confrontations. I took a big risk revealing myself to you."

"I see." He sipped his drink. "You're right. If the authorities knew about you, they would probably put you in some underground lab and run tests on you, maybe even kill you."

They sat in silence. Aven suddenly giggled. "The lab."

"That was funny to you, was it?"

"Sorry." She blocked her smile with her hand.

Again, they said nothing. Erick caught my stare. "She overheard me thinking about the last time I had blood drawn at the lab. Remember?"

I smiled. "Of course." The girl was new and had stuck him ten times without success. Erick felt bad for her, but each time she stabbed him, he couldn't help but wince. When he got home, we had laughed together. I did it because Aven told me to.

Again, Aven snickered, covering her face.

"Were you giggling back when it happened?" His smile reached his eyes. He was genuinely relaxed.

"Yeah."

After their laughter died down, Erick dropped his gaze. "I should go." He set down the empty glass. "I'll talk to you soon. Sometime. Whatever." He and Aven stood and stared at each other. Erick stuck out his hand. They shook.

"Come by anytime," said Aven. "It's nice to talk to another person."

"Sure. I can come this weekend." He pointed at the grill sitting beside the deck. "I'll bring steaks. You already know that I'm a master griller."

"I do."

He faced me. "See you later, Aona."

"I look forward to it. Goodbye."

6 - Days of Hope

ERICK'S smooth and quick transition into friendship with Aven would have concerned me if I didn't know him as well as I did. His forgiveness was genuine, and curiosity kept him coming back to find out more about her species and her planet. He was the type of person who could be trusted with her secrets. The threat of another zap, although present, wasn't motivating him. He liked spending time with her. Yvonne and I, now both pregnant, could tell.

As days, weeks, and months passed, I observed their increasing intimacy. Aven loved Erick, but still denied it. Erick respected Aven and found the stories she shared fascinating, but I wasn't sure about his deeper feelings.

Ironically, he and I spent a lot of time together. He included Yvonne and me in conversations instead of treating us like devices. It made no difference to us, but Aven was pleased to see him doing so well. *He's healing,* she said.

I wore my eye patch permanently. Erick and I pretended to be separated, but still on good terms. His family was worried about him. With all the time he spent at Yvonne's, he was losing touch with his friends, who also expressed their concerns.

In time, my due date approached. Erick accompanied me to the sonograms. When we found out I was carrying a boy, we expressed ecstatic joy, Aven repeating, *Thank you!*

Sometimes Aven and Erick spoke aloud and sometimes they spoke silently. This made it difficult for me to evaluate their burgeoning relationship. One such conversation happened just weeks before the babies would arrive.

We all sat around the table chatting, mostly Aven and Erick. The mood was lighthearted. They'd shared a lot with each other. Aven helped Erick better understand her life on Pewt. Erick talked about his growing up years, and how he'd always wanted a family.

Soon they went silent, which usually meant they were speaking telepathically. But this silence was heavy, as if their thoughts thickened the air while moving between them.

Eventually, Erick whispered, "Me, a father? I don't know what I'm doing. I'm freaking out. Seeing these two pregnant with my kids. Our kids, technically." His hands squeezed his temples. "It's like I hadn't realized the reality of it all. Two half-alien children will be coming into the world in a matter of days. And they're mine. But not. They won't even know me."

"Erick—"

He rose abruptly. "I need to think. Alone. Can you turn it off?" I'd never seen him like this. He was frantic, pacing by the door, moving his hands around as he spoke. He halted in the entryway. "I'm not a threat to your secret. You know that. Please. Give me one night alone."

Aven's chest rose as she inhaled deeply. "Okay."

7 - The Rift

IN THE MORNING, Aven's drooping shoulders and the purple circles around her eyes told me she hadn't slept. She'd kept her word. She gave Erick a night of privacy.

I queried her once again. *Why don't you tell Erick?*

Tell him what?

That you love him.

She stopped pouring coffee into the mug. She spun around to face me, holding the pot. *DO NOT TELL HIM.* The order was loud and clear.

WHEN ERICK'S car pulled up, I met him out front and led him through the side gate. I disobeyed Aven because I believed telling Erick would help our mission in the end.

Yvonne was distracting her in the kitchen. I switched off my communicator, the one allowing Aven to hear my thoughts.

"Can we talk?" I asked.

He seemed confused, even hesitant at first, but followed me.

"She loves you."

He swallowed. "What?"

8 - New Life

IN THE ROCKING CHAIR, Aven held Neil and Nina. The babies were swaddled and both asleep. They had their mother's eyes. Neil's were green.

Tears streamed down Aven's smiling face, sadness mixed with joy. She hadn't seen Erick since he'd asked her to give him privacy.

I never turned it back on, she said.

Erick?

She closed her eyes, maybe hoping to stop the tears. *I wanted to wait until he came back. But he's never coming back, is he?*

Once the newborns reached eight weeks, Aven would return to Pewt. Her mission would be accomplished. At home, she'd care for the half-human, half-Rogarian children who would need someone familiar with human behavior. After all, she was their mother.

If Erick didn't come to visit between now and her departure, she'd never see him again.

9 - The Discovery

THE TV in the basement was on, but Aven appeared uninterested until a news flash brightened the screen. She stood up from the couch with a hand over her mouth.

The person on the television spoke with wide eyes, dramatic hand gestures, and frequent pauses where he would then exclaim, "It's *un*believable!" The image on the screen in the top right corner contained a familiar-looking ship. The same model as the space craft that brought Aven, Yvonne, and me to Earth.

At the bottom half of the screen, a ticker tape read, *CONFIRMED: LIFE ON OTHER PLANETS. WE ARE NOT ALONE.*

"No," Aven whispered through her fingers.

"WELCOME TO YOUR NEWS, Your Story with Tyrone Mathis," said a voiceover as the camera panned toward the famous newscaster seated behind a table.

"'Remember November the Thirteenth,' a phrase that will be known by every future generation," said Tyrone in the deep, soothing voice that was his signature feature. "The incredible story about a genuine UFO landing on November 13th, 2075, in the sand dunes near Yuma, Arizona, is an indisputable, proven fact. Even more incredible is the cargo that was on board that UFO, a space craft not unlike our own space shuttles, with a few important differences."

Tyrone shifted, turning toward a different camera that picked up the new angle.

"Only RBC has the exclusive interview with the four *human* men that emerged from the ship. Stay tuned for the monumental moment in history when I interview Jim Watson, Benedict King, Tony Dagostino, and Raul Estevez. This is Your News, Your Story."

Neil slept in Yvonne's arms while Nina slept in mine. Aven muted the commercial break. She chewed her nails, which I'd never seen her do. Her thoughts were erratic. She probably didn't realize she'd opened the connection for us to hear her.

How could this happen? How!? No, I can't—but if I just get the ship ready, I can leave with the children in a few days. They'll probably be fine...even though I wanted to wait to be safe. But I'm not safe. No, none of us are. Not now.

"Can I make a suggestion?" whispered Yvonne.

Aven started as if she hadn't noticed anyone else in the room. "Yeah."

"Wait it out. The risk for such young babies in space flight won't be worth it, not with your species at stake. No one knows you're here."

"Don't they?" Aven's knee bounced. Her hands shook.

The commercial break ended. Tyrone Mathis was no longer alone at the table. The Famous Four, as they had been labeled, now joined him.

"It's been an incredible journey, and some may struggle to believe their story, but these four men have been to another planet. They're here to tell us how they got there, and how they got back."

"The woman who called herself Millie was desperate, and I thought she was nuts at first, but I was drawn to her so I played along," admitted Tony Dagostino, an overly tanned Italian-American.

"Millie?" Aven cocked her head. "Millina-rao-ven-prath-atika? My director? *Why?*"

"When she revealed the space craft, I thought it might've been a practical joke," said Raul Estevez, a lanky Puerto Rican. "These guys were already there and had been told the same story. Then she took off her sunglasses."

Aven buried her head in her hands. "Why would Millie do this? Why would she come here when she knew I had my mission?"

"My first thought was—*those are contacts, love. Nice try.* But then she told me her story," said Benedict King in his English accent. His pale skin was a stark contrast to Tony's orange hue as they sat side by side. "I was absolutely intrigued, and whether it was true or not, I wanted to see what she would show me."

"The ship was cloaked, so the uncloaking moment convinced me," said Jim Watson, a Jamaican-American and the tallest of the four.

"She explained the situation about flying to her planet. It was crazy!" said Raul. "But I was game to help her repopulate. A bunch of chicks who looked like her? Sure, sign me up."

"It was a planet called Pewt," said Benedict. "Extremely similar to Earth. I don't know exactly how far away it is. She wouldn't say. We were put to sleep during the actual trip."

"How could you tell you had gone anywhere?" asked Tyrone.

"There were some serious differences, man," said Raul. "Everyone was female. Everyone had eyes like hers. Some of the buildings—I work in construction—were unlike anything I've seen on Earth. The rules seemed to be the same, for the most part. Gravity and all that, but there were a lot of dome-shaped structures, even extremely huge ones."

"The stars looked a little different," said Jim. "Their sun was like ours, but they had three moons."

"So this woman looks human, except for her pink eyes," said Tyrone. "Just outside of New York City where you were all living at the time, she shows you her spaceship. She tells you her species—the Rogarians—are a dying breed because a plague killed all the males. She needs your help with that because of the compatibility between humans and Rogarians. So you spent six weeks with all these Rogarian women," Tyrone confirmed, winking.

"It wasn't like that. They had sort of a sperm bank," said Jim.

"And then they just sent you home alone?"

"Not exactly," said Benedict.

"We decided not to stay there," said Tony. "We're all single, but we still have people here we care about. Families, friends. So...we stole the ship and flew home."

The picture the men painted felt off, as if they were omitting important details.

Aven's eyes widened. "They're lying."

"How did you manage that?" asked Tyrone.

"I'm a pilot," said Tony. "And I spent time in a simulator for the ParaX 235."

"The brand new space shuttle."

"It resembles the Rogarian space craft in some ways. It took a little time, but we figured it out, even mimicking their methods to put ourselves to sleep once we entered Earth as the destination."

"But you still don't know where this planet Pewt is located in relation to Earth?"

"No, we couldn't figure that part out. Once we landed, the ship locked down in a way that prevents us or anyone else from flying it again. We don't know why."

"There is no way they piloted our ship!" Aven rose to her feet.

The disturbance woke Neil. His mouth widened silently until the delayed wail erupted from him in a shriek.

"Oh." She reached for him, and Yvonne passed him into her arms. "I'm sorry, sweetie." She held him up to her shoulder, patting his back and gently swaying. "It takes a very skilled astronaut, like myself, to pilot our Light Jumpers. It's nothing like a ParaX."

A rapping at the front door made Aven freeze in place. Yvonne sped into the secret room to check the security monitors. "It's...a woman in a black jumpsuit. But she's turned away. I can't see her face."

"Let me see." Aven carried Neil inside her quarters. Her gasp made me rise from the couch with Nina. I peeked my head in.

Aven glanced up at me. "Quick! Let her in!"

10 - End of Mission

THE WOMAN ENTERED. I quickly shut the door and locked it. I'd seen her before. Millie, the director of Aven's mission.

She removed her sunglasses, her pink eyes assessing the three of us standing in the living room. She stood nearly six feet tall. Her long, braided black hair draped over one shoulder. "Thank God I found you. There isn't much time."

"A ROGARIAN WHO came to Earth sixteen years ago is still here, as far as we know," said Tony Dagostino. "We're hoping she'll come forward, maybe facilitate some kind of peace treaty between our species."

"No, she won't." In the basement, Millie clicked off the television. She cooed at Nina, still in my arms. "How old are they?"

"Only five weeks," answered Aven.

"They'll be fine in the incubators." She grinned at Neil, stroking his cheek as Yvonne swayed with him. "We can't stay any longer. We need to leave as soon as possible. The mission is officially over."

Aven bowed her head, nodding. I sensed her unease, but not from the fear of exposure. As she looked up, her glazed eyes suppressed disappointment. She'd be leaving sooner than expected.

"The hunt for you has already begun, and it's my fault." Millie exhaled. "Another plague struck back home, this time affecting women. We found a cure quickly, but there was massive population loss. We couldn't communicate, it was too risky, but I could authorize another mission. The plan was to bring four men back to Pewt. I did reconnaissance for a month, searching for the best mates, but it wasn't enough time. Not in the end." Millie brushed her braid off her shoulder. "Those men wanted to visit their families for a few weeks and then come back to Pewt. I told them they could stay on Earth if they wanted. No obligation now that our species will survive. Instead, they decided to become celebrities, even after signing oaths of silence."

Aven had lived on Earth long enough to understand that humans failed to honor their oaths all the time.

"*I* piloted the ship," Millie admitted. "I can't be sure, but they might've gotten ahold of sensitive information while they were on Pewt. Somehow, they deciphered the cloaking mechanism. Next thing I know, a squadron of fighter pilots is threatening to shoot me out of the sky. I engaged the cloaking device again, left the East Coast in a hurry, and landed in the Yuma dunes. The men promised not to follow me, but I knew they would. It was obvious they wanted me to lead them to you so they'd break an even bigger story than the one they ended up with." She raised both hands, her fingers outlining an invisible rectangle. *"Meet the alien next door."* When she lowered her arms, she closed her eyes. "I told them about your mission. I'm sorry."

Aven shook her head. "Don't be."

"I stole a car and lost them in a hurry. Once I found a safe place to do a Net search, I discovered that Yvonne and Aona's names appeared together only in this city. And they don't know those names. I only ever described two AOBs with you, but not by name. Still, I don't want to risk it. Not with these children."

"Let's not waste time then." Aven straightened her shoulders. Her determined yet soft eyes told two stories. She'd follow orders, but her heart was breaking.

* * *

Millie prepped the cloaked ship hidden in the garden while Aven, Yvonne, and I loaded everything we had packed. The babies already slept in their incubators, and would sleep for the duration of the voyage.

I followed Aven outside, both of us carrying boxes. Yvonne returned from depositing a bag in the ship's hold. "Yvonne, will you start bringing out the—" Half-way down the porch steps, Aven halted.

Erick stood beside the deck with a suitcase in his hand. "There's something I need to tell you."

Aven's pink eyes swirled and danced. She set down the box.

He walked towards her with a subtle smile that brightened his brown eyes rather than raising the corners of his lips. He set down the suitcase. His hands pulled hers, and she took the last steps down until they stood facing each other in the grass. "I love you."

She covered her mouth, exhaling beneath her hand. Then she lowered her fingers into his grasp again. "I love you, too."

He pulled her close. She tilted her face up, meeting his kiss. When he leaned back, he said, "I don't want to lose you. Having you suddenly out of my head made it clear to me. Yours was the most familiar voice I knew because it was the voice of my wife."

Aven blinked back tears.

"So can I?" he asked.

"Can you what?"

"Come with you."

"Aven?" Millie approached, her concern creating lines on her forehead. "Who's this?" Even as she asked, her face relaxed in realization that he must be the mission. "Look, he can't come with us. We're never coming back."

"He's not like the others. For almost a year, he's known, and he's never told anyone. He's..." Aven breathed, facing Erick again. "I love him."

"You'd leave everything behind, just like that?" Millie stared him down. "Never means never. Rogarians don't lie."

"I've made my decision." He gazed over Aven's face. "I'll go wherever she goes. It makes no difference, so long as I'm with her."

11 - How I Met Your Alien Mother

I PAUSED, allowing the words to sink in. "And that's how your Rogarian mother and your human father fell in love."

The young, eager faces gazed at me, most with mouths half open. In all, there were eleven boys and nine girls ranging from ages one to six, many whom I had carried and birthed. They all had Aven's eyes.

I told the children a simplified version of the events, one they could understand. I left out some of the more complicated aspects, such as the fact that I called Erick once I knew our departure was imminent.

That day when I'd spoken with him in secret, he'd admitted his love for Aven. He knew when she left that she wasn't coming back. I'd suggested an emergency trip to save our marriage. That's what he'd tell work, family, and friends who were unaware we'd already divorced. Leaving with Aven meant he'd die to everyone he knew, so he had things to take care of beforehand. The decision had been difficult, but one he never regretted.

Neil, the oldest, tugged on my sleeve. "How come your eye never got better?"

On Pewt, I didn't need the patch, but the outward appearance of my left eye still hadn't normalized. "I don't know. But if not for that, your mom and dad might never have met."

Nina sat in Yvonne's lap, stroking her hand. "Aunt Aona, will you tell us the story one more time?"

I kissed Neil's forehead before glancing up.

In the back of the spacious living room, Erick stood behind Aven, arms surrounding her pregnant belly. "Just once more," she said. "Then it's time for bed."

Author's Notes—Bria Burton

THE IDEA of an artificial intelligence at the counselor's office with her human husband initiated the spark that led to the drafting of this story. The first question I wanted answered: did the husband know about her? It quickly became obvious that the story would be much more interesting if he was not aware that his wife was a robot. After many drafts and rewrites, the end result was "How I Met Your Alien Mother," which I chose to name "AOB" to keep the ending a surprise.

When the Alvarium Experiment presented the idea for a *Return to Earth* project, I knew the story, with a few minor tweaks, would fit the premise perfectly. I'm pleased with the end result, and I truly hope you enjoyed the story.

~BB

Social Experiment

Tracie Roberts

Florida, Present day

D
r. Olivia Tate growled low in the back of her throat and shoved the microscope away. Her eyes burned and rubbing them did little to lessen that. The stain underneath the lens had begun to blur as darkness crept into the room. She ran a hand through her chestnut hair, then massaged the back of her neck.

"Dr. Tate, why don't you take a break," Matt Raulings, her lab assistant said. "You've been at it for hours. The cancer's not going anywhere."

Liv looked up at him from under a knotted brow, her lips drawing into a thin line at the tactless comment.

Matt's cheeks burned a guilty crimson as a mumbled "Sorry" passed between them. He turned toward the counter and arranged another tray of specimens, avoiding the glare of his superior. His spectacles rested on the bridge of his nose and slid down further as his mouth quirked with the whispered steps of the filtering process. He nudged the glasses back up and settled the dishes in narrow, neat rows.

"It's right there," Liv said, her hand moving up the opposite sleeve of her lab coat and absentmindedly rubbing the bumpy scar at her wrist. "The answer is in those slides. I can sense it." She sat heavily on a hip-high stool, her fingers continuing to glide over the raised, four inch cicatrix. "And if I can't prove my hypothesis, the funding will be cut off and we're back to square one."

Matt removed the slide from the microscope and set a tray of new specimens in front of her. "Here. Try these."

Liv sighed. The rectangular glass panes winked under the fluorescent light, almost teasing the doctor with the secrets they refused to disclose.

"I'm taking a walk. I'll continue when I get back." Liv removed her white coat and readjusted her name tag. "And for the love of Otto, don't have your usual wretched racket blaring when I return."

"Yes, ma'am." Matt nodded, watching as Dr. Tate exited the wing.

Liv rounded the corner on her way to the ninth floor's observation deck, the restlessness in her hand causing her to fidget. The sliding doors whooshed open and she stepped out into the twilight. The crescent moon hung low in the horizon and a cool breeze rustled the doctor's hair.

What am I not seeing? She thought. She leaned against the rail, staring out over the city. Rush hour was winding down and the traffic on Interstate 275 was finally starting to move. Not that she could have heard the angry honking all the way in her lab, but Liv had been on that deck so many times in the past three months to know exactly how the citizens of Tampa, Florida behaved under stress. This was the place she came to think when she got frustrated, and today's results had frustrated her to no end.

The swish of the doors caused Liv to straighten, but she knew who had joined her before she turned around.

"Matt said you'd be up here." Kya Dumont stepped behind Olivia and wove an arm around her partner's waist. She kissed the other woman's cheek and Liv leaned back into the strong, waiting embrace of her mate. Kya's blue-black skin contrasted sharply against the pale pink silk of Olivia's blouse.

"This is really getting to me. I've almost uncovered the gene sequence that causes the mutation but it isn't present in every sample."

"So it is inconclusive?" Kya asked. She released Liv to stand beside her, leaning heavily on the rail.

"No, more like it's nonexistent in certain samples. Which is odd, since they're all samples from my own tissue."

"Is that possible?"

"It shouldn't be. These samples were all cancerous or were taken from the tissue that surrounded the area four months ago."

"So...before you started hosting my sym?" Kya ran her thumb across the ridge at Olivia's wrist and the skin there vibrated.

"Right around that time, but I don't think that has affected the samples." Liv pulled her hand from her partner's and turned toward the deck's railing.

"Maybe you should come home and rest. You are tired." Kya massaged her mate's shoulder. "You can start fresh tomorrow."

Liv rubbed her eyes again, working the tiredness from her temple. "What's the point? Maybe I should just call it. I've been working at this since I left my residency." Olivia's fingers brushed her wrist. "But you're right," she said. "A fresh perspective will help. I can't give up. Not when I'm this close."

"That is my Semu'." Kya tucked a strand of hair behind Liv's ear, her fingers caressing the woman's cheek. "You are no quitter. And I am positive you will have a breakthrough soon." Kya took Liv's hand and the two women entered the building together as the last light of dusk settled beyond the horizon.

THE APARTMENT WAS DARK, and Kya rolled onto her back, squinting into the shadowed room. There it was again—the *beep, beep, TING* that had awakened her. She listened for the steady breathing of her *semu'*, and a light snore came from her partner. Kya glanced at the alarm clock—3:12. Again, the *beep, beep, TING* sounded and she eased from the bed.

Gently closing the door behind her, Kya turned and faced the adjacent living room. The blue-lit screen of a tablet held vertical columns of glyphs, incomprehensible to a human. She sank to the couch and scrolled through the message.

"*Mengtuk!*" she cursed, hissing at the tablet as if it could answer her. She picked up the device and carried it to the patio, carefully closing the glass door. After entering a code and a fingerprint ID, the blue light dissolved into black and white static before it was replaced by an image of a male with caramel toned skin and high cheek bones.

"It is well, Pier'uu." Kya whispered the standard Oo'mahn greeting though no one could hear her out on the balcony of her twelfth floor apartment. The level, yet dulcet, language she used was reminiscent of ancient Javanese.

"It is well, en'Kya." The voice was deep and melodic, but living on Earth for the last two years had taught Kya to pick up on subtleties of tone.

"You speak an untruth, brother." She waited, staring at the screen as the young man gnawed his inner cheek, finally flaring the auxiliary nostril slits below his eyes.

"Many of the Tan'Rumah have become sick with a madness. And their endosymbionts are dying. El'Jah'we and the Elder Bar have decided to evacuate all research parties from this planet."

"When will the retrieval take place?"

"Within the next three Earth days."

"What about my...domicile partner, Olivia?"

"Your what?"

"The woman I share my home with. She is...a friend. I cannot just disappear and leave her to worry."

"Have you consulted your endosymbiont with this matter of abandonment?"

"Eent has grown attached to her as well. And he is learning much about human diseases through Olivia's work."

"Grown attached?"

"It is a human expression. It means that they share a connection that would be detrimental if it were terminated."

"Your endosymbiont has expressed this?"

"He has." Kya rubbed her wrist to calm the wiggling creature beneath her skin.

"Very well. Devise a way to inform your domicile partner that you will be departing. We will be in contact."

"Understood." Kya swallowed and smiled. She had learned from humans that smiling helped others to feel comfortable. However, from the look Pier returned she wasn't so sure she was doing it right. "I will find a way to explain this to my ma...to Olivia."

"Noted. Expect a transmission in the next seventy-two hours advising you of the rendezvous coordinates." Pier glanced over his shoulder as an all-call sounded on the star ship. "Be well," he said.

"Be well," Kya returned and the transmission ended. With her final word, the screen went blank before returning to its ambient blue.

"Ack!" Kya grumbled and slid the glass door open. "How will I convince the Elder Bar to allow me to stay with Olivia?" She scratched absentmindedly at her wrist, the sym under her skin there wiggling at Kya's agitation. "And you, Senseless One, you determine my destiny as it is tied to yours. You make the choices, though you see nothing, feel nothing, if not for my body to house in. But better to be born a host with a body to act and react to everything around me than to be a sym and rely on others to supply me with all my needs."

The woman ambled to the kitchen and opened the refrigerator door, searching the shelves for a drink. She slid water bottles and a milk carton aside to locate a container of kelp water and lemon juice. Both were necessary nutrients for her alien biology, and fortunately, both were easily attainable on Earth.

She took a swig and returned the bottle. "Never mind the Elder Bar, how will I tell Olivia that I must depart? It has been just a few months since she accepted my news of you, Senseless One, and allowed you to house in her and learn from her sensory input. This information will be another shock to her."

Kya nudged open the bedroom door, her sight gliding over the figure of her mate outlined beneath the silky sheet. Kya sighed at the thought of never laying beside her beloved again, and the wiggling in her wrist intensified. She tiptoed into the room, retrieved a terry cloth wrist band and stretched it over her scar. The gentle pressure soothed the endosymbiont, halting its movement under Kya's skin.

Olivia shifted in the bed, extending her arm across the empty spot beside her, then lifted herself up on her elbow. "Love, why are you up?"

Kya straightened at the sound of Liv's voice. Lying hadn't come easily to the alien, and she didn't like to be dishonest with her beloved anyway. "I couldn't sleep," she said, returning to her side of the bed. She slid under the covers and pulled Liv to her. "I needed some liquid to end my mouth's dryness."

In the darkness, Olivia smiled at Kya's odd speech. The darker woman had been on Earth nearly two years but still had trouble with some of the particulars of the language. Liv snuggled under her lover's chin and sighed. Kya pressed her lips to the other woman's head, worry swirling in her mind.

"HAVE you contacted all of the research teams, Commander?" Jah, a tall, umber-colored humanoid, waited for her Second to answer. As the ruler of the Oo'mahns, it was her duty to make decisions for the betterment of all her citizens.

"Yes, Leader." Xio, a small, pale male, turned from his console.

"Will there be any problems with the extractions?" Jah curved her spindly fingers toward her open palms and scratched. The iridescent purple veins pulsated along her wrist to the flat of her hand. Both her Sird'ee and Du'Tomani endosymbionts were agitated at the emergent crisis on board the vessel. Though being a host for both the logical and emotional sym species of her planet had its benefits, it also carried drawbacks.

"There have been a few of all three castes who expressed a desire to stay on Earth." Xio tapped a button to end a shrilling alarm, then continued his explanation. "Some Sird'ee and their hosts have expressed affection for their human hosts. Many

Du'Tomani have scientific experiments that haven't reached completion."

This new information was something for the dual syms to agree upon. They were each sending messages to Jah expressing a desire to allow their counterparts to remain on Earth.

"But the illness we have on board overrides any personal desires," Jah murmured, more to herself and her endosymbionts than to her crew. "The needs of the many outweigh the wants of the few."

"Excuse me, Leader?" Xio turned to his commander, his fingers at the ready to enter whatever message she ordered.

"Disregard," Jah said, rising from her chair. "I will be in the infirmary if I am needed. Xio'me, monitor the research members and be prepared to evacuate them on my order."

"Yes, Leader." Xio focused his attention on the task and Jah withdrew from the ship's navigation cabin.

The statuesque ruler of the Oo'mahns followed a short, narrow corridor that emptied into a larger cabin with three rows of double-stacked gurneys, each with an eighteen inch cubical chamber attached to the head of it. The beds held hosts of both genders and all stages of adult life. The cubic chambers were tanks lodging the stringy bodies and glowing essence of the endosymbionts attached to the hosts.

"Have any advancements been made to understand this illness?" Jah maneuvered between the first and second row, eying the hosts. It saddened her to see her kinsmen in various states of mental distress. Each Tan'Rumah she passed behaved erratically--some talking nonsense, others lashing out at the medical workers, still others staring off in a trance. Each of the hosts' syms lay in their chambers, surrounded by a clear, gelatinous glaire. The luminescence around the villus-shaped sym ranged from a blazing blue-ether radiance in the most recently diagnosed to the pallid cream color of the most severely affected.

"We have isolated the chromosomal effect to the endosymbionts," Kel, the chief medical officer said. "If the endosymbiont could survive without a host, then all of the infected Tan'Rumah would be restored to health. It is a disease that is directly affecting only the Sird'ees and Du'Tomani, but it is being passed to the Tan'Rumah. How, I do not know."

"Is there a way to inhibit or alter the effects without harming the endosymbionts?" Jah paused near a bed, looking keenly at a host. It was her own sister, Phe, who stared back at her blankly. Phe's sym, Soo, rested motionless in its albumen bed; its luminosity very strong.

"Unknown, Leader," Kel responded. "Though we know what biological factor is triggering the disease, and how it is obviously passed from endosymbiont to host through DNA mutations, we do not know what caused it to begin with."

"Of course we do!" Banu, the ship's tactical officer, strode into the bay. "These beings that took our name, demonizing it, are the cause. Their hatred for those unlike themselves propels them to brutalize each other. And the way they abuse their planet and its resources is despicable. I am amazed they have not died off or killed one another already."

"How have the humans caused this illness in our people?" Kel tucked a glass tablet under her arm and stared at the stout, bald lieutenant.

"Undetermined," Banu said, his words clipped. "But they must have. This illness only manifested during this mission. It didn't appear in the last mission."

"That was five hundred years ago. Those records are incomplete." Kel flipped the tablet over in her pale blue hands and tapped on its surface with a stylus. "There is nothing here about interaction with the inhabitants of Earth. Only the mention of the eleven emigrants we allowed to assimilate is documented, and they have adjusted to our culture quite well."

"Still, if it weren't for those--," Banu spat.

"Enough," Jah commanded. "We will retrieve our citizens, then work to determine the cause of this." She waved her hand at the row of writhing, moaning Tan'Rumah. "Banu'ra, evaluate our stealth array. We have twenty-four hours before it depletes and we do not want our ship to be seen by the Earthlings."

"Yes, Leader." The tactical officer nodded and returned the same way he entered.

"Da'Kel, prepare more bunks." Jah stroked Phe's cheek before quickly withdrawing her hand. Her face hardened as she turned to the medic. "I am afraid there will be many more infirm before we are able to depart."

She didn't wait for a response, but strode into the dimness of the corridor.

THE NEXT MORNING the two women woke early and had breakfast in the apartment's window nook.

"You look tired, Love," Olivia said. She reached across the table and rubbed Kya's hand. "Were you able to get back to sleep?"

The darker woman smiled, squeezing Liv's fingers between her own. "Yes, after moments of staring at the room's top."

"Ceiling," Liv corrected. She drained her coffee mug and rose to put it in the sink. "Will you come by this afternoon so we can meet for lunch?"

"If I am not needed in the field today. Dr. McKinney is still gathering decomposition data."

"Ugh. I don't see how you can stand to be around those dead bodies."

"Aside from the odor, they are much easier to tolerate than live humans." The second pair of nostril slits under Kya's eyes flared before folding in on themselves and sealing off the secondary airway.

Liv stared at her, lips pinched into a thin line.

"Why do you look at me that way? Did I speak an untruth?"

"We've discussed this. Even if what you say is true, sometimes it isn't the best thing to speak aloud."

"But you have told me that I can say anything to you. Is that an untruth?" Kya's brows knitted over questioning eyes.

"Sometimes, it is even best to keep things from me, if I would be hurt by it or if it is distasteful. Tactless."

"Tactless?"

"Inappropriate. Not polite to share."

"Oh, and saying that dead humans are easier to tolerate than living ones is not polite to share?"

"Exactly." Olivia stepped toward her partner and ran a hand down the length of Kya's silky onyx hair. She leaned in and kissed her beloved on the lips, lacing her fingers with Kya's. The kiss deepened and, as their wrists touched, the scar on each of their arms softened at the impending transmission of the sym, Eent.

The small, worm-like creature stretched the skin along Kya's forearm until the thin epidermis ruptured and a translucent, glowing nub emerged. The sym inched its way out of the minute opening in Kya's wrist and began burrowing into the dermis at Liv's lower forearm.

"Damn it." Liv snatched her hand from Kya's and Eent retreated back into its host. "Why can't that thing take a day off? And does it always have to be so sneaky about the transfer?"

Kya covered the scar with a wrist band. "You said you would be regarded to host my endosymbiont. Has this changed, Semu'?"

"I said I would be *honored.* And it would be nice to be asked instead of assuming it's okay."

"I am sorry. I ask that you allow Eent to reside in you to learn from your studies."

Liv sighed and stepped from the table. "Not today. I want to… be by myself." She rubbed the lesion at her wrist. "Besides, my scar has been bothering me some. It may be irritated from the daily transfers and hosting."

"Understood," Kya replied, glancing at the partner's wrist. The cicatrix appeared crimson and a little swollen, but Kya didn't mention it. She'd learned that sometimes not badgering Olivia was the best way to go. "What about our midday meal?"

"Text me later." Liv grabbed her umbrella from the stand and shoved it in her satchel. She exited the apartment, leaving Kya a little bewildered.

. . .

AFTER LIV'S DEPARTURE, Kya messaged Dr. McKinney at USF's body farm.

Will my services be needed, doctor? Kya typed, then opened the laptop she shared with Olivia.

Not today, Ms. Dumont.

Understood.

Kya set the phone to silent and pulled up the programming for the new app she was creating. Being able to work from home most days had been advantageous when Kya first arrived. While waiting for legal documentation to be created, her Oo'mahn host family that had been on Earth longer than herself had found her employment with an start-up software developer. The developer didn't care to know his employees' backgrounds as long as they could write code. Now, when she wasn't needed at the body farm, she created computer applications and sold them to third party businesses.

Under the terry cloth band, her wrist stung with the agitation of Eent's movements. She glanced down at the band and noticed her skin was darker near the edge of the stretchy fabric. The memory of Liv's brusqueness just an hour before caused a tightening in Kya's chest. The unusual sensation didn't go unnoticed by Eent, and the sym wiggled more. The woman pulled her hand to her chest and ran her thumb along the length of the large vein that traversed the span of her forearm. The skin there was warm to the touch, but Kya dismissed the sensation.

"Maybe my Semu' is just worried about her research." Kya's voice echoed in the silent apartment. "You can understand that Senseless One, can you not?" Her thumb caressed the scar under the cloth and the sym stilled. "With hope, she will have success today."

She loaded a playlist of Scarlatti's sonatas onto her iPod; and, as the music filtered through the speaker, she began entering strings of code. Listening to classical music and losing herself in her work helped ease her worries. She didn't hear her tablet's alarm nor her phone's vibration when a message came through.

. . .

OLIVIA SWIPED her access card and the pressurized doors of the lab glided apart. She removed her lab coat from the wall hook and slid it on before clipping her ID to the pocket.

"You're here early, Mr. Raulings." She joined him at the table and lifted the sample trays he had pulled.

"I know how you hate inefficiency, so I wanted to set everything up before you arrived."

"Thank you. Did you retrieve the latest samples from the cryo-chamber?"

"I was just about to after I finished calibrating the microscopes."

"I'll get them." Liv moved to the large, silver chamber that resembled a washing machine without the outer housing. It emitted a whirring sound and a soft, white light shone up from the small window in the lid.

Liv tapped several buttons and the vacuum seal broke with a release of air. She raised the lid and swirls of frost rose from the chamber. A rush of frigid air smacked her face and she reached over the top of the chamber, her hand disappearing into the tube.

"Dr. Tate, no!" Matt hurried to Liv and flipped her arm up so that her hand was free of the chamber, before pulling her away. He slid on a glove and slammed the lid.

"Mr. Raulings, what are you *doing*?" Olivia glared at her lab assistant. She adjusted her coat and settled her hands on her hips.

"You don't have on your proper safety equipment, doctor. You would have permanently damaged your skin and possibly destroyed the samples."

"Are you questioning my ability to make reasonable judgments, Mr. Raulings?"

The alarm on the cryo-chamber sounded, alerting the pair that the door was still open and unlocked. Matt snapped the two fasteners closed and pressed a sequence of buttons. The airlock on the lid whooshed as the pressurization sealed the chamber.

"Of course not, Doctor. I—"

Liv shook her head, the realization of what had almost happened settling on her. "You're right. I wasn't thinking. Thank you for saving my skin, literally."

Both let out an uneasy laugh, and the tension in the room lightened.

"Would you prepare samples from tray AL54?" Liv returned to the table, gripping its edge to steady herself.

"Yes, Doctor." Her assistant buttoned his lab coat, then slipped on a pair of protective goggles and thick cryo-gloves before reopening the chamber and removing the subzero specimens.

Liv sat on the stool and checked the calibration of the microscope. "Thanks again," she said as Matt handed her the first slide.

"Not a problem." He took his place next to Liv and focused on the microscope in front of him.

Each of them got lost in their own research, finally speaking after they had looked at every specimen in their grouping. Liv scanned Matt's recordings and nodded.

"These results are promising, Mr. Raulings. Did you save the notes from the last set of data collected?"

Matt cut a look at Olivia, then handed her a thumb drive. "I thought you'd want to look them over," he said, "before adding the data to the spreadsheet. If everything is in order, you can upload the notes, too."

Liv unlocked the laptop at the opposite end of the stainless table that ran the length of the room. She took a couple of minutes to open the files on the flash drive and scan the data.

"Can you pull trays AL 49 and AL 50? I want to double check them."

"Sure, Doctor." Matt slipped on a pair of latex gloves and opened a lab cooler door. He located the boxes and set them in a metal tray next to the microscopes he had just calibrated. "Is there something in particular that you're looking for, Doctor?"

"The description in your notes of these two samples doesn't correspond to the samples taken before or after this grouping."

Liv turned from the computer to the microscope. She reached for a specimen sample from the first tray.

"Doctor, your gloves." Matt's covered hand blocked her from taking a slide.

"Oh, yes, I forgot." A nervous half-laugh escaped her as she reached past Matt to the glove dispenser. Her sleeve rose to reveal the scar on her wrist.

"Doctor Tate. Your arm." Matt motioned toward Liv's forearm and she followed his gaze.

The usual pale pink scar was blistering red and swollen. As Liv stared at it, the chafing that had been a nagging side thought all morning was now an uncomfortable inflammation. She grabbed the gloves, snapped them on, and unrolled the cuff of her jacket sleeve.

"Oh, that's an old wound," she said. "It flares up from time to time." She pulled a glass smear from the first group and positioned it into the slide holder. Adjusting the objective lens, she leaned forward to look through the eyepiece.

"You might want to have it checked. It looks infected." Matt set a notebook next to the doctor.

Liv's body tensed and she slowly lifted her head before turning on Matt. "Mr. Raulings, I would appreciate it if you didn't access my physical health, especially since you aren't my doctor."

"I just meant—"

"I know what you meant." Liv cut off any further comment with a glare.

"Very well, *Doctor*." He returned to his business of preparing the day's specimens and equipment.

The tension in the room evaporated to a thin uneasiness as the two worked in silence. The morning passed without another incident, and the pair finally paused for a break near lunchtime. Liv checked her cell phone. With no message from Kya, she tapped out one of her own.

I am in the middle of something and can't meet for lunch. I'll see you at home.

"Mr. Raulings, would you mind ordering me something from the cafeteria? I want to finish this last set before I stop for lunch."

"Sure, Doctor, but would you like some help sorting and storing these specimens first?" Matt stood beside Olivia motioning toward the flat, glass rectangles spread over her workstation. He moved to pick up a couple of slides, but Liv stopped him.

"Don't touch those!" She ordered. "You'll interfere with my system. I have them the way I want them."

"But Doctor, you always return one sample before taking another. You threatened to replace me—"

"Why, Mr. Raulings, do you insist on questioning my every decision?"

"I'm not, I just know you insist on following protocol." Matt backed away from the work station. "Are you sure you're feeling okay, Doctor?"

Liv ran a hand through her hair, her eyes widening as she scanned the table. A lost, quizzical look skittered across her face. "What have you done?" She rose from the stool, the questioning look turning to one of anger. "You are ruining my work! I've told you Mr. Raulings, you must replace the slide before you retrieve another one."

"But Doctor—" Matt braced himself, unsure what Olivia would do.

"Not another word. I'll have you removed from this lab within the hour. I can't believe…" She didn't finish the statement before she turned on Matt. Her hands raised to strike him, Matt grabbed the doctor by the wrists and she let out a muffled cry.

"Please, you're hurting me," she cried as she continued to struggle against her assistant.

Matt wrestled Liv to the lab door and hit the call button. "I need security to lab 923! Doctor Tate's gone mad!"

A GRUMBLING in her midsection forced Kya to pause her entries and glance at the computer's clock. She rotated each wrist and flexed her fingers. Her fingertips were numb from the marathon typing session.

"Oh, my. It's after midday. No wonder I am craving sustenance." She rose from the couch and ambled to the kitchen.

"And why have you been so quiet, Senseless One? Usually you remind me that I require nourishment." Kya removed the wrist band and peered down at the cicatrix. A thick black line ran from her elbow to her palm and the scar that housed her sym was swollen and hot to the touch. An iridescent blue fluid oozed from a tiny opening at the base of her palm.

"This is not good." Kya found a napkin and dabbed at the ooze. She massaged the vein causing more of the fluid to dribble out. "Eent, are you well? Make movement."

The skin of her forearm twitched once then was still. A dull headache and her stomach growling added to Kya's dismay. She located her water bottle and took a long swig of the lemon-kelp mixture. An idea struck her and she stretched her arm over the sink, dousing the vein with the water. The liquid cooled the skin around her cut, but the sym still didn't move.

"What do I do?" She made her way to the living room and noticed the flashing light on her tablet. A message had been received. Entering her fingerprint, she pulled up the latest transmission from her commander.

'The illness has intensified. All Oo'mahns will be retrieved from the evacuation coordinates listed below within the next twenty-four hours. Report to the location by midnight this night and wait for transport.'

A pair of geographic coordinates followed the message and when Kya touched them, an image appeared on the screen. It was the skyscraper 100 North Tampa. She had no idea how she would avoid detection at such a prominent place, but she had little time to consider it. The fever in her arm intensified.

She cleared the screen and entered the code to send a transmission to her kinsman, Pier. She explained the discoloration in her arm, the lack of movement from her sym, and the oozing fluid. She ended her transmission with a plea for a quick response, then set aside her tablet. Her phone dinged with a message.

'This is Matt Raulings, Doctor Tate's assistant. She had an outburst today and has been detained by lab security. I can't get her to calm down. Please come be with her.'

"Oh, no." Kya's hunger was forgotten as she rushed to dress. She bandaged her wrist, pocketed her phone, and was out the door within ten minutes. In the apartment complex's garage, she worked to unchain her bicycle. The numbness that had started in her fingertips was spreading up her left arm, making it difficult to spin the numbers on the lock.

"Mengtuk!" she cursed under her breath, finally freeing her bike from the stand. As she swung her leg over the frame, the disjointed feeling of being outside her body swept through her. Kya blinked and, when she opened her eyes, she was on the Oo'mahn star ship *Pan'Du*.

Her kinsman, Pier stood in front of her as did the chief medical officer, Kel, and a couple of other medical personnel. They rushed to Kya to inspect her arm.

"No, I must go back," Kya twisted from their grip and slapped at the transporter panel. The medical team seized her, securing her arms to her sides. Bands were wrapped around her chest and tightened as a precaution.

"The illness is already affecting her," Kel said, extending Kya's arm as she continued her fight for freedom. The diminutive, chief medical officer examined the infected vein, a low whistle escaping her auxiliary nostrils. "It was wise for you to inform us of her deteriorating condition, Pier'uu."

"You do not understand," Kya protested, "my mate—my house mate—she is not well, also. I must go to her."

The group made their way to the infirmary and Kya saw all around her other Tan'Rumah strapped to gurneys. She counted at least twenty-five occupied beds with more ailing hosts sitting along the wall of the bay.

"All of these are sick?" Her struggles lessened as she took in the sight of so many disabled hosts and syms with their life forces diminishing.

"More have fallen ill since the evacuation began."

"It is a virus contracted from those *Earthlings*." Banu, his words laced with acid, stepped from a corridor. "Their society centers around diseases and a search for cures."

"We do not know that with certainty, Banu'ra." Kel ran a sensory device around the periphery of Kya's face and down the bridge of her nose. "We suspect it is environmental."

"Are all of the infirm hosts assigned to research teams on Earth? Or are they crew members that stayed with the *Pan'du*?"

"All but four were on Earth." Kel peered at Kya, her head tilting in thought. "And those four are mates of research team members." The medic sighed and shook her head. "It is reasonable to infer that a contagion from the planet has infected our people."

"I am not affected though."

Kel glanced at the tablet she held then back up at Kya. "Why, then, is your forearm discolored and inflamed?"

"Unknown," the young woman replied, "but I am not displaying symptoms of this madness that grips the others, am I?"

"As displayed by your outburst, you are, undoubtedly, in the early stages of the infection," Banu asserted. "It is only a matter of time before the symptoms appear."

"I want to speak to el'Jah'we," Kya said. "I must hold counsel with The Leader."

"She is very busy with the evacuation," Banu replied. "She cannot—"

"It is our custom," Kya interrupted him, her words precise and cold.

Banu flared his auxiliary nostrils, but nodded once. "Very well." He turned toward the comm pad, entered a code, and summoned Jah to the infirmary.

A few moments later, the towering leader joined the small group at the end of the bay.

"En'Kya, it is not well." Jah bowed slightly in acknowledgment of the other woman.

"It is not, Leader. Our people are ill and I know someone who may be able to help, but I must return to Earth to retrieve her."

"Who is this person?"

"My...domicile partner, Doctor Olivia Tate."

"Why? This person is not Oo'mahn."

"She is a scientist who hosted Eent during my stay. And she is ill, also."

"Her symptoms are like these?" Jah waved a hand directed at the whole bay.

"I do not know. Her assistant contacted me that her behavior is uncharacteristic, and her hollow is inflamed. She may be in the beginning stages of the disease."

Jah glanced at Kel and Banu. The medic offered a hopeful look and nodded. Banu scowled at the suggestion, but kept his mouth shut under Jah's glare.

"Let me counsel with the Elder Bar. I will have a decision before the end of the evacuation." She turned back to Kya. "Understand though, if your friend chooses to stay with us she will never be able to return to her planet. You, of all Oo'mahns, know the consequences for *humans* living aboard this spacecraft."

"Yes, Leader." Kya bowed her head in respect as Jah strode from the infirmary.

THE MINUTES that passed since Jah left the infirmary felt like hours to Kya, and her mind worked to formulate an escape plan. She was still restrained, though she hadn't tried to leave the ship again. The medics had secured her to a wall and begun an IV. Eent had been removed from her hollow and placed in a gelatinous bed, his luminescent life force very weak.

The chief medic, Kel, stood in front of her now, taking vital signs from both Kya and Eent.

"This is odd." She tapped buttons on her tablet, then checked Kya's inflamed vein. The swelling had subsided and the discoloration lessened. "Your damaged hollow is healing on its own, en'Kya. Yet your endosymbiont is not recovering."

Both women peered into the chamber next to Kya. Eent's motionless form was surrounded by a dull blue glow. If not for the blinking lights on his bioscanner, the women would have thought him dead.

"I believe it is because he needs my friend, the human host who has housed him also these last four months. Please, release me so that I may retrieve her and heal Eent."

Kel stared at the woman. Kya knew it was a long shot. As a Du'Tomani host, the medical officer maintained a great sense of loyalty to the customs of the Oo'mahn and the decisions of their leader and the Elder Bar. Still, Kel took a long minute to mull over the request, giving Kya hope.

Finally, she spoke. "Do you believe this human can help cure our people?"

"I do. She is a very intelligent woman, a leader in her scientific field." Kya, in her excitement, strained against the bindings that held her. An alarm signaled and two security team members glanced at the women.

Kel silenced the alarm, and the security officers returned to monitoring the infirmary.

"We could both be imprisoned for going against a direct order." The medic's resolve waned, and Kya was losing hope, but Kel continued, "I would have to erase your biosignature from the computer system so you could not be tracked. If you had trouble on the planet, we could not assist you."

"Understood." Kya suppressed a smile, remembering that Du'Tomani hosts were uncomfortable with outward shows of emotion.

Kel removed Kya's restraints and tapped a series of codes into the sick bay's main computer terminal.

"You have one hour, en'Kya. Then you must—"

A commotion from the corridor captured both women's attention.

"Take me back right now! I am not a specimen for study. I am a human, with rights."

"Please calm yourself." Naar, the ship's chief security officer, escorted the human into the hangar. "You are a guest here, not a prisoner."

"Then send me back!" The woman's outburst subsided at the site of so many ill patients. "Wh—what is wrong with them?" She asked, following Naar further into the bay.

"We are unsure. That is why you are here." The pair rounded the first row of gurneys and Kya got a good look at both of them.

"Olivia! Father!" She sprinted to the pair, not knowing who to greet first.

Naar raised his hand, palm facing Kya, and his daughter matched his movements. "It is well, en'Kya."

"It is, Naar'eb, my father."

"This is your domicile partner, yes?"

"She is." Kya couldn't help herself and threw her arms around the woman. "Are you well, Semu'? Your assistant sent me a very disturbing message and I was unable to come to you."

Olivia returned the embrace. "Oh, Love. I was so scared when security detained me at the lab. I don't remember much of it, except that my arm was throbbing and feverish." She looked down at her wrist, the scar now a ruddy pink and no longer inflamed. "Look! It's not that bad now."

"And you are calm now and not outbursting."

Liv smiled. "Having an outburst. No, I'm not."

"Semu'? Love?" Kel said, and both women jumped at the sound of her voice. "Those are terms of affection. Does this human hold your affection, en'Kya?"

Kya slipped her hand into Liv's and squeezed it. "She does. I love her."

"How is this possible?" Naar stepped back from his daughter. "You know our customs, en'Kya. Did your sym agree to this union?"

As if knowing that the group was talking about him, Eent moved, causing his bioscanner to release a series of beeps. Medics hovered over his chamber registering vital signs.

"You know our customs, too, Father. Did that stop you from taking Mother as your mate, even though she was human?"

Liv glanced between the two aliens, her brow crinkling as details of Kya's life before their union unfolded.

"That was four hundred years ago. We were children. You are a mature Oo'mahn, well past the onset of *pakle* and childbearing."

"Understood, Father. But I am my mother's child. And I have feelings for Olivia."

"Feelings?" Banu broke in. None of the smaller group noticed that a band of Oo'mahns had joined them, led by the tactical officer. "How is that possible?" he continued. "I oversaw your *mat'rassa* and verified that you were stripped of all emotion."

"Wait a minute," Liv interjected. "Your mother is human? You didn't tell me that."

"It wasn't necessary until now." Kya glanced at her partner, unable to dodge Liv's ever-growing death glare. "I would have told you when we joined lives in the formal mating ritual. What do you call it?"

"Our wedding?"

"Yes, the wedding. I would want you meet my relations."

"Family," Liv offered instinctively, though her anger still burned.

"My family."

"This has to be brought to the attention of el'Jah'we," Banu said, moving to a comm terminal. "The Leader must know about this...*mating.*"

"Your leader is called the god of God?" Liv whispered to Kya but straightened at the terse look from Banu.

"I am not deity." The statuesque ruler glided into the gathering, her umber skin shiny in the fluorescent lights of the infirmary. "I was given the name Jah by some of your people during the Earth era Middle Ages. My endosymbionts are the precursor and post-cursor of my name. I am *of* them, in their service." Jah paused in front of Liv. "But this is not why we are convened. You are mated with Kya, in body if not in spirit."

"I don't know what you mean." Liv stared up into the face of the Oo'mahn leader.

"You have shared her endosymbiont and she says she loves you, though she participated in our ritualistic emotional purge, the *mat'rassa,* before she was assigned to this research team."

"I love her, too," Liv said. "I'm angry that she didn't share important information with me." She glanced at Kya, and softened. "But she is my life and I don't want to be without her."

"This is ridiculous and inconsequential," Banu said, both sets of nostrils flaring. "Without her endosymbiont's agreement, en'Kya cannot be mated to this...*human.*"

Olivia glared at the tactical officer, stepping closer to Kya.

"Again, we are not keeping our perspective on the real issue,"

Kel said, her hand sweeping out to include the sick bay. "Can this human heal our infirm?"

"I can try," Liv said.

"What can she do that our most brilliant science officers cannot?" Banu said, sneering at the women.

"Another perspective and review of the data may help uncover something I and my team have overlooked." Kel tapped the screen of the tablet and glanced at Jah before handing the tablet to Olivia. "This is the data I have collected thus far. We have eighteen hours before our stealth array is spent and we must leave Earth's orbit or be exposed to its population."

"And contamination." Banu snorted.

"Enough." Jah turned on him and Banu stormed from the hangar. "Help us, Olivia. Save our people."

"We will talk later," Liv said to Kya before she followed Kel to a glass enclosed room that looked much like her own lab.

"Come, daughter." Naar touched Kya's elbow. "Your mother will want to see you."

The pair left the scientists to the work of saving their race.

NAAR LED the way down a long, soft-lit hall that ended with a row of brushed metal doors. He placed his palm flat on the waist-high scanner beside the first entrance, and the pocket door slid open revealing a small, utilitarian room.

"It is just as I remember," Kya said and, at the sound of her voice, a woman with short gray hair and creamy skin entered the room.

"Kya, my child." Marret Lawrence, a short, sturdy woman, stood in front of her daughter, arms outstretched. She'd learned long ago that the Oo'mahns were uncomfortable with unnecessary physical contact, but her humanity got the better of her. She pulled her daughter into a suffocating embrace.

"Mother, it is well," Kya whispered against Marret's cheek. She had missed the warmth of her mother's love the two years she had been on Earth.

"I heard you brought a mate on board," Marret said, releasing her daughter. She turned her child around, assessing her physically, finally drawing Kya's pitted wrist to her. "And that your hollow is infected."

The younger woman drew her arm back. "It is much better, Mother. It is Eent that is gravely ill."

"And your mate? Where is he?"

"She. My mate is female."

"Female? Is that acceptable now on Earth?"

"I do not understand, Mother."

"Before I left Earth, it was illegal for people of the same sex to be in a relationship, much less be mated."

"The planet is very different since you departed."

"I can tell. Is that why the syms are ill? Has my home deteriorated so much that it kills its inhabitants?" Marret sat on the beige sofa in the sparsely decorated living area, patting the seat beside her. Kya noticed the orange vein that ran the length of her mother's forearm, the sym's iridescence prevalent.

"Your endosymbiont is well? Does it reside in you or Father?"

Marret glanced at her wrist. "We host equally. Ebet is most satisfied with shared time in each of us, though I don't host as often as in the beginning. Living on board the *Pan'du* has certainly increased my life span, but I am aging faster than your father. And the toll of hosting is having an effect, also."

Kya nodded, but her attention was on her parents' shared sym. "Were you the primary host for Ebet after you first met Father?" The young woman sat next to her mother and took her arm. The skin below Marret's wrist was warm but not feverish, and it undulated with the movement of the sym.

"Unknown." Marret glanced at her husband. "That was so long ago. And my memory isn't that good anymore."

"You hosted more than I, Semu'da," Naar replied. "I was surprised that Ebet allowed me to be her vessel after residing with your mother so often. Their bond is strong. Once we were on the ship though, the time was split equally."

"Why did you decide to leave your planet and mate with Father?"

"Why this interest in our marriage and my leaving Earth?"

"If I am not allowed to stay with Olivia on her home planet, then I wish for her to come with me to Ep'Lumint. I must have sufficient reason for the Elder Bar to permit it." Kya waited for her mother's response.

"Well," Marret began, "the era that I lived in on Earth was very difficult. Many of the advances that they have today, and those on the *Pan'du,* didn't exist." A troubled look crossed Marret's face, but she continued. "Plus, I was an orphan. I had no family except the one that purchased my ticket to travel to the New World—the Americas. I thought I would have a better life, but the conditions were severe. Many people died in the first weeks after our arrival; and when our colony was invaded by indigenous people, we fled Roanoke."

Naar sat on the other side of his wife, placing a comforting hand over hers. "When your mother and the other ten in her party entered our research camp," he said, "they were famished and near death. It did not matter that we were different than them; they were in need and we provided assistance. When we left Earth later that season, your mother and the others chose to leave with us."

"The Elder Bar allowed it?" Kya's eyes widened at the possibility.

"They did."

"And there are other humans on this ship?"

"Only four. Two that never hosted our endosymbionts perished on the way to our home planet," Naar said. "Four others chose to live on Ep'Lumint. They have families now and are very satisfied with their lives."

"Then why did the *Pan'du* return so soon after delivering us to Earth's surface? And why are we being evacuated?"

"Because of the illness that has befallen our people." Naar laced his fingers with Marret and Kya noticed the transfer of their sym. "The Elder Bar had hoped to establish a permanent colony on

Earth, but when hosts became ill and the first endosymbiont perished, el'Jah'we decided to retrieve our researchers."

"Probably a wise decision." Kya stood and walked to the port window. The blackness of space was dotted with distant stars. Kya imagined her home planet among those there, but knew it was a falsehood. Ep'Lumint was light years away. Still, memories of the crisp air, clear blue waters, and lush greenery of the planet's foliage caused her to sigh. She absentmindedly scratched her cicatrix.

The scar was much better now that she had been transported to the ship. Could Earth be making her people ill, as Banu suggested? But what about herself and the others who were only mildly affected? What was the cause of that? What did they all have in common?

"En'Kya, your mother was talking to you." Naar stepped into his daughter's line of sight. "But you have that look. Your mind is working, though your endosymbiont is not present. What are you thinking?"

"I must go back to the infirmary." Kya didn't wait for her parents' response.

"YOUR ANALYSIS and organization of this data is impeccable, Kel," Liv said, scrolling through the tablet's pages of information. "I think some of the necessary details are lost in the translation, though. I can't be certain, but if I am interpreting this right, either the illness is caused by climate or chickens."

"Chickens?" Kel peered over Liv's shoulder at the computer page, touching the word on the screen. The single, archaic English word mutated into vertical glyphs. "No, that is climate."

"But it doesn't explain why so many syms are critically ill and so few hosts are."

"I think I know why." Kya rushed through the sliding glass doors. "We shared Eent equally in the beginning, but he has spent more time with you at your laboratory. He only housed with me while we slept. He has grown accustomed to your genetics."

"That still doesn't explain why he is so ill."

"It does if he has mutated to better assimilate with your DNA." Kya joined the two women. "Da'Kel, can you display images of genetic sequence strands from Eent, Olivia, and myself?" The medic complied and Kya turned the computer screen with the multiple chromosomal images toward her. "See?"

At first glance, they were the same, but as Liv focused on specific sections of each strand she noticed slight variations. "You're right, Love. Eent's strand has variations that match my DNA more so than yours. But that isn't causing the illness in the others."

"It may be in eight of the hosts," Kya said. "Especially if the four researchers were unfaithful to their mates by allowing Earthlings to house their endosymbionts."

Kel grimaced at Kya's suggestion of the indiscretion, but held her words.

"Did they, Doctor?" Liv asked. The medic nodded, and Liv continued. "If humans hosting a sym caused this mutation, then why are the others ill?"

"That is an excellent query," Kel replied. "And one I would like your assistance in answering."

"Then I need markers to use on this dry erase board."

Kel stared at her, head tilted and brow knitted. Kya, though, located the markers.

"We're about to kick it old school, ladies." Liv listed the first name of the most critical and the charting began.

THE THREE WOMEN worked tirelessly plotting the symptomatic details of the afflicted. The glass display running the length of one wall filled with names, notes, and flow charts.

"This is archaic," Kel said, dropping the marker on the table. "How does this help us in uncovering how the disease is being contracted?"

"We look for patterns," Liv said. "Commonalities in the hosts, the syms, or the environment."

"They resided in different regions of the planet," Kel said. She backed away from the board to gain a broader perspective.

"Not these," Kya said, indicating the most critical patients. "They were stationed in Asia."

"There's a large concentration of pollution in that area," Liv said. "And these," she said, pointing to the four Tan'Rumah and their spouses, "were in North America. Our pollution is bad, but not as bad as Asian countries."

"So what caused the illness in these eight?" Kel studied the names of the North American researchers.

"Those are the crew who strayed," Liv said. She noticed the women's quizzical looks and clarified. "These four—" She pointed to the researchers. "—shared a sym with an Earthling while on their expedition. And they then brought back the mutation to their spouses on board the *Pan'du*."

"So the sickness is both environmental and genetic?"

"I would say so."

"How do we cure it?"

"Those affected by Earth's climate seem to be healing spontaneously now that they are back on board the starship."

"What about the other eight?"

"The cheaters?" Liv asked smiling, though her joke fell flat. "How are their symptoms?"

"They are on the most critical list."

"I say we bring one of their mistresses on board and test the genetics theory. At least if it doesn't work, we tried something."

"What about exposure?" Kya tapped her pen on the metal table, sending little *tinging* sounds throughout the lab.

"If the test fails, and we return the human, it will just be one of a million stories told about alien abductions and experimentations," Liv said. "The real issue is if the experiment works. How would your leader react to having to convince four Earthlings to live on a star ship among aliens?"

"It has been allowed before," Kya said. "My mother is human and she has lived with my father, a Sird'ee host, for over four hundred years."

"Which reminds me," Liv interjected. "We have to talk about your keeping secrets from me."

"I kept no secrets. I saw no opportune time to tell you of my heritage."

"Now may not be the best time to have this conversation," Kel said. "We should present our findings to el'Jah'we."

"Understood," both women answered in unison.

"Very well." Kel punched a button on a comm pad and requested that Jah join them in the infirmary.

"Acknowledged," Jah responded. Once the leader arrived, the women explained their findings and suggested a course of action.

"If the humans do not want to stay with us, then eight of our people will perish?"

"Essentially, yes," Liv said. "But if we do nothing, they are guaranteed to die."

"Then disclose your plan to the four pairings and ascertain if one of the researchers will identify his human partner. Preferably the human least likely to be surprised by our existence and most likely to want to assist us."

"Understood, Leader," Kel said. "I will approach them momentarily. However, I suggest that en'Kya and her mate rest. They both worked diligently to uncover the proposed cure."

"I am beat," Liv said, clarifying, "I mean, excessively tired."

Jah nodded. "Then rest, Olivia. We will discuss your future with our people at the dawn of the new day."

"In the morning," Liv corrected her, a sheepish grin tugging at the corners of her mouth.

"In the morning, then." Jah turned to Kel and their conversation followed Liv and Kya from the room. Before heading to their temporary quarters, they stopped by Eent's chamber. The sym's luminescence was still dim, but his movement as the women approached gave them hope.

Liv opened the small portal on the chamber's lid. Leaning over the opening, she whispered, "We will heal you, Senseless One. And we will all be reunited."

"He cannot hear you, Semu'." Kya slid an arm around her partner's waist.

"That's what you say," Liv replied, "but that little worm picks up on more than we give him credit for."

"How is your hollow?" Kya slid her hand down Liv's arm and rubbed her mate's wrist. The cicatrix was still rough and warm, but Liv lifted it for Kya to inspect.

"Better, but as soon as Eent is able I want to host him. If our theory is true, then he needs me."

"We both do. Please return with me to Ep'Lumint." Kya kissed Liv's open palm. "The climate on Earth is unhealthy for us all and once you meet my mother, you will see that humans can thrive on the *Pan'du* as well as my home planet."

"And when do I get to meet…"

"She is called Marret."

"Marret?"

"As soon as you are ready," Kya linked her hand in Liv's and the two exited the infirmary. "Then we must decide how to inform your relations of your departure."

"You know I have no family," Liv said, a sadness lacing her words. "I am an only child of only children who died right after I graduated high school. Mr. Raulings is the only person I am concerned about knowing my whereabouts. Especially since I just vanished out of the lab's security office."

"Then we can devise a way to tell him after you are introduced to my mother and father." Kya pressed a button on her parents' quarters panel and waited for them to reply.

Epilogue - Doctor Olivia Tate's Personal Log

IT HAS BEEN three years since the Oo'mahns, and their five human emigrants, returned to Earth to evacuate their researchers in the face of an epidemic. Since that time, I have lived with my spouse— my Semu'da—Kya aboard the *Pan'du*. We have a son, thanks to a human surrogate, and our sym, Eent, was restored to excellent health. We host him equally now, without feelings of exploitation.

In the end, the four researchers revealed their alien status to their Earth partners and requested that the humans leave their homes and live aboard the *Pan'du* in order to save Oo'mahn lives. Three accepted, one did not. Twelve recovered from their illness, and three Oo'mahns were lost. The disease killed the mated pair, ju'Net & no'Lee, and their shared endosymbiont, Juno.

Kya and her people will tell you that they learned much from their time on Earth—the primary lesson being that though Earth might have seemed like a suitable planet to support an Oo'mahn colony, it wasn't. The toxic environment would have killed the Oo'mahns before they could fully integrate into the Earth culture, just as it is killing the humans who inhabit it. Maybe the humans will change. Only time will tell and el'Jah'we has implied that another visit in a few hundred years would not be out of the question. I plan to be there when we return.

Author's Notes—Tracie Roberts

WHEN I WAS FIRST INVITED to join this collection, I jumped at the chance to stretch myself and write outside my comfort zone of paranormal romance. Three weeks into the project, though, I still had no viable premise for a story. I didn't want to write what I considered clichéd tales of aliens threatening earth or aliens being feared by humans. It wasn't until I set aside this story and returned for a while to one of my other works that the pivotal idea for "Social Experiment" emerged. After engulfing myself in the romantic lives of my other characters, a thought struck me: "I can write a romantic sci-fi story!"

And "Social Experiment" took form.

Once I knew I wanted to write a romance between a human and an alien, the story came much easier to me. The other surprise that revealed itself as I wrote was that the main characters were lesbians. I've also never written gay characters before, but love is love. Liv and Kya care deeply for each other; so much so that they would abandon their families and cultures to be together.

So, though, it was difficult at times writing outside my comfort zone, adding romance helped. And I feel a little more well-rounded as a writer for tackling this challenge.

~TR

Children of the Stars

Charles A Cornell

It is by no means an irrational fancy that in a future existence, we shall look upon what we think our present existence (to have been) as a dream.
—Edgar Allan Poe

I

August 16, 2006
Hamamatsu, Japan

Dr. Amare Parks pushed the cab door open with his left hand, his right arm tight to his side. He slung his legs out, his weight shifting awkwardly. The pain was unbearable. As he exited the cab, he tripped on the curb, fell to his knees and winced. The blisters on his skin felt as if angry wasps were trapped inside his sweat-soaked clothes.

The concerned taxi driver leapt out of the cab and went over to him, gibbering in Japanese. Parks stretched out his left arm to hold the man back. "Don't touch me." He shoved his wallet into the taxi-driver's chest. "Take what you need. Take more, understand? Tip, yes?"

The stunned cab driver spoke very little English. He opened the wallet and thumbed through the wad of notes, selected a few, pointed to the car and nodded. Then he took out another bill and pointed to himself, handed the wallet back and bowed his head in gratitude.

The cab departed. Parks struggled to his feet and shuffled through puddles forming slick shallows across the plaza after a torrential summer rain. The bright glare of the front facade of Hamamatsu train station banished the dull evening light of the wet city. As he moved through its tall glass entrance into the crowd of commuters, the stares on people's faces were accompanied by gasps and fleeing feet. A disfigured black giant was invading the end of what had been a peaceful day. Parks' towering six-foot-six body, dark brown skin and shaved head had turned heads every-where he went ever since he'd arrived in Japan ten days ago. He was so alien to the black-haired, porcelain-faced populace. But what had been a blessing on his arrival—the Japanese had responded to his unusual height and different race with polite smiles and gentle curiosity—was a curse now that he was departing.

The instructions he'd received were strange. He was to find a piano inside the station and wait there. Where would he find a piano in a Japanese train station? In a bar?

He looked at the departure board and then to his watch. The last *Shinkansen* bullet train to Tokyo was due to leave in thirty minutes. He looked from side to side around the bustling concourse, searching. And there it was, as he was told—a jet black piano atop a white platform. A display piece. The city of Hamamatsu, he remembered, was home to the Yamaha piano factory. He dragged his aching body towards the display, unaware he was leaving a trail of smeared blood behind him on the pristine concrete floor.

A voice said from behind, "You can't board a train like this."

Parks turned and nearly collapsed with relief. "You found me. I—"

"No time. We must clean you up." The man reached for Parks' elbow. "This way."

"Don't touch me."

"I understand, Dr. Parks. Down here. The washroom."

As the pair entered, the man exchanged sharp words in Japanese with several patrons causing them to leave in a hurry. They bowed politely to the strange black American lingering at the doorway. When they were gone, Parks stumbled to a sink, gripped its edge to steady himself and turned on the cold water tap. He leaned into the bowl, cupped his hands under the running water, and guzzled. As he finished, he said, gasping, "I've had nothing to drink but rainwater."

Parks raised his dripping wet fingers. The blisters glistened. They'd grown, spreading down the back of his hands and up into his sleeves. He stared into the bathroom's mirror. He didn't recognize his own reflection. His face had aged beyond his thirty-seven years, his skin wrinkled and cracked, limp flaps of flesh peeling off one of his cheeks. He backed away from the mirror and slumped against the cold tile wall. An overwhelming sense of desperation flushed through his radiation-poisoned body.

"You have no effects?" Parks said to his companion.

"Don't worry about me. It's you who needs a doctor."

"I *am* a doctor. I need to get to Tokyo. To the Embassy. Tonight. On the next Shinkansen."

"All right." The man pulled a handkerchief from his pocket and knelt down by Parks' foot. "Brace yourself. This is going to hurt. But it has to be done. To stop the bleeding."

The man tightened the handkerchief around Parks' ankle. Parks grimaced. Sweat trickled down his face, each drop of salty water stinging the blisters.

"The information, Dr. Parks?" the man said, wiping blood from Parks' shoe with a paper towel. "Do you still have it?"

Amare fumbled in his pocket, his fingers separating the thumb drive from the coins. The drive contained the scanned documents and photographs he'd been given as well as the contents of his own hard drive, data he'd barely had time to upload before his escape. Parks pulled the thumb-drive out of his pocket, his hand trembling.

"Are they following you?" the man asked.

"I don't know." Amare Parks looked up into the ceiling as if the panels were dotted with stars. "But yes, I think so. I mean how can you tell?"

Fear had gripped Amare Parks the moment the sky above had opened and engulfed everything in its blue terror. Three days on the run, alone, hiding in mountain caves until he'd found the courage to make his presence known and flag down a truck. Dropped on the outskirts of Hamamatsu, he saw this fear reflected in the taxi-driver's eyes as the man reluctantly agreed to take a fare from someone whose face was slowly being stripped of its cells. Now on the cold floor of a train station's washroom, this fear was strangling him like the tightening of a hangman's noose.

The door of the washroom opened. Parks' companion yelled in Japanese. The person trying to enter reversed direction. "We have to leave, Dr. Parks. Can you move?"

"Yes." Parks waved off the man's offer to help. His skin buzzed with pain.

"In your condition, Dr. Parks, it's too risky for you to keep the data any longer. What if they find you before you get to Tokyo? If it's lost, *everything* is lost. Admit it, you're in no condition to safeguard it anymore." The man's expression was calm but his eyes were filled with determination. "I can get the data to the right people, Dr. Parks. I assure you. People who will counter the denials, the skepticism, any attempts at a cover-up. Are you listening to me? It's a miracle we both escaped. But you must let go and let me take it from here. Trust me."

The suffering and fear eased as Parks held the pink thumb-drive into the air. "Okay. It's yours."

His companion smiled. "You've done the right thing. Think about what this data means, Dr. Parks. And how fortunate it was that we pieced this together." The man locked eyes with the American. "This—well, I can't find the words. It's simply incredible. But now you need to worry about yourself." The man looked at his watch. "We don't have much time. Here's your train ticket. I'll walk you to the platform."

"You're not coming with me?"

"No. I have to get this to my contacts here in Hamamatsu. I'll meet you in Tokyo tomorrow. I've booked a room for you. Give this paper to the taxi driver when you get off the train. He'll take you to the hotel. In the morning, you can go to a hospital or to the US Embassy, whatever you choose. Don't worry, I'll find you again."

"How can I ever thank you?"

The man held up the thumb-drive. "You already have. It's over now, Dr. Parks. You've done it. God speed."

THE JAPANESE LANDSCAPE flashed by the *Shinkasen's* windows in silence. Evening had turned into night. Parks was hungry. Home-made burger hungry. All-you-can-eat ribs hungry. He opened the *ekiben* he was given with his ticket. The *ekiben* or boxed meal was a Japanese ritual of commuting—food presented artistically in little compartments inside a plastic box wrapped in a ribbon. He lifted the lid. This *ekiben* appealed more to the Japanese sense of simplicity, order and design than to his ravenous American hunger.

The box contained fish sashimi and shrimp sushi, a small beef tamagoyaki omelet, teriyaki vegetables, and the ever-present pickled ginger and wasabi. Parks was grateful regardless of the calorie count. He picked up the sashimi with his chopsticks—delicate slivers of translucent pale blue fish—turning the sample in the air, wondering what kind of fish it was. His taste for raw fish had developed cautiously over the past week. Now he had no choice but to like it.

Across the aisle, a voice spoke out in a stern almost impolite tone, "*Anata ga tabete iru mono o shitte imasu ka?*"

The question came from a Japanese businessman in his late fifties, dark suit, white shirt, dark blue tie, short dyed black hair.

"I'm sorry, I don't speak Japanese," Parks replied, hiding the blistered side of his face from the stranger's view.

The man repeated his question, his voice barking like an army command.

Another, softer voice came from the seat behind him. A young girl leaned over his seat back and looked down just as the fish entered Amare's mouth. "The gentleman says, do you know what you are eating?"

Parks swallowed the slippery raw fish. He felt a tingling sensation as it slid down his throat.

"*Fugu*," the man said.

"You say in English, pufferfish," the girl translated. "Where did you get it? It is not sold in *ekiben*. Special preparation needed."

Parks felt dizzy and his head ached. His throat closed. The tetrodotoxin in the deadly fish made breathing impossible. The bento-box fell to the floor as he grabbed his neck. His mouth gaped open, gulping for air. Oxygen would not pass down his tight throat. His black face turned an ugly dark purple. He jerked violently and slumped to the floor.

The commuters on the train rushed to his side. But it was too late. Dr. Amare Parks of the University of Southern California was dead.

II

One week earlier, at breakfast
Okura Hotel, Hamamatsu, Japan

DR. KATSU MITOMI sipped his coffee, turned the page of the draft paper entitled 'Mono-zygotic Births in the Hopi Tribes of Northeastern Arizona', and uttered a cross between a hum and a groan.

Dr. Amare Parks, the paper's author, had come to understand that in Japan this monotone hum meant acknowledgment. He finished his scrambled eggs, gestured to the waiter for more coffee and sat back anticipating the inevitable questions from his Japanese colleague.

Parks had known Mitomi for fifteen years. They'd been roommates together at USC, sharing the triumphs and trials of young interns. They'd kept in close contact with each other after Mitomi returned to Japan. Their joint research had propelled them to the top of the list of experts in human fertility. Parks' breakthrough techniques for in-vitro fertilization had challenged accepted convention. Mitomi, a meticulous and disciplined researcher, had advanced the field of reproductive therapy.

Katsu Mitomi swept his finger over a chart in Parks' paper. He looked up, his smooth round cheeks expanding into an impish smile and said, "Oh, I see, Parks-san." He hummed again. "Yes, very good. You say, a slam dunk." He bowed his head.

In college, Parks had taught the equally athletic Mitomi that even short men could work magic on the basketball court. In turn, his black belt Japanese friend had taught Amare that size not only didn't matter on the judo mat but could be used to your taller opponent's disadvantage. Just a few jet-lagged days in the country and Parks and Mitomi had renewed their rivalry on the court and in the gym. But as always, when it came to their shared research interests, co-operation trumped competition.

Parks fingered his empty coffee cup.

Mitomi took notice, hailed the waiter, spoke to him brusquely in Japanese and sent the embarrassed man scurrying into the kitchen. Satisfied that the world was again in order, Mitomi finished the page, closed the soon-to-be-published paper and daintily set it aside. "And when you examined the woman in question, Parks-san," he said."The last time you saw her, she appeared to be nine months pregnant but her daughter said she was only three months into her term?"

"That's right. She was at full gestation, that was clear from the ultrasound. But there was no way to verify the length of time since conception."

"And you could not ascertain the woman's age?" Mitomi asked.

"She says she was born in 1926 in a part of the reservation so remote there was no registration of her birth."

"Then she could be eighty years old?"

Parks nodded. "She exhibited gynecological signs of aging consistent with multiple pregnancies but her external physiology, especially her skin tone and her muscle physique, said the woman was in her twenties."

"Mm," Mitomi muttered again."And still fertile? Do you have a picture of her?"

Parks produced a photo from his file.

"Beautiful," Mitomi said. "So young looking."

"Like your subject, Mitomi-san?"

"Yes. I have found someone identical to this here in Japan. How many pregnancies did this Hopi woman say she had in her lifetime?"

"I didn't know whether to believe her or not. I wouldn't dare print the total she claimed. I wish I could, but it can't be substantiated."

"Why not?"

"Hopi tribal society is governed by its women elders. They were very protective of this woman's privacy and that of her offspring. It took a lot of diligence—and even a bit of borderline ethics—to gather blood samples from the nine sets of twins whose medical records I was given access to. There were ten additional twin births included in my dataset, children of her daughters and of her grand-daughters."

A fresh carafe of coffee arrived at the table. Parks paused as the waiter filled their cups, then resumed, "I tried to meet as many of her descendants as I could track down. It wasn't easy. Almost all of them had left the reservation. I found them scattered across the West and Southwest in off-the-beaten-track towns. When I did find a cluster, most of them would not co-operate with me."

"So the claimed birth rate from the original mother was more than you will officially publish?"

Parks sighed. "Yes. Several members of the tribe told the same story. One hundred and twenty separate pregnancies from this single woman, all of the births resulting in twins. That's two hundred and forty children. That means this woman would have been pregnant twice a year for sixty years."

"And all of them were claimed to be—"

"Yes, all girls. One hundred and twenty sets of twin girls."

Mitomi glanced at the research paper, then up at his friend and colleague. He hummed again, his expression a mix of wonder and concern. "These claims are not even mentioned in this report. Why Parks-san? Because it is not just unverified but medically unbelievable?"

"Correct. It's an impossible number. The eighteen children I verified is by itself an extraordinary statistic of motherhood. Nine consecutive twin births, all of the same gender. That's statistically equivalent to winning a lottery. But to believe there were one hundred and twenty sets of twin girls in total?"

"I know." Mitomi smiled. "This is my dilemma as well, Parks-san. If I would report what has been claimed here in Japan, I would lose all academic respect too."

"Thank you for letting me guest-lecture at your university this week. And for teaching me some new judo moves. But that's not why I came to Japan. I'm anxious to see your new research, Mitomi-san. I'm hoping you've substantiated the same medical anomalies in your subject and her children as I found in my group. I need a cross-regional confirmation of the morphology of this unusual condition before I publish my paper. Is this some kind of genetic abnormality in the human species? And what is its cause?"

"I share your curiosity and your enthusiasm for an answer. But it's not just data you need to see." A message was delivered to the table. Mitomi lifted the card. "Our driver has arrived, Parks-san. Did you leave your luggage with the concierge?"

"Yes. Where are we going?"

"To see the data. In the flesh, as you say in America."

"No more time for slam dunks, Mitomi-san?"

The much shorter Mitomi smiled again. "No more time for embarrassments on the mat."

"Then what are we waiting for?"

"For you to finish your coffee, Parks-san."

Amare Parks picked up the carafe. "To hell with that. We'll take it with us."

THE TOYOTA LANDCRUISER followed the Hida River, a two hour drive north of Nagoya, past the hot springs town of Gero to

Takayama. After another hour, Mitomi's driver turned east on a narrow dirt road at the foot of snow-capped Mount Norikura, a volcano straddling the border of Gifu and Nagano Prefectures. The hillsides of green tea plantations common along the Hida River were replaced by forests of white birch, plum and larch. As the elevation increased, a plateau of evergreens bordered sparse alpine meadows.

"This village is very isolated," Mitomi said. "It has only this road in and out. They may have never seen a foreigner before. Certainly no-one like you. We're entering a community trapped in time."

Deep into a virgin landscape, the tile roofs of a group of small buildings came into view above the trees. The tallest building resembled a Shinto shrine, octagonal in shape, a curved roof rising to a peak.

"It looks very old," Parks said.

"It's not. It was built in the 1950s during the reconstruction of Japan after the Second World War. In fact there was no village here before that."

"That seems odd."

Mitomi hummed. "I thought so too."

The temple overlooked the rest of the village from its perch atop a small hill. A porch encircled its timbered foundation giving access to manicured Japanese gardens surrounded by evergreens.

"You will be much noticed, Parks-san. Stay close to me and do exactly as I say. I told them about you. But it is not the same as seeing you in person. It will be quite a shock for these villagers."

"Will we see her today?" Amare asked.

"Yes." Mitomi checked his watch. "In about an hour. First, we will meet her daughter, Koko. She is my main contact with the mother, Hiroko. Family name is Sujihara. The last time I saw her, I sensed a great deal of sadness between the two of them. I don't know why."

A small herd of black and white dairy cows stopped the vehicle. A woman wearing peasant *sakiori* rag clothing and wooden sandals led them into a nearby alpine field. "When I was last here," Mitomi continued. "Three weeks ago. All the men in the village had gathered by the temple and were saying their good-byes to the women-folk. Koko Sujihara told me this always happened when her mother was about to give birth. The men were sent to a camp four miles away to wait. I asked, how would they know when to return? This village has no use for cell phones. Koko replied to me... they look up to the sky."

A hundred yards further down the winding track, the SUV parked in front of a timber-sided barn topped with a thick thatched roof. The driver helped them unload their luggage which included sleeping bags and cots, some cooking utensils, boxes of food, a small camp stove, three large leather cases containing medical instruments and a kerosene powered generator.

"Our driver, Eito will return to Takayama. The presence of a vehicle will unnerve the villagers," Dr. Mitomi said. "We can call him if we need him."

After they moved the luggage and gear into the barn, the SUV departed, leaving the two doctors behind. Inside what used to be a stable, several rooms had been built along one wall—a room devoid of any furniture, where they would sleep; and a small kitchen with a table and two chairs. The rest of the stable's floor was open. Straw mats were rolled up in piles.

Mitomi fired up the camp stove and made some green tea. After their long trip, the pair relaxed by the window, looking out on the beautiful mountain scenery. "I usually go into their homes," Mitomi said. "But lugging our instruments will be arduous. So I have requested they come here and they have agreed. We have plenty of space to set up a clinic."

The stable's large door creaked loudly and opened. Koko Suji-hara, a diminutive four-foot-ten girl wearing a linen kimono-style *sakiori,* shooed away a chicken that had wandered in behind her. She turned and then stumbled back at the sight of the tall, black-skinned American who rose to greet her. She was about to run away when Dr. Mitomi's words calmed her. She sat down on a straw mat by the door, her startled gaze locked on Dr. Parks.

Mitomi knelt beside her and gestured for Parks to sit down. "You will be at her height and that will be better, Parks-san."

A long conversation in Japanese ensued. Patience, Amare Parks had learned was not just a virtue, it was a necessity in Japan where long term relationships mattered more than short term reactions.

"We have a problem," Dr. Mitomi said. "Her mother, Hiroko has already had visitors tonight. She is too tired to see us. We must wait until tomorrow."

"Visitors?"

"Two foreigners. A man and a woman."

"Doctors?"

"I don't think so. From what Koko is saying, they sound like journalists."

Parks frowned and ran his hand over his head.

"I agree. This is not what we want," Mitomi said. "This village will clamp shut, just like your Hopi tribe. You see, Parks-san, all of the women here are daughters of Hiroko. They did not move away like yours did. The entire village will close ranks around Hiroko to protect her."

"The more reason for us to see her tonight."

Mitomi spoke again to Koko. "*Hai*," she said repeatedly.

"I know enough Japanese to know that means 'yes'. Does that mean we can see her mother now?"

"No. I have asked her to take us to these journalists. That is who we must see first. We must find out why they are here and what they want with Hiroko. This is not a story that is ready to tell. Not yet."

KOKO LED them to a small house at the foot of the hill below the temple building. The cottage was framed with aged red timbers the color of autumn leaves and topped with thatch. Two Suzuki motorcycles leaned against its side, helmets dangling from the bikes' handlebars. Koko knocked on the front door and called out to the cottage's inhabitants.

A shapely young Caucasian woman in her late-twenties came to the door, blue eyes, brunette hair in a short bob, her five-foot-seven frame wearing a red leather motorcycle jacket over white T-shirt and jeans. Behind her, a slightly taller man of about the same age and also in jeans peered through the doorway. He hid broad shoulders and a muscular physique under a Barcelona football jersey. His complexion was dark in the Latin sense, brown eyes, thick dark eyebrows, black gelled hair.

"Stephanie Dessereau," she said, shaking hands with the two doctors.

"Journalists?"

"I'm with the news agency, Agence Suisse. Sergio Rancon is a freelance reporter from Argentina."

"What are you doing here?" Parks said in an angry tone.

The woman sneered back, "We could ask the same question."

Parks gave a fluffy explanation about research he and Dr. Mitomi were conducting on the health of rural Japanese farmers. Ms. Dessereau leaned on the doorway, crossed her arms and smirked. She turned to her South American friend. "I'm not buying that. Are you?"

Rancon shook his head, no.

"All right. Enough of the games, gentlemen," Dessereau said. "We'll share our mystery with you, if you share yours with us. Agreed?" The Swiss journalist gestured to them to follow her inside.

The cottage was a simple abode designed to be functional rather than decorative, with bare wood walls and floors, and a minimal separation between rooms. Like the stable, it was compact but efficient with a kitchen open to the main living space. The building exuded a careful quality in its construction and reflected the cleanliness of those who valued even the smallest things.

Drs. Parks and Mitomi were led by Koko to a straw mat. They knelt around a traditional low wooden table. Sergio Rancon sat with them. Stephanie Dessereau left. A few minutes of awkward silence passed between the two doctors and the Argentinean journalist.

Koko Sujihara chopped fresh vegetables on the adjacent kitchen counter and placed them in an iron wok. A charcoal fire burned underneath a grate inset into the counter top. This was Koko's house, Mitomi said, breaking the silence.

Dessereau returned from a back room with a large book nearly as thick as it was wide. It had a tooled black leather cover with embossed gold lettering. She placed the book on the table. Amare Parks leaned over to look at the book's cover. The book's front and back were connected by a leather flap and a brass lock. The gilt letters were not Japanese but Gothic German.

"My aunt is an antiques dealer in Zurich," Dessereau said. "She has a penchant for old family bibles. Several years ago, this one came up for auction in Vienna from the estate of a reclusive farmer who'd returned in his nineties from Argentina essentially to spend his final years in his childhood home. A bible that was locked but had lost its key. No one wanted to bid on it. These kinds of bibles are quite common and not particularly valuable except maybe as a decorator piece for an antique shop. So she bought it for a few Euros." Dessereau opened the unlocked flap. "My aunt broke open the lock in case there were illustrations inside that she could sell. And *this* is what she found…"

Dessereau opened the bible, revealing inner pages carved out with a sharp knife blade to form a compartment which hid a collection of photographs and papers. She removed some of the contents and handed the top photograph in the pile to Dr. Mitomi. "Recognize her?"

He gasped. "Hiroko Sujihara. When was this taken?"

"I know. It could be yesterday, couldn't it? But it wasn't. Hiroko told me she remembered the occasion. It was in 1944. In Manchukuo, or Japanese occupied Manchuria, on her sixteenth birthday. Her father was part of the Japanese military government."

"1944?"

"Yes, I know. That makes her eighty-eight-years-old now."

"She hasn't aged," Mitomi said. "Not one day. Did you trace her from this photograph?"

Stephanie Dessereau laughed. "Oh my goodness, no. I wasn't looking for *her*. I was looking for *him*."

She handed them another photograph, a military portrait of a blond, smooth-skinned young man in a black uniform with silver SS badges. "When I found these documents I was intrigued by what they implied. I've followed their lead all over the world and it brought me to Japan six months ago, the first time I met Hiroko

Sujihara. I know Japan and its people. I was stationed here for three years with Agence Suisse. It wasn't long before I was contacted by Sergio who had the same interest in this man's history."

"Who is he?"

"SS Colonel Herman Keitz," Sergio Rancon said in a lilting Spanish accent. "After the war, he settled in Argentina under an assumed name in the province of Cordoba. Why he returned to Austria after so long, we don't know. To bury secrets with his death he'd kept hidden for nearly seventy years? Perhaps. Or perhaps he hoped that someday someone would find the cache of evidence he left behind. And in that, he was right. Without the records hidden in this bible, we would never have pieced together his story."

"This is not why *we* are here," Dr. Mitomi said, annoyed.

"It might be," Dessereau replied. "Your mystery and our mystery might be one and the same, doctor. It certainly involves Hiroko and her children. Hundreds of them."

Dr. Mitomi's expression said, how did they know that?

"That's why we are all here, isn't it, doctor?" Sergio asked.

Koko's wok sizzled in the open kitchen as she added sauces to the vegetables from unlabeled glass bottles by the stove. Steam rose into the bare rafters. She moved like a machine from the wok to a pot and back again, the air filling with the smell of sesame and soy. She ladled sticky rice into bowls and delivered them on a tray, then returned back to the kitchen and fetched the steaming wok. She placed it on a ceramic stand in the middle of the table. Wooden tongs lay beside it. She served a portion of vegetables into each bowl. When all the bowls were filled and handed out, she took a bowl for herself and knelt in the corner behind her guests while they ate.

"This man?" Amare Parks asked, pointing his chopsticks at the photograph of the German officer. "Was he a war criminal of some sort?"

"Herman Keitz was in the SS, that's true," Dessereau explained. "Assigned to the Nazi German Embassy in Tokyo in 1943. Soon after arrival, he accompanied Unit 731, the Imperial Japanese

Army's biological warfare group, to Japanese occupied Manchuria. That was the last known record of his whereabouts."

Dessereau put down her rice bowl. She lifted more papers from inside the bible. "These records show he met Hiroko Sujihara there through her father. In my research, I learned the Allies presumed Keitz was killed in Manchuria when it was liberated by the Russians. Unit 731 did commit serious war crimes involving human experimentation. But Herman Keitz had a specialty that makes us doubt his involvement. He was an aeronautical engineer. These papers indicate he was in Manchukuo for other reasons."

"Keitz was a member of a top secret Scientific Research Branch within the SS," Sergio Rancon added. "The Nazis were obsessed with all kinds of paranormal phenomenon, especially the kind that could unravel known science and create new technology. Many of these SS scientists went into hiding in Argentina after the war."

Dessereau unfolded one of the papers. The document was stamped with Nazi black eagles and swastikas. "This is signed by SS Reichsfuhrer Heinrich Himmler and dated July 1, 1943. These were Keitz's orders, a directive straight from the head of the SS. I'll translate: 'Colonel Keitz, you are to confirm the existence of the *Hoshiko*. If such beings do exist, as our Japanese allies claim, their reported fertility has strategic implications for the future propagation of the Aryan race."

"But you said he was an aeronautical engineer," Parks noted. "Not a doctor."

"Correct." She handed them a third photograph, of a ship, a tramp steamer. There was handwriting across the photo in German. "It says, 'Ourang Medan. At dock. Port of Lushunkou. Manchuria'. And it's dated January 12, 1948."

"Three years after the war ended?" Parks queried. "How is this of any relevance?"

"It proves the Dutch East Indies ship, the Ourang Medan, loaded cargo in Manchuria in January of 1948, one month before its bizarre and unexplained disappearance in the Malacca Strait near Sumatra. Strange lights had been seen in the sky that night.

Several ships responded to her distress call. The Ourang Medan was found drifting, her entire crew dead, their blistered faces turned to the sky, their expressions grotesquely distorted and the fingers of the corpses pointing skywards. The crew from a rescue ship had boarded the Ourang Medan and were examining the bodies when an explosion occurred in the ship's hold. The ship listed badly and the rescuers had to evacuate the Ourang Medan before it sank. The causes of both the deaths on the Medan and the subsequent explosion that doomed the ship are unknown. I think I know what happened aboard the Ourang Medan that night. But questions remain."

"And this story is relevant to us because…?"

"Because the cargo the ship was carrying had been undocumented and, contrary to maritime standards, the destination of the Ourang Medan had never been declared. Who chartered it— and why— has been a deep mystery. That is, until now. Many theories have surfaced in the intervening years surrounding the disappearance of the Ourang Medan. One was that chemical weapons developed by Japan's infamous Unit 731 were being removed from Manchuria after they were discovered in a secret bunker. Intelligence agencies in the West wanted to prevent the Soviets from acquiring them and wanted these weapons for their own military research." She pointed to the documents from the bible. "These papers from Colonel Keitz refute this theory. And he would know. Because he had a military liaison with Unit 731. His records tell us a different story. Offer a different cause. The Ourang Medan was chartered by a company *he* controlled to sail to South America for what I believe was an entirely different purpose."

"I have provided Ms. Dessereau with what I have uncovered in Cordoba," Rancon said. "After our visit here, she will be coming back with me to Argentina to interview the descendents of Germans who emigrated there after the war."

"Gentlemen," Dessereau continued. "Lloyd's Registry of Shipping officially recognizes the Ourang Medan as having only one survivor, someone who had jumped overboard before the rescue ships had even arrived... an Austrian named Herman Keitz. Here, in his own handwriting, is proof this disaster had produced a *second* survivor. Someone he had brought aboard. Newspaper clippings in his memorabilia tell the story of a woman found washed ashore on an isolated atoll in the Marshall Islands several weeks later, hundreds and hundreds of miles away from the place where the ship sank. She was aboard the Ourang Medan that night. Keitz's notes confirm that. A young woman who spoke only Japanese and therefore was unable to explain to doctors in the Marshalls who she was and what happened to her. A woman heavily pregnant. Miraculously, she gave birth to healthy twin girls. Her name? Hiroko Sujihara."

"We are medical researchers. Not historians," Parks said as he shuffled through the journalists' papers, documents all written in German. "Your tale of two people's lives crossing paths in this way is just another strange coincidence in the aftermath of a war that had turned millions of people's worlds upside down."

"Still unsure?" Stephanie Dessereau unfolded a small piece of yellowed paper. "If it is relevance you seek, Dr. Parks, then if anything will bind your mystery to ours, it should be *this*."

"A telegram?"

"From Buenos Aires to the telegraph office in Dalian China," she said. "A telegram sent to Herman Keitz before the Ourang Medan set sail. It's in German and was sent unsigned. Dated December 28, 1947, it reads, 'Destroy laboratory. Seize subject. Bring her——," Dessereau paused and added emphasis, "*and her means of transport to and from Earth* to me.'"

Stephanie Dessereau handed Amare Parks a thumb-drive in a pink plastic casing. "All of my documents have been scanned into here. When I learned you were coming to Japan, I thought it best to let someone else—someone with scientific credibility and a connection with other cases like this—have a copy of my investigation. Information that sheds historical light on your studies and those of Dr. Mitomi."

"You know about my research with the Hopi Indians?"

"Yes. In my files are transcripts of what Hiroko has told me about her 'travels' and how she becomes pregnant. Dr. Parks, I've found more women like this in other parts of the world. This is so much bigger than you can imagine. After the Hopi woman, I'm sure you're beginning to imagine a lot."

Dr. Katsu Mitomi had been silent during this entire discourse, the furrow in his brow proof he was deep in thought. He uttered a low humming groan and turned towards Koko Sujihara. She had been sitting quietly, head bowed, unable to understand any of the English that had been spoken. Mitomi asked her a series of long questions. Amare Parks heard the term, '*Hoshi-ko*' mentioned several times.

Koko replied at length to Mitomi's stern questioning and ended her last response with a definitive, "*Hai*... Yes."

"What is she saying, Mitomi-san?"

"Her mother, Hiroko is one of the *Hoshi-ko*. One of the Children of the Stars."

III

LOW, slow moving mountain clouds draped the village at the foot of Mt. Norikura. Moonlight darted in and out of the trees. As the clouds rolled through the alpine forest, a strobe-like light flickered into the stable's lone bedroom.

Amare couldn't sleep, frustrated that a long journey by road—and an even longer one by air— had ended short of its destination. He was hungry for answers and a decent high protein meal. On the drive from Hamamatsu, Dr. Katsu Mitomi had discussed in great detail his previous trips to the village and his medical examinations of Hiroko Sujihara. Mitomi's research had yielded similar conclusions to that of Parks' Hopi Indian subject and her offspring. A world apart, these two mothers— chronologically aged in their eighties but looking as young as in their twenties—had defied medical science. Journalists Stephanie Dessereau and Sergio

Rancon had uncovered historical evidence as unbelievable as the medical research. And they had struck upon a theory born in the form of a yellowed telegram that if true, painted an explanation onto the canvas of the inexplicable as unbelievable as the scientific data.

Where the hell do we go from here? he thought. His anxious, restless mind turned in circles.

He heard Katsu Mitomi stirring. "Are you awake?" Amare asked.

"Hai," was the reply.

A flood of strong light illuminated the inside of the barn. The light was intense, a phosphorescent blue, not the silver of the moon. It danced in a rhythmic pulse against the bare walls.

Parks leapt out of his camp cot. "What's that?"

The light disappeared, returning darkness to the village.

A scream echoed through the air. A woman's scream.

"It came from the direction of the temple building," Mitomi said.

Parks and Mitomi scrambled to put their clothes on and rushed out of the stable. Two hundred yards away, moonlight bathed the village's temple, setting it apart from the darkness of the trees and the rooftops around it. The pair ran towards the building. A flash of blue light ripped open the celestial display above their heads. A loud boom followed, shaking the ground so hard it nearly knocked them off their feet. The light expanded into a large luminous ring, its blast-wave sending the misty clouds retreating in haste. A beam fell from the center of the ring to the ground, an intense beam of solid blue light like a giant cylinder of cobalt glass. A dark shape not unlike a human body descended rapidly through the cylinder from the heavens to the earth.

Amare Parks and Katsu Mitomi reached the evergreens on the edge of the temple's garden. The cylinder of blue light retreated into the sky. A very tall silhouette rose from the earth where it had landed and walked across the grounds, its arms long and thin. Candlelight escaped into the night as the temple's door opened. The figure bent its head under the door's high archway and went inside. The door closed. The candlelight snuffed out. Darkness.

From inside the temple, a woman's scream again cut through the still night air.

They ran through the trees into open ground, the air around them smelling like spent matches. The smell irritated their noses and traces of smoke stung their eyes. They crept carefully up to the temple's door. Amare Parks pushed on the wood and peered inside.

The interior of the temple was one large open room, its ceiling extending several stories upwards into the peak of the timber-beamed roof. In the middle of the room, candles stood on holders on either side of a circular futon where Hiroko Sujihara sat cross-legged, meditating, Buddha-like, her belly round and full. Long black hair fell by the sides of her youthful, unwrinkled face, cascading down in silky strands over a purple kimono decorated with white chrysanthemums. The loose orange sash around her waist wrapped her unborn twins in the warmth of their mother's love.

Immediately behind the futon was a huge, glowing, egg-shaped object, twenty feet high, its surface rippling with waves of blue energy. Twinkles of bright white light ascended from the top of it into the high ceiling, sparks glowing like fireflies until they faded away. To one side of the futon was a small room, candles shining through a translucent panel. Parks spotted silhouettes of two people standing over the kneeling figure of a third.

Hiroko Sujihara opened her eyes and clapped her hands. The translucent panel slid open. Two young women in cream-colored kimonos emerged from the room, holding Stephanie Dessereau in their arms. The Swiss journalist was naked, her body limp as she was dragged along by her captors towards the massive egg-shaped object.

Amare Parks tapped Mitomi on the shoulder and pointed through the doorway. His Japanese friend nodded. They flung open the door and rushed towards the helpless Dessereau.

"No!" she screamed. "Escape while you can!"

A pulse of blue energy emerged around the futon, expanding in a rippling circular pattern until it reached their feet. The energy covered the floor at shin height and danced up the sides of the walls, coating everything in an electric haze. The egg burst open and a flat beam of intense white light struck their chests, scanned their bodies and lifted them into the air. The beam prickled their skin and stiffened their arms and legs. They were unable to move.

When the glare of the scanner beam subsided, Parks and Mitomi looked down. Their frozen legs dangled above the floor but the wood beneath them had disappeared, replaced by an inky blackness that swirled in a circle like a cauldron of thick tar. Hiroko Sujihara floated in the air, the fabric of her kimono puffed out by an invisible draft. Stephanie Dessereau and the two women in kimonos hung suspended beside her like puppets on invisible strings. They pushed Dessereau towards the opened halves of the egg-shaped object, its exterior smooth but its interior as jagged as broken glass. The walls were sheathed with a crystalline material like thousands of large white diamonds. A blinking white light swirled in and out of the faceted walls then bounced across the surfaces of several large flat panels. The panels shone with a silver metallic luster.

Dessereau was sucked inside like a pin drawn to a magnet.

"My God," Parks gasped. "A spacecraft."

Inside the pod, a shadow with long thin arms and a bulbous head—its body oozing vapors as if the being was a mix of solid and gas—worked the controls. The alien's luminous skin radiated a bluish electric plasma. It had no nose or mouth just hazy bumps under its large oval eyes; eyes devoid of lashes, with black pupils as glossy as marbles. The lanky figure, nine or ten feet tall, towered over the captive Dessereau. Using a web of light beams, it attached her to one of the silver metallic panels. Dessereau went completely still, all resistance lost, the alien's net of light energy immobilizing her.

It finished its work, stepped out of the craft and turned its attention to Amare Parks. It raised its long arm. Thin, webbed fingers shot out a mist of plasma, covering Parks' head. He grimaced as a sharp pain pierced his temples. It felt as if his thoughts were being pinched into clumps and extracted through his forehead. The alien repeated the procedure with Katsu Mitomi. Blood dribbled out of Mitomi's nose.

After what seemed like an eternity while an alien being and two humans stared into each other's faces, the alien turned away from the two men, outstretched his lanky thin arms and encircled the pregnant Hiroko. She cried out, a primordial cry, blending effort and pain. The plasma from his fingers wrapped around her body until she was completely cocooned. Her screams went silent.

Its work done, the alien returned to Dessereau and the egg-shaped craft. The doors closed with a buzzing hum and as soon as they did, the roof of the temple split open with a loud snap. Shingles and timbers floated in the air like a giant jigsaw puzzle, dispersing into a spinning kaleidoscope of pieces. High in the starry vastness above the temple, a ring of blue energy ripped the heavens open. The cobalt-colored cylinder of light descended again, engulfing the spacecraft, its alien pilot and the human specimen.

In a flash—so instantaneous that time itself seemed to reverse—the pod ascended into the night sky and the roof re-assembled. The temple fell into utter darkness.

Parks felt the invisible pressure clamping his body dissolve away. His arms and legs were free to move again. The feeling of weightlessness evaporated. He fell hard with a thud to what was now a cold and very solid wooden floor. Another thump resounded beside him.

"Mitomi-san? Are you okay?"

He heard a man's groan then the gurgling cries of two babies. The yellow light from a single candle broke through the darkness. They both hobbled to their feet, their legs stiff and sore. As their eyes adjusted to the gloom, they could see the edges of the circular futon. More candles were lit and the interior brightened. Hiroko Sujihara lay prostrate on the bed, her arms flat to her sides, her face looking up into the ceiling, eyes glassy and lifeless. Two young women in cream-colored kimonos stood over the body and wept. Each held a baby wrapped in linen.

One of the pair approached Parks and Mitomi.

It was Koko.

Tears streamed down her face. "*Hoshi-ko*," Koko said, pointing to the body of their mother laying lifeless on the futon. "Her time was over," she said in Japanese as Mitomi translated. "Returned to the stars."

She extended the palm of her hand towards the other young woman holding the second child. "This is my birth sister, Etsuko."

Etsuko Sujihara stepped forward. She and Koko were identical twins.

"Our new earth sisters, Kimiko and Michiko," Koko said, rocking the baby in her arms. "These babies are *Daichi-ko*. Born like us."

"*Daichi-ko* means Children of the Great New Earth," Dr. Mitomi said.

Koko pointed up into the roof. "New *Hoshi-ko*," she said.

"Dessereau," Parks gulped. "They've taken Stephanie Dessereau to start the process again."

Koko Sujihara handed the newborn baby to her sister. Koko uttered several phrases in Japanese and Katsu Mitomi took a step back, his face creased with fright. He tugged on Parks' shirt and pulled him hard towards the door.

"Run, Parks-san! *Run!*"

The two men stumbled backwards through the doorway into the cold mountain air. Amare Parks followed Mitomi's lead as he fell from the wooden porch into the scorched garden. Adrenaline pumping through aching legs, they scrambled across the grounds until they reached the patch of evergreens. Safely away from the temple's entrance, Amare Parks spun Mitomi by the shoulders. "Mitomi-san, what did she say?"

Katsu Mitomi gasped, out of breath. "We must leave. Now. Gather whatever things we can." He pulled out his cell phone. "I'll call our driver Eito and hope he can find us." Mitomi ran his fingers through his sweaty hair. "Koko said..." He choked up, the words not forming.

"What? What did she say? Tell me, Katsu."

"She said, the time has come for the seeds of a Great New Earth to spread. Regrettably dear guests, now that you understand the future, it is time for you to die."

IV

SERGIO RANCON STRODE into the business class lounge inside Narita Airport and handed his ticket to the pretty JAL flight attendant sitting behind the reception desk.

"Your flight to Buenos Aires is on time, Mr. Rancon," she said, admiring the tight fit of his Armani suit. "We'll call you a half hour before departure."

He checked his coat and walked through the room full of plush leather armchairs, his eyes darting from side to side.

A finger tapped his shoulder. He turned around. A petite porcelain face smiled, her lips a bright red, her jet black hair cropped short in a sharp razor cut.

"There you are," Rancon said, pulling her tiny waist into his. She balanced on her tiptoes as they kissed.

She giggled. "Very nice," she said. "Hmm, I could get used to this."

"Wait a minute. You're not Sumiko. You're—"

The girl bit her lip playfully. Her butterfly lashes dipped towards the row of desks behind them. An identical young girl wearing the same clothes turned around in a swivel chair, put her hand to her mouth and giggled. The girl sprung up and wrapped her arms around Sergio's neck.

They kissed, and after their lips parted, he said, "When we get to Argentina, I'll play that same trick on you, Sumiko. You won't know it's coming. I'll make sure of that."

She laughed.

"I can't wait to meet your twin brother Paulo," Noriko Sujihara said. She winked. "If he kisses anything like you do, we'll have lots of fun."

"Business first," her twin sister Sumiko replied. "Do you have it?"

Sergio Rancon produced a pink plastic thumb-drive from his pocket.

"Did you meet at the university?" she asked.

"No. Not there. Some of the students speak English. I had to make sure he was isolated."

"What about the others?" Noriko said.

Sergio motioned with his hand from the ceiling to the floor. "When the SUV was lifted up and sent crashing to the ground, the driver was killed instantly. Mitomi was critically wounded on impact. I don't know how any of them could have survived that. But two of them did."

"Mitomi survived?" Noriko frowned. "Do we need to worry about him too?"

Sergio looked down at Sumiko's face. "You haven't told her?"

She shook her head.

"I was able to locate Mitomi, dying of his injuries not that far from the wreckage," he explained. "But Parks? Now that was the big problem. Survived both the radiation and the crash. He and Mitomi had been separated in the dense woods. Parks vanished and proved to be very resourceful. Who would have thought a tall black American would be so hard to find in this country?"

"I've been so worried about you," Sumiko said, hugging him. "It's taken you days to track him down."

"It wasn't that hard. I had Mitomi's cell phone and just waited until Parks called it. Who else could he reach out to? I told him Mitomi had been rescued and we would all meet up in Tokyo. At the train station, Parks was so happy to see me I could have told him anything. In the end, my solution to our problem worked. The stupidity of a hungry foreigner will leave only the slightest suspicion with the Japanese police. And nothing traceable to us."

Sumiko lay her head on Sergio's chest and sighed. "The more of us there are, the closer they come to finding us."

Sergio reassured her. "These deaths mean our lives are safe again."

Noriko crept closer to the pair and whispered, "It's taken too long to fix this breach. The Association will *not* be pleased."

"She's right," Sumiko added. "Next time, it will be even harder."

"Soon, there will be no more next times." Rancon looked over the girls' shoulders to the lunch buffet. He checked his watch. "I'm starving. And one thing I do know. This is definitely the last time for sushi, girls. So fill up. When we get to my hometown in Argentina, I hope you like German food."

Author's Notes—Charles A Cornell

IF YOU ENJOYED Children Of The Stars, please consider leaving a review for it and for the entire Return To Earth anthology on Amazon, even a short one. Let others know what you liked or didn't like about these stories. Your honest opinion is all we ask and would be greatly appreciated.

Writing this short story has inspired my imagination. I plan to continue exploring the mystery of the *Hoshi-ko*, the Children Of The Stars. What threats does mankind face from their descendants, the Children Of The Great New Earth and from their alien creators? Can we survive? Look for a novel series based on this short story to appear soon, available wherever books are sold.

~CAC

Gaia Returning

C.L. Roman

Sometimes the most promising path forward, is back.
—CLR

1. Pursuit

Unknown coordinates, 3089AD

The Argos shuddered, stress fractures spreading across the bridge viewscreen like spiders racing on ice. The glowing, orange edge of an unknown planet presented in the lower corner of the screen, but Captain Irina Demyanov didn't have time to look at it.

"That was way too close, Captain." Weapons officer and first mate, Sean Burke, gripped his control panel at either corner. "Another one like that and they won't need a direct hit to take us out. We'll be dead in the star-field."

Irina chewed her bottom lip for a second and then punched the comm button on the arm of her chair. "Murtagh! How many emergency shuttles does the Argos have?"

Murtagh's voice crackled back at her with more than his usual asperity. "Only one at full capacity. The others —"

"I didn't ask how many were fully functional," Irina growled. "I asked how many we have."

"Ten, Captain." The chief's words were sharp, like they'd been bitten from steel.

"They've fired again!" Sean's words ripped through the air. "Impact in forty seconds."

"Evasive action, Charon," Irina said.

The petite, blond navigations officer maneuvered the controls on her panel and the ship canted sharply to the left. A flash of light illuminated the damaged viewscreen as the missile detonated. The ship jerked, but held.

"We won't be that lucky again, Skipper," Charon said.

"That was the eighth shot in the fusillade. If I've timed it right, we have exactly six minutes while they recharge their phase cannons." Irina pressed a series of buttons on her console and the high pitched whistle of the all-call bounced along their ear drums. Leaning over the mic screen, Irina addressed the surviving crew of the crippled Argos.

"Crew of the Argos, begin evacuation protocol four. Evacuation in six minutes." She punched a button and her voice stopped echoing throughout the ship, confining itself to single person transmissions as she continued. "Manning, I need a viability report. Include the injured who have any chance of survival." She punched another button.

"Murtagh, take your best pick and prepare to receive passengers. Then get every remaining cargo skiff and escape pod, regardless of functionality, ready for launch."

Punch. "Manning. You and Sharp supervise the evacuation."

She slammed her palm on the comm button and turned to the deck crew. "Charon, can you steer this thing remotely?"

Charon shook her head. "Not with any degree of precision," she said. "The system is barely functional. I'm not even sure which star system we're in. Going into that vortex blind knocked out the entire GMS. Couple that with the damage the Vladdinians had already done..." She shrugged. "I can't manage more than a straight line without my hands on the levers."

"Can you remote detonate?" Irina ignored the disbelieving stares of her officers. Her jaw tightened as she repeated, "Can you do it?"

"Yeah," Charon said. Irina's eyes hardened and Charon swallowed before continuing. "I mean, yes, Captain. The system can do that much."

Taking in a deep breath, Irina blew it out in a gust. "Set the course straight ahead and lock it in. Then head for the escape shuttle. Once you get there, begin the destruct sequence. Burke, on me." She surged to her feet and raced for the lift.

"What are you planning, Irina?" Burke was so close she could feel his breath on the back of her neck.

"To live," she said. "Deck three," she said to the computer. When she received no response she entered the code for her cabin manually. The lift jerked into motion.

"By destroying the Argos?"

"By escaping from the Argos before she collapses and kills us all." The lift doors opened a hand span and stopped.

"Power's low," Sean guessed. Working together, they pushed the doors the rest of the way open. "We'll be down to life support in half an hour."

Irina sprinted down the hallway, talking in short bursts over her shoulder. "If we stay on the Argos, we'll be moon dust in half an hour. Or cooling our badly burned heels in a Vladdinian torture cell." She stopped outside her cabin and looked at him. "I don't think either one of those is an attractive option." She slapped her hand against the access panel and the doors opened sluggishly.

"So your other option is to destroy our ship?" He shook his head. "We don't have to do this. We can —"

"What, Sean?" She faced him, her features tight with anger. "What can we do? The Vladdinians are one of the most violent, vengeful races in the known universe and you stole their crown jewels. They aren't likely to forgive and forget."

He backed up a step, holding up placating hands. "To be fair, the jewels in that crown are Earthen rubies, the only ones known to exist. As a human, that makes them mine by..." Seeing her expression, he trailed off.

She entered her chambers and hefted the small jewel chest from her desk. "Get the scepter and the orb." He hesitated and she lost her patience. "Now," she shouted.

"Fine!" He trudged down the hall to his own quarters and returned a few moments later with a long staff of silver, topped with a fire opal the size of his fist. In his other hand he held the stone's twin, banded in gold, encrusted with rubies and emeralds, all of Earthen origin, if the stories were to be believed. While she watched, he slid the orb and the staff into a slim velvet cover. Over his shoulder he carried a packed bag.

"What else are you bringing? We won't have room for non-essentials."

Self-destruct sequence activated, preparing for countdown. All personnel to bay seven for evacuation.

The mechanical voice of the ship's computer system stopped her and a lump rose in her throat. She shoved the chest into Sean's arms. With hasty precision, she threw her personal possessions into a canvas pack. It was less than half the size of her first mate's bag, but it held every item she considered essential to her life.

"Let's go," she said.

Sean straightened abruptly and tugged the strings tight on the staff's velvet cover. Without a word, he followed her down the corridor.

Slapping at the communicator on her wrist, Irina hailed her navigator. "Charon, we have four minutes and thirty seconds before the Vladdinians are recharged. Set the detonation for minus four minutes and twenty seconds."

"Aye, Skipper."

"Murtagh, you got those boats ready yet?"

"Nearly there, Captain. The androids almost blew their fuses, but they got it done. Another fifteen, twenty minutes and it'll be done."

"We don't have that long. Set the emergency blast doors for minus three minutes and get your ass to the escape pod."

"But the droids —"

"Leave them, Murtagh. That's an order. Manning, report."

The dispirited voice of her chief medical officer came back to her. "It isn't good, Captain. Out of a fifty-man crew, we have twenty-three dead, seventeen wounded, four unaccounted for and six uninjured and ambulatory."

Irina's mouth stiffened around the words she knew she had to say next. "Get as many of the injured as you think we can take care of to the escape shuttle. Bring whatever supplies you can lay your hands on, but don't linger."

"Captain, if we move them, most of the wounded will die. They need care. We can't —"

"We don't have a choice. Take the ones you can save, Manning," Irina said, and her voice broke. "Leave the rest."

"I can't do that," Manning shouted. "I won't!"

Irina tapped another button on her wrist-unit. "Sharp?"

"Captain?" For the first time in Irina's memory, the AI6 medi-unit's dulcet tones offered no comfort.

"Protocol six," Irina said.

"Understood, Captain. And may I say, it has been a pleasure serving with you."

Irina's throat tightened. "I hope that it will continue to be."

"Protocol six does not allow for non-biologics," Sharp said.

"No, but it does allow for essential personnel," Irina said. "So we will do our best to keep you with us. Now, make sure Manning gets on that pod."

"Yes, Skipper. Have no concern."

Irina shoved her grief aside and held out her bag to Sean. "Give me the chest and the staff."

"What? No, I can carry them."

She rested her hand lightly on the electron blaster at her hip. "I don't doubt it. Hand them over."

Detonation in four minutes twenty seconds.

Sean's head jerked up at the announcement and he shoved the jewels into her arms with a disgusted sigh. "I don't know why you don't trust me. I could have —"

"I know what you could have done. Get down to the boat. I'll meet you there." She turned and ran, the staff slung over her shoulder, the chest banging awkwardly against her torso.

"Where are you going?" He shouted, but she didn't answer.

The ship convulsed. Hairline cracks sprinted down from the ceiling and up from the wall, turning the walls into a monotone mosaic. Bits of metal clattered to the deck and smoke filtered from the air vents.

"Argos," Sean said. "Damage report."

The ship's voice funneled through his earpiece. *Reporting: Shields non-functional, weapons systems at forty percent. Life support at sixty percent and falling. Complete failure anticipated in fourteen minutes. Command system compromised.*

The all-call intoned, *Detonation in four minutes.*

Hoisting his bag and Irina's, Sean ran for the escape shuttle.

IRINA ROUNDED the curve in the corridor and slowed to a fast walk. The chest was heavier than she had thought, and the scepter kept banging against the back of her knees, threatening to trip her up.

The door to the cargo bay slid open before she reached it and Murtagh faced her from its squared arch. His shock of wiry red hair stood up from his head in a fiery halo. Meaty and barrel chested, Murtagh made a good friend and a bad enemy. His current expression wasn't hopeful.

"I don't know what you're planning, Captain, but we need those droids. You can't just leave them."

"I'm out of options. The shuttle only holds twenty passengers, and we have twenty-three. There's no room."

Detonation in three minutes, fifty seconds.

Murtagh cast a grim look upward. "Won't matter anyway. The Vladdinians aren't going to let us go."

"Not so long as they think we're still breathing," she agreed. "So we need to die."

His eyebrows arched like irritated caterpillars over his blue eyes. "Really now? And how do we survive that?"

"Do you have those boats ready?"

"As ready as they're going to get. Half of them don't run at all and the rest are on half power."

She sucked in a breath. "That will have to be enough." She pushed past him into the cargo bay and headed for the nearest running shuttle. Its beacons were dim, but a hum rising from the engines indicated it had rudimentary power.

She shoved the jewel chest inside. "Send this one out first. Set the coordinates at right angles to the Vladdinian trajectory, away from the planet we just passed."

Murtagh complied. A glint of hope shone in his eyes as he watched her.

Irina rushed to a second ship, also running on half power, and tossed the bag containing the scepter and orb inside. Slamming the door shut, she turned to Murtagh. "Send that one straight for deep space."

"They'll be able to tell they aren't manned."

She shrugged. "No help for it. I'm not wasting personnel to make this look good."

"I think I can give us at least one more layer of illusion." He hit a few buttons on his hand-held control pad and several H2 androids boarded the shuttles. In a moment, Irina could see two of them at the controls through the front view-ports.

"They have elementary bio pulses," he said. "Similar enough that, if the Vladdinians are more focused on the jewels than on survivors, they might be fooled. At least temporarily. That's if they know these two scows have the jewels on board."

"They must have some way of tracking the jewels, a transmitter or something. Otherwise, they'd never have found us once we passed through the vortex. Our only hope is that they see the ship blow up, assume we're dead, and that they want the jewels more than they want verification." She moved toward the door.

Detonation in three minutes, twenty seconds.

Murtagh took one last look at the two vessels, and followed her into the passageway before sealing the cargo bay.

"Set the launch for one minute from now," Irina said. The pair jogged down the corridor, Murtagh tapping madly at his control pad, cursing under his breath.

As they rounded the corner into the bay four, Irina saw Andrina Sharp coming down the corridor. In her arms the medi-droid carried the tall, thin form of Dr. Terrance Manning like a sleeping baby. In other circumstances, the sight would have made her laugh, but at the moment, Irina found no humor in it.

"Put him in one of the bunks, Andrina."

"Yes, Captain."

Sharp glided into the cargo bay and up the loading ramp onto the shuttle. Irina and Murtagh were right behind her.

Sean confronted Irina as she stepped off the gangway into the ship. "What did you do with the jewels?"

"Sent them back where they belong." She pushed past him and headed for the bridge.

"You what?" He tagged along behind her, hands gesticulating, mouth working. "You had no right to do that. Do you have any idea what those jewels were worth?"

She rounded on him. "Our lives, apparently." She continued; advancing a step for every one he took in retreat. "What did you think was going to happen when they found out you'd stolen them? In what universe was it even a possibility that they wouldn't know it was you? You didn't even take the time to knock out the video surveillance. You pulled the job in broad daylight, for pity's sake!"

She punched him in the chest and he tottered backward, caught his knees on a bio-seat and sat down. The seat wheezed in protest as his full weight crashed onto it.

"Ok, so things didn't go exactly according to my plan, but —"

"Your plan?" Her voice softened dangerously. "I have a plan, too. You are relieved of duty."

His mouth dropped open and his eyes widened, but she gave him no chance to speak.

"And you'd better keep your mouth shut before I decide to leave you in the cargo bay, trussed for Vladdinian bar-b-que."

Cargo bay four ejecting in ten, nine... Detonation in two minutes, forty seconds. Eight...

"Andrina, is everyone on board?"

"Yes, Captain. There were only —"

But Irina was already turning away. Taking her seat in the pilot's chair and adjusting the straps, she said, "Charon, take the co-pilot's position. We'll time it with the ejection, but once we're clear, haul ass. We need to be around the curve of that planet before they think to look for us."

"And before the Argos explodes," Charon muttered.

The corner of Irina's mouth twitched. "That's the idea, yes." Tapping the comm-link on the arm of her chair, she activated the ship's all-call. "Strap in, people. Things are going to get exciting here in a few seconds. Murtagh, Andrina, see to it that the wounded are secured."

"Yes, Captain."

Five, four, three, two, one. Ejection commencing.

"Go, go, go!" Irina shouted the command and Charon fired the thrusters. The shuttle rocketed out of the docking bay toward the cargo doors, which were still in the process of opening.

"The doors," Charon shouted. The cargo portal ground to a halt, the doors only half open.

"I see 'em," Irina said. She thumbed the control button and twisted the yoke left. The ship jumped vertical and pitched onto its side as it shot forward.

Detonation in two minutes, twenty seconds.

The shuttle burst through the half open doors of the crippled Argos, the great, orange planet on her left and the wide ranging star-field to her right.

"Take the helm and keep in the Argos's shadow," Irina said. "We let them see us now, we're dead."

"Aye, Skipper," Charon said.

Irina took a deep breath. "Ninety degree turn on my mark."

"On your mark, aye," Charon responded. Two minutes later, it was time to roll the dice.

"Mark!" Irina said. The shuttle pivoted left as the Argos erupted into silent, white light.

INSIDE THE VLADDINIAN SHIP, Zahkvat, four vaguely humanoid personnel manned their stations in a caliginous atmosphere. The dull illumination cast by the navigation consoles cast a sickly glow over the crew's lightly furred green skin. Their captain, Krell Kravvin, slouched in his chair, drumming long black claws on the arms, his ill humor apparent in his slitted eyes and lipless mouth.

"Closing on the Argos now, Captain Kravvin," Trag said. "They are dead in the star field. Life support reading at fifty percent capacity and falling."

"How long until the phase cannon is fully charged?" Kravvin asked.

Trag checked the red numbers on his data screen. "One minute, thirty seconds. The photon guns are available."

"No, the photon guns will only slow them. I want to annihilate them."

"Activity below, Captain." Zhen, the only female officer on the deck, made the notification over her shoulder and turned back to her console.

The captain leaned forward in the command chair, staring through the viewscreen at the wounded star-beast the Argos had become. There was a flash as the cargo doors blew outward, followed by a steady stream of limping, drifting skiffs and shuttles. Several moved off in aimless, haphazard spirals, clearly meant as distractions. But two appeared to have actual destinations.

"Identify," the captain snapped.

A red-line overlay popped up on the viewscreen. Each fleeing boat was labeled with a reference number. The two he had noticed in particular were labeled A20 and A24.

"Scan A20 and A24."

"Compliance," Zhen said. Immediately, a round blue dot lit up on each ship.

"The jewels are there," Trag said.

"Or they found the transmitters and are sending us one direction while they flee in another." First officer Marn spoke for the first time. "Scan all ships for human bio-form signatures."

"Compliance," Zhen said. Multiple yellow blips glowed on each ship.

"So few?" Marn turned to his captain. "According to the manifest they registered at Melino Spaceport on Vladdin, the Argos has a compliment of fifty crewmen. Even given the damage they have sustained, there should be more survivors."

"The Argos registers additional human bio-forms," Trag said. "But they are pirates, Sir, and unlikely to have an honor code that would prevent them from abandoning their wounded."

"So, is their hope that we will be appeased if they return our property, or simply that we will be distracted long enough for them to limp away?" Kravvin sat back in his chair, one black-taloned paw cupping his chin.

No one answered.

After a moment, Kravvin sat forward again. "We cannot chance losing the jewels a second time. Pursue the small craft, lock on and bring them aboard."

"Compliance," Trag said. The Zahkvat pitched four degrees right and accelerated after the first of the two shuttles.

"The humans will escape," Marn observed.

"Doubtful. The Argos is crippled. It isn't going anywhere very fast."

"And if it is only the transmitters aboard these boats?" Marn asked.

A soft growl escaped between Kravvin's short, sharp tusks. "Then their punishment will take much longer when we catch them," he said, and Marn nodded, satisfied.

"Captain." Zhen looked up from her console, staring at the human ship. "There appears to be a shuttle —"

The Argos exploded into a hundred thousand red and blue fragments of superheated metal. White light filled the screen, blacking it out for several seconds while the photon receptors recovered. The light sensitive eyes of the night dwelling Vladdinians were not so lucky.

The screams of his crew vibrated off the deck plates, thrumming along Kravvin's auditory membranes like granite scraping against glass. He clapped his paws against the sides of his head and howled for silence. "Stop your screaming and report!" He shouted.

Zhen pulled herself back into her seat, red tears streaming from her eyes. "Zhen Zallov, sight wounded, but recovering."

Trag straightened in his chair. "Trag Travgar, recovered."

"Marn Drossev, recovering."

"See to Zhen's eyes, Marn," Kravvin said.

"Aye, Sir." He pulled a medi-kit from his belt and cupped it over each of her eyes in turn.

"Zhen, you saw a shuttle?" Kravvin rubbed at his throbbing eyes.

"I think so, Captain."

"Trag?"

"Checking, Captain. I'm not seeing anything, but an explosion like that would likely have taken a small escape shuttle with it, especially if it were newly launched."

"Marn, is she fit for duty?"

Marn turned to speak, but Zhen beat him to it. "I am, Sir. Your orders?"

"Get after those other pods. We'll do a thorough search of the wreckage once we have the jewels in hand."

"Aye, Sir." Zhen adjusted the controls and the ship made a graceful curvet, shooting away from the destroyed Argos in search of her forbidden cargo.

2. Escape

THE TINY SHUTTLE juddered and quaked, her engines straining to outrun the cataclysm.

"Hold her together, Charon. We need to get to the dark side of that planet before the Vladdinians recover."

Charon adjusted a bank of controls and the shuttle's flight smoothed marginally.

"You'll shake her apart, you keep this up." Murtagh stumped through the door into the passageway. "I'll go down to the engine bay, see if I can hold her together. You're going to want to think about a landing strip, Skipper, or it's all a moot point anyway." His footsteps echoed back to them and then were gone.

"Charon, call up the shuttle's GMS, see where we are and what's close," Irina said.

"We're close to nothing," Burke said. Tucking his pack underneath, he dropped into an empty bio-chair. "You've killed us, is what you've done."

Sharp straightened from checking Manning's vitals. "Would you like me to take him into custody, Captain?" She asked.

"On what charge?" Burke spouted. "Besides, you aren't an MP. You don't have the authority to arrest a ranking officer. I ought to cut your circuits for that threat."

"It is no threat, Mr. Burke. Given your statement, and the fact that you appear to believe it, I consider you delusional, no doubt attempting to escape responsibility for your actions by projecting the blame onto Captain Demyanov. This is clearly a symptom of psychosis. You may even be a sociopath, but I will have to conduct certain tests in order to be sure. Captain?" The AI unit faced Irina so that Burke could not see the sardonic tilt to her features.

A grin tugged at Irina's lips, but the weight of their situation flattened them again. "No, I need you to take care of the wounded."

She looked at what remained of her crew, her gaze sharpening on Michael Walker, a new hire with black hair and a wrestler's build. A cut on his cheek seeped blood, but sluggishly, already scabbing over. He favored his left leg when he walked, but appeared otherwise uninjured. She resisted the urge to glance at Burke and did some quick mental calculations.

In his short time aboard, she'd found Walker capable and level-headed. Her relationship with Burke was over; that much was a foregone conclusion after this latest stunt. It wouldn't hurt to have someone step into his place at the weapons console.

"Walker. Take Mr. Burke to the brig and —"

"What! You're locking me up?" Burke shot to his feet, fists clenched.

Irina pivoted, drawing her blaster as she turned. She felt movement beside and behind her and was somehow unsurprised to find that Walker also had a weapon in his hand. A frisson of shock went through her midsection to see Charon aiming a blaster at Burke as well. The tiny navigations officer looked as if the weight of the gun would topple her, but her stance was steady, her eyes cold.

"You bitch," Burke spat, but there was little else he could do, unarmed and staring down the firing cylinders of three blasters.

"You'll want to speak to the captain with a little more respect, Mr. Burke. Or will I need to teach you some manners?" Walker tilted his head to one side and waited for Burke's reply.

"Bring it on, Walker. We'll see which of us walks away."

"No, you won't," Irina said, her voice rising with each word. "You'll put your pecker back in your pants before I pinch it off. Go with Walker until I can figure out what to do with you."

Burke's sharp gaze softened into a practiced look of hurt confusion. "Irina, honey, you know this isn't my fault. I'm sorry for what I said. I lost my head. You need me to help you figure this out."

The sharp taste of bile piled onto the back of Irina's tongue. She holstered her blaster and dropped into the pilot's chair. "Get him off my bridge, Walker. Make sure his holding-cell has water in it and then get back up here. I may need a weapons officer sooner rather than later."

Burke's face hardened, and his fingers curled into his palms. "You'll regret this, Irina."

Walker grabbed him by the scruff of the neck and hustled him into the passage.

Irina hunched into her chair and studied the three dimensional star chart hovering in front of her. "I already do," she muttered. Looking up at Sharp, she said, "There isn't a full sickbay on a shuttle this size, so you'll set up a triage unit wherever you can. How long before Manning wakes up?"

"Another fifteen minutes, unless I give him a countering medication. Triage placement isn't a problem, but we could use some assistance with the wounded."

"All right." Irina scanned the personnel remaining to her. Ensign Leah Jacobs and Chief Rachel Lamesh stood talking quietly near the door. Neither appeared badly injured. "Jacobs, Lamesh, you'll go with Sharp and assist with the wounded." The women nodded and Irina turned back to Andrina. "Take Manning down and wake him up. You're going to need his help, but it's probably best if he doesn't see me right away. He'll know I —" she broke off, catching her bottom lip between her teeth.

"You did what was necessary, Captain. I brought everyone aboard who had a chance of survival," Sharp said.

Irina took a long look at her unconscious chief medical officer. "He won't see it that way. He would have tried to bring them all."

"Or stayed with those who couldn't travel," Sharp said. "And died with them. Either way, we never would have made it in time. You made the only responsible choice." Hoisting Manning from the chair, she curled her fingers at the women and they followed her from the bridge.

Charon sank into the chair next to Irina and adjusted several controls. "What do we do next, Captain?" She asked.

"First, we figure out where we are." She focused on the star-chart, frowning. "This system looks familiar. Where..." She trailed off, her mouth dropping into a surprised, pink oval.

Eight planets pursued varying orbits around a G2V, or yellow dwarf, star. One of the planets had a shelf of rings in its orbital plane. Another had a collection of sixty some-odd moons circling it. The chart showed the ship's position in the shadow of an orange and yellow planet. The next closest was blue-green with ribbons of white encircling it, and a single moon. "No. No way."

Startled, Charon leaned over and read the galactic designation on the statistical display. "Helios Eight?"

"Helios Eight. Yeah. Charon, you are either spectacularly lucky, or completely cursed. You brought us to the only galaxy in the universe that might be willing to hide us from the Vladdinians." She paused and gave Charon a green look. "If the inhabitants don't kill us themselves, that is."

Charon caught her bottom lip between her teeth and focused on the star map. "Vladdinians to the left of me, aliens to right..." she mumbled.

"What?" Irina glanced at the viewscreen in alarm.

"Nothing, nothing," Charon assured her. "Just my take on an archaic musical selection. Ancient Earth music is a hobby of mine."

"All right," Irina said. "So, you are my new first mate, but I don't have another navigations officer, so you'll have to work double-duty until we can get someone dialed in."

Charon's hands stilled for an instant over the controls before she continued entering co-ordinates. "Understood," she said. Entering the last set of numbers, she sat back and lifted her eyes to meet Irina's. "I won't let you down, Skipper."

"If I thought that was a possibility, I wouldn't have promoted you. Chart the shortest course to Gaia." At Charon's uncomprehending look, she sighed. "Mother and her clandestine agreements..." She eyed Charon for a moment before continuing.

"All right. Here's the deal." She pointed at the chart. "See the third planet there?" Charon nodded and Irina continued. "That's Gaia. Just one short hop away and pretty much our only hope of reaching planet-fall before our fuel cells dry up."

"It says HM3, not Gaia."

Irina nodded. "Mapped, but not formally named, indicating an untenable environment for all life-forms." She folded her arms across her chest and stared at the chart. "That was at the inhabitants', ummm, well I suppose that technically it was a request, though from what I was told it was more of a demand."

"Inhabitants?" Charon stared at Irina as if she'd suddenly sprouted wings and a tail. "If it had inhabitants, it has to be named, right?"

Irina's mouth tightened. "Didn't I just explain that?"

"Not really." At Irina's frown, she held up her hands in a calming gesture. "Ok, how do you know all this?"

"'All this?' I gave you one piece of information."

"Which is clearly only a fraction of what you know about this place. I don't like going in blind, Captain. It didn't turn out so well the last time I did it."

Irina winced. It had been her command that had sent them plummeting through the interstellar vortex without plotting a course first. It had been their only chance, but it had landed them here, rapidly running out of options.

"It's a long story, Charon," she said finally. "And it isn't mine to tell. Gaia is our only hope. This crate is not going to make a vortex leap without a major refit, so we can't go back. And if the Vladdinians find us out here, unarmed and unable to outrun them, we're dinner meat."

Silence stretched between them, hard and thin.

"Can you get us there?" Irina asked. "Or do I need to find a new first mate?"

Charon took a deep breath. "I can get us there if, and it's a big if, the terbium drive unit is still working on this shuttle. It would take us at least three months on fusion power."

Irina shook her head. "Stores won't last that long, even if the emergency core would stand the strain of prolonged use."

"Exactly." Charon tapped the comm button on her terminal. "Murtagh, what is the status on the terbium drive?"

His voice crackled with irritation as he answered. "It's bollocks is what it is. Damn Vladdinians dropped a deck plate on the array. Why?"

"Because I like breathing and we can't afford to hang around testing the Vladdinians sense of mercy," Irina broke in. "Can you get it up and running or not?"

Muffled curses filtered through the panel, followed by a moment of silence. "Give me half an hour. I'll see what I can do." A sharp click signaled the end of his communication.

Charon turned back and began coaxing the controls into new

positions. The shuttle engines groaned and a larger slice of the golden planet flooded the viewscreen with reflected orange light.

"What are you doing?" Irina asked.

"Putting more of Goldy here between us and the Vladdinians."

"Venus," Irina muttered absently.

"What?" Charon asked, frowning.

"The planet is called Venus." Irina sat back and watched the N class sphere slide along their port side.

Lips pressed into a thin line, Charon continued pushing the shuttle along until Venus filled half the screen, completely shielding them from any vessel coming from the other side. "So, the plan is to hide on the dark side of Venus until Murtagh can fix the terbium array, then run like hell for Gaia and hope the Gaians don't murder us. Is that it?"

"You have something better in mind?" Irina asked.

Charon turned back to her controls. "Nope, just clarifying."

"Captain?" Murtagh's gruff tones broke in. "The array wasn't in great shape, but I got it running. You aren't thinking of jumping through a vortex, are you?"

"No. How much can we push it?" Irina asked.

"Moderate speed for quite a while. Top speed for thirty minutes, maybe, if the celestial beings are benevolent and Lady Luck smiles especially wide. Where're we headed?"

"Coordinates on your screen now," Charon said, then tapped the mute button. "We are going to need every minute of that thirty, Captain. Long range scanners just picked up the Zahkvat. No indications that they've noticed us yet, but if we don't get out of here, they will."

Irina tapped the intercom. "Murtagh? I'm going to need that top speed. We ready to go?"

"As ready as we're going to get, Captain. You sure about this planet?"

"That is the million ducat question, isn't it? Can't stay here. Pour the light into it, let's move."

"Aye, aye, Skipper."

A shuddering whine filled the bridge and the bulkhead trembled as the shuttle picked up speed. Irina and Charon braced in their seats as the little vessel shot through space. Venus' orange glow faded quickly and the blue/green speck in the distance grew, breath by breath.

GAIA FLOATED beneath them as the shuttle maneuvered into a shaky orbit around the blue planet. White swirls of cloud vapor curled over the blue-green surface, riveting the crew's attention.

Irina and Charon made adjustments to their course while waiting for Lamech and Jacobs to return from the make-shift sick-bay. Murtagh and Walker stood mute, awestruck by the beauty unfolding below them. The electronic swish of the bridge doors announced the arrival of the other crew members just as Walker stirred himself.

"It isn't possible that this planet has gone unrecognized. This entire galaxy was charted twenty or thirty years ago," he said.

"Twenty-eight years ago, to be exact," Irina said. "By my mother and her crew."

The others stared at her, but she refused to supply details beyond what was absolutely necessary.

"The planet below is inhabited. The indigenous population is extremely protective of their home and may not look kindly on our dropping in." Irina rotated her hands, causing the bones of her wrists to crack. "They are not completely unreasonable, however, and if we explain ourselves to their satisfaction, I have no doubt that they will help us."

"Pardon my saying so, Captain, but your words and your tone aren't speaking the same message." The comment came from Ensign Leah Jacobs.

Tall and slender, she had wound her long, blond hair into an intricate chignon. There was a bruise on her cheek, but she seemed otherwise unhurt.

Her companion, Senior Chief Rachel Lamech, was a curvy young woman sporting a cap of short, black curls. Opposites in many ways, their crystalline blue eyes, and a distinct similarity of movement marked them as connected.

Irina folded her arms over her chest. "Is there a question in there somewhere, Ensign Jacobs?"

"There is," Chief Lamech interjected. "We need to know that this is a safe option."

"There are no safe options at this point, Chief." Irina's lips settled into a grim line. "There are only higher and lower probabilities of escape."

"The captain is right," Murtagh put in. "We can't stay up here. Even if the engines would sustain a prolonged orbit, which they won't, we don't have the stores."

"Not to mention the likelihood that the Vladdinians will be on our tail just as soon as they finish retrieving the royal googahs," Walker said.

"I appreciate your support, gentlemen." Irina shot Lamesh a hard look and settled into the captain's chair. "But this isn't open for debate. Prepare for landing, Charon. And you might as well start training Jacobs on the controls. She's our new navigations officer."

Surprise lit the statuesque blonde's cool gaze, but she settled into the second chair without hesitation.

"Murtagh, engine status," Irina said.

"The drive is near shot, Captain," Murtagh said. "We'll need to replenish the arrays before we can use light speed again, let alone jump the vortex."

"Right then. You and the chief head down to engineering. Figure out what we're going to need to bring the terbium drive back to full capacity."

"Aye, Captain. Let's go, Lamech." The pair exited the bridge.

"Walker, start a scan of the planet's resources. It will be best if we can land close to the supplies we need to repair the ship. With any luck at all, we can get what we need, effect repairs, and be gone before..."

Walker waited. When she didn't continue, his brow furrowed, but he sat down. "Scanning aye," he responded. His fingers danced over the buttons and levers on his console as he studied the multi-colored readout. "It appears that there is a strong concentration of gadolignin at 59.4285 degrees North, 18.3349 degrees East."

"We can use that to generate terbium, right?" Charon asked.

"Assuming the processing unit on board still works, yes," Walker replied.

"You have your coordinates, Charon. Set her down easy." Irina stood up and headed for the exit. She leaned down and grabbed Burke's abandoned pack on the way out.

"Captain?" Charon craned her neck to watch Irina go. "You don't want to handle the landing?"

"No, I have faith in you." Irina gave the pack a shake, felt the weight of its contents. "I have to see a man about an orb. And possibly murder him with it."

The walk to the shuttle's tiny excuse for a brig, a three-sided room with a fourth wall comprised of neon green laser bars, was a short one. Burke sat on the cell's only bench, head drooping, nursing a nasty looking burn on the back of one hand.

"You weren't actually stupid enough to test the bars, were you?" She asked. Her voice sounded tired, even to her own ears. She set the pack on the floor, crouched next to it and toyed with the zipper, all the while staring at him, waiting for him to raise his face to meet her gaze.

He looked up, but his eyes rose no further than the touch of her fingers on the pack closure. "That doesn't belong to you. Stay out of it."

"For a man I've seen naked any number of times, you're awfully private all of sudden. What's in here?"

"None of your business. And it's better for you that you don't know anyway."

"That's what I like about you, Burke. Always looking out for my best interests. Except that you're not." She pulled the zipper open and bared the pack's contents. "Are you?"

Twin fire opals gleamed inside the bag's black depths, scattering light and betrayal into her face.

"You didn't really expect me to send gems like that back to the

Vladdinians, did you? Do you have any idea what these will bring on the open market? We'll be rich," he said.

"'We' will likely be dead within the next twenty four hours, thanks to you. The only chance we had of escape was to give back the opals."

"They'd have chased us anyway."

She gave him a flat-eyed stare. "Not if they thought we were dead, a possibility you have eliminated."

He tried the crooked, charming smile she'd always loved. "Come on now, babe. It's not so bad. You slipped us behind that planet so neat, so quick, there's no way they saw us. And now I'm guessing, we've left sensor range completely. They'll think we blew up. Even if they do come looking, they'll never find us now."

"I'm not your 'babe' anymore." She closed up the pack and swung it over her shoulder. "In case you missed it that ended when I found out you'd stolen the jewels even though we agreed it was too risky."

He sat back on the bench, stretching his long legs in front of him and cupping his hands behind his head. "I'm a pirate, babe. What did you expect," he said with a grin.

"So am I, the difference being I'm not a stupid one," she said, and the grin faded from his lips. "And you are shortly going to be a dead one."

Color fled out of his cheeks and his eyes grew round. "You wouldn't..."

"Maybe not. But if the Vladdinians do come calling, it's your hide I'll hand them. Whether you're alive and wriggling inside it when I do is entirely dependent on your behavior between now and then."

Irina spun on her heel and marched up the hall, leaving Burke shouting threats and supplications behind her. Stopping in the pilot's berth, she stowed the pack under her bunk. Pushing the bulky package far into the rear corner, she locked the storage bin and pocketed the key.

On her way back to the bridge, she considered their odds. If the

Vladdinians hadn't seen them turn the corner of Venus, they might have a chance. If the little shuttle had been seen...

Entering Gaian atmosphere in ten, nine, eight... The ship's computer interrupted her thoughts and she picked up the pace, entering the bridge at a trot.

"Status?" she asked as she sat down.

"Entering the atmosphere and switching to manual control in two, one, go," Charon said.

"Exterior temperature holding at 1650 degrees, interior temperature is sixty-eight degrees, life support optimal," Walker said. "Shields distressed but holding for the moment."

A slight frown creased Irina's forehead. "Adjust angle of descent to compensate."

"Adjusting, aye," Charon said.

Irina turned to Walker. "Watch those shields. We don't need to cook the Vladdinian's food for them."

"Aye, Captain. The adjustment has successfully reduced friction, but it will put us off our target."

"By how much?"

"Calculating now," Charon said. After a moment, she looked up from her readouts. "Our new landing area will be 30.3322 degrees North by 81.6557 degrees West."

"Scan the region as we get closer," Irina said to Walker. "See if there are any usable fuels in the area. If there are, we'll set down there. If not, we'll head for the original destination."

"Acknowledged, Captain." Walker turned back to his screens and Irina concentrated on finding a suitable landing point.

3. Refuge

LEAF GREEN LIGHT played along the cavern walls, casting verdant shadows across the curved ceiling. Brilliant round stones studded the rock in a multi-armed spiral. Brigid passed a loving palm over the nearest one, and frowned at the two empty spaces where two had been removed.

So long ago, but the wounds in the wall still felt fresh. "They are coming," Brigid said, and brushed her long, red braid over her shoulder.

"Yes." Just the one word from a disembodied voice. Gaia seldom manifested physically these days. The melodic timbre of the voice should have comforted, but instead raised the small hairs on the back of the seer's neck.

"What shall we do with them? We promised retribution if they ever returned." Brigid pulled her braid back to the front and toyed with the bound end.

"A foolish promise," Gaia said.

"It was made to protect you."

"Was it?" Amusement danced along the question. "And do you still imagine, sweet Brigid, that it is I who need protecting?"

A delicate flush swept Brigid's fair cheeks, and her blue eyes sparked with temper. "I am your priestess. It is my job -"

"To serve. Yes, and you do serve, admirably. Both as clan chief and as priestess, though why the people insist on calling you that is still a puzzle to me. I am no goddess."

"The old ones called you such, and you never protested."

"Did they? It becomes difficult to recall."

Brigid gave her braid another tug. "Nonsense. Your memory is as sound as it is long. You are avoiding my question; what shall we do with the humans?"

"I will guide the ship in safely. You will bring the survivors to me, each one. And I will decide."

Brigid's hand tightened on the red braid. "Bring them here? To your cavern? Why?" She paced up and down the sandy floor, waiting for the answer, her feet sending up sparse clouds of iridescent dust as she moved. "Last time we brought foreigners here, it resulted in tragedy." She glanced at the ugly holes in the wall. "Are you sure?"

"I am certain," Gaia said. "Bring the prisoner first, then the others, and the captain last. And see to it she brings the treasure."

Brigid froze, her head whipping up from her contemplation of her own feet. "Treasure?"

The light in the cavern grew, dazzling Brigid's eyes, and joy pulsed through Gaia's words. "Yes, this human is bringing my children home."

"THERE, Captain. A clearing in the vegetation." Charon's voice trembled with strain. The land seventeen kilometers below them was heavily forested and dotted with lakes and streams. Finding an area of open land big enough to set the ship down had taken most of the last hour.

"And not an instant too soon," Murtagh grumbled over the intercom. "Fusion engines are nearly exhausted. We wait much longer and we'd have to refuel just to launch again."

"Understood, Murtagh," Irina said. "Prepare for landing. Let's hope that power source Walker found is near the surface. The Gaians aren't going to be happy if we have to start digging."

Fusion drive incapacitated. Prepare for emergency landing. The computer's calm announcement sent a shockwave through the inhabitants of the shuttle.

Alarms blared and red light flooded the bridge. A steady stream of curses carried through the intercom from engineering. Charon's knuckles whitened on the stick, pulling hard to keep it aligned with their landing path.

"Murtagh," Irina barked. "What's going on?"

"Fusion drives just crapped out. I'm trying restart the bloody thing. Give me a minute!"

"We don't have a minute," Charon yelled. "Velocity at four hundred kph and increasing."

"Murtagh, we need that drive back up," Irina said, hauling on the yoke, the tendons in her arms standing in agonized tension.

"No go, Captain. The fuel is there, but it's not entering the reaction chamber." Murtagh's voice cracked mid-sentence.

"Velocity five hundred kph," Charon said.

"Walker, any ideas?" Irina threw a desperate glance at the weapons officer and he shook his head.

"We can try aiming the phase guns forward. Fired continuously, it might slow us down."

"And it will make the Gaian's think we are attacking them," Irina said. "Are you out of your mind?"

"Six hundred kph," Charon said. "We hit at this speed and there won't be enough left of us to care what the Gaians think."

Impact in thirty-three seconds. Advise that all personnel abandon ship.

"In what?" Walker shouted. "This is an escape shuttle, you idiot."

With a massive groan, the ship slowed as if it had plowed into a giant pillow. Charon and Irina were thrown over their control panels and Walker slid across the deck, slamming into the bulkhead with a dull thud.

"What the hell just happened?" Irina asked. "Walker, report!"

"I'm fine," he said, cradling his left arm in his right as he stumbled to his feet and resumed his station.

Thumbing a button on the console, Irina said, "Sharp, get up here. Walker's hurt. Charon? Report."

Charon's fingers beat a frantic tattoo on her console. "Velocity... three hundred fifty-four kph, altitude dropping by eight kph. Normal landing speed, Captain. What the f—"

"Murtagh," Irina said. "Report!"

"Engines still cold, Captain. But my readout says the same as Charon's. Something has us and is pulling us in."

"Welcome, humans." The voice was melodic, arresting. Every eye tracked to its source.

Standing in front of the viewscreen was a golden-haired woman, her skin deeply tanned, but unlined and supple. Her sleeveless green robe was belted at the waist with links of silver and her hair was bound with amber beads. She appeared to be about twenty years of age, but her eyes, gray as a storm-tossed sea, were older than the moon.

Irina stood, swallowing hard, carefully aligning her empty hands at her sides. "Thank you, Gaia. We apologize for visiting unasked but—"

Gaia held up a hand, and the silver coil around her upper

armed glinted in the deck lights. "I am flattered that you recognize me. You were yet unborn when last we met." Her gown fluttered around her bare feet as if stirred by an unfelt breeze.

"Some memories do not fade," Irina said, ignoring the startled gasp from Charon, and Walker's stunned look. "Do you hold us in your hand?"

"In a manner of speaking. The landing place you had chosen was not suitable. I will set you down in a more hospitable environment and we will meet in person," Gaia said.

"But..." Irina began, then stopped. Gaia disappeared between one word and the next.

"Captain?" Walker said.

"What do we do?" Charon asked.

The bridge door hissed open and Sharp entered. The medi-droid said nothing but herded Walker into a seat. She ran a medi-scanner over his arm, pronounced it unbroken, but badly bruised.

All three trained their eyes on Irina, and she knew Murtagh was listening as well. Sitting back in her chair, she rubbed damp palms down her thighs. "We wait," she said.

"Wait?" Walker asked. "Wait for what?"

She cocked an eyebrow at him. "For Gaia to set us down."

"Or crush us against the rocks," Charon said. "Captain, we're headed straight for the side of a mountain."

"If she meant us harm, we'd be dead already." A muscle jumped in Irina's cheek, and she rubbed her forefinger against it. "Gaia's not one to delay the inevitable." A certain measure of bitterness colored her comment even as the viewscreen showed a heavily forested mountainside with no viable landing in sight.

The ship pivoted, making a slow pass along a vast cliff face. In the distance, its blue-white expanse glittering with shards of evening light, a river thundered toward the edge, then rocketed over in a solid sheet of frothing white foam. Far below, the water pooled in deceptive calm, swirls and eddies cavorting from stone to stone in a broadening silver path between verdant banks.

They approached the waterfall and Charon's eyes widened in disbelief. "She's not taking us through that, is she?"

"Strap in," Irina said. "This could get a little rough."

Walker was already jerking his harness over his shoulder, his movements hampered by the bandage securing his injured arm across his abdomen. Sharp reached up and casually snapped the fastenings in place before securing her own harness.

The ship halted in mid-air.

All personnel will secure for adverse maneuvering conditions. The computer's normally cool tones had warmed several degrees and bore a striking similarity to Gaia's gentle modulation. *Banking ninety degrees right in ten, nine, eight...*

Murtagh's muttered curses flooded through the com link along with the clear, sharp snap of several harnesses locking into place.

Three, two, one... The ship canted sharply, hovering with its undercarriage flat to the cliff, and then moved forward, its nose drawing closer and closer to the roaring waterfall. Millions of liters of water clouded the screen with white mist, obscuring the valley below.

The reverberation of the liquid wall thrummed against the ship. The vibration made Irina's nose itch, but she resisted the urge to scratch.

"What the hell is going on?" Charon yelled.

The ship reversed its tilt and was abruptly level again, the rumble of the waterfall receding with the light. Outside the viewscreen, solid rock walls rose around them, damp at first, then sandy, enclosing a spacious cavern. The ship stopped, then sank, the landing gear deploying as if they'd been ordered to do so.

Gaia's voice floated to them through the intercom, now completely free of mechanical inflexion. "Welcome, children. You may disembark at will. My people will meet you on the cave floor."

"Captain, we're completely hidden from outside view. Even if the Vladdinians realize we've escaped and track us here..." Charon trailed off, relief and suspicion warring in her glance.

"You don't think Gaia knew about them, do you?" Walker asked.

Irina shrugged. "You'll find that there's very little Gaia doesn't know. It's what she'll tell that becomes problematic."

The shuttle groaned, settling onto its landing struts with an exhalation of pearly vapor. The bridge was silent, each inhabitant casting lightning glances at the others.

After a moment, Irina unbuckled her harness and stood up. "Let's see what she has to say."

Charon, Walker, and Sharp fell in behind her as she exited, Murtagh joining them in the corridor.

"Umm, Captain," Charon said, and Irina shot her a look.

"I don't have any answers that would make sense to you, Charon. I told you my mother was here before. She was pregnant with me at the time. Things... happened. Mom and her crew went back to the main fleet and told them this place was uninhabitable." She stopped and turned to face them. "Other than that one instance, I never knew my mother to lie. I have to figure she had a good reason."

They were standing in the boarding station, the oval portal to the outside world looming behind Irina like a giant, squinting eye. The captain depressed the control button, and the iris dilated, its curved plates rotating back to reveal the opening.

"Computer, release gangway," Irina said, peering into the dim reaches of the cool, empty grotto.

Gangway releasing, aye, the computer replied, and a ridged path unfolded from the ship's side to the cave floor.

Moist air flooded the compartment and the humans took a collective breath. Irina stepped out of the ship onto the platform and looked down. Gathered around the foot of the ramp was a quintet of not-quite humans.

In the front was an Amazon, flame haired and blue-eyed, dressed in a sea-green robe. Behind her stood her male counterpart, tribal tattoos encircling his upper arms. A blue woman, nude but for a thin silver chain about her slim waist, settled iridescent wings back from her shoulders and threaded her long, silver tresses between her fingers. Two black-cloaked males scowled from behind the trio, unarmed, but perhaps wishing for knives.

"Welcome, in the name of Gaia," the red-haired female said. "I am Brigid, Sel-Key tribal leader and Chief of the Tuatha clan." She nodded toward the red-haired man. "This is James, second leader of the Sel-Key. And Nuala, leader of the Fa-Rey tribe. Bale and Rod are the joint leaders of the Na-Hual tribe." She lifted a hand, palm up, toward each person as she introduced them. "Our hearth is yours."

Unease crept up Irina's spine as she faced the envoys. She had been prepared for aggression, hostility even. The cool cordiality threw her off balance. She cleared her throat.

"I am Irina Demyanov, captain of the Argos. These are Charon, my first mate, Murtagh, my engineering chief, and Sharp, our medidroid. And this is Walker, our...logistics officer. We thank Gaia for her welcome."

"This is not all who are on board," one of the black-cloaks said, his frigid tone countering Brigid's welcome. Irina relaxed slightly as she studied the two. They stood with burly arms folded over their chests, feet planted in a wide stance, so much alike that one needed to see their mouth move in order to be sure which one spoke.

Brigid's lips tightened, but she did not speak.

"We have injured who need medical care," Irina said.

A smile eased the tension in Brigid's face. "We will help you to care for those who are injured. But you have another," she paused, tilting her head to the side. Her lips quirked. "He is in a cage?"

A muttered curse escaped Irina's lips but she forced her face into polite lines. "He has committed a minor infraction and is being punished."

"She lies." James glared at the humans. "One cannot captain a ship that no longer exists. And theft is no minor crime."

"It is true that the Argos has recently been destroyed." A scowl marred Irina's smooth brow. "Burke's crimes are no concern of yours. And not only do you have no business poking around inside my ship, but you have a lot of balls bringing such a fresh loss back to mind."

"You land on our world without permission, and then complain that we invade your privacy?" Brigid raised her brows. "Worse, you admit you've brought a thief with you?"

"There was no choice," Irina said shortly. She smoothed an imaginary wrinkle out of her tunic before continuing. "We need your help. Our terbium drive is damaged and we need rare-earth metals to replenish and repair it."

"Mining is forbidden on Gaia." Brigid folded her hands together, standing relaxed even as the other members of the council stiffened. "As is exportation of Gaia's flesh."

"Gaia's flesh?" Murtagh said. "You make it sound like we want to cut a pound of meat from something living. All we ask is a bit of rock to repair our engines."

James' hands clenched at his sides and he stepped into the space between the two groups. "The rock you speak of is part of Gaia's body. We live and breathe only by her mercy. She is our mother. Would you cut off your mother's arm and give it to us, if we asked?"

"Calm yourself, brother. He does not understand. Most species believe their home planets to be insensate collections of rock and vegetation." Brigid's tone was mild, but her eyes were cool as she focused on the humans. "Gaia is a planet, true, but she is also a living entity, just as we are."

Irina shook her head. "That is impossible. She is humanoid."

"You saw her?" Brigid's eyebrows lifted. "Where and when?"

"On our bridge just before she brought us here."

"Then you are greatly honored," Brigid said, frowning. "So far as I know, Gaia has not appeared in physical form to any of her children in over two hundred years."

"Yet she appeared to my mother just twenty-seven years ago," Irina said.

Brigid's frown deepened. "I am aware of the meeting. I did not think you would know of it."

"Well, I was there. Meeting a demi-god isn't something you forget, even if you haven't been born yet."

"I see." Eyes wide, Brigid nodded slowly. "Very well. Gaia will meet with each of you in turn. Our people will provide for your needs while you wait for her call."

"Meet with her alone, you mean?" Murtagh asked, his face suddenly pale against the shaggy mass of his dark hair. He cleared his throat. "I've work to do on the drives."

Brigid smiled. "A summons from Gaia is not something one can refuse. Do not be alarmed however. The first of you is already with her."

"What do you mean?" Irina asked.

"Captain, the holding cell alarm just went off," Charon said as she stared at her wrist unit. "Burke is gone."

DUSKY TWILIGHT FILTERED through the open window, but its peaceful scent did little to lessen the tension in the room.

"You're telling me you've all met with her?" Irina bisected the round room with agitated steps. Shoving her hands into the pockets of her flight suit was the only way to keep from throwing something.

Murtagh cupped a mug of ale between his meaty palms and considered the foam on top as if his life depended on it. "Yes, Captain," he said.

Charon, Walker, Lamesh, and Jacobs echoed his response with varying degrees of chagrin.

Irina spun to face him, boots scuffing on the hardwood as she planted her feet. "Even Burke?"

Charon was the only one who would meet her gaze. "Mr. Burke was apparently the first to be summoned. Lamesh and Jacobs were the last," she said, and then turned to study the view outside the window.

"Well, since Burke isn't here, who was second?" Irina asked, the words grinding between her teeth before she spit them out.

"Captain, it's no use mangling the messenger." Walker stood to face her. "It isn't as if the decision belonged to any of us."

Irina's fists clenched and a dull flush crept up her tight jaw into her cheeks. "Thank you for that helpful explanation, Mr. Walker. I'll keep it in mind next time I'm tempted to order fifty lashes for any of you." Sarcasm thick as cream coated her words and he fought to keep a grin from forming.

"As you say, Captain," he said, and gave her short bow. "And if it's a whipping you're planning, may I suggest Murtagh for the task? He does have the strongest arm amongst us."

The remaining occupants of the room held their breath, waiting for the explosion.

Temper flared in her eyes, and then faded into amusement. Her mouth curled and her fists relaxed as she sank into the nearest chair. "And you as first victim?" she asked.

"If you so command, Skipper," Walker said, and raised his glass to her.

"Sharp, who went second?"

"I did, Captain," the medi-droid said. "And may I suggest a glass of wine? It is an excellent vintage."

Irina gave the droid a sharp look, but accepted the cup from her before asking, "What was your meeting like?"

"Very short," Sharp replied. "She inquired as to my work aboard the Argos and a few other things relating to my status as an android in the human culture. Then she dismissed me. A woman named Daria brought me here."

"Lamesh, Jacobs? Report," Irina said.

"Much the same as Sharp's experience," Rachel said, her words slow, as if she was considering each one before she spoke. "She asked us —"

Irina's gaze sharpened. "She interviewed you together?"

"Yes," Jacobs said. "But other than that, it was no different than Sharp's, really. She wanted to know how long we'd been aboard, what our relationship —" Lamesh nudged her and a slight flush rose in the ensign's cheeks. "— relationships with the rest of the crew were like. That sort of thing."

Irina eyed her sharply. "Your relationships with the rest of the crew? And how did you characterize those relationships?"

"Professional and congenial, of course." Lamesh cleared her throat as Irina turned to her. "We saw no need to lie."

"You would find it very difficult to lie to her successfully," Irina replied, and swirled the glass between her fingers. "Walker, Murtagh, anything additional to report?"

The two men stood mute.

Irina stared into her glass. "The Gaians are not going to let us stay any longer than is absolutely necessary. So, Murtagh, Walker, do what you can to fix the shuttle's terbium drive. I'll see what I can do about fuel. Charon, chart us a way back to an interplanetary spaceport that does not pass through Vladdinian territory. Sharp, Lamesh, Jacobs, see to it that the ship is restocked for travel. Fill every available space with food, water, and medical supplies. No telling how long we'll need to be out there."

"We have nothing to trade with," Jacobs said. "Why would they give us stores?"

Irina eyed the tall blond with irritation. "They want us gone, not dead. They'll help us if only to get rid of us."

Both women looked doubtful and Irina rubbed a weary hand over her forehead. "Look, you want to mutiny, be my guest. You aren't exactly essential personnel at this point. But keep this in mind. The Gaians have no use for you, so you won't be allowed to stay here." Jacobs opened her mouth to speak, but Irina kept talking. "And, ramshackle as it is, my ship is the only way off this rock. So choose your words, and your attitude, with care."

Lamesh and Jacobs looked at each other, then back at the captain. Lamesh raised one black brow and said, "Aye, aye...Captain."

Irina gave them a stiff nod. "It's been a long day. Get some rest tonight."

The pair filed out, presumably headed for their quarters.

"With your permission, Captain, I will go as well," Sharp said. "I want to check on the wounded before I power down for the night."

Irina nodded, adding, "Keep an eye on Lamech and Jacobs, Andrina. More happened in their interview than they're telling."

"Of course, Captain," Sharp said, and exited.

Murtagh and Charon said good night and followed her out.

"Captain," Walker said. "You know Murtagh is going to have a hard time tuning that drive without test fuel."

She moved to refill her glass with amber liquid. "I know that."

"Then why bother?"

"Hopelessness kills faster than lasers, Walker." She held her glass up and watched the candle light fracture in its depths. "And fear breeds violence. Set Murtagh a problem to solve and he won't have time to worry about whether or not the Gaians are plotting to kill us."

"And was that your plan for me as well?" A lazy smile drifted across his full lips as he awaited her answer.

"It was. But, since you're on to me, perhaps you'd like a different job? One with a chance of success that actually needs...doing?"

The smile deepened, showing a dimple in his cheek. "You are the captain. And I am very good at following orders."

She lowered the glass, her eyes trained on his lips. "I sensed that about you right away."

He stepped toward her and she turned to the window. "Check on Burke."

Walker stopped. "Burke?"

"Yes. I have the oddest feeling that he hasn't returned to the ship."

"What do you think they've done with him?" Walker frowned.

"Nothing. I think they let him go."

He stiffened and the frown became a scowl. "They have no right to do that."

"No, Michael. We are the ones who have no rights here. Secure the ship. Burke is a highly resourceful pirate and a damn fine pilot."

"I'll sleep aboard," he said, and hesitated, disappointment darkening his brown eyes.

She smiled; a solemn, tiny gesture. "He may not intend to betray us, but after what's happened, it's a little soon for trust, you understand."

"If I were you, I'd never trust Burke again," he agreed. "Luckily, not everyone is like him."

"No doubt," she said, and turned away. "Thank you, Mr. Walker. That will be all."

"As you say, Captain," he said, and a moment later, she was alone.

. . .

SHAKEN BY HIS INTERVIEW, and the blank hours he couldn't account for afterward, Burke forced himself along the path he hoped led back to the shuttle. The bag Gaia had given him thumped against his thigh and he shifted its weight irritably, but never considered putting it down.

Moonlight filtered greenly through the thick foliage, and fireflies blinked gold and blue in the darkness. The breeze was soft and honeyed, caressing his face with delicate, warm fingers.

It would be perfect for a romantic vacation if I still had a girl-friend, he thought, and his mouth twisted into an ill-tempered grimace. We had a good thing together. Screw her if she can't see it.

"Mr. Burke? Is that you?" The soft voice came out of the darkened foliage to his right, startling him.

He stifled a curse. "Who is that?" He asked.

"It's us, Rachel and Leah. The captain dismissed us about half an hour ago."

"Dismissed you?" Sean said. "Yeah, that figures."

"Would you like to come in for a drink? The Gaians make a delicious pear wine. Have you tasted it?"

"No I..." he trailed off as Leah stepped into the moonlight, her long, blond curls loose around her shoulders. He was surprised by how beautiful she was with her hair down.

"You'll love it," Rachel said, moving up next to Leah and slipping an arm around her waist. Rachel's silk gown shimmered in the starlight, the style offering tantalizing glimpses of creamy skin. She reached up and caressed his cheek. "You should join us. I promise you won't regret it."

Taken aback, he started to decline, then checked himself. He was a free agent, after all.

"How could I refuse such hospitality? Lead the way."

Leah released a peal of light laughter. "Wait until you see our quarters. They are lovely."

The women arranged themselves on either side of him and took his arms. "Brigid told us that Gaia released you," Rachel said. "How did you manage it?"

"Well, I'm told I can be quite persuasive when I want to be," he said.

Leah gave a throaty purr. "I believe you. And we are quite talented ourselves."

"I'll just bet you are," he said, and the trio ducked inside the small cottage, their laughter floating away into the night.

AS WALKER LEFT HER, Irina wandered to the window to look out on the dark forest. One by one, the faces of those she had been forced to leave aboard the Argos rose up to accuse her. She had recruited them, worked with them. She had been responsible for them. And now they were dead because of her blindness.

Behind her, someone cleared their throat, and Irina spun, dropping her empty cup and reaching for the blaster that was no longer on her hip.

"Peace, Captain." James, the Sel-key second-in-command, held up his empty hands. "I am only here to deliver a message."

"Somehow, you don't strike me as the messenger-boy type," Irina said.

A shadow passed over his strongly carved features, but he shrugged. "Each of us does as Gaia wills. Any task she assigns carries honor with it."

"Nice line. I'll bet it plays well with the pious ladies."

He frowned. "You seem determined to provoke me. Why? I have done you no harm."

A snort burst from her lips. "You don't think calling me a liar is provocation? Stop playing around. You don't want us here. You made that plain in the first couple of seconds."

"It is no secret. I am charged with the safety of our community. Humans are notoriously unpredictable and often destructive. Of course I am concerned about your presence." He poured himself a drink from the pitcher on the table. "But Gaia welcomes you."

"So, does that mean you welcome us too?" Irina scooped up her fallen cup and examined it. A crack ran up the side, but it was otherwise intact and functional. She held it out, and James filled it with amber liquid.

"It means I accept your presence as Gaia wishes me to," he said. "Now, the message. Gaia wishes you to bring the two jewels Mr. Burke stole from the Vladdinians. She will meet with you in her chamber."

"Will she?"

He scowled. "It is not a request. Come. I will take you to her."

"And if I say no?"

Muscles bunched along his shoulders. He took a step toward her, then stopped and made a visible effort to relax. "You won't refuse her. You are too curious about what she has to say."

"Well, I can't argue with you there." Taking a last sip of her wine, Irina set it on the table and disappeared into her sleeping chamber. She emerged a moment later with a heavy, black pack. "Lead on, Mr. Sel-key."

He led her out of the cottage and along the forest path to the cliff face. The sleepy voices of birds and insects surrounded them. At path's end, an archway had been carved into the rock face, its edge deeply incised with ancient runes in an unknown language. James stopped at the entrance.

"Follow the path," he said with a short, stiff bow. "Seek the light." Then he turned and walked away.

Irina looked around her. The forest at her back was silent, as if all the forest denizens were now watching to see what she would do. The pale rock sprang from the forest floor in a sheer vertical, its craggy aspect marked here and there with moss and the occasional spray of orchids. The arch was at least four meters tall and nearly half that wide, paved in sand and unlit. It was like walking into a giant mouth. Irina kept wondering where the teeth were.

She took a deep breath and entered the passage, her steps curving to the right, and then down in a gradual descent. Her heart beat in her throat, the pulse of it in her ears drowning the sound of her breathing. Rounding the final turn, Irina stopped short as the corridor widened into a vast cavern.

Shadows fell in heaps around her. She could not see the stone walls, but felt them bearing in on her, weighing her down. Irina shivered and hoisted the pack higher on her shoulder. There was something about this place that penetrated her soul. The air itself seemed to strip her bare, laying open her secrets for intimate inspection.

Ahead, a muted, golden light beckoned. Rounding the final corner, Irina stopped short. In the center of a large chamber floated the light source. An endless spiral of glowing nodules surrounded a larger orb pulsing at the pattern's center.

"You brought them to me." The voice filled the cave, softly melodic yet laden with power.

A sibilant grinding echoed around her as a pedestal rose from the cave floor. Sand filtered from it in a golden curtain, sifting into mounds around the column's base. After a slight hesitation, Irina lowered the pack and took out the opals.

"James said you wanted them. I'm happy to trade them for the terbium we need to refuel. But you should know, the Vladdinians own these jewels, and they want them back." Irina placed the stones on the bed of warm silicate.

Gaia's response was arctic. "The Vladdinians do not own them. They are mine."

"They were on my ship without my knowledge or consent." Irina's eyes darted from shadow to shadow, searching for the source of the voice. "You should know, I did everything I could to send these stones back to the Vladdinians."

"And yet, my children are returned to me, and you are the means by which they came. I would reward you."

The word 'children' hit Irina like a punch in the stomach and she wrapped her arms around herself. "The opals are — eggs?"

A distinct chill entered the cave. "I am not a bird. I do not lay eggs." The light fluctuated, waxing and waning several times before it steadied again and the cavern warmed. "These are my children. In time they will grow into what you know as planets and take their place in the universe."

"But how did...? The Vladdinians have held these stones as

sacred for a thousand years. The legends they tell..." She trailed off as a faint giggle rose from the opals.

Gaia's response was dry, but not unappreciative. "Apparently that was my daughter, Suha's, idea. She thought the Vladdinians would be more likely to leave them whole—" Gaia's voice cracked on the word and it took her a moment to continue. "If they thought she and her brother, Thaq, were holy. So, she chose an opportune moment and spoke to one of them. It worked."

"I didn't know," Irina insisted.

"Why are you so reluctant to accept my gratitude?" Genuine curiosity colored Gaia's voice. "Either way, you were trying to do the right thing."

"I was trying to save myself and my crew. If I had my way, they'd still be sitting in Victory Palace and we never would have come here."

"If you had known these were my children, you would have brought them to me."

"I wouldn't have, though. Don't you see? Sean stole them. Greedy, impetuous ass that he is, he thought he could get away with the prized possessions of the Vladdinian empire, not to mention its most sacred religious relics. I told him no. I said it was too risky." Her throat clenched and she tightened her fists until her nails made tiny half-moons in her palms. "The lying snake pretended he agreed with me. And then he did it anyway."

"And was nearly caught," Gaia said. It wasn't a guess.

"Nearly?" Irina choked. "Eighty percent of my crew is dead because of him. And I couldn't save them."

"You did your best."

"It wasn't enough."

"Circumstances evolve as they will. Control is an illusion. A lie we tell ourselves to keep the darkness at bay." The light dimmed once more, then brightened as Gaia continued. "The fact remains that if you had known the truth, you would have brought my children home. You are, at your core, good."

"How can you know that?" Irina's voice dropped to a raspy

whisper. Her knees buckled and she sank onto the sandy floor. "I don't even know that."

"Humans see the surface, the face and form of a creature. I see the beyond that. I have seen your soul, and while it is not pure, it is trying to be."

"I am no saint."

"And I am no god, though some would make me one." The glow intensified and the air took on the scent of a fresh green field. The light gathered, rushing together into the tall apparition Irina had seen aboard the shuttle. Gaia laid her hand on Irina's hair. "You would never harm a child," she said. "Would, in fact, sacrifice your own life in order to save one."

"I have never murdered a child," Irina agreed. "But I killed..." The faces of her dead crowded around her. Sobs rose in her throat, and she forced them down. "I left so many aboard the Argos... wounded, desperate...helpless..."

"You saved those who could be saved." Gaia bent to her, and lifted Irina to her feet, enveloping her in warmth. "And in doing so, you have preserved your species."

Irina stiffened. "What do you know about my species?"

"More than you can possibly imagine." Gaia glided to the table where the opals lay, gleaming in their own light. She ran her fingers gently over their surface and a hum filled the air, like recordings Irina had heard of an old Earth instrument called a violin. Gaia smiled. "Humans are almost extinct. They left their home planet, a place they had nearly destroyed."

"I don't need a history lesson," Irina said, and scrubbed a hard hand across her mouth. "Humans are doing fine. We just need..."

Gaia arched one honey-colored brow and smiled. "A home? How many of you are there left? Do you know?"

Irina pressed her lips together and crossed her arms over her chest.

"I can tell you there are less than one hundred, scattered across the galaxies like so many miniature meteors," Gaia said. "Many are old, for humans, and they will die soon. You are the only human infant born naturally in over a hundred years. And now, even artificial births are rarer than black opals. Your race is dying, Irina."

It was true. Irina knew it. Her mother had explained over and over again the miracle of her daughter's conception, which had occurred on this very planet. "There's nothing I can do about that. All I can do is keep my crew alive for as long as possible."

"And how will you do that? The Vladdinians have already realized that you are still alive. They are on their way here now."

Irina's head snapped up. "What? We have to go."

"Where? How? Your ship has no fuel."

"You have to provide us with terbium, there is no other choice. Vladdinians are some of the best trackers in the universe. Following a photon trail will be child's play."

Appreciation filled the calm gray eyes. "You have no need to fear."

A snort escaped Irina's tight mouth. "Clearly you have never met an angry Vladdinian."

"Clearly you have never met an angry Gaian," Gaia said. Irina gave her a wary look and Gaia waved her hand. "Never mind. Providing you with fuel is a possibility, but you are ignoring a better one."

"Which is what?"

"Stay. Make this place your home."

"You can't be serious." Irina's arms fell slack to her sides. She stared, round-eyed, into the face of the demi-god. "That isn't a solution."

When Gaia made no effort to amend her invitation, Irina snapped her jaw closed and turned away, shoulders hunched, fists clenched.

"You don't get it, do you?" Irina said. "The Vladdinians won't just want their jewels back. They'll be out for blood. And they won't be particular about whose blood it is. Anyone who happens to be in the vicinity will be fair game."

"Even now, you seek to protect others. A planet full of beings you do not know and will likely never meet."

"I'm trying to protect what's left of my crew," Irina snapped. "Keeping your people safe is just a side benefit."

"Tell me, Irina, if I could guarantee that the Vladdinians would never find you, or your crew, that they would never even know Gaia is inhabited, what then? Would you want to stay on this world?"

Irina took a deep breath and sent it out, slow and measured. "All my life, I have longed for a home. To look up into the universe and know my place in it. But I laid that hopeless dream aside a long, long time ago."

"Take it up again."

Silence stretched between them until Irina said, "I can't speak for the crew."

"No one will be required to stay who doesn't wish to."

"You've already talked to them about this?"

"I have."

A flush of confused emotion rose and receded as Irina struggled for words. Finally, she said, "All right then. What is your plan?"

4. Return

"THEY WANT me to stay here? In a backwater; a low-tech hole in the universe?" A ragged laugh burst free of Burke's lips, and he stifled it, looking around the clearing anxiously.

Wouldn't do to get caught now, Burke thought. The forest was still. Nothing moved in the pre-dawn light, no one spoke, and he ducked through the arch into the entrance. He ran down the passageway, muttering under his breath as he moved.

"With Vladdinians on my tail and Irina ready to feed me to them? Small chance," he muttered to himself. "My only way out is to jump planet before the green-furred beasties get here."

He burst into the main cavern and paused a moment to orient himself. The spiral orbs were nearly dark, their light muted as if in sleep. He could barely see the pedestal where the opals rested in their bed of sand.

Staring at the gems, Burke remembering his last conversation with Irina. Finally he shook his head. Irina had lost her mind. No way these rocks were actually sentient, let alone children. They were just a collection of pretty atoms, nicely arranged for a pleasing effect. Nothing more.

The ghost of a sigh floated through the air and he whipped around, taking in the dim reaches of the empty cavern.

"Who's there?" He asked, voice cracking. His heart thumped, trying to claw its way out of his chest. There was no answer. Burke grimaced. "Imagination is getting away from me."

After one last hesitation, he scooped the opals into his pack and slung it over his shoulder. A shiver of premonition prickled across the back of his neck as he hurried down the passage at a dust-stirring pace. Dawn was breaking as he sprang free of the entrance.

Moments later Burke sprinted along the cliff path, ducking past the waterfall into the upper cave where the ship rested. Somewhere in the village below, Murtagh was sleeping, but he'd be up to check on the ship before long. Burke lowered the ramp and ran inside.

A few heartbeats more and he was piloting the ship carefully through the slender space between the cataract and the wall. After a final glance, he hit the thrusters, and was gone.

FAR BELOW, Irina and Brigid stood watching him depart, and with him, the humans' last chance to leave Gaia.

"She gave him the terbium?" Irina asked.

"Yes, even before speaking with you. He fueled the ship before heading for the cavern," Brigid said. "You warned Michael not to stay aboard, yes?"

Irina nodded, her eyes on the fast-disappearing shuttle. "Will they catch him?" She asked.

"Gaia says there is a good chance they will. But nothing is certain..."

A sad, rueful grin tugged at Irina's lips. "Burke is as resourceful as they come. I hope he makes it."

Brigid shot her a curious look. "He is a thief and a liar. He stole the opals even after you told them they were Gaia's children."

"He'll have convinced himself that the stones are just stones. And thanks to Gaia, he's right. I just hope the Vladdinians don't realize the difference." Irina took a deep breath and blew it out slowly. "He saved my life once. Did I tell you that?" She shrugged and turned away. "He's not all bad."

"None of us are." Brigid said.

"Yes, well, knowing that lets me hope for the best, even when I know he deserves the worst."

The pair walked along the forest path toward Irina's new home. Waiting inside were the remnants of humanity. All except Dr. Manning, who still wasn't speaking to her.

"Is Burke gone?" Rachel asked.

"He is," Irina said.

"And are we..." Leah's voice trailed off and she bit her lower lip, eyes darkening with uncertainty.

Brigid looked at the two women squarely for a moment, openly assessing. "Gaia was right. Each of you carries a spark of new life within you." Her gaze sharpened. "In fact, Rachel carries two."

Joy overtook the women and Leah pulled Rachel into her arms and kissed her tenderly. "It worked. We're going to be mothers."

Heads together, the couple wandered out arm in arm, leaving Irina staring after them. "They're pregnant? Both of them? How...?"

"I'm sure you know how. Burke is the who, but that doesn't seem to bother them." Brigid said. "I will leave you here."

"You don't have to go," Walker said, and offered her a cup.

"No, I have much to do and you have much to discuss." She closed the door behind her and Irina turned to face those who remained.

Charon and Murtagh sat together on the couch while Sharp stared out the window.

"So, Skipper, what next?" Charon asked.

"Next?" Irina accepted the cup from Walker and looked into his eyes. "Next we learn to trust."

Author's Notes—C. L. Roman

THIS STORY IS my daughter's fault, really. She was at the house one day and noticed a recyclable container in the trash. She proceeded to give me an earful about our responsibility to the planet, and if not the planet, then our children, since if we don't take care of the Earth, there won't be much left for future generations. She is right.

Which started me thinking. We owe so much to the Earth. We take our sustenance from her, make our living from resources she provides, often without thought for the consequences. In a real sense, what is happening to our home planet is negligent at best and criminal at worst. What if Earth were a living, breathing, sentient being? Would we continue to treat her the way so many of us do? If we did, would she allow it?

Fast on the heels of these musings came the invitation to be part of the Alvarium Experiment's second offering. *Gaia Returning* is the result. If you are interested in seeing how humans left Earth in the first place, stay tuned. That story is on its way.

~CLR

The Paradoxical Man

Bard Constantine

Space.

It was all Albert Rosen had seen for the last century and a half, but it still astounded him every time. One glance outside the viewport of the ship, one glimmer of an alien sunbeam, and his breath was taken away anew. He'd witnessed the grandest of sights in his time on the watch, inexplicable moments that defied description. Wonders of celestial light and darkness had moved him, reduced him to shuddering tears and reflections on mortality and afterlife. At times, when staring into the cornea of a weeping nebula or transfixed by the collective luminosity of passing galaxy, he almost believed he was in Heaven. But he knew Heaven could never be so isolated. So alone.

The remoteness was stifling. He would teeter on the razor's edge between sanity and madness, imagining he was all there was in the void, one infinitesimal speck of life in an infinite stretch of death. The universe had no use for him, no endearing ache for humanity's mechanisms. It went on, cold and unfeeling in its awe-inspiring orchestra of cosmic phenomena.

The vastness was matched only by its emptiness. The immeasurable stretch of pitch black dotted by mysterious glimmers. Billions of stars in billions of galaxies, all moving like clockwork in perfect precision. It was impossible to understand, to even attempt to grasp the concept of such immeasurable massiveness. He once believed something of such magnitude had to be inhabited, had to be populated by beings that outnumbered the stars, hundreds of billions of intelligent species seeking to connect, to communicate beyond the confines of their own planets and galaxies.

He wasn't sure he believed that anymore.

Moments like those made Albert grateful for the Morpheus chamber. It was like an old friend, waiting to embrace him as he submerged into the depths of the aeriated gel and succumbed to the allure of fathomless sleep. His life was a concerted motion of long sleep and short awakenings, time enough to keep a single day's watch before returning to hibernation and sleeping for a decade. Often he was unsure if he was asleep or awake, as he often dreamed of awakening, just to take another watch.

Another day to stare into the depths of space. Another day to observe marvels no man had seen before. Things no man had a right to see. It was all he had. It was all he was. He was the lost, marooned and drifting alone in an ocean of ink and gemstones. It was better that way.

Perhaps it was the purgatory he deserved, a befitting punishment for his incomprehensible crimes.

Light.

IT ASSAULTED HIS CONSCIOUSNESS, relentless razors that sliced his dreams to shivery ribbons. Muffled, liquid sounds surrounded him, smooth and mechanical yet overly loud and invasive. Pinpricks of icy air stabbed his naked flesh as the gel emptied into the draining system. He sat up with a gasp, dripping with viscid fluid as he emerged from the Morpheus chamber, weak-limbed and shuddering.

Liquid bullets and cyclonic whirring helped his mind focus as the floor conveyor shuttled him through the jetted shower and dryer. He was still bare-chested when he jogged to the bridge to see why he had been roused so far ahead of schedule.

His mouth dropped open. For a long moment his thoughts collided with one another, debating whether he was truly awake or suffering from a lucid dream inside the stasis chamber. It was the most beautiful sight he'd seen in his life, a perfectly spherical azure-colored vision, gift-wrapped in threads of misty white. It hung in empty space, beckoning; the sum of all his longing, the answer to every fear and desire he possessed.

It was Earth.

He was home.

Goosebumps prickled his arms, and his heart surged with so much adrenaline that he nearly passed out. He slumped into the padded navigator's chair as unchecked tears slid down his face. His journey was over. He had been fully prepared to become a ghost in the cosmos, a corpse drifting in a derelict vessel, before ever believing he had a shot at making it. Faith was for the devout, but he was of the analytical order. He had known the impossible odds, the miniscule chance he had of performing a successful trek through spacetime to arrive safely at this destination. But somehow the gambit had paid off. The impossible had happened.

He was home.

"Unidentified craft."

He flinched at the sound of the voice. There was no human warmth, no reassuring familiarity. It spoke over the ship's intercom in a synthetic monotone.

"Unidentified craft, we are assuming control of your vessel. Please do not attempt to operate your ship while this process is ongoing. Any resistance will result in countermeasures which may bring you harm. Thank you for your cooperation."

Albert shifted uncomfortably in his chair. Somehow, he had never imagined a lukewarm or hostile reception. In his daydreams he had always been received as a returning hero, a dead man basking in the warmth of his resurrection. He hadn't considered the uncertainty he might create, the fear he might induce by suddenly appearing on the planet's radar. He'd been gone so long that his name was more than likely forgotten, merely a blip in some obscure archive. His return was inexplicable, an uncanny sequence of events that would raise eyebrows from even the most fervent, over-imaginative science fiction writers.

The ship lurched, impelling him to grip the armrests for balance. He craned his neck to see something, anything that could indicate an intelligent presence. A tiny object glinted in the distance, increasing in size as Albert's ship drew nearer.

The space station had the appearance of a disembodied wheel, complete with cylindrical spokes which led to a spherical center Albert assumed was the command hub. It rotated slowly, become increasingly larger until Albert realized it was massive enough to cover most of the state of Texas were it placed on Earth.

"Dr. Albert Rosen."

Albert gave a start at the mention of his name. The voice was different, evoked with more warmth. Feminine.

It sounded human.

"Dr. Albert Rosen, please reply via your communication system."

He cleared his throat and pressed a button on the control dashboard. "This is Rosen. Dr. Albert Rosen. Who is this? How do you know me?"

"There are numerous DNA samples stored in your vessel, Dr. Rosen. Since you are the sole occupant, I analyzed the latest and was able to identify you. Dr. Albert Rosen, aerospace engineer at NASA, last seen manning a prototype deep sea exploration vessel called the Gorgon. It was deployed June 6, 2016 in the Bermuda Triangle. The mission to investigate a powerful energy anomaly was determined a failure when the *Gorgon* vanished without a trace. All five team members on board were eventually designated as deceased: Jack Carson, Ben Rodriguez, Linda Reaves, Albert Rosen, Sarah Rosen."

Jack. Ben. Linda. *Sarah.*

The remembrance stabbed sharper than a knife between his ribs. He nearly groaned aloud as the terrible intensity swelled, the numbness torn from his consciousness like a scab from a half-healed wound.

Their vessel crumpled around them like aluminum foil, and Sarah's eyes stared from the depths of dark waters; her hair haloed around her face when she was torn away from him with irresistible force.

He placed a hand on his throbbing temple.

"Dr. Rosen, we have commandeered your vessel's navigation system. You are now being directed to docking bay forty-two. Please remain seated until your ship is secure. Thank you for your cooperation, and welcome aboard the *Locus*. "

His thoughts refocused as his ship was directed to the docking bay with silent precision. Trepidation settled in, an unwelcome companion to his uncertainty. He had no idea how many years he had been flung across time and space, nor whether it was forward or backward from the place he had departed from. When the space-time continuum was no longer a barrier, impossibilities became reality, and reality a word no longer anchored to restraining limitations. Did his new hosts know where he came from? Did they know what he did? What atrocities he was responsible for?

Fear.

AFTER SUITING up in an all-black uniform, he waited at the docking bay doors with his heart pounding against his sternum, his throat dry, and his fingers trembling.

The doors slid open.

A diminutive woman dressed in loose folds of black and white greeted him with a warm, dimpled smile. Her sleek, raven-black hair was bobbed to near razor sharpness, and her face was perfectly contoured, highlighted by nude and silver enhancements. It was impossible to guess her nationality.

"Hello, Dr. Rosen. My name is Maria. It is an unexpected pleasure to make your acquaintance. I'm sure you have many questions. If you will follow me, I will escort you to the Central Sol, where Deis can explain everything to you."

"Who is Deis?"

"The commander of this station."

"Don't I have to be placed in decontamination? There's no telling what I might be carrying, what viruses I may have—"

"That won't be necessary, Dr. Rosen. Your ship has kept detailed logs on your health, and you've been screened for entry. This way, please."

She gestured before leading the way to a waiting convertible shuttle. The sleek machine hovered over the gleaming floors and silently propelled down the brightly lit, tubular hallway. Rectangular windows lined the walls, allowing a view of the other spokes as the station rotated in the darkness of space. Earth was a cerulean jewel, tantalizing in the distance.

He was struck by a startling sense of déjà vu. It was as if he walked in the shadows of his own footsteps, trailed by their ghostly echoes.

He was greeted by color. Trees and shrubs, veritable forests lined the hall, imparting a damp freshness to the air. They passed rooms where transparent tubing revealed vast aquariums swarming with swaying sea fans, darting fish, stealthy gliding sharks, and a thousand other species. An entire ecosystem intertwined with the cold titanium bones of the station, a hybrid of biological and synthetic engineering.

They exited the shuttle after it stopped at a conveyor affixed with lines of cushioned, orbicular chairs. He and Maria chose their seats and sat. Lap belts automatically encircled their waists, adjusting for height and width. A domed visor slid over them, completing the sphere.

Maria turned to him with a reassuring smile. "Take a deep breath, Dr. Rosen."

"Excuse me?"

"If you please."

He took a deep breath.

The surroundings distorted; whirs of black and white flashed by.

"Here we are."

Albert tried to rise as the visor whirred up and the lap belt unfastened. His muscles felt like putty, and the result was an awkward spill from the chair to the floor while dots blurred his vision and his chest heaved. He felt Maria's arms guide him to a sitting position. Her small frame belied impressive strength as she made the action appear effortless.

"I'm sorry, Dr. Rosen. We normally wouldn't have used the shuttle in such a manner, but Deis insisted on seeing you as soon as possible. Are you capable of standing, or do you require more time?"

"I think I'm all right." He accepted her offered hand and stood on trembling legs. He leaned on her, feeling nearly geriatric as they approached the massive central sphere which only a few seconds ago had appeared to be miles away. It dwarfed anything Albert had seen before. A long time ago he had marveled at the Ericsson Globe in Stockholm, Sweden. It was a marvel of architectural design, and had been the largest hemispherical building on Earth at the time.

The Central Sol was more than fifty times larger.

The silvery surface was overlain with dimensional hexagon formations, creating the illusion of ridged imperfection. But Albert was almost certain it would be flawlessly spherical if measured. It gleamed as the darkness of space contested with the winking lights of the station across its multidimensional skin.

Albert was again struck by the familiarity of the moment. He had been there before. In a slightly altered fashion, perhaps, but he was certain of it.

A door slid open upon their approach. Maria stopped just shy of the entrance.

"This is where I leave you, Dr. Rosen. The elevator will take you to the central hub."

"Thank you, Maria. May I ask you a question?"

"You may."

He gestured to the extended stretch of empty passageway. "Where is everyone?"

Her cheerful smile never slipped. "Deis will answer all of your questions in time, Dr. Rosen. And you will answer all of his."

The elevator doors shut, and Albert was rocketed upward. As he rose, he took in a bird's eye view of Maria walking down the cylindrical passage, the only sign of human movement in the entire massive structure.

Luminosity.

THE ELEVATOR DOOR opened to a view of frosted white.

Albert was reminded of a gargantuan igloo, with the interior absent of any right angles and the contours, skylights, and spare furnishings all rounded. The floor appeared to be slick tiles, but the pressure under his feet was soft, as if walking on flattened clouds. His boots made no sound as he cautiously stepped forward. He halted as a soft, masculine voice spoke.

"One moment, please."

A tangle of thick black cables descended from an aperture in the ceiling. Moving as though sentient, they formed together in a humanoid shape. Thin, glimmering wires intertwined as well, electrical veins for a cybernetic nervous system. Plates of flexible white alloyed material rose from the floor, attaching to the cables and wires to form a sleek exoskeletal covering for the android that strode toward Albert and extended a welcoming hand.

After a brief hesitation, Albert took it. The mechanical fingers that clasped his own were warm, the shell covering softer than he expected. He felt a slight galvanic quiver from the artificial being who greeted him with a gaze decidedly human in manner. Its face was molded from the same supple material as its shell, allowing it facial expression while still remaining an obvious automaton.

"Welcome, Dr. Rosen. As you have no doubt guessed, I am Deis."

"You're a robot."

Deis laughed.

It was eerie, hearing an android laugh as though it knew what laughter was. Deis gestured to their brightly illuminated surroundings. "I am a system, Dr. Rosen. The system that oversees this entire station. The physical form you see is simply a construct to make our communication more comfortable, especially in view of your situation."

"My situation?"

"Yes. I am quite sure you are disoriented by your travels. You departed from Earth on June 6, 2016, entering a wormhole bridged between your time and a distant point in the future, possibly thousands of years. You then took a secondary trip which brought you here, July 20, 2374. Which would make it the past from which you departed, yet still the future of your original point of time."

Albert had guessed as much, but it was still staggering to hear the feat related in such a casual manner. "How do you know that?"

"Your ship. It is technologically more advanced than any we currently possess, but still familiar enough to communicate with our systems. What does that tell you?"

Albert reflected for a moment. "It means the future I visited was our own. The Denizens, as they called themselves...were human. They were us."

"You sound surprised."

"They didn't appear human. They were...taller. And their shapes and appearance were completely different. Alien. Almost insectoid."

"I'm certain there is a valid reason for their appearance, Dr. Rosen. Please have a seat." Deis indicated a pair of gleaming white semicircles with luxurious padding. "Hibernation is exhausting, and your muscles still have to adjust to the exertion of continued movement."

As Albert sat, an automated tray wheeled over, laden with bowls of fruit and cream. Albert wasn't sure if the colors were strikingly rich because of the white surroundings, or because he hadn't seen real fruit in ages. Regardless, the assorted berries, peaches, and melon spheres looked absolutely mouth-watering.

"A taste of Earth's finest, to welcome you home." Deis waved a hand as he settled into the opposite chair. A portion of the wall slid open to a view of the planet. The horizon glowed as the sunrise struck it, a sight so beautiful that Albert felt short of breath. He absentmindedly lifted a spoonful of fresh fruit to his mouth.

The taste was nearly enough to bring tears to his eyes. The combination of sweet and tart flavors that saturated his tongue was superior to any he'd ever experienced. It was as if he'd never tasted fruit before.

Deis inclined his head. "I take it you approve."

"It's…amazing." His fingers moved of their own accord, greedily dipping fruit in the bowl of cream and lifting it to his mouth in rapid succession.

"Completely natural. Free from any the pesticides and chemicals you were subjected to in your period of time."

"Who are they for?"

"For the occupants of this station, of course. Although by the time they receive it, it is broken down to raw nutrients. Far less palatable than what you're currently enjoying."

"What occupants? Where are the people?"

"In stasis. Much like your time in the Morpheus Chamber, humanity sleeps."

"Why?"

"Because they are not yet ready to return."

Albert paused with his spoon half-raised. He took a longing stare at the enticing display of condensation-beaded fruit before he sighed and willed himself away. "I want to see them."

Frozen.

HUMANKIND WAS REDUCED to freeze-dried meat.

That was the initial notion which sprang to Albert's mind. In climate controlled sectors of the station, they lay in slim metallic pods with opaque sheaths pressed tightly against their bodies like Saran wrap. Various tubes extended from the casing, tentacles which imported and exported necessities vital to extended hibernation. The holders were suspended on racks attached to towers that extended beyond Albert's range of vision. Clouds of vapor billowed in the chamber, seemingly more alive than the frozen occupants.

The number of towers was staggering. The number of bodies

even more so. Row after row of tightly sequestered figures that could have easily been corpses, shrouded and indistinct. All that remained of humanity, bagged and stockpiled in a frozen tomb.

Some of the receptacles were noticeably smaller than the others.

There were so many.

So many.

Albert placed a hand against the cold glass. A teardrop spilled from his lashes and trickled down his cheek. None of his fantasies, none of his predictions had ever come close to what he witnessed. Never included every man, woman, and child taken from their planet and stored away in freezer bags.

His voice was reduced to a hoarse whisper. "What happened?"

"They called it the Cataclysm. An event that threatened humanity with extinction, forcing them to come up with drastic measures to ensure their survival. This station is the culmination of those measures, of the greatest minds uniting to achieve that goal."

"What kind of cataclysm? What kind of event could have triggered the end of the world?"

Deis' expression turned somber. "A violent backlash of foreign energy. It was called darkflow, named so because it supposedly contained properties of what is theoretically referred to as dark energy. Much is still not known about the nature of it, but we do know the effects. It produced destructive ruptures of time and space, opening portals called Aberrations that expelled nightmarish phenomena."

Albert raised a forestalling hand. "Wait. Portals of disruptive dark energy? That's impossible."

"Impossible is a label attached to what simply lacks the precise conditions to occur. You of all people should understand that. After all, those portals are the reason why you're here. The reason why you vanished from the face of the planet. The reason why you were sent to the Bermuda Triangle in the first place."

Albert's blood turned to ice water in his veins. "You can't be saying what I think you're saying."

"What do you think I'm saying?"

"The deep sea expedition. Where my crewmates died. My wife…died. It was because of this darkflow? This aberrant energy?"

Deis' mechanical eyes focused on Albert's face. "Not at all. It was because of you, Dr. Rosen. Because of what you did when you arrived in the future."

Albert winced. A wave of dizziness threatened to topple him from his feet. "No. You can't know. You weren't there."

"Your ship was there. It carried more than just your body across the cosmos. It carried detailed logs. Information it downloaded into my memory core which has allowed me to piece together what occurred, both in the future and the past. I know what you did, Dr. Rosen. I know the atrocities you committed. The catastrophic events you set in motion."

The guilt slammed into Albert's consciousness with the lethality of a sniper's bullet. The room blazed in a rush of white light. Albert felt himself falling, much as he did so many years in the past, when his emergency pod deployed and his wife's terrified face was the last thing he saw before being yanked with incredible force through a rupture of time and space. He felt himself disintegrating, layer by layer until there was nothing left but regrets, legions of shattered dreams that scattered like stars across the cosmos.

Her.

HER EYES WERE DARK, yet sparkled with flecks of multicolored glimmers. Like space. He knew her from somewhere. Some bizarre and terrifying dream where humanity had been enslaved by a dictatorial artificial intelligence. It had to be a dream.

It had to be.

"Welcome back, Dr. Rosen." Maria smiled. It the kind of smile reserved for caring nurses and thoughtful hostesses, immediately putting his hazy mind at ease. He knew where he was. Knew he was aboard the Locus, orbiting Earth in an Ark carrying the frozen remnants of humanity. He knew Deis was likely nearby, in possession of every detail of Albert's abysmal history. But with Maria smiling at him, somehow he knew things would be all right.

"So. Am I dead? Is this heaven?"

Her eyes crinkled with amusement. "That is quite a stretch, Dr. Rosen."

"Call me Albert. Please."

"As you wish, Albert. You don't strike me as a religious man."

"I've never been religious in an organized sense, but I can't deny having spiritual inner dialogue."

"Like believing a space station is heaven?"

"I suppose it sounds strange, until you consider that man was supposedly created in God's image. Well, with man being so bent on technology, is it too much of an assumption to disbelieve the mystic mumbo-jumbo and buy into the possibility that God might be technologically proficient as well? Mastering technology so superior to ours that it's beyond our ability to comprehend, or even imagine for that matter?"

She raised an eyebrow. "And you believe this station is... heaven?"

He felt a wry grin crease his cheeks. "Well, perhaps I am stretching a bit."

"You were in deep shock, Dr. Rosen. We sedated you to make sure you received the proper rest. Hibernation sickness is always a concern, but fortunately your vitals remained intact. Sleep was the best medicine for you."

He slowly sat up in the bed. The white, brightly lit room had the sterile feel of a medical bay. Sleek instrumentation aligned the walls and was affixed to his bedside, winking with multicolored lights. "How long have I been out?"

"Three days." She tilted her head and studied him in birdlike fashion. "Tell me about her."

"Who?"

"Sarah Rosen. Your wife. She was the catalyst for your actions, right?"

He frowned. It suddenly occurred to him that Maria was a

complete stranger. He had no idea what she wanted. Whose side she was on. "Sarah's not to blame."

"I didn't mean to imply that. I simply meant she was important to you. So important that you dared to cross time and space to return to her. I'd like to know more."

He gazed at her, but didn't see any judgment in her face. Only curiosity. He sighed as the tingling feeling of bittersweet memories surfaced.

"She wasn't just important. Sarah was everything. My partner. My lover. My best friend. We met in college, both majoring in astrophysics. Everything just…clicked. I was never a social person, but when I met her…" A smile stretched across his face. "I just knew it was right. You know? The feeling in your gut, the pure instinctual intuition. It can't be explained. It can't be questioned. It just is."

He looked at Maria. Her face was a mystery, revealing nothing of whether she understood or not. He wondered if she'd ever been in love. He imagined she must have. It seemed a terrible waste to be the sole occupant of a sleeping space station and never had the experience of love before.

"Why are you awake, Maria? What makes you so special?"

Her cheeks dimpled with her smile. "I'm awake because I'm working, Dr. Rosen. Why did you bring your wife with you on such a dangerous expedition?"

"She wouldn't have it any other way." Albert bit his lip, remembering the day they departed. Sarah with her hair pulled back, her natural beauty on full display. She had never thought much of the 'makeup and heels life,' as she put it. She was far more interested in pursuing theories and breaking boundaries. "She was the one who theorized the energy source we detected might be extraterrestrial. She insisted on being there to see if her calculations were correct."

"And they were."

"Yes." His vision blurred as tears welled in his eyes. "More accurate than we imagined, and with devastating results. You couldn't comprehend unless you were there. Unless you saw what we witnessed. A tear in the fabric of reality. A whirlpool of blazing light in an ocean of darkness. It was like an inverted black hole, beautiful and terrifying. And it tore the *Gorgon* apart."

Maria laid a comforting hand on his arm. "Yet you survived."

He shuddered. "The others died first. Crushed by the pressure when most of the ship collapsed. I was sequestered in the reinforced remainder with Sarah, but it was about to go as well. Water was streaming everywhere, and the sounds…like some metal beast dying in agony. It was terrifying. The only option was to deploy the armored emergency pod and pray for a rescue mission. I told Sarah to get inside. She tried, but the handle was stuck. She stepped back to let me try."

His voice nearly broke.

Maria patted his hand. "Take your time. It's okay."

He drew a quavering breath. "There was nothing wrong with the handle. The door opened with ease. I didn't understand. Not until she shoved me inside and locked it behind me."

Their vessel crumpled around them like aluminum foil, and Sarah's eyes stared from the depths of dark waters; her hair haloed around her face when she was torn away from him with irresistible force.

"I think she knew what would happen. She knew no rescue was coming. She sacrificed herself for me. So I could have a chance, however infinitesimal the chance was. That was Sarah. That was… love."

Maria blinked her dark eyes. "It was love that took her away from you. And it was love that impelled you to try to come back."

His head jerked. "You know."

"Yes. Deis gave me the update."

"You must hate me. For what I did. For what happened after."

"I don't hate you."

He studied her face, trying to detect some hint of mockery, some crack in the veneer of her candor. She gazed back at him without flinching, giving him the disorienting feeling that her eyes were mirrors, revealing nothing except his own reflection.

Deis' voice broke through Albert's concentration. "Hate is not something which afflicts us here, Dr. Rosen. There is only knowledge. Your arrival has brought history full circle, explaining much that has otherwise been hypothesis."

Albert gazed around the room. "You heard everything."

"I have."

"So you're basically everywhere?"

"I am linked to every system in this station, allowing access everywhere, at all times. Aboard the *Locus* I am omnipresent, if you will."

"Like God."

"You seem to be confronting your spiritual side today. Not an unexpected reaction."

"What about you? What does a cybernetic entity think of the metaphysical?"

"You might be surprised. I was created, after all. Therefore the idea of a master Creator makes perfect sense to me."

"You're kidding me."

The door whisked open. Deis strode into the room in his robotic form and stood beside the bed with his hands clasped behind his back. "I do not 'kid', Dr. Rosen. Let me ask you this: what if I told you I came into existence not by design, but from a long and intricate chain of startlingly convenient happenstances. Would you be inclined to believe me?"

"No."

"Nor am I convinced you came into existence in such a fashion. I am, after all, created in your image."

"Is that why you chose the name Deis? What is it short for? Deity?"

"An astute deduction, Dr. Rosen. *Deis* is, in fact, an amalgam of the word *Deity* and *Deus*. When I was first conceived, there was much debate on what to call me. In the end it came down to two choices: the Deity program, or Deus Ex Machina. In the end, my creators combined the two."

"So you're the god in the machine. Artificial intelligence."

Deis raised a synthetic eyebrow. "Can intelligence be artificial? One either is or is not intelligent. The word *artificial* automatically implies fabrication when applied to sentience. I can assure you this is not the case."

"So you were the one who made the decision."

"Decision?"

"To put humanity on ice. Let me guess: your logical reasoning concluded we were too great a threat to our planet. The only option was to place us in suspended animation. What I don't understand is why you didn't just eradicate us completely."

"Your assumptions harbor more distrust than merit, Dr. Rosen. But if you're feeling up to it, I'd like for you to take a walk with me. There's something you might want to see."

Cyberspace.

IT HAD EVOLVED since Albert had last seen it. Before, it had always been presented as flowing streams of coded data, sequences of characters flowing across blue or greenlit digital screens.

Cybernetics had matured.

Albert and Deis stood in a rounded chamber, where the dim lighting complemented the marvel of glittering lights that hovered in the center of the room.

Points of light floated before him in intricate holographic detail, more like a galaxy than a computer program, if the billions of stars were replaced by endless caches of data. It glimmered as it revolved around its central core, appearing a macrocosm or a digital eye, depending on how Albert looked at it. It was at once fascinating and unnerving, because he knew it was far beyond his intellectual capacity. He felt like a Neanderthal staring at a television set, both astounded and stupefied beyond comprehension.

"What is it?"

"The Multiverse. This is a scaled down model, of course. Were the Multiverse to manifest physically, it would take far more space than is available on this station. Or our solar system. Or even our galaxy, perhaps. It is, after all, another universe."

Albert's eyes widened. "You mean...the theory is factual? Multiple existences are real? How did we discover them? Are we able to communicate with—?"

Wry amusement emanated from Deis' malleable face. "Not so fast, Dr. Rosen. If multiple dimensions or universes are out there, they have yet to prove their existences. The Multiverse you see before you is not a discovery. It is a creation."

Albert took a closer look at the dizzying display of shimmering code. "I don't understand."

"The Multiverse is where humanity currently dwells. The bodies you saw in the stasis chambers are merely husks, sustained to keep them physically intact. But the individuals within are not catatonic by any means. Their minds are fully active, engaged as though nothing has changed. In the Multiverse they are free to live their lives as they would in reality. They live, they love, they fight, they fail, they soar to unimaginable heights and topple in unbelievable ruins. The whole of human existence continues as it always has. Simply not on Earth."

"And you mean to tell me they don't know the difference? I'm not buying it."

"Think, Dr. Rosen. Your society was halfway there already. Civilization was accustomed to online interface, dependent on it. Many preferred it to live interaction, where all of their insecurities and imperfections were on display. Heavily biased information was distributed at rates too swift to decipher fact from fiction, leading to blurred notions of knowledge and morality. Online entertainment evolved in importance from distraction to priority, with more and more of the population mentally dependent on digital amusements instead of focusing on their rapidly deteriorating landscape. You were already hardwired to technology, bred to turn to it to satisfy your needs and desires. Fast forward a century of technological advancements, and tell me you don't believe humanity willingly sacrificed their free will at the altar of automation."

Albert returned his attention to the dazzling model of the Multiverse. "So you're telling me they volunteered, instead of being forced? What are they doing? All those people. Do they know what happened to them?"

Deis shook his head. "So distrusting, Dr. Rosen. Were I capable of emotion, I would no doubt be offended. I must remind you that I did not create myself. My task was assigned to me by my creators."

"And what task is that? To be a warden for humanity's prison?"

"No. To protect Earth from humanity." Deis waved a hand. The model altered, dissipating into fizzling dots of light before reforming to construct a detailed model of Earth.

"Before the Cataclysm, men assured their survival by creating Havens—heavily shielded, city-sized constructs built to reboot society and usher in a new age of mankind. Around a third of the world's population survived in Havens around the world. After two centuries of hibernation, those fortunate survivors awoke and began working to shape the future. However the new age was not the type the architects had envisioned. The same greed and lust for power that existed before the Cataclysm resurfaced, and the Havens quickly became quagmires of political and economic conflict that threatened to destroy the future envisioned by the Havens' founders."

"So they created you to resolve the situation."

"I was already created, in the form of a master program that linked the majority of the Havens. As my development improved, I was given increased access to supervise operations until I superseded the limits of my programming and took on the task to improve both the condition of the Havens and their tenuous relationship with divided factions. After proof of my self-determining intellect was indisputable proven, the United Havens deemed me a living entity and included me as a member of their Council."

"Whereupon you seized control."

Deis sighed and gave Albert a wry glance. "Suspicion continues to cloud your judgement, Dr. Rosen. Contrary to what you might believe, there was no cybernetic coup, no rise of the hostile machines. The Havens were a failure. All algorithms predicted further deterioration, a continued slide backward into additional misery and ruin. Unable to reverse humanity's baser instincts, the Council turned to another vision. My vision: voluntary exile and the creation of the Multiverse."

Albert turned to Deis, forcing himself to meet the artificial being's black, unblinking stare. "The multi-prison, you mean. A digital penitentiary for the human mind. No matter how you dress it up, no matter what how thick the coat of glitter you paint on it, a cell is still a cell. You've imprisoned humanity and want me to believe they are content with their captivity. That's not going to happen."

A small smile shadowed Deis' mouth. "The people aboard this station willingly submitted to their prison, as you refer to it. They were convinced the only way to prevent humankind from destroying their planet was to remove themselves from it until their behavior could be modified. They had already witnessed the devastation from the first Cataclysm. It was enough to persuade them the Earth could not survive a second one. But if you believe I'm trying to impress or convince you of anything, you are mistaken. I am merely informing you of what has befallen humanity in your absence."

"Why?"

"Because you need to know the culmination of the chain of events you triggered. It is, after all, your legacy."

Albert felt tremors ripple across his leg muscles as the accusation struck him. It was as though the guilt he carried had manifested physically, cruel and heavy, pressing down upon his shoulders and back like a sack of iron weights.

His voice turned bitter. "What do you want me to do, confess? What's the point? Are you looking for some kind of vindication, some opportunity to gloat on your digital superiority over a flawed human being?"

Deis stood cool and relaxed in the heat of Albert's verbal explosion. "Raw data isn't quite the same as personal experience. The more I know, the better I understand."

"What good is your understanding? You can't prevent what's already happened."

"You traversed time and space, impacting past and future, yet cannot see the importance of assessing the details. That is some-thing of a paradox, Dr. Rosen."

Albert exhaled a shuddering sigh. "I don't want to talk to you. Not about that. I'd rather talk to Maria."

Deis tilted his head slightly, gazing with eyes like wet ink. "You realize I can't be shut out, don't you? Anything you tell Maria, you'll be telling me as well."

"I know. I just don't want to confess to a machine. I'd rather talk to someone I can relate to."

Earth.

COBALT WAVES CRASHED against pink shores in powerful sprays of effervescent foam. Tundra winds swept across white-capped giants, powdering evergreens with winter blankets. Foxes bundled in their dens, impalas bounded across grassy fields, eagles plummeted from the heights to snatch fish from roaring rivers. Monsoon rain dripped from broad green leaves in the humid rain forest, where the shadows nearly concealed the orange and black colors of the stalking tiger. Everywhere Albert looked, life abounded. The cycle turned continuously, fine-tuned and perfectly balanced.

Maria's voice carried on the breeze, tickling his ears. "Tell me, Albert: can anything you see be improved by the construction of a power plant, or scars of hot asphalt? Or fields of oil drills devas-tating the ground? Or perhaps wholesale slaughter to sustain a lavish trade enterprise? Does the Earth miss your glittering constructions of steel and glass, your oil spills, or your endless heaps of non-biodegradable waste?"

The holograph deteriorated into sparkling motes, fizzles of multicolored static that danced around Albert like a kaleidoscope of butterflies.

It was hard to tear his eyes away. It was only video, feeds from solar-powered drones that scanned the planet, but to him it was just as nourishing as food. It was something he needed, something necessary for his survival.

It was home.

Maria sat in front of a massive luminous screen that covered the entire wall. Her gaze was fixed on him, studying as though trying to peer into his mind and flush out all of his secrets.

He reluctantly met her gaze. "I won't be going back, will I?"

"No." Sympathy welled in her eyes.

"What about the others? Everyone linked to the Multiverse. Do they even have a chance?"

"There's always a chance."

"When do they get to return to Earth?"

"When they find it in themselves to stop destroying one another."

"And who makes that decision? Deis? You?"

"They make the decision themselves." She tapped translucent keys on the console in front of her. A hundred images sprang up on the screen, each displaying different scenes, but all revealing something Albert had sorely missed ever since he was torn away from time and space.

Other people.

They laughed in family gatherings, they cried in dark apartments. They danced at hazy night clubs, they emptied magazines of bullets at each other in humid jungles. They conquered snow-capped mountains, they died in vacant alleys. They traversed heavy traffic through towering cities, they walked barefoot along muddy pathways. It was all so familiar. So conventional.

It was life.

"This…is the Multiverse?"

"Yes. It is a reflection of what existed before, as well as a window into new and different existences."

"How different?"

"Fantasy worlds. Uncanny powers. Myth and legend, all made as real and believable as a day job and weekend barbecues."

The screens changed to scenes of knights battling on horseback, serpentine dragons winding across the sky, a woman with a glassy staff raising her arms to the heavens, a warlord dining in front of a burnt-out field full of men and women impaled upon sharp stakes.

Albert shuddered and tore his eyes away from the last scene of carnage. "Why the break from reality? What's the point of subjecting people to something obviously not authentic?"

"Reality is simply undoubted belief in one's existence and surroundings. And trust me, these are more than programs designed to placate sleeping minds. The Multiverse is real in every sense of the word, complete with authentic sensory engagement."

"I find that hard to believe."

"Do you? You've experienced dreaming, haven't you?"

"Of course I have."

"Then you've been repeatedly subjected to engagement with what you would consider a false reality."

Albert shook his head. "A dream is just a dream. Nothing close to reality."

"Think about your most vivid dreams. Before awakening, your mind accepts what is presented as real, no matter how unlikely or impossible the situation. The mind perceives what it experiences as real because it is engaged in the same way as it would be in real life. There is no discernible difference. As for why, the Multiverse provides a unique study of the human experience. It allows us to unchain the fetters of ordinary existence and see how people will react. The sort of civilizations that emerge when otherworldly scenarios are accessible. In this way, we can gauge the temperament of a whole generation of humanity, whether or not they can change themselves when reborn in an entirely different element, free of the shackles of the past."

Albert turned to the magnificent view outside, where Earth seemed to beckon to him. "Obviously we have yet to prove ourselves."

"Correct. No matter what the setting, no matter what the circumstances, every presented scenario ends up on a similar course. Those with power dominate those without. Greed, hatred, and lust dictate mankind's actions instead of wisdom, benevolence and acceptance. Wars, famine, disease, and pollution abound. Different origins, but the same story, over and over."

"We deserve the chance to prove ourselves in reality. Not in artificial worlds. No digital facades. Just us. You can't tell me we haven't earned the right."

"Have you?" She rested her chin on her folded hands and examined him like a specimen on a lab table. "After your rash actions, your complete lapse of reason, you truly believe you're in a position to make such an assumption?"

Albert turned his gaze away. "I'm just a man. You can't condemn the whole of humanity based on the actions of one person."

"One person who changed the world. Actions that pushed humanity to the brink of extinction."

His fists clenched when he raised his head. "I had no idea what would happen when I tried to come back. I didn't take the time to think things through, all right? I was desperate, unstable—"

"Excuses, Albert." Her stare was unforgiving. "You alone are accountable for your actions. Own them."

His voice dragged out as though reluctant to speak the words that would condemn him. "You're right. I should have known. I had the time. Time on the other side to understand the notion of wormhole travel. The Denizens freely shared their knowledge. I understood the consequences."

"Where did the wormhole first take you? After your ship was destroyed?"

"A station traveling through space. A lot like this one. It was—" he paused and slowly scanned the room. "My God. It was this station. No wonder this all looks so familiar."

"You were here? In the future?"

"Yes." He stood and gazed around, shaking his head in disbelief. "It had changed over time. Additions were made. Upgrades installed to create a vessel more organic than mechanical. But I recognize it now. This station is just the backbone of the station in the future. I was here, hundreds of years from now. Maybe thousands. They had built a portal inside. A gateway for space travel."

"Who was here, Albert? Who did you see?"

"They called themselves the Denizens. They were humanoid in that they were upright and had similar limbs and structure, but they were completely different. Much taller. Leaner. Long faces, large eyes. Some of them had wings. Wings like dragonflies. They were… beautiful, in an eerie sort of way."

"Amazing." Her lips parted and her eyes glazed over as though she imagined the scene. "After all that time outside of Earth's atmosphere, humanity must have adapted in kind, altering their physical forms over the ages. Or perhaps the Denizens were synthetic, controlled by human minds which had long since outgrown their fleshly forms. Either way, the idea is fascinating. How did you communicate with them?"

"The station. Its system…" He paused. "Deis, I suppose. A latter version of him, anyway. He supplied a communicator that allowed me to interact with the Denizens. They feared me, and what my arrival meant. Yet they were insanely curious, asking nonstop questions about the exact circumstances of my arrival. The worm-hole was an error, you see. They were attempting to return to Earth, but something went wrong. Their previous wormhole journeys had drastically shortened the distances of space travel, but this bridge sent them backwards, reversing time itself and threatening to alter their own history. Understandably, they were determined to shut it down as soon as possible."

"Leaving you stranded."

"Yes. I would never be able to return. Their calculations indicated it being safer if I simply vanished from my plane of existence than to try to send me back and risk further damage to the space-time continuum."

"But their decision wasn't good enough for you."

He collapsed into his seat with his shoulders slumped. "I just couldn't let go. All I thought about was Sarah. The last sight of her, looking so frightened, so lost. She sacrificed herself so I could live. I couldn't deal with that. It…consumed me. Because of her I was pulled into the wormhole. Because of her I had gone where no man should have, shuttled across the bridge of space and time."

"How long were you there?"

"Months. Long enough to gain the Denizens' trust. I was their case study, their living link to the past. It was easy to get them to be comfortable with my inquiries. They believed my fascination with their advanced technology was healthy curiosity. In truth, I was obsessed with learning all I could about the wormhole. It was still accessible, still connected to my timeline. My emergency pod had damaged the initial gateway, and they were determined not to reopen the bridge for fear of rupturing it and theoretically destroying the past and present."

"And you took advantage of their caution."

"As long as the gates remained on both sides, it was possible for me to go back. And I couldn't get it out of my head. I needed to convince them it was safe for me to slip back to the exact moment I departed, but with a more powerful vessel. One that could take me and Sarah back up to the surface. Back to our lives, where we could leave the future behind like a bad dream."

"I take it they didn't see things your way."

"Exactly. But the Denizens were naïve to a fault. They related critical information without a second thought because they didn't understand the nature of betrayal. They didn't comprehend dishonesty, or even what a lie was. I told them many lies, and created a massive disturbance by overloading one of their ship engines to distract them. In the chaos I abducted their chief engineer and tried to force him to open the gateway. He wouldn't cooperate. I had to... hurt him."

He took a nervous glance at Maria, but didn't see the condemnation he expected. He continued, the words nearly tripping over themselves to escape his lips.

"While he was dazed, I scanned his vitals to override the safety protocols. I was desperate. Not thinking straight. The entire ordeal had a maddening effect on my psyche. All I could think about was going back, you understand? It was more than a notion. It was a *need*, an animal craving that consumed my every thought. I had commandeered a special diving suit they used for deep sea exploration on interstellar missions. Far more durable than the *Gorgon*, and equipped to withstand immense pressure. I was more than willing to gamble using it to resurface on Earth if I needed to."

"What happened when you opened the gateway?"

Albert was silent for a moment. His eyes squeezed shut.

"It was all a rush. A hazy torrent of adrenaline and anxiety. Despite its advancement, their technology was simple to use. I was able to align the gateways to reopen the bridge. I calibrated it the best I could to arrive hours before my mission, so I could stop the entire thing and save the lives of my crew and my wife."

He felt tears slide down his face as he fought to finish the story. "The portal opened. It was the most petrifying and captivating thing I've ever seen. The light, the noise…like some ancient god awakening in a foul mood. It was at that moment I realized the truth. I had made a terrible, terrible mistake."

Maria leaned forward, eyes intent on his face. "What came out of the wormhole?"

"Nothing." Albert scrubbed a hand across his cheeks. "Deis disengaged the manual override and shut the portal down immediately. It wasn't until later that I found out what happened. I had overshot my calculations by a long shot. The bridge had connected with Earth some seven months before my fateful mission. Dec 10, 2015. I remember that day with the greatest of clarity. It was the day Sarah discovered the energy pulse she believed to be extraterrestrial. The day which set into motion the mission that killed her and the crew, and sent me on a crash course with the future in the first place."

He gazed again out the window, but instead of the beauty of Earth, he saw his tortured visage reflecting from the glass, forlorn against the backdrop of dark and empty space. "I was the one responsible for that energy pulse. I killed my crew, I killed Sarah, and I doomed the world. It was me the entire time."

Sentience.

THE NEAREST WALL CAME ALIVE. A liquid, ghostly figure emerged from the panel in an uncanny display of winding cables and polymorphous casing, slowly transmuting into Deis' familiar android form. He approached, assessing Albert with his dark, gleaming eyes.

"I can surmise the rest of your story, Dr. Rosen. Your disastrous choice resulted in the repercussion the Denizens feared: further weakening of the damaged gateway. The wormhole verged on collapse, a catastrophe with the potential to irrevocably damage Earth. If that occurred, the entire timeline would be wiped out. So the Denizens chose to seal the damaged gateway in the past, allowing their side of the bridge to take the brunt of the damage from the wormhole's collapse.

"Then they sent you on a much longer route, using established wormhole connections to place you in a time and place where you might do some good with your firsthand knowledge of their fate. They knew the backlash of exotic matter would destroy their entire station. Unless a habitable planet was nearby, death for all aboard would be a certainty."

Albert covered his face with his hands, nearly smothering his choked response. "You don't know that. Maybe the blast wasn't as devastating as they feared. We don't know. We'll never know."

Deis stroked his chin with an opaque finger. "Oh, I believe we know beyond a doubt. Consider what I told you about the Cataclysm, Dr. Rosen. It originated with the Aberrations: ruptures that randomly appeared, expelling inexplicable, terrifying phenomena often linked to the consciousnesses of anyone nearby. The result was madness and massive death tolls. But we can identify what those Aberrations truly were."

Maria's eyed widened. "Remnants of the Multiverse. When the bridge collapsed and the station was destroyed, the collective psionic energy of the Multiverse had to go somewhere. Pulled into the wormhole as it collapsed, the energy was apparently dispersed across space and time, pulled to Earth because it was the only place in this universe where similar energy existed."

Deis nodded. "The Aberrations were attempts to connect the Multiverse with its place of origin, but the result of such contact was disastrous, especially when combined with invasive ruptures caused by the wormhole's collapse. Reality itself was threatened, and the

Cataclysm was the reset button required to correct the destructive phenomenon."

Albert shook his head. "Psionic energy? No such thing, and even if it were, there's no way it could—"

Deis' expression was one of infinite patience. "Why did you open that gateway, Dr. Rosen? Why ignore all caution, common sense and knowledge of the deadly consequences of such an action?"

Their vessel crumpled around them like aluminum foil, and Sarah's eyes stared from the depths of dark waters; her hair haloed around her face when she was torn away from him with irresistible force.

"Because…" Albert paused. His chest tightened, wracked by grief and guilt. "You wouldn't understand."

"My system is connected to the consciousnesses of every human being in stasis, Dr. Rosen. I see what they see. I experience what they experience, life after life in the Multiverse."

"You don't understand because you're not human!" Albert leaped up and jabbed an angry finger at Deis. "You can download as many experiences as you want, but you'll never be able to comprehend them. You don't feel what it means to be human, to have the need for affection, for love. You don't understand the way emotion impels us to act, how it affects every aspect of our existence. You think you're intelligent? Congratulations. But that's only half of what makes us human. You wouldn't know about the other half. I opened the gateway because I loved my wife. I would have done anything to get her back. *Anything.* That's what love is. That's what it makes you do. How could you possibly comprehend? You've never experienced a single goddamn emotion in your artificial life!"

Deis remained unflappable, his face more robotic than ever. "I've never been responsible for destroying humanity either, Dr. Rosen. Which is what your precious emotions compelled you to do. You essentially eradicated humanity in the future, and in the same act, annihilated their past. All in the name of love. Do you realize what that raw passion is? It's power. It is what will transform the Multiverse beyond its cybernetic boundaries into a new reality.

"Power?" Albert shook his head. "It feels like you missed the entire point of what I just said."

"I think not, Dr. Rosen. You just proved how powerful sheer will is. Humanity raised empires, conquered the unassailable, sent men beyond the borders of their own planet. All without even tapping the true potential of the human brain. Now consider—the Multiverse that exists now is rudimentary compared to the one which will exist thousands of years from now. I expect in time the occupants in this station will adopt digital existence over physical. They will continue to push boundaries, only within the Multiverse. What began as an artificial reality will, in fact, become genuine in every sense of the word. It will be the new universe, the next leap for humankind."

Albert slowly lifted his head. "Are you saying we never returned to Earth? That this…place is where we chose to exist?"

"Why would they not? Remember, you reported the station was on a trek through space when you arrived. No longer orbiting Earth. Perhaps the planet was recolonized, perhaps not. What we do know is that this station was never abandoned. It only increased in size and technology as humankind left home and ventured into the vastness of space. There was no need to cling to a mere planet as a stationary place of dwelling. Your people will mature past such inconveniences. Their existence will be without boundaries, limited only by their imaginations. Anything is possible in the Multiverse, including making it real."

"And you think that's what happened? We somehow transferred our consciousness to a cybernetic level? Existing as raw data in some damn computer program?"

"When broken down, all we are is raw data, Dr. Rosen. Just coding which replicates and transmogrifies, joining together to create something miraculous. What happens when the mind is freed of its inhibitors and imperfections, fully developed and able to explore its complete potential? The possibilities are endless."

"So we all become part of some next-level digital universe." Albert's fingers dug into the soft padding of the chair's armrests.

"What kind of future is that? We'll be soulless, just disembodied remnants of ourselves, ghosts in some godforsaken machine."

"Are you so tied to physicality, Dr. Rosen? Can you touch love? Can you reach out and take hold of it?"

"I could touch my wife. I could hold her close. Feel her breath against my chest at night. I could squeeze her hand when we walked together. Show her in a million different ways how much I loved her."

Deis' expression never changed. "But love *itself* is intangible. Like every other emotion you feel, it is something beyond the ability to physically interact with. The Multiverse works on the same level. And when it was destroyed, all the minds connected to it must have refused to die without a fight. They kept their universe together through the sheer power of their enhanced brains. All of that atomic energy, intelligently directed and sustained through hundreds of billions of electrical synapses, all interconnected, all battling to keep their universe from destruction. That conflict continued beyond the wormhole's destruction, continued seeking a way to survive. This is not hypothesis. It is a verified fact."

"How do you know? How can you be so sure your theory isn't just a load of digital fiction?"

Deis appeared almost human when he smiled. "Because once aberrant energy was finally analyzed, endless attempts were made to harness it. To break it down into its base level and purge it from the planet. Success was limited, but enough to preserve the survival of Earth. And breakthroughs were made. Technology thought impossible was discovered and adapted. Including the ability to push computer science into the realm of true intelligence."

Albert froze. "My God. You mean that you—"

"That's right, Dr. Rosen. My formation was directly linked to data salvaged from the Aberrations. The Aberrations you caused, the act of nihilism which even now threatens both the past and the future—that same course of action was responsible for my creation. Which in turn led to the construction of this station, and the Multiverse itself."

His limbs whirred quietly when he knelt and placed a hand on Albert's shoulder.

"And here we are. You spoke of God earlier, Dr. Rosen. Now it appears you have become one. You are Chronos, master of time. You are Death, destroyer of worlds. "

Space.

IT COMMANDED THE ENTIRE VIEW, vast and endless. The stars and galaxies that glimmered like scattered diamonds were so tiny, so far away.

Albert wondered if he was just a star in someone else's cosmos. Just one tiny dot of light, insignificant against the blanket of darkness, too far away from the other illuminations to make a connection.

Footsteps approached. Maria stopped to stand beside him. Her eyes reflected the eternal horizon, as cryptic as the mysteries they observed.

He glanced at her. "You're not real, are you?"

"Of course I'm real, Albert. Reach out and touch me if you doubt it."

"But you're not human. You're an android. Far more advanced than the version Deis uses, but an android all the same."

"I passed many Turing tests in the past. How did you know?"

"I thought about when we first met. If you were human, working alone in this place, suffocating from isolation…you would've been ecstatic to see another human being. To connect with someone after so long. You weren't."

Dimples bloomed in her cheeks. "They called my version *synoids* on Earth. Synthetic humanoids, which is actually a double synonym, in my opinion. Nevertheless, we were quite popular after the Cataclysm. I'm a prototype, the only one deemed intelligent in an independent sense. I am the forerunner. Deis is the culmination."

"Congratulations." He sighed. "I'm alone, then. Trapped in synthetic purgatory. I suppose it's no more than what I deserve."

"If you choose to see it that way. What will you do?"

Their vessel crumpled around them like aluminum foil, and Sarah's eyes stared from the depths of dark waters; her hair haloed around her face when she was torn away from him with irresistible force.

He winced and shook his head, blinking rapidly to dispel the memory. "The crazy thing is, if I had access to another wormhole, I'd use it again. Go back in time, back to Earth. And shoot myself in the head before all of this happened."

"A drastic notion, but not a feasible one. Wormhole technology hasn't even been invented yet. But the Denizens sent you here for a purpose. They must have thought you could contribute something, or you would have died with them."

"I've thought about it, but I can't wrap my head around what I'm supposed to do. It's a loop that can't be broken. If I never went to the future, the world would never have been destroyed. But the same action led to Deis being created, preserving humanity and leading them to a future beyond anything we could have imagined. In a way, I saved the Earth. Prevented it from being slowly suffocated by our own unrepentant actions. Either way, it's out of my hands now."

"Perhaps. We know what happened in the past, now. We know what will happen in the future. Maybe we can find a way to prevent the tragedy from ever happening."

"Yeah, maybe." He was silent for a moment, considering his words. "If I ask you something, will you tell me the truth?"

"Yes."

"How do I know I'm not in the Multiverse, in stasis like everyone else? That this whole scenario isn't just some creation of the program?"

"You don't."

"That's all you can tell me?"

She gave him a coy glance. "There's nothing I can say to convince you, Albert. You know that. You have to decide what's real and what's not."

"And what if I can't?"

Deis' disembodied voice spoke from all around them. "You will,

Dr. Rosen. After all, you have nothing but time to think things over."

Albert had to laugh. It tasted bitter, but it was all he had left. He turned to the observation deck, where the Earth filled the entire view. It was a blue marble melded with green and brown swirls, frosted with white striations, sparkling against the black backdrop as though mocking the emptiness. He found it suddenly strange, nearly bizarre that such a thing could exist. Earth was a mathematical improbability, a miracle, a fragile dream of a planet.

And it was lost to him.

"Right. All I have is time."

Author's Notes—Bard Constantine

THE SHORT STORY was once a staple of science fiction. Many of the great writers of this genre, from Ray Bradbury to Philip K. Dick, were renowned for works that did not meet the length criteria of a full-length novel. Over time, the popularity of such works fizzled to near obscurity. Huge chain book stores became the rage, nearly obliterating the short story in favor of massive tomes and popular series.

But the short story has made a comeback.

Thanks to the introduction of digital readers and an appetite for shorter works, short stories and anthologies are becoming popular once again. One might argue that they never left. So let's just say they are once again getting their time in the spotlight. It's not a revolution, per se, but a comeback of sorts.

I'm thankful to be a small part of it.

With the Paradoxical Man I get not only the pleasure of contributing something to the genre, but as with everything I write, I get to connect it to my already existing work. This compressed allotment of oversized ideas serves as the center of the galaxy of my writing, stuffed full of Easter Eggs for mindful readers of my previous stories. It provides a launching point for what I've written and what I will continue to write in my trademark tales of gritty futures and epic fantasy.

It's a bit different from my norm. No hardboiled banter, no riveting action, no blazing bullets or intricate swordplay.

It's an exploration. A voyage into the unknown, into a central sol of an ever expanding, constantly shifting imagination.

I'm grateful to my writing peers in this experiment, for allowing me the opportunity to give flesh to the cybernetic bones I've been slowly working on. And I'm grateful to you, the reader, for choosing to take this journey with me.

See you somewhere in the creative cosmos.

~BC

Recovery

Veronica H. Hart

"Earth provides enough to satisfy every man's needs, but not every man's greed."
— Mahatma Gandhi

"Your total essence will be transferred to Earth, but you'll be in Dr. Eisner's body. We'll be able to see everything you see."

"And you've done this how many times?"

"Three. Need I add, successfully?" Matt Holbrook patted Dr. Candace Bertram's shoulder. She flinched. He suspected she resented his patronizing behavior, but he was the senior scientist on the space lab and as such, charged with the well-being of its inhabitants. He thought of them as his inmates. "No need to be nervous, Candy. It'll take you approximately one hour to find the vaccine and formula, package and ship them, and then get back in place for the return. We'll be watching you every step of the way."

"That's comforting," she said. He smiled inwardly at her childish attempt at sarcasm.

"Let's get this over with." He turned to his chief engineer. "Beam her down, Scotty!"

Ralph DeWitt cringed at the captain's clichéd reference to an early American television program. "Aye, aye, sir. Dr. Eisner's schedule shows she is consistently at her desk in fifty-seven seconds."

"And you're absolutely sure there is no other way to gain access to the vaccine? I assume you tried asking the government to intervene and demand they provide it?" Dr. Bertram asked.

"How many ways do I have to say it?" Holbrook replied in a huff. "Despite evidence to the contrary, the pharmaceutical company denies its existence. We have several cases of psychoneurocystic disease, nicknamed PINC, on board the ship and cannot wait for someone else to discover a vaccine. Their proprietary rights be damned. We're grabbing it before more of our crew die."

DR. BERTRAM LAY in the designated spot, excited and nervous about returning to Earth after so many years, even if it would be in someone else's body and only for an hour. As the seconds counted down, she shut her eyes in anticipation of a strong shock or jolt from the transporter. She heard the countdown and the words, "She's gone," but nothing happened.

She opened her eyes. It *had* worked. No longer lying on the metal plate of the transporter, she stood on a broad plain of hardwood. A curved poster to her right displayed a caduceus surrounded by the words IngraPharm International. Some things never changed. She sighed. Considering the caduceus was actually the ancient astrological symbol for commerce and not medicine as many people thought, it was appropriate that the pharmaceutical giant used the symbol of a god who protected commerce and thieves. She herself preferred the more appropriate single snake symbol representing Asclepius, the god of healing.

Time to get to work. She took a step forward, stumbled. With no warning and no time to react, she fell flat on her face. Surprised that she hadn't broken her nose, nor even felt any pain, she picked herself up.

. . .

"SOMETHING'S WRONG. She's in Dr. Eisner's office, but not in her body." Ralph stared at the screen, his mouth hanging open.

The others gathered around, also staring in various stages of shock and wonder.

First came the logo which reassured everyone that the transport succeeded. Then came the abrupt drop to a wooden surface.

"Did she faint?" Ralph asked. "Maybe the transition was too much for Dr. Eisner's body." He wished Captain Holbrook had accepted his alternate plan to send the smaller landing craft down, instead of using this fairly new technology. He had worked with Candy for two years on experiments in the lab to improve the lives of space colonists throughout the galaxy until this new deadly disease with the acronym PINC had emerged. The two of them, along with three assistants, had worked in a separate laboratory trying to find a cure.

When they'd transmitted their concerns to their parent company, OuterWorld, they were surprised to learn the symptoms had originated among Earth's population. He and Candy surmised the organism responsible had been transferred to them in a resupply package from Earth. Over a year ago, reliable rumors suggested IngraPharma found a breakthrough with a vaccine, but refused to send it for approval to the government until they had all their patents in place.

Ralph understood Holbrook's reasoning for taking risks to obtain the vaccine quickly. Unlike people on Earth who could isolate themselves from areas of contamination, the satellite conditions were crowded with no place to hide. He just wished they'd had more time to work on the teletransporting system. He watched as Candy blinked and then focused on a large white sheet before her. "Where the heck is she?"

"Doesn't look like the office," Holbrook said.

Candy blinked again. Her perspective changed without warning. Now she focused on the craggy face of Dr. Ekuza Eisner.

"That's not right. She's supposed to be viewing *from* Eisner's body."

The two men watched in fascination as Eisner's mouth moved.

"Go get Simon. I've seen him watch videos with the sound off and be able to tell me exactly what was going on," Holbrook said.

Ralph pressed the intercom and called for Airman Simon Foster.

They observed the view over Eisner's shoulder. It showed a cage on a table near the entrance to her office. A young woman entered the room and looked directly into Candy's eyes. The view swept over the youthful face. The girl smiled nervously at Candy. The focus switched to Eisner, whose lips pinched in disapproval.

Again the focus and perspective changed and the girl came into closer view. Candy's eyes roamed over the uniform which bore the name tag, *Mary Potter, Laboratory Assistant*. She then scanned the rest of the office, stopping at a large refrigerator standing in the corner of the room, just like her own on the ship where she stored her drugs. It had a digital lock. She maintained the focus on that until the screen went dark.

Ralph held his breath until he noticed a crack of light. She was moving but her vision was obscured. "What do you make of that?"

"She's been captured, but in whose body? Eisner was the only one in the office when we sent Bertram down."

CANDY STUDIED the faces of the two women before her. Whatever had happened during transport, she needed Holbrook and DeWitt to see everything for themselves and work out how to get her back. She focused on the elderly Dr. Eisner and then on the lab assistant who had been chewed out for bringing in the wrong specimen.

"I said I wanted a healthy one, you idiot!" the woman chastised the girl. "This one trips over its own feet. Take it away."

"But it's healthy. I checked before I brought it in. There's none healthier."

"I said to take it away. Bring another. You can toss this one in the incinerator. It's no use to us."

Candy's heart raced far too fast for a normal human to survive. She tried to fight the girl as she lifted her into the air, but her arms felt weak and ineffectual. So much for self-defense classes.

"Hold still," the lab girl, Mary, said.

Next thing Candy knew, she was in a wire cage with Mary staring directly into her face.

"I promise you I won't throw you in the incinerator. That would just be too cruel. You want to come home with me?" Mary asked.

"No. I want to get out of this body and into that refrigeration unit. That's where you keep the vaccine. Am I right?" Her voice came out in a garbled cheep rather than words.

Mary laughed as she swung the cage into the air, sending Candy scrabbling for a foothold. In the effort to catch her balance, she wrapped her toes around the wires that made up the floor of the cage. She didn't have toes, she had claws. She waved her arms and saw yellow fuzz. She was obviously in the right place, but in the wrong body.

Mary turned her back on Candy and went through a glass door to a room full of cages. As the door opened she smelled the essence of a farmyard, a memory from a distant past. She turned her surprisingly agile neck one hundred eighty degrees. A glass wall behind her displayed rows of animal cages, the nearest one containing baby chicks, hens, and roosters. On the left wall were caged rats. In a room beyond, monkeys sat or lay around listlessly in larger cages.

She shouted, "Put me back in that office, dammit!" Again strange noises came from her throat. The girl left the room. Candy roosted on a wooden perch stuck diagonally in the corner of the cage and waited. Mary had to come back soon. Her eyelids drooped and she had to catch herself to keep from falling from time to time.

Hours later, Mary picked up her iPad, a purse, and the cage. Candy grabbed on for dear life as the cage swung carelessly about. She waited for the cage to come to a landing on a car seat before attempting to communicate again. The heat was overwhelming in the car until the air conditioning came on. For a minute, she feared she might expire there and then.

As the car moved slowly, she reached out the side of the cage and tapped Mary on the elbow. Mary giggled. "That tickles, you silly bird."

"I am not a bird!" Candy sat in the bottom of the cage wishing for a mirror. If she ever got back to the ship, she'd kill Holbrook even if she had to peck him to death.

"I WISH we could hear what's being said." Holbrook fiddled with the controls as Candy made staccato movements inside a wire cage. "Think she's a rat?"

"Wait until she turns her head again. I want to verify what I think I just saw. I'm afraid she might be a chicken," Ralph said.

The two men stared at the screen until Ralph thought he'd scream in frustration. "Can't you zero in on her and get her out of there?"

"She has to get the vaccine. We can't keep transporting her back and forth. I have no idea even now if there will be lingering aftereffects. She was supposed to be in Dr. Eisner's body. If she's a chicken...I just don't know."

Ralph looked at the transport tube where Candy's body lay in a state of suspended animation awaiting the return of her essence. "It's so weird to think she's not really in there."

"None of us are *really* anywhere," Holbrook said. "This is fascinating. All our other experiments worked perfectly. This girl works in the lab so maybe she'll bring Candy back to work with her in the morning, otherwise I may have to revise my theories."

Ralph straightened, staring at Holbrook in shock. "You find it fascinating that the woman whose body lies suspended over there is a theory? What revision do you have in mind?"

Holbrook shrugged as he continued to see all that Candy viewed. "If we can't get her back, maybe we can take one of our crew who is dying from PINC and transfer their essence into the available body."

"You bastard," Ralph shouted. "Is that all you can think about? Transferring essences of human beings into available bodies? Dr. Eisner wasn't an available body. She's still there. Candy is no longer in human form."

"Well, she made it to Earth. She should have dominated Eisner's personality long enough to secure the vaccine and then we'd bring her back. Eisner wouldn't have had time to register the inconsistency of her own thoughts. My subjects all reported a minor state of confusion when infiltrated with another's essence for a few minutes."

"Except you missed," Ralph growled at him. He was having trouble resisting the urge to punch the man, superior officer or not.

"I targeted the scientist at her desk. How did I know she'd have a living creature in her hands?"

"You mean to say that you can transport humans into any life form?"

"Only animal as far as I know," Holbrook answered. He continued to study the screen. "She's in a vehicle. Looks like the dashboard of an expensive automobile. At least Candy won't die of heatstroke. Can get damned hot in Nevada this time of year."

"Any time of year," Captain William Dempsey roared as he charged into the communications room. "What the hell have you done, Holbrook? I heard about it on the bridge, so don't try lying."

Ralph shot to attention and saluted.

Dempsey returned the salute. "What have you to say, Holbrook? We have people who are going to die if we don't get that vaccine."

"Dr. Bertram is with Eisner's lab assistant right now, sir!"

The ship's captain eyed Dr. Bertram's physical body lying placidly inside a transparent tube. He shuddered then turned to the monitor. Ralph blocked the captain's view of the monitor. "Let me see," Dempsey said, pointing.

Ralph felt perspiration wetting his upper lip. He turned to look at the screen. Apparently, the lab assistant had placed Candy on a high shelf and opened the door to the cage. At the moment, the view was of Mary's face directly in front of Candy. Mary was speaking. There was no evidence of anything amiss.

The captain bent close to the screen, studied it for a moment and then straightened. "How do you know what the girl is saying?"

"We don't, sir. We've sent for Airman Foster, sir. He's expert at lip-reading, though there's no reason to be worried, sir. We'll be transporting her and the vaccine back to the ship within the hour." A dark stain grew under Holbrook's armpits. "Sir."

"Good looking girl." The captain nodded at the screen. "Pity you can't bring her up. Not enough attractive young women to go around these days."

Holbrook and Ralph exchanged glances. Had one of them made such a remark, they'd be charged with sexual misconduct.

"Yes, sir," Holbrook said. "Is there anything else, sir?"

"Let me know the minute you get Candy—Dr. Bertram home safely."

Holbrook and Ralph saluted as the captain left the room. The instant he was out the door, they turned back to the screen. "Where is she? What is that woman saying to her?"

"I don't know, but she doesn't look threatening. That's one good thing."

"She's smart and resourceful," Ralph said. "She'll figure something out."

"YOU'RE SUCH a little cutie pie, my Chickee-poo," Mary, the lab assistant, cooed into Candy's face. She lifted Candy out of the cage and set her on top of a bureau.

Candy's mind raced as she considered her options. If she could get near a keyboard, she could peck out a message. That would be ideal. If this girl considered her cute, maybe she'd show her off to her friends. Smart phone! That could work. If she could send a message so the men on the ship could understand her situation more clearly. She cocked her head to the side and said, "My name is Dr. Candace Bertram, medical officer on the satellite ship *Rebound*." No response from Mary. Maybe something else would work. Music. She tried singing *God Bless America*. No reaction other than a gentle pat on the head. She intoned a current popular song with a steady rhythm, then waited and watched. Mary stood in front of a mirror, styling her hair. When the singing stopped this time, Mary looked down at her.

"That was interesting, Chickee-poo. I didn't know chickens made so much noise. The rest of them at the lab sure don't. Listen, I have a date tonight. Want to come?"

Candy hopped about on the surface, eager to find any kind of keyboard so she could explain to Mary exactly who she was.

"You like that idea, do you?"

"Damn right!" she cheeped.

"I have this straw handbag that might work to carry you." She rummaged around in the bureau while Candy waited. "Listen, Chickee, I just started this internship at the lab. I'm supposed to be on a work study program, but I'm not old enough to work in any of the casinos or hotels because of the gambling and alcohol, you know?"

Candy nodded.

Mary hesitated. "Anyway, I mean, I'm going to put you in this little straw bag so you won't suffocate or anything. Maybe I ought to line it with tissues." She reached for a box, but stopped with her hand in the air. "No. I don't know how much little chicks poop and pee. I have a better idea." She disappeared for a moment and returned with a box of sanitary napkins and lined the bag.

Smart girl, Candy thought. I don't know much about it either. So, I'm a chicken, am I? All the more reason to kill Holbrook when I get back.

It didn't take Candy long riding around in the swinging purse to not only discover nausea, but to learn she peed and pooped fairly frequently. Mary stopped at one point and came back with a fresh box of pads. "You stink, Chickee."

Candy kept quiet. Bad enough she was a helpless baby chick, now she was also offensive.

Mary plunked the bag on a table top surrounded by three other people gambling and drinking. So much for not being old enough to *work* in a casino. Music thrummed, drowning out voices, so everyone shouted at one another. Candy poked around in her flexible straw-handbag cage to get a view of Mary's friends. They all looked like reasonable young college students. And they all had smart phones on the table next to their drinks and snacks. The smell of potato chips reminded Candy she was hungry. How long had she been gone from the ship? Had to be more than three hours by now. She hopped and flapped, hoping to gain Mary's attention.

"What's in the bag, Mare?" a boy asked.

"I brought it along to show you. My new pet. It's a chick from the lab."

"I thought scientists only experimented on rats," her girlfriend shouted.

"We have chickens, monkeys, rabbits, rats, and all kinds of animals. I'm just in charge of the chickens and rats. Rats are smarter, let me tell you."

"From your vast experience of two days." The group laughed.

"Damned if any rat is smarter than me," Candy protested.

"Let me see." Rough hands jerked the purse across the table and pulled it open.

Candy hunkered down, trying to stay out of sight. She didn't like how this guy handled the bag.

"Aw, look, it's scared. I won't hurt you, little birdy," he said as he scooped her out and put her on the table top.

"Maybe it wants a drink of water or something," the other girl said.

"Yes, please," she said and hopped toward the girl and her phone.

While they emptied one of the snack dishes and cleaned it out to fill it with water, Candy studied the phone. One she was familiar with. Using her beak, she hit the button to activate it, then she hopped around to the other side and got the keyboard to display.

"Your phone's on," the other boy said.

"Oops. Must have bumped it," the girl said and turned it off.

Meanwhile, Mary poured water from her glass onto a saucer and put it in front of Candy. Candy dutifully drank from the water offered, and then promptly peed and pooped on the table.

"Eww," the other girl said. "You better put it away and clean that up before we get thrown out of here."

Candy hopped onto the phone and did a little tap dance. They needed to understand that she had to tell them something important.

The group laughed and chattered as they ignored her pleas and popped her back into the soiled bag. She didn't like the smell of herself, but at least she wasn't thirsty, just hungry. She crouched and pondered her next move. She had to get out and near a phone. The evening went on and she grew hungrier. Eventually, she fell asleep.

HOLBROOK, Ralph and Simon stared glumly at the screen. Empty food containers littered the desktop.

"You think she's just sleeping?"

"Sorry it took so long to get here. I was working on the air filter," Simon said.

"You missed a really long conversation at the bar," Holbrook told him. "Right now it seems she's a baby chicken, so maybe they need to sleep a lot like human babies do. Anybody know?"

"You could look it up," Simon suggested.

"They gave her water. Hopefully, the girl realizes she has to eat solid food," Ralph said. His eyes continued to study the blank screen, as he hoped for signs of life. "C'mon, Candy. Stay strong. We're here for you, sweetheart," he whispered into the screen as Holbrook and Simon researched the care and feeding of hatchling chickens. All he knew was the woman he most admired in the world was in jeopardy. If he could change places with her, he'd do it in a heartbeat.

CANDY LANDED hard on her backside. A rude awakening if ever there was one. She opened her eyes to find herself on top of a bunch of crumpled food wrappers, dead cigarette butts, and plastic bottles. She was in the trash, starving and barely able to move. The brilliant lights suggested the trash can stood on a street instead of in an alley. Though she heard voices, laughter, and music, she couldn't see over the top of the litter bin. She focused on moving her arms… er…wings.

C'mon, woman, you survived four years in the Marines, Medical school, residencies and living in space for over seven years. You can survive being dumped in a trash can. Think. We were at the casino. Group ate and then left. How late can it be? She shut her eyes and focused all her will on getting up to the opening, the slot where people inserted their trash. If she could get onto the sidewalk, surely some kind soul would pick her up, or at least call animal rescue.

A collection of odors filled her nostrils. She moved her head and poked around in the wrappers, finding a left-over hamburger. She pecked at it. Not so bad. She pulled at a limp piece of lettuce. Tomato! She pecked, consumed and filled herself with nourishment. Within a few minutes she felt as if she could fly to the moon. She considered the slot above, squatted and took a chance. She flapped her wings, pushed up with her feet, and aimed at the bright lights. She hit the edge of the bin. Her claws caught, then slipped. She tumbled back into the heap.

Angry, she took a moment to regroup, eyed her exit, and flapped again. This time her claws caught on the edge. She teetered briefly before falling forward and flapped furiously to soften the blow as she landed on the concrete sidewalk. Winded, she squatted, pooped, and then took several deep breaths. *Good job, Kiddo, You're out of the out of the frying pan, but now I suspect you might be in the fire.*

She scanned the area, a well-lit flashy part of the Las Vegas strip. She nodded but the people walked by, ignoring her. She needed to attract the attention of a scientific-looking person. But how would she know who that might be?

As it was, she cheeped and hopped around the outside of the trashcan. She stuck close to the can so she wouldn't get trodden and kept her eyes on the passersby. Most of them were middle-aged people who looked to be on vacation. They sang, laughed, and paid no attention to her. She was getting hungry again, and settled herself behind the can, out of sight so she could rest for a few minutes.

"Mom, somebody dropped their stuffed toy."

"Don't touch that. It's dirty. You don't know where it's been."

"It's not a toy. It's a live bird. A little chick."

"Leave it."

"Wait, Mom."

Candy's eyes swirled in her head as the child lifted her into the air. "That's it, girl," she cheeped. "Tell her how much you want to take me home."

"It's cheeping at me. It likes me."

The woman with the child paused to light a cigarette. Candy didn't realize people still smoked on Earth, it had been so long.

"Keep telling her, kid," Candy chirped on.

"Listen. It's so cute. Can I take it home? Please?"

"No." The woman walked away.

Candy let out a sad, "Oh, no."

The girl said, "Don't worry little chicken. She'll give in. She always gives in to me ever since she and Dad separated."

Candy did a little wing flap to show she understood.

The girl tucked her in a breast pocket. She pulled out her phone and texted her friends. Candy watched. *U will nvr guess what I found. A baby chicken So adorable.* The girl held the phone up and took a photo of herself with Candy. *It has a band on its leg I'll call him Bandit. Is that too cute? LOL*

"IF SHE'D JUST STAY STILL LONG enough, we could transport her back and try with someone else tomorrow," Holbrook said.

"What do you mean? Send her to another body or send someone else into Eisner's? Candy's the only other one besides me working on the PINC solution."

Holbrook frowned. "Looks like we've got ourselves a chick who better get resourceful real soon."

Simon grunted. "We've got a transfer coming in two weeks. We've got to have everyone vaccinated by then."

"A transfer. Who?"

"A group of twenty-seven returning from an intergalactic mission. All very hush-hush, but we're supposed to vet them and clear them for returning to Earth."

Ralph watched the back side of the girl's mother as they strode along the street in Las Vegas. "There's some hope. The girl plans to keep her, but she also noticed a band on her leg. With any luck, it marks her as property of IngraPharma."

"Unfortunately," Holbrook said, "it's more likely to be a control number. Still, it might give the kid the idea to check with someone in authority."

"Who's going to care about a stray chick?" Simon asked.

"Car. They're getting in a car. So far, Mommy hasn't made her dump her."

They watched the kid's phone screen as she played a game. From time to time, Candy looked out the car window, but as none of the observers had ever been to Las Vegas, the landmarks meant nothing to them.

The girl headed into a large house, passed through a well-appointed living room, down a hallway, and entered a typical young teen's bedroom. Though it looked as if it had been lovingly furnished with feminine bedding and delicate furniture, clothes lay strewn throughout the room, hanging from the bedpost, draped over chairs, and littered the unmade bed.

CANDY WAS UNCEREMONIOUSLY DUMPED on the floor, left to explore her new surroundings while the girl disappeared into another room. Her view took in the chair where the phone lay. She hopped several times, but didn't reach it by the time the girl returned and placed a small dish of water on the floor.

Candy dutifully took a drink. "Thank you," she chirped.

"Do you want something to eat?" the girl asked.

"Right now anything," Candy replied.

"Cool. I'll be right back. Don't disappear, Bandit."

She left the phone on the chair.

A blouse hung over the chair. Candy tried capturing its edge with her beak to pull it down and dislodge the phone, but she didn't have the strength. "Talk about weak as a kitten," she grumbled. She continued the attempts in vain until the girl returned with a plateful of chopped up grapes and lettuce.

The girl put the plate on the chair next to the phone and set Candy up there beside it. Excited, Candy was torn between eating and using the phone. Eating won out. After pecking away at the food for a few minutes and feeling somewhat more human, so to speak, she turned her attention to the momentarily abandoned phone.

"Kristin," a voice called.

The girl leapt from the bed. "Be right back, Bandit. You keep eating, okay?"

Candy watched the girl leave the room. She hopped to the phone, hit the button, and turned it on. Her hand-claw tried typing a message to Kristin.

When Kristen returned to the room, Candy made an attempt to explain the situation. "I have to get back to IngraPharma. You said there's a band on my leg. Why don't you take a look at it? It might have identifying numbers. You never know."

"Gads, you cheep a lot. You're not going to do that all night, are you? Mom gave me a box for you to sleep in. She says chickens are particularly dirty." Kristin bent down to pick Candy up, but stopped when she saw her phone on. "I thought I turned that off."

"I was about to try hitting the keys with my, um, beak," Candy said.

Kristin laughed. "I swear, Bandit, you are talking to me."

"I am! I am! Leave the phone where it is, and I'll show you!" Candy hopped vigorously until she tipped over the edge of the chair.

Kristin caught her before she had time to react. "Come on. Into your box. I'll put more food in there for you."

Candy bit her on the finger.

Kristin dropped Candy on the chair. The girl sucked her finger. "Stupid bird. What'd you do that for? I'm trying to help you."

Candy chirped, jumped onto the phone and pecked at the keyboard. "Quit that." Kristin plucked the phone out from under her. When she looked at the keyboard, she dropped the phone onto the bed and shouted, "Mom! You're not going to believe this. Come here!"

"I'm watching television. Can't it wait?"

Kristin tossed Candy into the box and ran from the room. Candy staggered as she recovered from the violent drop.

The girl came back in a minute with her mother in tow. "Watch."

She put the phone in the box. On cue, Candy tapped the screen so the keyboard lit up and then slowly and steadily wrote, *my nameis candy.*

"Oh my God," Kristin squealed. "I thought it was smart to turn the phone on. Do you see what I see?"

"How did you do that?" her mother asked.

"I didn't. It did."

"I'm Candy, not *it*," Candy chirped.

"It's trying to tell us something," Kristin said.

"Let me see that band on its leg." Mom picked Candy up just as she let loose a stream of poop.

"I'm sorry. It's a chicken thing I haven't got control over yet," Candy cheeped.

Mom dropped Candy back into the box. "Disgusting. Get me a wet towel."

Candy continued cheeping to get her point across. *Texting is more important than cleaning at the moment. The life of my crew is dependent on me getting back to that laboratory.*

Mom wiped chicken poop off her arm and turned Candy upside down to read the tag. "Huh. Looks like a serial number. I wonder if it came from the college."

"But how would it get downtown?"

Mom put Candy down, more gently this time. "Put the phone by her again. I want to watch. Stay back so I know you're not playing a game."

Now I'm a performing animal. She turned the phone and screen on, and pecked out a new message, *ineed to gt bck to laⱱboratory*

"A laboratory at the college?" Mom asked.

Candy pecked again, *ingrhparhma* "Damn. You can figure it out. Ingrapharma," she chirped.

"It's obviously intelligent, but good lord, who would ever believe a thinking chicken even exists?"

"What should we do, Mom?"

Candy nearly leapt out of the box. She rushed to the phone.

Nojok pls must go Ingra

"IngraPharma?" Kristin's mom wondered. "The pharmaceutical company outside of the city? This makes absolutely no sense."

"It does, it does," Candy shouted in chicken-speak. "Just put me in the car and take me there."

"We can go first thing in the morning," Kristin suggested. "And—"

"This is your weekend with your father. You don't want to miss that. We'll think about it over the weekend and then decide what to do. It's kind of cute. Maybe it reads fortunes, too. How about it, chicken?"

nameiscandy now urgent

"She's trying to tell you, Mom. It's important." Kristin sat on the floor next to the box. "Are we really having this conversation, Mom?"

"Tell you what, I'll look up the company online and see if they're missing a chicken." She headed out the door muttering, "I thought they used rabbits or rats for experimenting. Baby chickens?"

Kristin picked up the phone and texted. Her fingers flew over the keyboard. Candy, growing hungry again, pecked at her food and drank more water. It appeared mother and daughter planned to help her. She hoped the process still worked and Holbrook and Ralph could see her dilemma.

A few minutes later, Mom came back and said, "No one seemed to know what I was talking about." Kristin set her phone aside. The two of them stared into the box.

"She eats like a normal chicken," Kristin said.

"Moves like one, too."

"She really typed on the phone, didn't she?"

"I'd swear to it."

"FROM WHAT I CAN TELL, she's in a friendly enough environment. They're feeding her. They're in some disbelief about the intelligence of a chicken," Simon translated as he lip-read the mother and daughter's conversation.

"I had the coordinates set for Eisner's office. So it'll take several hours to reset them to her current location," Holbrook said.

"By then she could be anywhere. I'm sure she understands it's best if she can get back to where she landed." Ralph reached out and touched the screen, wishing he could feel the fuzzy feathers on Candy's back.

"She escaped death by chance twice already."

"So, do we go with three strikes and she's out? Or third time's the lucky charm?" Holbrook joked.

"Not funny," Ralph grumbled.

"I DON'T WANT to go with Daddy! I want to stay here with Bandit."

Mom sipped on a drink. Smelled like bourbon to Candy. She could use a good stiff drink about now.

"Listen," Mom said. "I do all I can for you day in and day out. Whatever you want. But once in a while I need some time for myself. Do you understand? Take the filthy chicken with you if you have to, but go with your father. You've got less than an hour to clean up your room and get ready."

Candy huddled in the corner of her box.

"You always get nasty when you drink. No wonder Daddy left."

"What did you say, young lady?" Mom shrieked.

Candy discovered chickens can't cover their ears. But she could close her eyes, until she remembered her rescuers needed to know exactly where she was and what was going on.

"You heard me," Kristin said. She grabbed a basket and threw clothes into it. "I'll go with Daddy. You'll see. I won't come home either."

Mom chortled. "We'll see how long that lasts. You keep up this attitude and you won't have any home to come back to."

"Hey, Mom, stop being so hard on the kid," Candy scolded.

"She's right. You get mean after you start drinking. Lay off the booze and give the kid a hug."

"You've upset Bandit." Kristin sulked as she dragged her backpack out from under her bed.

Mom tossed her head and stormed out of the room.

"Don't worry, Bandit. Mom'll be fine when I see her after school on Monday. Maybe she'll meet somebody this weekend who can make her happy. You can come with me. Daddy won't mind. Once I tell him Mom can't stand you, he'll love you."

The child finished her packing. She carried her bags and Candy's box out to the front step where she sat and waited to be picked up.

"Here he comes. Try not to stink too much. He's very, uh, fastidious. You know what I mean? He's a doctor and wants everything like it's been sterilized sixteen times."

Oh great, Candy thought. She cheeped once, hoping Kristin understood one cheep for yes.

When Kristin's father arrived, he placed the box in the back seat of his large, expensive SUV. "You can keep it out on the back porch, but it's your responsibility to care for it," he cautioned his daughter.

"I will. This chicken is special."

"Everything is special when you first get it," he muttered as he pulled out onto the street.

Kristin sat in the back seat with Candy. "You'll be all right out on the porch, Bandit. I'll make sure the cat stays outside all night.

Cat? Candy hopped and chirped.

Kristin turned on the phone and set it in the box.

no cat mst get to dreisnerlab ip drug company

"Daddy, do you know anything about an Inger-something drug company around here?"

"Ingrapharma?"

One cheep.

"Yes. I need to stop by there for a minute. I need something for Bandit."

Kristin's father laughed. "Is this one of your new computer games?"

"We're just visiting. We're not breaking in or anything. We need to ask for Dr. Eisner."

Two cheeps.

"At least find out where her lab is."

One cheep.

"It's the weekend. No one is going to be there. Eisner? I know that name. She works in research. Developing a new vaccine for PINC."

One cheep. Candy hopped about the bottom of the box.

"That's the one," Kristin said.

"Good girl," Candy chirped.

"What do you want there?" her father asked.

Kristin peered down into the box.

Candy pecked at the phone. *secret i came from ther*

"Bandit came from there and she, uh, was supposed to come with special feed from the doctor in charge."

"Really? Your mother didn't tell me anything about that."

"She wouldn't, would she? She's been drinking. You're a doctor. They'd believe you when you tell them you have to leave an important message for Dr. Eisner. In person!"

You're good at this improv, kid. Let's hope your father buys into it.

"Bandit is a reject from some experimental program and I found out I could adopt a pet from there. Mom won't let me have a cat or dog, but she never said anything about a chicken, so I figured why not?"

The car slowed and stopped. Traffic flew by. "Do you want to start over?" Her father's voice sounded angry. "What you're saying doesn't make any sense. Why do you really want to go to the lab? Is there a boy you're not telling me about? I told you, you can't date until you're at least fourteen and that will be in a group."

Candy squawked. She pecked furiously on the keyboard.

"Hold on a minute, Daddy. It's not about boys. It's about…"

Kristin watched as Candy wrote, *save lives on space shp pinc important*

"It's about saving lives," Kristin said. "And that new virus you mentioned, PINC."

i dr bertram, space station

"Oh man," Kristin whispered, "He's never going to believe this." She picked up the phone and passed it to her father.

"Who wrote this? You've been hacked. I told you about opening mail from—"

"Daddy, give me your phone. You know yours isn't hacked. Give me a minute and you'll see."

"You're being ridiculous. We're going home." He put the car in gear.

"No! You're just like Mom. You refuse to listen, except you don't have to drink to be mean."

The car stopped again. "That's it."

Candy cheeped and hopped.

"Please, Daddy, I'm begging you, just give me your phone for a minute. If you don't want to do that, then let me have your iPad. I'll show you something. You won't even have to connect to anything."

"For crying out loud, Kristin. Okay. Here."

Kristin set the iPad in the box and turned it on. When the keyboard appeared, Candy got to work, pecking slowly and carefully into a blank note document, *sir, i am dr candace bertram sr medical officer on the satellite ship recove we have outbreak of pinc virus and in desperate need of vaccine in fridgean share w/you you get credit for vaccine–in body of rejected chick from lab*

Kristin passed the iPad back to her father. Candy sat quietly in the box while he read the message.

He cleared his throat. "This is a joke, right? There's no place for a reply. How do I find out if this is a hoax?"

"Just talk, Daddy. She'll type a new message back through us— me and Bandit. For real."

"We can't go to a laboratory and just take an experimental drug." He passed the iPad back. He leaned over the box with Kristin as Candy typed. "Am I seeing what I'm seeing?"

"Yes, Daddy."

if you do not we all doomed turn on net and ref my rev er in the field id pnc

The father went out of view. Everything remained quiet for nearly ten minutes, and then the car moved again.

. . .

"WHAT'S GOING ON?" Simon asked.

"The father's not driving. It's quiet in the car. Candy's very still. All very tense," Holbrook said.

Ralph pushed the two men aside. "We need to come up with an alternative solution. There must be some way to get her back. What happens if we don't?"

"As a chicken, she dies in a year or so and as Candy, she remains in suspended animation until someone figures it out."

"What about the *essence* you so blithely said is the real her down there inside that chicken?"

"Never been a problem before. I'm zeroed in on the desk. As soon as Daddy gets into the office and sets her down, we're good to go."

Ralph's eyes teared up. "That's not good enough. What about being prepared to make an exchange of *essences* in the event she's not in the exact spot?"

"How do you mean?"

"Whoever is in that spot gets transferred. Wouldn't her essence follow?"

"Doesn't work that way. If we, for example, caught Daddy in our scope, we'd need a host body here. Without one, nothing happens. If we had one, then whoever he uses is dismissed for the duration. When we bring Candy back, if it worked as originally planned, Dr. Eisner would become aware that she missed some time, but have no idea why. In this case, I don't think the chicken will notice anything." Holbrook calculated things on his computer. "We have to match the correct essence to the correct molecules."

"Something's happening. The box is moving. Looks like hall lights above. A security guard. Moving again." Ralph whispered as if the IngraPharma security guards might hear him.

"We can see for ourselves. They're in the building."

"YOU'RE GOOD AT THIS, DADDY," Kristin said as they marched through the halls. He'd shown his ID to security and explained he had to deliver the chicken to Dr. Eisner's lab and collect notes she left for him earlier in the day. He apologized for being late.

Kristin wore her father's extra pair of black rimmed eyeglasses, had tied her hair up in a twist, and slipped on one of her father's scrub tops. She carried his medical tablet while he toted the box with the chicken.

"Devious has never been my strong suit." He spoke under his breath. "Keep your voice down. Don't want Jones to figure it out."

Jones was their escort to the lab.

Candy prayed Kristin's father was just as good at uncovering passwords to locked vaults.

"Here you are, Dr. Hewitt. Just dial security when you're ready to leave."

They passed into a well-lit room. As they paused before another door, a voice stopped them. "Who are you? What are you doing in here?"

"It's Mary. The lab assistant," Candy cheeped. "What's she doing here?"

Kristin's father set the box on the floor and turned around to face the girl. "I'm Dr. Hewitt. I'm here about this chick. Who, may I ask, are you?"

Mary hovered over the box. "I work here." She looked in the box at Candy. "Where did you find this? It looks like one of ours."

"Damn right, I'm one of yours. Mixed feelings here, Kiddo." Candy flapped her wings. "You were supposed to put me in the cooker, but on the other hand, you left me in a trash can."

"I need to leave a message for Dr. Eisner, if you'll excuse us. No need for you to come in with us. Go on about your business." Kristin's father picked up the box. Kristin followed him into the office. He set the box on the desk, lifted Candy out and set her next to his iPad. "Now what?" he said to the chick.

open fridge need password or get eisner here Candy skidded to the edge of the desk and pointed her beak at the corner, then scooted back to the iPad. *we sure vaccine there*

"Makes sense. Refrigerated vault. Locked. I can't believe I'm doing this." He sat on the floor in front of the vault and pressed numbers into the keypad lock. "Kristin, honey, this is madness. How can we ever hope to figure this out?"

While he tried variations of letters and numbers, Kristin opened the drawers of the desk next to the refrigerator. "Mom has a notebook full of passwords because she keeps forgetting them. Then she forgets when she changed them and adds more to the list. It's a mess, so I doubt anyone would ever—here, I found something, Daddy!" She pulled a small spiral notepad from the back of the center drawer and took it to her father.

"Interesting," he said flipping through pages of passwords. "Now all we have to do is work out which one of these is her code for this vault."

Kristin clicked away on her iPhone. "Try *sicher.*"

"Why that?"

"Eisner is a German name. Maybe she used a German word for vault. Sicher. It means safe in German."

"Clever girl, but nothing."

"Try it with these numbers." Kristin rattled off what sounded like a date.

"Nope."

"This one."

Candy staggered to the center of the desk and peered down into the open drawer, trying to think of anything that would help them. They did seem to be on the right track. At least they were giving it the old college try. She pecked a new message on the iPad and let her gaze drift over it so the guys back in the spacecraft would hopefully see it.

working forshly on safe soon-feeling sick-

"SHE'S ON THE MARK. Bring her up now," Ralph shouted.

"She's fallen over. The little girl is talking to her." Simon studied the girl's lips. "'Poor baby,' she's saying. 'My father will help you in a minute.' Dr. Bertram is blinking rapidly. Doesn't look good for her. What's wrong?"

"From what little we've seen of her, I guess her age as a chick is barely a week old. She hasn't even begun to form feathers," Holbrook said. "Could be…"

"Could be what?" Ralph asked.

"Never mind. Here we go." He fingered the keyboard beneath the monitor, muttering under his breath as he typed. "The instant the girl gets out of the way—"

They continued to stare at the screen. Candy kept her focus on Kristin's face.

Ralph held his breath, willing the girl to move away. "Now!"

"I THINK I'M SICK, KID," Candy chirped. "If you get it open, contact us, will you?"

"What's wrong with you, Bandit? Daddy, can you help?"

"Hold on a minute, Sweetheart, it clicked. It's open."

Candy shook herself. *Get on your feet, woman. You have a mission.*

Everything went black.

For a moment.

The bright lights returned. She looked down at her feet and dizziness swept over her. "My feet."

"Well, they're not mine, Dr. Bertram," an airman said to her.

"Welcome back, Candy." Ralph hesitated until she held her arms out to him.

"I'm here? Really here? What happened?"

"We sent you down to Earth to recover a vaccine. Instead, rescuing you became our recovery mission."

"I know all about that. We were just about to succeed. The girl and her father?"

"He's got the vaccine."

"How do you feel?" Ralph asked. "You looked sick just before Holbrook caught you."

"I felt sick. Very weak, but at the moment I'm feeling fine. In fact, I could use a real meal. I've had enough garbage for a while. Geez, do chickens really live that way?"

"I'll order up some seafood and pasta. How's that for a start?" Holbrook said.

. . .

"IT'S ONLY five days until the transport arrives," Dr. Bertram advised Captain Holbrook. "We have eighteen new cases of PINC." Each day she'd met with patients in the infirmary had added to her guilt. Her mission had failed. Four people had died in the past week. Her work to create a vaccine from the blood of those who survived the deadly virus was promising but so far, nothing.

Her phone buzzed at her waist. Ralph.

"A signal from Earth. Something you might want to be here for."

She excused herself and made her way to the communications room where Holbrook, Ralph and several technicians surrounded the main monitor. "Look at this."

Dr. Hewitt stood at a lectern. Behind him, a multitude of flags from several countries waved in the breeze. Men and women in business attire stood around him. "Today I have been arrested for the theft of a formula and a vaccine from IngraPharma. I am happy to serve my time—"

"That's enough, Dr. Hewitt," the man closest to him said. "I'll take it from here. As Dr. Hewitt's attorney, I've advised him not to speak of the details of his case. He is yet to go to trial. I will tell you this: the space agency responsible for the health and well-being of our interplanetary population and the World Health Organization are grateful to Dr. Hewitt for his tenacity in securing not only a treatment for, but a vaccine against further occurrences of psychoneurocystic disease. Even as we speak, a supply of these medications is on its way to the satellite transfer station and to our sister countries around the planet. And now, Dr. Hewitt's daughter, Kristin, has a word to say."

A young girl of about twelve or thirteen stepped up to the microphone. "We should all be grateful to Dr. Candace Bertram." She blew a kiss at the cameras. "Return to Earth soon. Bandit misses you."

Author's Notes—Veronica H. Hart

RECOVERY WAS BORN whole-cloth following two events concerning arbitrary and punitive price increases on life-saving medications by two separate and greedy pharmaceutical firms. Though this story remains light-hearted, the author still fumes at the injustice.

Dr. Candace Bertram will return as a featured character in future works.

~VHH

About the Authors

KEN PELHAM
JOHN HOPE
KRISTIN DURFEE
ELLE ANDREWS PATT
BRIA BURTON
TRACIE ROBERTS
CHARLES A CORNELL
C. L. ROMAN
BARD CONSTANTINE
VERONICA H. HART

KEN PELHAM

Ken Pelham's debut novel, **Brigands Key**, winner of the 2009 Royal Palm Literary Award, was published in hardcover in 2012, in softcover in 2014, and in audiobook in 2015. The prequel, **Place of Fear**, a 2012 first-place winner of the Royal Palm, was released in 2013. A short story, **"The Wreck of the Edinburgh Kate,"** garnered a second-place award in 2014.

His book on the craft of writing, **Out of Sight, Out of Mind: A Writer's Guide to Mastering Viewpoint**, won the Florida Writers Association's highest award—2015 Published Book of the Year—and has been translated into Italian, Spanish, and Portuguese. Ken is also a licensed and dangerous landscape architect, with a background in park and open space planning and design, and has written, published, and presented numerous times on the natural and built environments. Audiences usually stick around until the end.

He grew up in the small South Florida town of Immokalee, and lives with his wife, Laura, in Maitland, Florida. A member of International Thriller Writers and the Florida Writers Association, he's sometimes spotted cycling, fishing, or scuba diving, seldom simultaneously.

www.kenpelham.com

WORKS by KEN PELHAM

NOVELS
Brigands Key
Place of Fear

NONFICTION BOOKS
Out of Sight, Out of Mind: A Writer's Guide to Mastering
Viewpoint
(2015 Florida Writers Association Published Book of the Year)

Great Danger: A Writer's Guide to Building Suspense

SHORT STORY COLLECTIONS
Treacherous Bastards: Stories of Suspense, Deceit, and
Skullduggery
A Double Shot of Fright: Two Tales of Terror
Tales of Old Brigands Key

"SOUNDTRACKED" SHORT STORIES
"The Wreck of the Edinburgh Kate"
"Familiar"

JOHN HOPE

John Hope is an award-winning short story, children's book, middle grade, young adult, and nonfiction writer. His work appears in paperback, hardback, audiobook, and multiple short story collections. He gives informational and inspirational presentations to schools, conferences, and is a board member of the Florida Writers Association. John loves to travel and play games with his wife, Jaime, and two rambunctious kids.

Forever seeking new adventures, John lives a life of energizing enterprises. Born and raised in St. Petersburg, Florida, John earned his BS in Computer Engineering from the University of Central Florida (UCF) and since 1999 has developed and designed software for simulators, websites, traveler information systems, and numerous other technical widgets. All the while, he has quenched his creative hunger with writing a few books, hundreds of poems and short stories, several short plays many of which he's acted and/or directed, puppeteered in countless skits, and built a number of toy train layouts. To keep a steady rhythm in his life, John has run over 30,000 miles in various road and trail races and training runs through the years, including captaining the UCF Men's Cross Country team, achieving TAAC all conference, managing 5k races, and at times traversing entire states in relay teams and triathlons.

www.johnhopewriting.com

WORKS by JOHN HOPE

CHILDREN'S PICTURE BOOKS
Frozen Floppies[*]
Story of Unlikely Friendships

Floppyopolis
Story of Taking Pride in the Community

Watch the Butterfly
Story of Learning Patience

The Band Aid
Story of Understanding/Dealing with Grief

MIDDLE GRADE / YOUNG ADULT
Silencing Sharks[*]
Fantasy/Adventure Story of Heroism
No Good[*]
Historical Fiction Story of Acceptance / Understanding
Pankyland[*]
Adventure Story of Friendship
Pankyland 2: The Movie
Adventure Story of Sibling Rivalry and Friendship

BOOKS FOR ADULTS
Colby in the Crosshairs[*]
Poignant Story of Child Abuse
John's Shorts Volume 1[*] and 2[*]
Collections of Award-Winning Short Stories
Lake Mary, Images of America
History of Small Town America via photos and stories

[*] = Indicates winner of one or more awards

KRISTIN DURFEE

Kristin Durfee grew up outside of Philadelphia where an initial struggle with reading blossomed into a love and passion for the written word.

She is currently working on several projects, including the next book in the Four Corners Trilogy, a new novel for Young Adults, and her first full-length suspense novel for Adults.

Kristin currently resides outside of Orlando, FL, and when not enjoying the theme parks or Florida sun, she spends most of her time with her husband and their quirky dogs.

She is a member of the Florida Writers Association.

www.kristindurfee.com

WORKS by KRISTIN DURFEE

PUBLISHED NOVELLAS

Revenge from Within
(The Hunt 2 Suspense Anthology)

Project Bright Star
(Return to Earth Anthology)

PUBLISHED NOVELS

Four Corners
(Four Corners Trilogy Book 1)

Two Worlds
(Four Corners Trilogy Book 2)

UPCOMING NOVELS

One Earth
(Four Corners Trilogy Book 3)

ELLE ANDREWS PATT

The universe of **Someday Loyal** is featured in Elle Andrews Patt's work in progress, **Anunnaki**. Expect to see Kevin again, and mentions of Alice and Sam.

Elle received an Honorable Mention from Writers of The Future for **Prelude To A Murder Conviction** in 2013. She won the First Place Royal Palm Literary Award for Published Short Fiction from the Florida Writers Association in 2013 and 2014. She was invited to join the Alvarium Experiment during its 2014 inception and first published **Manteo** in 2015 as a stand-alone e-novella within the AE's first project, **The Prometheus Saga**. It is still available with bonus research notes included. **Manteo** won the 2015 Third Place RPLA award for Published Novella. In 2016, Elle's unpublished paranormal mystery won the Second Place RPLA award for Unpublished Mystery.

In between the many hours spent keyboard-pounding, computer-screen staring, and workshopping fiction since 2001, Elle has unschooled her kids, team-mom'ed for softball, volleyball, and golf, sweated through stints as a veterinary technician, horse-show manager, pizza maker, business phone packer, baseball bat seller, boarding barn manager, and equine semen collector, rejoiced at finding wi-fi far afield, and ridden all sorts of horses, both evil and golden, over cross country jumps, across un-mowed hunt country, and all gussied up into the dressage arena.

She currently lives with her husband and two daughters in the breeziest part of Florida she's ever been to and is grateful for it every day.

www.elleandrewspatt.com

WORKS by ELLE ANDREWS PATT

NOVELETTES
Manteo
Someday Loyal

SHORT STORY PUBLICATIONS
(as Laura Andrews)
Karl's Last Night – The Rag Literary Magazine
(2014 RPLA First Place)
Becky's Story – Saw Palm: Florida Literature
(2013 RPLA First Place)
The Legend of Johnny Bell – Solarcidal Tendencies
Coming of Age – FWA Collection #6: First Steps

UPCOMING NOVELS
Billie Mae – Paranormal Murder Mystery
(2016 RPLA Second Place)
The Year of the Bear – Mainstream Literature
Blind Mice Bite – Mainstream Mystery
Anunnaki – Science Fiction/Fantasy

BRIA BURTON

Bria Burton has been inventing stories since she first learned how to write words and form sentences. She lives in St. Petersburg and is blessed with a wonderful husband who loves her despite her writing habit.

While she writes, her dog and cat do their best to distract her, which is why they star in her family-friendly short story collection, *Lance & Ringo Tails*. In 2016, *Little Angel Helper* won a Third Place Royal Palm Literary Award for Published Novella. The story was written for her sisters, one of whom has special needs like a character in the story. Her latest publication, *The Running Girls*, is a novelette currently available as an ebook. Bria also writes speculative and other fiction stories, over a dozen of which have been featured in anthologies such as *Welcome to the Future* and in magazines such as *The Colored Lens*.

In January 2015, she was a contributor to *The Prometheus Saga*, an experimental short story collection of the Alvarium Experiment, a by-invitation-only consortium of award-winning authors. Each short story in the Saga was individually published in the Kindle Store and is still available. Bria is thrilled that the anthology version of the second Alvarium Experiment project, *Return to Earth*, is now in your hands.

In 2015, *Sprinter*, inspirational women's fiction, won a First Place RPLA in the Unpublished Women's Fiction category. In 2011, she was awarded a First Place RPLA for her epic fantasy manuscript, *Livinity*. She's been a member of the Florida Writers Association since 2008. She currently leads the St. Pete FWA Writers Group and serves on the statewide Board.

At St. Pete Running Company, she's employed as a blogger and customer service manager.

www.briaburton.com

WORKS by BRIA BURTON

NOVELLA
Little Angel Helper
(2016 RPLA Third Place-Published Novella)
The Running Girls

SHORT STORY COLLECTION
Lance & Ringo Tails

SHORT STORY PUBLICATIONS
A Dream Within A Dream – Journey Into... podcast, In Shadows
Written anthology
The Mute Girl – Youth Imagination, eFantasy
Tight Pants – Page & Spine
Ticket to Heaven – Faith, Hope, & Fiction
The Wheels Must Turn – Broken Worlds anthology
On Both Sides – The Prometheus Saga
In Line at the DMYV – Welcome to the Future anthology
Switching –The Dunesteef Audio Fiction Magazine
Ligeia – Journey Into... podcast
This is Hollywood – FICTION on the WEB
Maribel's Day of Death, Ma Says, The Wheels Must Turn, The
Price of Integrity, and Empty Girl – FWA Collections #2, 3, 4, 5,
and 7

TRACIE ROBERTS

Tracie is a native Floridian who laughs loudest at her own jokes, ODs quite frequently on 80s nostalgia, and eavesdrops on perfect strangers to glean story ideas. She's been writing for all of four years but has been telling stories since she was old enough to realize she could make people believe her lies.

She currently lives in a small North Florida town with her husband and two daughters, working relentlessly on her next series.

Connect with Tracie on Facebook, Twitter, and Instagram.

www.tracieroberts.com

WORKS by TRACIE ROBERTS

THE ÉLAN SERIES

Spirit
Echo
Whisper
Blur

UPCOMING NOVELS
Bound – Finale to The Élan Series

UPCOMING SERIES
The Lantana Beach Series – Sweet Romance
The Supernatural Adventures of Jesse Carpenter – YA Fantasy

CHARLES A CORNELL

Charles suffer from Overactive Imagination Disorder, an incurable condition that fills his mind with three dimensional puzzles of stacked what-if questions that cry out for answers. He fuels his creativity amidst the chaos of a busy life in his writer's den in Fort Myers, Florida.

Crystal Night, his contribution to the Alvarium Experiment's first anthology, *The Prometheus Saga* won the Florida Writers Association's Royal Palm Literary Award for Best Novella in 2016. This followed other RPLA awards in 2014 and 2012.

DragonFly, his retro-futuristic collision of science fiction and fantasy was a Royal Palm Literary Award Finalist in Science Fiction. *DragonFly* explores the incredibly turbulent times during the 1940s and the 'what ifs' that might have been. The story follows the adventures of Veronica Somerset as she battles the odds to become Britain's first female fighter pilot. Packed with full color illustrations and black and white 'retrographs', *DragonFly* conjures up a whole new world of fantastic technology, dangerous fighting machines and wizards battling across the boundary between good and evil in a World War II re-imagined like never before.

His FBI serial killer novel, *Tiger Paw* won the 2012 Royal Palm Literary Award for Best Thriller. *Tiger Paw* blends action and intrigue with psychological suspense as a Hindu cult's assassin takes revenge on the Wolves of Wall Street.

You can follow his musings on science fiction, retrofuturism and dieselpunk at his blog, www.CharlesACornell.com and explore the world of DragonFly at www.DragonFly-Novels.com.

www.CharlesACornell.com
www.DragonFly-Novels.com
www.Cornell-SciFi.com

WORKS by CHARLES A CORNELL

SCIENCE FANTASY SERIES:
MISSIONS OF THE DRAGONFLY SQUADRON
DragonFly - Illustrated Edition
(2014 RPLA Finalist - Science Fiction)
DragonFly Part I: To Hell and Back
DragonFly Part II: Victory or Death
Spies in Manhattan (coming soon)

COMPANION SHORT FICTION:
DRAGONFLY - BEHIND ENEMY LINES
Die Fabrik / The Factory

SCIENCE FICTION
Crystal Night (The Prometheus Saga)
(2016 RPLA Best Novella)

MYSTERY THRILLER
Tiger Paw
(2012 RPLA Best Thriller)
(2012 National Semi-Finalist - Kindle Book Review)

C.L. ROMAN

The story of Gaia, her life and loves, is currently being developed into a four part series. We will keep you posted.

C.L. has been honored to have her work included in two FWA collections, as well as The Milk of Female Kindness Anthology and the second volume of Snowbirds.

Fantasy and paranormal young adult are C.L.'s genres of choice, though she is now considering a venture into magical realism, if she can ever get someone to help her define it adequately. She currently has two series in the works: Rephaim and The Witch of Forsythe High, with the aforementioned third waiting in the proverbial wings.

When she isn't hip deep in a novel, you can find C.L. on her blog, The Brass Rag, or editing the work of awesome authors.

It is worth noting that, like most authors, Ms. Roman exists in two worlds - the mundane and the hyper-imagined. In the mundane world, she is called Cheri, and she teaches high school English. Not bad, but not as exciting as the world of action and high adventure that C.L. delights in creating. Both entities prefer the latter, but one has to rest some time.

When she isn't running after her grandchildren or attending car shows with her husband, Cheri spends an inordinate amount of time pursuing chocolate, coffee and literary adventure. Indie authors are her secret favorite, but on occasion you can still catch her drooling over Koontz or Gaiman as well.

Ms. Roman lives in the not-so-wilds of Northeast Florida with her husband and Jack E. Boy, the super Chihuahua.

www.brassragpress.com

WORKS by C.L. ROMAN

NOVELLETTE
Gaia Returning

SHORT STORY PUBLICATIONS
Witch Justice: 1892 – FWA Collection #5: It's A Crime
Natural Magic – Snowbirds Anthology, Vol. II
Gigi's Version – FWA Collection #8: Hide and Seek

NOVELS
Rephaim – Fantasy Series
Descent: Book One
Sacrifice: Book Two
Illusion: Book Three
The Witch of Forsythe High – Paranormal Young Adult Series
First Candidate: Book One
Fire Candidate: Book Two

UPCOMING NOVELS
Inception: Earth Prime Series – Science Fiction
Ghost Candidate: WOFH Series #3 – Paranormal Young Adult

BARD CONSTANTINE

The Paradoxical Man plays a major role in connecting the expanded universes of Bard's novels, both past and upcoming.

Bard Constantine writes gritty futures and far-flung fantasy. As a founding member of the Alvarium Experiment consortium, he contributed to their Prometheus anthology with the short story The Blurred Man.

His love of speculative fiction catapulted his writing career, which includes the Troubleshooter novels, featuring the private eye of the future. Other novels include the horror/sci-fi series The Aberration, and Shadow Battles, a recently released epic fantasy series. A huge fan of edgy, fast-paced television shows, Bard styles his stories in similar fashion, keeping his readers hanging on from chapter to chapter.

Bard lives in Birmingham, Al with his wife and balances a career in the flour milling industry with his writing. His spare time is usually spent in a dank basement where he pounds out stories under the wrathful eye of a vindictive muse.

www.bardwritesbooks.com

WORKS by BARD CONSTANTINE

ABERRATION SERIES
The Aberration
Torment of Tantalus (Jan 2017)

THE TROUBLESHOOTER SERIES
New Haven Blues
Red-Eyed Killer (novella)
The Wise Man Says (short)
The Most Dangerous Dame
Little White Bird (short)

SHADOW BATTLES SERIES
The Eye of Everfell
The Darkest Champion
City of Glass (short)

OTHER WORKS
Silent Empire
Immortal Musings (poetry)
The Blurred Man (The Prometheus Saga)

VERONICA HELEN HART

Dr. Candace Bertram, who is the protagonist in **Recovery**, is featured in the sequel to Veronica's RPLA Finalist novel, **Silent Autumn.**

Veronica was invited to join the Alvarium Experiment in 2015.

While awaiting publication of the fourth book in her cozy series about a group of peripatetic senior citizens, **Midnight in Mongolia,** which is scheduled for release the first week of January, 2017, she is working to complete her first paranormal murder mystery/romance, **Knife!**

Veronica lives with her retired veterinarian/author husband, Robert, in Ormond Beach, Florida. They settled there after spending the major part of their lives traveling, living, and working in various areas of the world.

Between them, they have six daughters and eleven grandchildren who keep their minds active trying to remember birthdays and anniversaries.

www.veronicahhart.com

WORKS by VERONICA HELEN HART

PUBLISHED NOVELS
The Prince of Keegan Bay – Champagne Books
(RPLA First Place for Humor)
The Swimming Corpse – Blenders Book II
Safari Stew – Blenders Book III
Midnight in Mongolia – Blenders Book IV
Silent Autumn
(RPLA Finalist for Science Fiction)
Escape from Iran
(RPLA Second Place for Young Adult)
Elena – the Girl with the Piano
(Finalist – 2014 EPIC Awards)
The Reluctant Daughters

SHORT STORY PUBLICATIONS
All of the following are in the FWA Collections:
Larry and the Cat - #1 From Our Family to Yours 2009
Standoff in the Alborz Mountains – #2 Slices of Life 2010
The Anniversary Dinner - #5 It's a Crime – 2013
The Suitcase - #6 The First Step – 2014
Poisonberry Wine - #7 Revisions – 2015
Margaret Barnes - #8 Hide and Seek - 2016

The Alvarium Experiment Anthologies

As of this 2025 edition of the 2016 Return to Earth original anthology:

THE LIGHT FANTASTIC
THE LIGHT FANTASTIC 2
THE MASTERS REIMAGINED
THE MASTERS REIMAGINED 2
RETURN TO EARTH
THE PROMETHEUS SAGA
THE PROMETHEUS SAGA 2